"Who's tha[t]... asked

As the litter neared the pyramid, slaves dropped immediately and placed their foreheads on the sand.

One old man, stumbling under the weight of a stone, didn't prostrate quickly enough to suit the overseer standing next to him. The overseer swept his metal-encased whip handle across the old man's face, drawing blood and knocking the old man to the ground.

Kane prostrated himself on the first level of the pyramid. But he still looked up.

The fear remained in Bakari's voice. "As I told you, that litter carries no man. It belongs to the god Set."

The passenger pushed open the shrouds of the litter and stepped down onto a slave's back, then onto the sand. He was dressed in a hooded black robe that hid his face from view.

Kane watched with increased curiosity as the figure reached up and pulled his hood back. When he saw the man's features, Kane's breath locked in the back of his throat. Although he had never seen the creature alive, Kane knew who he was.

Other titles in this series:

721/07

JAMES AXLER

OUTLANDERS®

PRODIGAL CHALICE

A GOLD EAGLE BOOK FROM
WORLDWIDE®

TORONTO • NEW YORK • LONDON
AMSTERDAM • PARIS • SYDNEY • HAMBURG
STOCKHOLM • ATHENS • TOKYO • MILAN
MADRID • WARSAW • BUDAPEST • AUCKLAND

First edition February 2002
ISBN 0-373-63833-7

PRODIGAL CHALICE

Special thanks to Mel Odom for his contribution
to this work and to Mark Ellis for his contribution to
the Outlanders concept, developed for Gold Eagle Books.

Printed in U.S.A.

PRODIGAL CHALICE

The Road to Outlands—
From Secret Government Files to the Future

Almost two hundred years after the global holocaust, Kane, a former Magistrate of Cobaltville, often thought the world had been lucky to survive at all after a nuclear device detonated in the Russian embassy in Washington, D.C. The aftermath—forever known as skydark—reshaped continents and turned civilization into ashes.

Nearly depopulated, America became the Deathlands—poisoned by radiation, home to chaos and mutated life forms. Feudal rule reappeared in the form of baronies, while remote outposts clung to a brutish existence.

What eventually helped shape this wasteland were the redoubts, the secret preholocaust military installations with stores of weapons, and the home of gateways, the locational matter-transfer facilities. Some of the redoubts hid clues that had once fed wild theories of government cover-ups and alien visitations.

Rearmed from redoubt stockpiles, the barons consolidated their power and reclaimed technology for the villes. Their power, supported by some invisible authority, extended beyond their fortified walls to what was now called the Outlands. It was here that the rootstock of humanity survived, living with hellzones and chemical storms, hounded by Magistrates.

In the villes, rigid laws were enforced—to atone for the sins of the past and prepare the way for a better future. That was the barons' public credo and their right-to-rule.

Kane, along with friend and fellow Magistrate Grant, had upheld that claim until a fateful Outlands expedition. A displaced piece of technology…a question to a keeper of the archives…a vague clue about alien masters—and their world shifted radically. Suddenly, Brigid Baptiste, the archivist, faced summary execution, and

Grant a quick termination. For Kane there was forgiveness if he pledged his unquestioning allegiance to Baron Cobalt and his unknown masters and abandoned his friends.

But that allegiance would make him support a mysterious and alien power and deny loyalty and friends. Then what else was there?

Kane had been brought up solely to serve the ville. Brigid's only link with her family was her mother's red-gold hair, green eyes and supple form. Grant's clues to his lineage were his ebony skin and powerful physique. But Domi, she of the white hair, was an Outlander pressed into sexual servitude in Cobaltville. She at least knew her roots and was a reminder to the exiles that the outcasts belonged in the human family.

Parents, friends, community—the very rootedness of humanity was denied. With no continuity, there was no forward momentum to the future. And that was the crux—when Kane began to wonder if there was a future.

For Kane, it wouldn't do. So the only way was out—way, way out.

After their escape, they found shelter at the forgotten Cerberus redoubt headed by Lakesh, a scientist, Cobaltville's head archivist, and secret opponent of the barons.

With their past turned into a lie, their future threatened, only one thing was left to give meaning to the outcasts. The hunger for freedom, the will to resist the hostile influences. And perhaps, by opposing, end them.

Chapter 1

The crack of the whip echoed through the fetid swamplands. The bits of jagged metal braided into the leather strands at the whip's end easily cut into the victim's back.

Crouched in the shadows of a lightning-blasted cypress tree whose branches were filled with Spanish moss, Kane listened to the woman's shrill screams of pain. Tall and rangy, he resembled a wolf in the way he carried most of his weight in his shoulders.

His dark hair hung in damp ringlets from the incessant humidity. His blue-gray eyes took in the details of the scene while his mind kept the raw emotion at bay. Kane readied the M-14 rifle he carried. He wore a loose-fitting, long-sleeved chambray shirt in mottled denim over a Kevlar vest, and his patched jeans were tucked into combat boots. A Colt Government Model .45 rode at his right hip in a paddle holster. The large canvas rucksack at his feet held spare ammunition clips, as well as other weapons.

The small boy beside the woman cried out and reached out to hold on to his mother. The boy's efforts to help his mother only hindered her. She tripped over a gnarled root in the inches-deep muck of the swamp that was quickly drying out now that the summer season was upon the land. That was a source of part of the humidity. The other was their relative proximity to the Gulf of Mexico.

"Mama!" the little boy squalled, trying to wrap his mud-encrusted arms around his mother's leg. "Mama!"

The woman was gaunt, and her skin was reddened from the sun. Mud and leaves matted her long brown hair, turning it into a snarling mess. Still, she was young enough and probably attractive enough once she was cleaned up that she would bring a good price in the slave markets near what had been the Grande River before the nukecaust transformed the world on January 20, 2001.

Kane shifted in the shadows of the cypress, his stomach clenching at the sight of the slave line stumbling through the muck of the dying swamp. Farther east, the swamps were thicker, filled with harsh, flesh-eating acid rain and mutie alligators. But the land here held the oppressive heat and dangers of its own.

The whip cracked again, targeting the small boy this time. The metal braided into the ends cut deeply into the boy's cheek. Blood ran down the side of his face and dripped onto his scrawny chest. Instinctively, the boy cowered, dropping to his knees in the muck and falling face forward. He wrapped his skinny arms around his head and screamed out in pain. Chained as he was to the twenty-three other slaves and given that they were all nearing exhaustion, the boy held up the line.

The slaver drew back his whip and cracked it again, opening a new bloody welt across the boy's shoulders.

The new onslaught of pain caused the boy to dig more deeply into the muck as he tried to escape. His terror-filled screams reverberated between the tall trees and caused nearby birds to take flight.

"No!" the woman yelled, stepping protectively in front of her child. Clad as she was in a ragged pair of cloth pants and tattered T-shirt, she was also vulnerable to the whip. Her full, round breasts and slim hips showed through the thin material.

Clothing wasn't important to the slavers. Once the slaves were on the auction block, the buyers judged them by how healthy they were.

"Kane," Brigid Baptiste whispered from her position less than ten feet away.

Kane kept himself steady as he watched the brutality unfolding. They had come across the slavers' trail by accident only a few hours ago. They already had a mission of their own, but the evidence of footprints of at least three small children had set them into this hunt.

As a former Magistrate in Cobaltville, Kane had an intimate knowledge of brutality in all its forms, and slavery was a common sight in the Tartarus Pits, located in any of the nine baronies.

However, the recent wars had taken their toll on the labor force available to the barons. Since Magistrates weren't going to be sent out as slavers, several of the barons, including Baron Samarium, who ruled the local barony, had started subsidizing slaver rings to bring in the new slaves. Slavery wasn't a new endeavor in the Outlands, which encompassed all areas outside the baronies proper, but lately it had become more aggressive.

"Kane," Brigid called again. "We've got to do something."

"We will," Kane promised.

The nine slavers all had the look of hard men familiar with the life's work they had chosen. They were better fed and in better condition than the two dozen slaves they herded. They rode horses and were armed with assault rifles and pistols.

"Don't you hit him no more, Luther," the mother ordered as she stood in front of her son. "He's just a boy. This trip's hard on him. If you'd stop and give him a little rest, he could make it."

After trailing the slavers the past twenty minutes, Kane was certain Luther was the leader.

Rawboned and twitchy, Luther showed all the signs of a heavy jolt addiction. Down in the swamplands, there were plenty of places to pick up the addictive drug, and it was almost accepted that anyone who had the jack would be a user.

"I should have chilled that fuckin' titsucker when I first laid eyes on him," Luther declared harshly. "I been in this business long enough to know if a kid ain't old enough to walk on his own, he ain't gonna make it."

The slaver leader twitched his whip again, and bright metal

shards gleamed in the merciless sun. Sweat beaded his face and neck, and his skin color was flushed with anger and the strong drug moving within his system. The horse stamped its feet tiredly, and the hooves splashed the thick mud.

"I ain't going to let you chill my son," the woman announced.

The boy cried out and reached for his mother.

A grim grin carved Luther's narrow face. "I don't see how you can stop me, bitch."

"You'll have to kill me, too, and I know you don't wanna do that," the woman said.

Brigid shifted in the brush nearby, and Kane hoped that none of the slavers would hear her. She wasn't used to this kind of work, but Kane knew she was getting better at it. Brigid had been an archivist in Cobaltville less than two years ago, before being recruited by Mohandas Lakesh Singh to join the group of rebels in Cerberus redoubt. In their war against the baronies, they were fighting the tyranny and deceit of the baron—and their mysterious backers.

Now a fugitive, Brigid knew how to kill, but she still lacked finesse when it came to timing an ambush.

Kane glanced to the other side of the trail. Even with his keen eyesight and knowing that Grant was there, Kane couldn't see his partner of many years. But he trusted Grant implicitly. When the chips were down, Grant would be at his side.

This day would be no different.

Lifting the M-14 combat rifle he had chosen from the Cerberus Kane centered the open sights on Luther's neck. His finger settled easily over the trigger and took up the slight slack. He snugged the rifle butt up against his shoulder and settled into his crouching position.

Luther laughed, throwing his head back and whinnying like a horse. The other slavers laughed, as well.

"Woman, you got what we call an overinflated sense of yourself," Luther said. He raised the battered Colt CAR-15 carbine and pointed it at her. "You see, I'm in charge of this

here expedition. Anybody who gets in my way gets fuckin'
chilled. And that's an ace on the line. Hell, I'll load you and
that damn titsucker up on the last train headed west myself."

The woman stood uncertainly for a moment, gazing around
at the other twenty-two slaves. All of the other slaves dropped
their heads and looked away from her.

Kane didn't hold their decision against them. Chained and
unarmed, they stood no chance at all against the slavers. It
would be mass suicide to side with the woman and her child.
To their way of thinking, it was better to be sold as a slave
than to die where they stood. At least there was some chance
of escape from the Tartarus Pits.

"Step away from the titsucker," Luther ordered, peering
over his rifle.

"No!" The woman pulled a rock from the muck and threw
it at Luther.

The rock hit Luther's horse in the muzzle. Startled, the
animal reacted by bucking. Luther cursed and grabbed for the
saddle horn in an effort to keep from being thrown. The effort
failed, and Luther flew from his mount, crashing to the ground
nearby.

Kane followed the man with the M-14's sights.

"Stupe bitch!" Luther roared as he got to his feet unstead-
ily. His anger made him shake all over. He pulled the assault
rifle to his shoulder. "Now you're gonna get chilled, bitch!
Keep standing there in front of your brat like that, and it won't
take but the one bullet between you!"

Kane saw the man's finger whitening on the trigger.

"Kane!" Brigid implored.

This time, the slavers heard her.

Cursing, Kane followed his target's swinging head, knowing the other slavers were already targeting their positions. He
squeezed the trigger and rode out the M-14's recoil, moving
on to his next target because he knew with grim certainty that
Luther would no longer be in the game.

The M-14's steel-jacketed 7.62 mm slug cored through his
target's throat, smacking into the spinal cord and shoving it

in glistening shards through the back of the man's neck. Luther collapsed like a puppet with its strings cut as Kane centered the rifle's sights in the middle of another slaver's broad chest.

Kane snapped off the round too quickly because the man was already in motion. Knowing he had missed his target, Kane threw himself to the left, toward Brigid's position because he didn't think she knew the danger they were in.

A swath of bullets hammered the area behind the cypress tree where Kane had been hiding. The bullets clawed finger-long chunks of bark from the tree to reveal bright white patches.

Just as Kane had thought, Brigid stood behind a tree but was coolly taking aim with the Copperhead she was carrying. The close-assault weapon was gas operated and had the potential to cycle 700 rounds per minute through the barrel. However, the magazines of 4.85 mm ammunition held only fifteen rounds. In the hands of an amateur, someone not trained to fire in 3-round bursts, the assault rifle would be emptied in nothing flat.

Brigid Baptiste, beautiful and now deadly, had learned how to fire 3-round bursts. She put two tribursts into the slaver nearest her, punching her target off the horse.

From the corner of his eye, Kane noticed for the first time that not all of the slavers were men. As the slaver that Brigid had shot tumbled to the ground, pale blond hair shook free from under her floppy hat and neckerchief. The woman slaver flailed out weakly, tried to push up twice, then collapsed to the ground.

By that time, another of the slavers ripped a gren from the bandolier across his chest and threw the explosive toward the tree Brigid took cover behind. Brigid was so intent on protecting the slaves that she didn't notice the lobbed gren.

Kane scooped her up in one long arm as he rushed by her. His momentum pulled her along with him, and he drove his feet hard against the ground, trying to put as much distance between himself and the explosive as he could. Bullets ripped through the leafy canopy above their heads. Then an unseen cypress root caught Kane's foot and sent them both sprawling.

Recovering quickly, Kane shouldered the M-14 as one of the slavers rode toward him, an Uzi subgun in his right hand. The Uzi stuttered and jerked in the slaver's grip, and 9 mm rounds sliced through the air.

Kane registered the heat of a bullet passing his face even as he squeezed the rifle's trigger. It had been that close.

The heavy 7.62 mm round caught the approaching slaver in the upper chest and knocked him off the back of the horse. Freed from the rider, the big animal got its head and ran to Kane's right.

"Why did you do that?" Brigid demanded as she pushed to her feet.

Before Kane could explain, the gren went off. The explosion ripped through the swampy forest with deafening intensity. All sound evaporated for just a moment, and Kane's head filled with staticky white noise.

The explosive had been an antipersonnel charge. The pellets spread in a killing radius of thirty feet, tearing through brush instantly. The horse was broadside to the blast, and the pellets tore through its rib cage, ripping its lungs to shreds.

Knocked from its feet, already dying, the horse fell within arm's reach of Kane. Blood sprayed from the animal's nostrils as it breathed its last.

Kane's hearing returned in a rush. He heard the distinctive roar of Domi's .357 Magnum revolver, backed up by Grant's Copperhead.

"I didn't know," Brigid said, gazing down at the dead horse. Her reddish-gold hair was pulled back in a ponytail and hung at shoulder level. Although slender, she was full-breasted and stood nearly as tall as Kane. Her olive-drab T-shirt was tucked into military-style camouflage pants. Her emerald-green eyes peered at him anxiously from her beautiful face. "Are you all right?"

"No foul, Baptiste," Kane replied, then turned his attention to rescuing the rest of the slaves.

The surviving slavers had fled to the forest, taking advantage of the cover there. The slaves, however, had not been so fortunate. Linked by collars and chains, unified by a single thought but not a single mind, the slaves had tried to rush in all directions at once. They only succeeded in becoming a confused jumble in the center of the clearing.

Seeking to vent their anger and fear on something or someone, the slavers opened fire on the slaves. Their bullets chopped down a man and a teenaged girl. With those bodies attached by the chains, the slaves had even less chance than before.

"Grant!" Kane yelled.

"Go!" Grant responded in his deep voice.

Kane surveyed the tree line the slavers had chosen for cover. "I'm going to flush them out."

"Do it," Grant replied. "I got your six."

Moving forward, Kane quickly searched the corpse of the man he'd shot from the horse's back. The dead man's bandolier held two more grenades. Kane took them both, guessing that they were probably antipersonnel, as well. He glanced up and saw Brigid looking at him.

"Stay here," Kane said. "If you get the chance, see if you can free those slaves. They're too exposed where they are." He scanned the tree line again and noted the shadows shifting among the trees.

Evidently, the slavers were certain how many people they were up against and thought perhaps they might still be able to salvage some of their human cargo. And if they couldn't, Kane knew there was every chance that they would try to kill the slaves as payback for the people they had lost.

Kane moved expertly through the brush, keeping his eyes and ears open. The earlier explosion still caused ringing in his hearing, but it wasn't anything he couldn't compensate for by watching.

A horse snorted somewhere in the tangle of brush ahead of him.

Kane kept moving swiftly, taking advantage of the cover

offered by the trees along the way. A line of bullets tore through the branches over his head. He hunkered down behind the nearest tree, and then felt it vibrate as more bullets slammed into the trunk.

"Grant," Kane called, then heard the sudden roar of Grant's Copperhead burning through an entire magazine at once. It wasn't something Grant did without extreme provocation. Magistrates were chosen and bred for their military abilities, and then they were drilled until the day they died.

"Can't help," Grant replied. "Brigid's making her bid at a one-percenter."

A one-percenter was a common term among Magistrates. It generally referred to the chances a Magistrate had of surviving a chosen course of action.

Kane craned his head around the tree and peered toward the area where he'd left the former archivist. Her reddish-gold hair flashed in the sun as she raced across the clearing to the slaves. Bullets from the concealed slavers smacked into the thick mud around her.

The mother who had tried to protect her son now crouched over him protectively, her arms wrapped tightly around him. On one side of her, a dead man lay facedown in the mud. Chained to the dead man, she had no hope of getting her son or herself to safety. The little boy screamed and kicked his feet against the mud, crying out so loudly now that his voice broke.

It was a trap, Kane knew. The surviving slavers had deliberately left the woman and her child in the open as bait. They probably thought Brigid was family, hell-bent on rescuing them.

Without warning, one of the slavers spurred his horse into the clearing. He was young and lean, and lay down over the top of his mount like another layer of hair. He rode straight for Brigid, a long-barreled pistol coming up in one hand.

"*Brigid!*" Kane shouted. But he knew the warning was too little too late. He started to get up, then a bullet smashed into his sternum. The breath left his body in a heated, rushing gasp.

Even as everything started to go black, Kane saw more men approaching at a quick trot. The slavers had been closer to reinforcements than Kane had expected.

Chapter 2

Mohandas Lakesh Singh stared at the huge Mercator map on one wall in the command center of the Cerberus redoubt, which was located in the Bitterroot Mountain Range in Montana. A headache throbbed at his temples, and he finally turned away from the map. If there were any answers there to the problems that he faced now, he didn't see them. Nor had he seen them in days.

The command center represented his own personal world within the world that was represented by the huge Mercator map. Inside the command center, Lakesh had control of everything that went on. It was a microcosm that he had both learned to appreciate and hate over the years.

Periodically, the long room with its high, vaulted ceilings was still small enough to feel like a prison. Perhaps, had the imperator not offered him a glimpse of his youth and briefly reawakened all those memories of what it had been like to be young and full of passions, he would not feel so trapped some days.

The command center held walls full of comps and electronic devices that had allowed him to access worlds of knowledge that included the past and the present. Amazingly, Lakesh had lived in both of those worlds. Before the nukecaust that devastated the world, he had been part of the Totality Concept, a secret government program set up to use incredible technology ostensibly given to them by an alien race that called themselves the Archons.

As a young genius, Lakesh had been heavily recruited and finally drafted into the treachery that had been the Totality Concept. His fields of physics and cybernetics placed him with Project Cerberus, the division that dealt with matter transfer via hyperdimensional travel.

Lakesh glanced at the mat-trans unit at the other end of the room. The brown armaglass walls gleamed dully. His research had been partially responsible for the final design of the mat-trans units. They had been secretly built and scattered around the world, hidden away in redoubts just like the one here at Cerberus, allowing for instantaneous transportation of people and materials.

But the gifts of the Archons hadn't come without price. The Archons brought about the world war that had destroyed all the superpowers and plunged human civilization back into the Dark Ages.

That human civilization, however, had proved incredibly resourceful. For the past two centuries, the survivors of skydark had been crawling back up to the top of the food chain.

Immediately after the nukecaust, Lakesh had volunteered to be cryogenically frozen and placed in the Anthill, the Totality Concept's largest hidden facility. He was supposed to be part of the subsequent Program of Unification, an effort designed solely to take over what was left of the world.

Once he had been revived, Lakesh saw the errors in his judgment. As senior archivist in Cobaltville, he had spent years plotting against the ruthless designs of the Archons. It had taken almost fifty years to find a group of people with enough strength, cunning and resources to stand against the baronial alliance. And the group he had gone to such pains to select often did not agree with the goals he set or the means with which he chose to pursue them.

Lakesh glanced at the Mercator map again. The world was so big, and yet there had to be some way to set everything aright that he had unwittingly helped go so horribly wrong. That guilt colored everything he did, and his confidence that he would find a way kept him going on day after day.

This day was one of the days Lakesh felt trapped. The need to be out and doing something was incredible.

He paced the room and tried to work off some of the excess nervous energy.

"You're going to give yourself a coronary if you keep that pacing up," an amused female voice stated.

Recognizing the voice immediately, Lakesh turned and faced the woman. "Good afternoon, my dear Dr. DeFore. Welcome to my sanctum sanctorum."

DeFore smiled warily. "'Said the spider to the fly.'" She wore the one-piece white uniform common throughout the redoubt. She was deeply bronzed by natural coloration, and it contrasted sharply with her braided, ash-blond hair. She was buxom and stocky.

Lakesh frowned at the woman. Their relationship was awkward at best. Like Kane and the others, DeFore did not take well to the his organized leadership and centralized control.

"I must assure you, Dr. DeFore, sarcasm does not well suit you."

"Let's split the difference and call it a genetic deficiency because I find my sarcasm very entertaining. The only thing I find lacking is a good audience." DeFore glanced at him and smiled. "However, I usually find a dearth of ammunition."

"As you can see, I am quite busy. If there's anything you need…"

"There's some scuttlebutt going around the redoubt about the latest mission you sent Kane and the others on," DeFore said.

Lakesh stiffened in displeasure. "I see. And you're down here to assuage curiosity on the behalf of the other people here."

"No, I'm here acting in a professional capacity." DeFore crossed her arms over her breasts and glanced at the mat-trans unit. "When I found out Kane and the others had jumped out of here through that thing, I figured I'd come down here and see what kind of damage to expect when they jump back through." She looked at Lakesh. "They *are* jumping back, aren't they?"

"My dear doctor, I appreciate your enthusiasm for your professional responsibilities, but I assure you this is nothing more than a—what do Kane and Grant call these sorties?"

"A soft-probe recon," Donald Bry called from his workstation. He was the leading tech at the redoubt and usually oversaw all of the group's away missions. He was a small man in a white lab coat with rounded shoulders and copper-colored hair.

"Do you see, my dear doctor?" Lakesh asked. "Even the name is innocuous."

DeFore changed her attention to Bry. "Where are they?"

"Almost as close to what used to be Houston as they can get," Bry said, "without stepping off into the Gulf of Mexico." He watched the comp screen in front of him.

"And they're well?" DeFore asked.

"Dr. DeFore, if Kane and the others weren't all right, surely you would realize they would already have been down to visit you in the med bay," Lakesh said irritably. He never liked being questioned, especially about things that he intended to keep private. Despite the fact Cerberus personnel all ultimately worked toward the same goals—those goals being, for the most part, the goals that Lakesh designed—not all of them needed daily updates.

"I figured that depended a lot on how many pieces of themselves they had to find first," DeFore stated.

Lakesh let out a long breath. "I'm afraid, Dr. DeFore, that I no longer find your sarcasm inviting in any manner whatsoever."

"I just want to know more about what's going on," DeFore said.

"You'll know when you need to know, my dear doctor."

"'All animals are equal but some animals are more equal than others.' Is that what you're implying?" DeFore gazed steadily at Lakesh with arched brows.

A brief spate of quiet and contained laughter came from Bry at his workstation, but he quickly covered it by feigning a cough.

Lakesh shook his head. He really didn't want to deal with this now. Ever since Kane had arrived at the redoubt, his rebellious ways had seemed to spread. Everything would work so much easier if all those involved would simply recognize the fact that someone needed to be in control.

"The quote," DeFore said, "is from a book called *Animal Farm*. It was written by a man named George Orwell, and he had a view of society that I find very appropriate to your way of conducting operations here at Cerberus redoubt."

Lakesh said nothing.

"If you're not familiar with the book," DeFore suggested, "I'll lend you a copy. In fact, you may find that it's getting very popular around here."

"Dr. DeFore, *really,* I would expect you to find better uses for your time."

"Than reading?" DeFore shook her head. "No, I don't think I can give that up. I find it entirely too enlightening."

Deciding that discretion was the better part of valor, Lakesh capitulated. He gazed up meaningfully at the huge Mercator map. "As you're aware, this map shows the locations of all known mat-trans chambers throughout the world."

"If you're so sure that all of the gateways are shown on this map, then why did you send Kane and the others down to the Gulf of Mexico to investigate a mat-trans unit?"

"If you had all the answers, then why did you come here with questions?"

"You can't believe every rumor that goes through this place," DeFore said.

"Obviously, if people have so much time on their hands for idle chatter, I don't have enough for them to do. Perhaps you would like to help me correct that oversight."

"What is so important about this mat-trans unit?" DeFore asked. "I know that Kane would not have wasted his time or risked his ass on this mission if you hadn't made a believer out of him."

"Actually, friend Kane made a believer out of me this time," Lakesh admitted. "A few weeks ago, friend Bry noticed that an until-now malfunctioning mat-trans unit suddenly went on-line. It's not located in any of the nine baronies."

"Then what are Kane and the others doing down around the Gulf?" DeFore asked. "That's in Samariumville, and definitely one of the baronies."

"Jumping straight to the now-functioning mat-trans unit that we want to investigate didn't seem like such a good idea to Kane and Grant," Lakesh said.

Bry spoke up unexpectedly, still with a little humor in his voice. "They especially didn't like the idea after the probe we sent through was destroyed. Kind of put a damper on the whole picnic."

"Instead," Lakesh said, "Kane and Grant, along with Brigid and darlingest Domi, chose to pursue their investigation in another manner. One that they hoped would be less risky." He walked over to the Mercator map and pointed to a redoubt located west of what had been the Texas-Louisiana state line. "The redoubt here was located on the Grande River. It's little used by any of the baronies because it's located in harsh territory filled with deadly dangers."

"And this is the *safest* route?"

"This is the route that Kane and Grant elected to travel from." Actually, DeFore's comments reawakened Lakesh's own misgivings about the course of action. The redoubt by the Grande River was not safe by any means. Of late, the area around Redoubt Delta had become a hotbed of slavery.

Seeking to replenish slaves in the Tartarus Pits at Cobaltville, Baron Cobalt had underwritten a massive slave-procuring operation west of the Redoubt Delta area and close to the coastline. To meet the increased supply issues, villes had sprung up in the area.

The Grande River redoubt wasn't used for the slave transportation routes, and in fact was seldom used at all. Crews were outfitted and sent north through what had been Oklahoma and on into Colorado. The Redoubt Delta slavery operation wasn't the only one going on. Several others had been established in the Western Isles and along the Atlantic coastline in Sharpeville.

Slavery operations based in the northern reaches of Cobaltville, Mandeville and Snakefishville staged raids into Ragnarville on a semiregular basis, taking advantage of the fact that Baron Ragnar had been killed by TARA and the barony was leaderless and in a state of flux.

"Baron Cobalt only runs Magistrates and equipment through the Grande River redoubt two or three times a month," Lakesh said. "It's not used often, and I do have access when it's in use. It was simple to arrange a jump to the Grande River redoubt without Baron Cobalt's knowledge."

"So where is this mysterious mat-trans unit?" DeFore asked.

"It's on the northeastern side of the Yucatán Peninsula," Lakesh said, "in the Gulf of Mexico area. Friend Kane and friend Grant intend to liberate a sailcraft along the coastline and sail it to the Yucatán Peninsula to investigate."

"How much do we know about those areas down there?" DeFore asked.

"Historically, the Yucatán Peninsula is a fascinating place." Lakesh smiled, warming to the subject. "It was the land of the Maya. Most scholars believe the Maya originated sometime between 2600 and 1000 B.C. Most believe that the original people who came to be called the Maya migrated from North America. That is, of course, after they originally migrated from Asia across the Bering Strait when a land bridge connected Alaska and Siberia. In the beginning, what scholars called the Preclassic period, the Maya people were not organized. However, some time during that age, they started to band together, and when they did they recognized chiefs and kings. The idea of royalty followed after that. Their society quickly became very similar to the European nations. They had warriors, nobles, architects, administrators, merchants and farmers, as well as other classes. Later, during the classic period, the Maya people made a number of advances in construction, cosmology, art and science.''

DeFore looked at Lakesh. ''Weren't the Maya people the ones who believed in Quetzalcoatl?''

''No, that was the Toltecs and Aztecs,'' Lakesh replied. ''He was also called the feathered, or plumed, serpent god. The Aztecs believed Cortez was Quetzalcoatl returning to fulfill an ancient prophecy.''

''But it was only the arrival of the Spaniards,'' DeFore said.

''Exactly,'' Lakesh agreed. ''The Maya called him Kulkulcan, and he was also known as the feathered or plumed serpent. The Toltec of Tula, which was an ancient city in a country called Hidalgo before the nukecaust, moved south into Campeche, the same area that Kane and Grant are headed into. Kulkulcan became their leader in occupied Chichen Itza. Chichen Itza is centrally located in the Yucatán Peninsula and was built around two large cenotes.''

''I'm not familiar with that term.''

''Cenotes are natural wells,'' Lakesh supplied. ''Chichen Itza is believed to have been an astronomical observatory.''

''Didn't the Maya also believe in human sacrifice?'' DeFore asked.

''Yes,'' Lakesh answered.

DeFore studied the Mercator map some more. ''I don't suppose there's any chance that Kane and the others will run into any Maya?''

''My dear doctor, there's very little chance of that. Campeche was, until skydark, a tourist area and a source of oil. As I recall, considerable interest was directed to that area because of the offshore oil rigs out in the Gulf. The people who depended on the tourist trade hated the oil refineries that sprang up in the area. The Gulf is also home to a lot of hurricane activity, and there were several accidents involving offshore rigs that affected the wildlife in the area, as well as the tourist trade.'' Lakesh shook his head. ''The people in that area had probably lost most of their cultural attachments long before the nukecaust. After two hundred years of barbarism since that time, I'd think the last thing our friends have to worry about is becoming a human sacrifice to Mayan gods.''

"Then what's your interest in the mat-trans unit in Campeche?'' DeFore asked.

"A nonfunctioning mat-trans unit simply does not go back on line after more than two hundred years.''

"Are you sure that it hasn't been functional in the past two hundred years?''

Lakesh hesitated. He hated being uncertain, and he hated even more being uncertain in front of others. "No, I can't say that.''

"Then why worry about one mat-trans unit going on-line?''

Lakesh shrugged. "I don't think either friend Kane or myself is especially worried about this mat-trans unit, but it could be a good thing to know.''

"Do the barons know about this?'' DeFore asked.

"Not that I'm aware of, my dear doctor.'' Lakesh knew DeFore was referring to the eavesdropping system Bry had established through the communications linkup with the Comsat satellite Cerberus had access to.

It was the same system and same satellite they used to track information from the subcutaneous transponders implanted within Cerberus personnel, which relayed location, as well as heart rate, respiration, blood count and brain-wave patterns.

Bry had been working on a system for a long time, and had recently developed an undetected method of patching into the wireless communication channels all of the baronies had in one form or another. The success rate wasn't one hundred percent, but they had been able to eavesdrop on some of the villes and some of the baron-sanctioned operations in the Outlands. They monitored different frequencies on a daily basis. Lately, all the talk among the different baronies had been skewed toward rebuilding much of what they had lost.

"Lakesh!''

Turning toward Bry, noting instantly the agitation in the

little man's voice, Lakesh scanned the comp screen at the workstation. "What is it, friend Bry?" he asked.

"It's Kane," Bry said. His stubby fingers rattled the keyboard in front of him. "His heart just stopped."

Chapter 3

Brigid Baptiste ran for her life, but she also ran for the lives of the mother hunched protectively over her child in the center of the clearing.

Pumping her arms, sprinting for all she was worth, Brigid heard the detonations of rounds cycling through different weapons, amazed at how she could identify nearly all of them. She had been born with an eidetic memory that had proved itself basically photographic over the years, so remembering something when she had seen it or heard it wasn't astounding. What was astounding was how much she had been exposed to over the past two years.

As an archivist, she had led a very sheltered life in some respects. She knew about the black-clad Magistrates who patrolled Cobaltville, but she'd had little interaction with them. And she'd had even less interaction with the slaves who toiled in the Tartarus Pits.

Since joining up with Kane and Grant and accompanying them on some of their missions away from Cerberus redoubt, she had learned a lot about cruelty and death. She had learned a lot as an archivist reading all the files for Baron Cobalt. However, that training was nothing like the face-to-face confrontations that Kane and Grant lived.

While hiding in the brush waiting for the proper moment to ambush the slavers, Brigid had felt guilty when the mother stood up for her child. Brigid had known Kane and Grant were delaying for a reason, but waiting had proved hard when she thought it was going to cost the life of the mother.

And maybe Kane *would* have waited.

That was one of the major differences between them. There

was no doubt in Brigid that Kane would save the slaves if at all possible, but she also knew his Magistrate training would allow for sacrifices to be made—if necessary for the greater good.

Now, closing in on the mother and her child, and listening to the drum of gunfire all around her, Brigid knew she had made more than one mistake in the past two minutes. The woman and her child had been left deliberately.

Brigid's breath burned the back of her throat as she ran. Pulling up short, feeling the thick mud skid from under her boots, she looked at the fearful mother holding her child.

Quickly, Brigid aimed her Copperhead at the chain linking the woman and her child to the dead man beside her. The Copperhead danced in Brigid's hands as she squeezed the trigger and held it down. The bullets sparked against the chain, making it jump, but shattered the links.

Brigid grabbed the woman by the shoulder and pulled her to her feet. "Go," she ordered. "Get out of here. Get your son out of here."

"Brigid!"

Recognizing Kane's voice, Brigid looked up just in time to see a horseman bearing down on her.

The slaver hauled up his right arm and pointed a revolver at Brigid. A snarling smile covered his face, partially obscured by the horse's flying mane. He was young, but he had a mouthful of splintered and missing teeth. Huge clods spewed out behind the horse as its hooves raked mud from the drying swamp.

Automatically, with an alacrity that both disturbed her and made her proud, Brigid pulled the Copperhead to her shoulder. She didn't bother to sight the weapon but relied on instinct and past experience. Her finger slid over the trigger— and she squeezed, just as Grant and Kane had taught her.

The Copperhead remained mute.

The assault rifle was empty, she realized. She had blasted through the whole magazine cutting through the slave chains.

Death came for Brigid Baptiste on drumming horse's

hooves. She watched the slaver's right hand bounce as his arm took on the heavy pistol's recoil.

The heavy-caliber bullet cut through the air and ripped out the outside thigh of Brigid's camouflage pants. For a moment, she thought she'd been hit, and then she realized she was still standing.

The slaver came on, only a few feet away from her now. His thumb raked forward and pulled the hammer back to fire again.

The pistol was a single-action revolver, and maybe that saved her life.

Moving quickly, Brigid reversed the Copperhead and held it by the heated muzzle. Luckily, she hadn't fired enough rounds to seriously overheat the barrel and didn't suffer any burning.

Brigid stepped to the side, pulled the assault rifle back like a baseball player she'd seen on old vid in the Cobaltville archives and swung with everything she had. The Copperhead's abbreviated stock slammed against the slaver's gun wrist. Brigid distinctly heard bone splinter a split second before the sharp report of the pistol.

The slaver lost his grip on the pistol and it spun through the air, catching the sun.

Brigid lost the Copperhead, as well, surprised at how much impact there had been with the contact. The horse stumbled on the dead man lying at Brigid's feet and fell into her, catching her in the chest with its muscled shoulder.

Knocked from her feet, Brigid sailed through the air and splatted onto the swamp mud with bruising force. Her lungs searched desperately for air and her vision swam with black spots. She willed herself to move, remembering the trajectory of the falling pistol and where it had to be.

The horse fell completely to the ground, whinnying in terror. In the next instant, three heavy slaps smacked into its haunches and blood spurted in a trio of miniature artesian wells.

"C'mere, bitch! I ain't done with you yet!" Incredibly, the

young slaver rose from the swamp bed. Mud clung to him in
great clods and fell from him as he whipped a long-bladed
hunting knife from his belt at his back. A necklace of shriv-
eled flesh bounced against his stained shirt. He grinned at her,
exposing diseased gums and stubs of broken, black teeth.
"I'm gonna take your ears back with me, and that's a fact."

Brigid made no reply. She dived for the pistol lying only
a few feet away. On the other side of the clearing, Grant
leaped from cover and ran toward the slaves, screaming something that Brigid found unintelligible at the moment.

The pistol lay half buried in the mud. Brigid recognized it
easily as a Colt Single Action Army knockoff of the Peace-
maker. The revolver had first been introduced to an American
Army in 1873, and the cartridge pistol had changed the world.
Until that time, the United States Calvary had been using
black powder pistols, which made reloading much slower.
The model P-1940 lying in the mud was chambered in .44-
40 Magnum rounds and held six shots.

As she grabbed the pistol's butt, Brigid remembered that at
least two rounds had been fired—maybe more. Footsteps
slapped the mud behind her, closing rapidly.

The pistol felt incredibly heavy in Brigid's hand as she
dragged it from the swamp bed. Thick mud dropped from the
weapon as she raised it and spun to meet her attacker.

The slaver held his heavy-bladed knife in his left hand but
looked to be entirely comfortable with it. "Gonna diiiieeeee!"
he yelled as he charged toward her.

Coolly, ignoring the fierce, throbbing fear knotting her
stomach, Brigid thumbed back the big pistol's hammer and
slid her finger inside the mud-caked trigger guard. With the
hammer eared back, the necessary trigger pull was no more
than a twitch.

The hammer fell as Brigid remembered the pistol had been
in the mud and she didn't know if the barrel was clear. There
was every chance that the shell would detonate and explode
in her hand.

The slaver was less than two feet out from Brigid when the

.44 fired. For a moment, Brigid thought the pistol had exploded in her hand. She fully expected to see only twisted flesh and broken bone at the end of her wrist when she next looked at it.

Instead, the big .44 roared and a foot-long muzzle-flash leaped from the barrel and touched the slaver's face. At the same instant, the heavy round smashed into the slaver's gaping mouth, breaking through rotted teeth and punching through his palette. Gray and crimson matter erupted from the huge hole in the back of his skull.

Without another sound, the slaver jerked to a sudden stop, his corpse slammed back by the impact. He fell backward.

Brigid glanced at her hand and saw that she still somehow held on to the Colt.

"Brigid!"

This time the voice belonged to Grant. He moved toward the tree line where Kane had headed.

Recovering, Brigid scanned the surrounding ground and spotted her Copperhead lying half buried under the wounded horse now struggling to get to its feet. She kept hold of the .44 with her numbed hand but made her way over to the assault rifle.

After slipping the heavy Colt between her belt and the waistband of her pants, Brigid reloaded the Copperhead with a fresh magazine and readied the weapon. Painful pinpricks signaled a return of feeling to her numbed hand. She turned and scanned the tree line. At least four of the slavers were dead from her and Kane's efforts.

That left, at most, five more.

The line of slaves ran toward the opposite side of the clearing. They worked together to pull on the chain, dragging three corpses and at least one wounded person after them.

Sprinting, Brigid ran to the tree line to her left. She fell into position behind a thick-boled tree and prepared to give Grant covering fire.

Standing four inches over six feet, Grant was a veritable mountain of a man. He was thick and broad shouldered, his bare arms showing corded muscle. But there were scars on his coffee-brown skin that spoke of past encounters with bullets, knives and searing fire. Gray dusted in his short-cropped curly hair. A gunfighter mustache framed his mouth and chin.

He wore jeans and a green sweatshirt with the sleeves hacked off. A canvas rucksack, the second of the war bags that Kane and Grant had filled from Cerberus's stores before they'd made the mat-trans jump, hung over one broad shoulder. Besides the Copperhead in his hands, he carried a Colt Government Model .45 that was a twin of the one Kane carried as a backup weapon.

The muzzle of a .30-30 slid around the tree in front of Grant and took aim.

Without hesitation, Brigid opened up and placed two 3-round bursts into the tree, then six inches behind the tree. The bullets slapping into the tree served as a warning to the shooter and splintered the bark so there would be no confusion as to how close Brigid had come. The three rounds behind the tree were hopeful.

A moment later, a man stumbled from hiding with both hands wrapped around his bleeding throat. He fell to his knees in the clearing, crimson threading through his fingers. He fell into the mud and twitched spasmodically.

That was six. Confirmed.

Domi broke cover to Grant's right with the lithe stride of an attacking cougar. Her appearance was striking. At first glance, she looked like a child. Domi stood only a couple inches over five feet in height. She kept her bone-white hair cropped short, and her fine, delicate features made her look like a porcelain doll, especially since she was a true albino and had paper-white skin.

She wore winter camouflage pants patterned in white, gray and black splotches, and a tight-fitting deep purple tank top under a baggy black lightweight jacket. Her camou pants were tucked tightly into the tops of her combat boots.

Halfway to the tree line, Domi raised her .357 Magnum revolver in both hands and ripped off three rapid-fire shots.

The three reports rolled like thunder through the trees. In the next instant, Domi disappeared into the forest, with hardly a leaf stirring in her wake.

Brigid risked a glance at the freed slaves hiding in the brush on the other side of the clearing not far from her position. She caught a quick glimpse of the mother and son huddling behind a fallen tree.

Spotting Grant pulling up short beside a tree, Brigid watched as a sudden spray of bark and white splinters exploded toward the clearing.

"Reinforcements!" Grant yelled as he shoved a fresh clip into his Copperhead.

"How many?" Brigid was already on the move, gathering up the war bag she and Kane had left behind earlier and circling within the tree line to reach a position near Grant's.

"Can't tell." Grant readied his weapon. "Enough to take all the fun out of this." He paused. "And while we have the chance, let me tell you that play you just did has got to be the riskiest thing I've seen intentionally done in a long time."

Brigid didn't know whether to feel insulted or appreciated. With Kane and Grant, sometimes it was hard to tell.

As she rounded the next clump of brush, she spotted the new arrivals. They were on foot and moved through the forest as if they'd been born there. Given the circumstances, Brigid believed they probably had been. Still, they didn't seem to be as well armed as the initial group of slavers.

Brigid counted eleven men as she lifted the Copperhead. She aimed at the unsuspecting man in her sights and fired without a second thought. The slavers in the area were killers. That had been confirmed by reports Bry had overheard in communications from Cobaltville.

The 3-round burst snapped the man's head back, and blood misted over the leaves and branches behind him.

"I count ten," Brigid said as she whirled back around the tree. Several rounds cored into the tree and through the brush around her. Even as the shooting slowed and the man checked to see if they had hit her, she stepped away from the tree to the left and remained within the brush, dropping into a duck-walk to stay below cover.

"Ten," Domi called out. "Was eleven but not no more."

Suddenly, Brigid realized she hadn't heard anything from Kane since he'd first called out the warning to her. A small quiet fear dawned within her. She tried but couldn't shake it off. The clearing and the surrounding forest was filled with the stench of cordite and refined gunpowder. Her right hand still tingled from the .44's recoil, but the feeling was coming back.

"Grant," Brigid called.

"Yeah," Grant growled from somewhere off to her right.

"Where's Kane?" When the answer wasn't immediately forthcoming, the fear grew inside Brigid.

Kane and Grant had watched each other's backs for so long that it seemed one could hardly be anywhere that the other did not know. Part of it was the Magistrate training they had undergone in Cobaltville, but they had also developed special combat senses over the years of their partnership.

"Don't know," Grant answered. "Lost him when he went into the brush."

Brigid pushed her breath out. She remembered seeing Kane step into the forest near the position she held now. And if he had, he had to have run into the men now moving through the forest around them.

Or had they run into him?

Heart beating a little faster, Brigid peered through the forest. The thick canopy overhead muted sunlight that came down harsh and glaring into the clearing. Light in the forest took on a hazy green ambience and angled through the branches in small columns no thicker than her wrist.

A pistol barrel moved through the brush to Brigid's left. Reacting immediately, Brigid lifted the Copperhead and pointed into the brush. She squeezed off 3-round bursts that emptied the assault rifle's magazine. Even as the body fell backward on the other side of the brush, she fished out another magazine and slapped it into the Copperhead.

"Nine," Brigid called out.

"Eight," Domi said in a singsong voice.

Brigid knew the albino had resorted to her knives. In the brush, they were just as effective as her pistol and didn't give away her position as easily.

But Brigid's mind kept drifting back to Kane and wondering where he was. Prowling through the forest like this, fighting for his life—those were the things that he excelled in.

Nothing, she told herself, could have happened to him. But as his location remained a mystery, she found she had to work to believe it.

"Hey!" a man's voice roared out of the wilderness. "Hey, let's dicker a little about this situation."

"Ain't nothing to talk about," Grant yelled back. "If you don't want to get killed, pick your asses up and leave the forest."

"Now let's look at this a little bit," the man said. "Last thing you want to be doing is going off half-cocked. The way I look at it, there's enough slaves here for us all. The barons, they're all paying a fair amount of jack these days. And there's plenty of slaves if a man knows where to look and is willing to risk a little."

Brigid moved forward cautiously, her thoughts sliding through her mind as she worried about Kane's disappearance and getting out of the present confrontation alive. She knelt down over the man she had just killed. Keeping an eye peeled, she ran a hand over the man's body, checking for weapons that she might use. The only thing he had was the .22 Colt Woodsman that he had aimed at her.

"We got more people than you people have," the speaker said.

Remembering some of the information she had read about weapons while at Cerberus, Brigid took the .22 Colt Woodsman. Checking it, she found there were still seven .22 long rifle rounds in the magazine. She drew a small knife from her boot and quickly cut the man's shirt off him.

Working quickly, she wrapped the shirt into a ball and

placed it over the end of the target pistol. She took the roll of ordnance tape from the war bag and looped it around the wadded shirt, securing it to the Colt Woodsman's barrel. She stood, slinging the Copperhead over her shoulder, then went forward with the .22 clasped in both hands.

"Seven," Domi called out. "Mebbe not so many now, huh?"

A sudden burst of gunfire ripped the quiet that had descended on the forest surrounding the clearing.

"Your guy missed," Grant taunted. "Doesn't say a lot for believability, does it? Or accuracy, either."

A twig snapped in front of Brigid less than ten feet away. Holding the .22 Colt Woodsman in both hands, Brigid moved as gracefully as a dancer and stepped into the sheltering cover of the brush circling a cypress tree. The Spanish moss hung thickly over her head. The sweet, rotting smell of bougainvillea filled her nose as the brush closed over the front of her.

"Wasn't my guy," the speaker objected. "Was one of that original bunch you people braced."

"You were out here sniping, is that it?" Grant sounded aggravated. "How am I supposed to trust someone lying in ambush and trying to get the same thing I was after?"

"You ambushed them first. You got no call to be saying you can't trust me." The man's voice held a whine.

Two men stepped in front of Brigid. They both held lever-action rifles at the ready and faced away from her as they surveyed the forest carefully.

Calmly, Brigid pushed her arms out and held the .22 Colt Woodsman level. She let out half her breath and held it. Wrapped in the shirt as it was, she knew the pistol's noise was going to be negligible. Hopefully, it would be enough to give her the advantage of time she needed to take care of the second man. The drawback was that the .22 long rifle rounds had almost no knockdown power.

Brigid strode from the tree silently, pressed the shirt-wrapped pistol barrel against the back of the second man's head, and squeezed the trigger three times in rapid succession.

The .22 cycled through all three rounds with no problem. Hollow pops echoed in the immediate vicinity as the man's head jerked with each impact. Still, the noise was enough to draw the attention of his companion. The man turned quickly, bringing up his lever-action rifle.

Brigid closed on the dead man before he could fall. She grabbed the back of the shirt collar with her left hand, slammed her body against his to help with the support and thrust the .22 Colt Woodsman over the dead man's shoulder. Holding the corpse up and using him as a flesh-and-blood shield, Brigid aimed at the other man's head. Only a head shot would take him out because the .22 rounds would just flatten out against the man's sternum.

The shirt wrapped around the Colt Woodsman smoked, and embers actually caught fire as Brigid fired again. She felt the corpse shiver against her as the other man's rifle round hit him. All four of the .22 rounds smacked into her adversary's face. At least one of them got him in the right eye, and another penetrated the thin bone above the bridge of his nose.

The man crumpled to the ground with a low moan. His body jerked for a moment, then lay still.

Brigid tossed away the empty weapon and slid the Copperhead from her shoulder. She quickly verified that both men were dead. The .22 rounds had a habit of bouncing around inside a person's skull once they got there, never getting out again and cutting the brain to pieces while they were in motion.

"Five," Brigid called out, still on the move. "Didn't lose count. I took down two of them that time."

"Hey," Grant called brightly. "Did you get that? Maybe we should take a minute and discuss whether or not I'm willing to let you out here with your ass intact."

The silence drifted through the forest.

"Four," Domi reported. "Guess I got one doing all talking."

"How about it?" Grant asked. "Anybody else feel like being the leader?"

Brigid froze as she heard the sudden movement in the forest. She took herself to the shelter of a nearby tree and waited, concentrating on breathing slowly. Kane's whereabouts never left her mind.

"They gone," Domi called.

Peering around the tree, Brigid saw shadows running through the forest away from the clearing.

"Yeah, well, maybe they're pulling up stakes for now, but I got a feeling those people may be back," Grant offered.

Brigid stepped out from behind the tree and looked at the two dead men lying nearby.

"Brigid," Domi shouted. "Come quick! I found Kane! He's not breathing!"

Plunging through the brush and swinging around the trees, Brigid homed in on the albino's voice. "Where are you, Domi? Keep talking so I can find you."

"I'm over here. Near the clearing. Don't know how missed Kane."

Grant crashed through the heavy underbrush, having an easier time of it because he was big enough and strong enough to push it all out of the way. Without a word, he gripped Brigid's upper arm and guided her through the forest. They crossed the bodies of two of the men Domi had executed with her knives.

There, at the edge of the clearing, Kane lay unmoving.

Brigid threw herself down on her knees beside Kane. She scanned him frantically, but saw only scratches and superficial wounds.

As Domi had said, Kane wasn't breathing. His skin took on a bluish tint from him being cyanotic as she watched.

"He was shot," Grant said.

"Where?" Brigid demanded. "I don't see a wound."

Grant dropped to the ground beside her, raking a knife from his boot. With his free hand, he pointed to a piece of flattened metal embedded in the Kevlar vest over Kane's heart. "He was shot here. Big gun." The knife in his hand flashed, cutting through the ties holding the Kevlar vest together. "Vest kept the bullet from ripping into his heart or lungs, and probably saved his life, but the hydrostatic shock stopped his heart. Must have hit him between beats. I've seen it happen before.''

Brigid knew all about hydrostatic shock. After she had started going out of the field with Kane and Grant, she had read up on wounds and injuries that military men could suffer. Although the Kevlar vest had stopped the bullet, it hadn't stopped the kinetic energy the bullet had delivered. It was like getting hit with a blunt object; there would be no penetration, but the hydrostatic shock was considerable. At the very least, Kane would be bruised and hurting for days.

Grant stripped the Kevlar vest from Kane, revealing the dark bruising already taking place across Kane's upper chest.

Judging from the impact area and the bruised, purple-and-red flesh, the bullet had struck Kane squarely over the heart. Brigid knew from her reading that such injuries could be deadly. Professional boxers and men trained in martial arts could deliver the same kind of blow with a fist. If the blow hit at the right time, it could stop a man's heart.

Her agile mind processed that information in the space of a drawn breath—a drawn breath she was only too aware that Kane didn't draw. How long had he been like that? She didn't know. She struggled to guess at how long it had been since he'd called her name to warn her. Had it been that long?

Had it been *too* long?

His eyelids flickered, twitching slightly.

"He's not dead," Grant whispered.

Brigid thumbed one of Kane's eyes open. The blue-gray iris stared back at her without seeing. The black pupil contracted and expanded rapidly, reminding Brigid of a crow taking wing for some reason.

A crow was often regarded as the symbol of death, she thought, then pushed the nugget of information from her mind. With her memory, everything stuck. Including useless details that cropped up at the oddest of times.

Red filmed the white of Kane's eye, spreading from the tiny burst capillaries. Brigid was suddenly aware of how her hand stuck to the side of Kane's head. She pulled it away, gazing at the bright blood on her palm.

"What?" Grant asked.

Tilting Kane's head, Brigid relaxed a little. The blood came from a laceration at the back of Kane's skull, not from a bullet hole. She remembered how easily the .22 rounds had penetrated the heads of the two men she had shot. Those holes hadn't been large, either.

"Has he been shot?" Grant asked.

Brigid ran her fingers over the wound. There was only swelling, no puncture. "No. He must have hit his head when he fell." Her quick eyes spotted strands of Kane's dark hair threaded into the tree bark next to him even as she cupped the back of his neck and tilted his chin up. "I need you to administer CPR, Grant. Otherwise we're going to lose him."

Grant nodded and moved closer. His big face remained impassive, but Brigid suspected seeing Kane like this was taking its toll on him. She peered down Kane's throat, making sure there was no obstruction, then leaned down and put her mouth on his, breathing into his lungs twice.

There was no response except the continued eye twitching.

"Start the chest compressions," Brigid ordered, glancing over to Domi and seeing that the albino was already standing watch over them. Domi's fiery red eyes roved over the forest restlessly. "Give me fifteen for every two breaths."

Grant nodded and placed his hands together, one over the other, took his measurement from the bottom of Kane's rib cage, then fell forward, using the weight of his shoulders to drive his hands against Kane's chest.

"One…two…three…" Grant counted as steadily as a metronome, as if it weren't his friend lying on the ground in unfriendly territory trapped somewhere between life and death.

Brigid took another deep breath and leaned down to breathe into Kane again. When she drew back, she saw that his eyes were still twitching. It was REM, she realized suddenly, not some kind of reaction to a concussion. The rapid-eye movement indicated that he was dreaming.

But dreaming about what? Brigid wondered. How could he be lying there dreaming when he was dying?

She leaned down and breathed into Kane again, watching his chest rise in response. She pulled back, watching as Grant drove the wind from Kane's lungs again.

The carotid artery at the side of Kane's neck remained smooth, showing no signs of a pulse, but his eyes kept twitching.

"Kane," Brigid called desperately, hoping he could hear her voice and find his way back to her. *"Kane."*

Chapter 4

Kane heard his name being called and opened his eyes. He stared up into the wind and sunburned face of a young man looking down on him worriedly.

"My friend," the young man said, smiling uncertainly, "are you all right?"

Realizing that he was lying on the ground, Kane started to sit up.

The young man placed an open palm against Kane's chest, restraining him gently. "Easy. If you get up too fast, you could pass out again."

Pass out? The observation didn't make sense to Kane. He'd been shot. Passing out had nothing to do with it. He took a deep breath reflexively, remembering the incredible pain that had slammed into his chest. If he hadn't had on the Kevlar vest, the slaver would have killed him.

Then Kane grew aware of the sand under his back. It was sand, not the thick, muddy loam of the swampland. And the sand stuck to his back, his bare back. For the first time, he took stock of the young man watching over him.

The young man was in his late teens or early twenties. His body was thin and reddened bronze, but the lines of whipcord muscle showed through in his chest and arms, and in his thighs and calves as he squatted barelegged at Kane's side. An abbreviated skullcap covered his head, leaving his ears poking out the sides. His eyes were so dark they looked black. His face was sharp featured like that of a hawk. A stained white cloth wound around his loins, and leather sandals twined around his calves. Scars marred the young man's smooth skin.

"Where am I?" Kane croaked. His mouth felt as though it were filled with the powdery amber sand spread out around him.

The young man frowned. "You don't remember?"

"No," Kane assured him. For one teetering moment he grew afraid, remembering how things had been when he'd traveled to the other casements through the power of the Chintamani Stone. But this didn't feel like those journeys.

"These are the pharaoh's lands," the young man said.

"Which pharaoh?" Kane asked.

"Djoser," the young man said. He smiled curiously at Kane and shook his head. "Are you sure you're not playing a joke on me, Kanakht?"

"It's no joke." With the young man's help, Kane sat up and gazed around him.

At least a hundred other young men in similar garb toiled under the hot midday sun, all of them carrying blocks up onto the hill where a pyramid was being built. Overseers dressed in shirts and pants carried whips and stood in groups under small cloth tents.

"What is my name?" the young man asked, frowning a little more.

Kane looked at him. "I don't know you."

"Now isn't a time to be kidding around," the young man said. "I'm getting a little concerned about you. We've been working in this merciless sun a lot for the past few days, but Djoser's vizier is a damned harsh taskmaster."

Kane shook his head and felt mildly dizzy. He glanced down at his chest. Like the other man, he went shirtless and wore only a loincloth. His burnished skin was darker than he could ever remember it being. Where were Brigid, Grant and Domi? When he'd jumped to the other casements, he'd found them there, as well.

Automatically, Kane checked around for his weapons.

"What are you doing?" the young man asked.

"Looking for my weapons."

The young man held a finger to his lips and glanced quickly

at the nearest overseers. "What are you doing talking like that?" he whispered angrily.

Kane looked at the other man.

"Slaves don't have weapons, Kanakht," the young man whispered. "If the pharaoh's men even guessed what we have, they'd kill us."

"Slaves?" Kane's mind wobbled and he remembered the slaves they'd saved in the clearing in what had been Texas. Maybe they'd saved them, he amended. The play hadn't turned over the last card when he'd checked out.

He wondered if being shot had caused the hallucination he was now having. In the past, there had been visions of past lives. Usually in those, Brigid had been there, as well. He gazed around, watching the heat shimmer over the endless sand dunes around the pyramid area.

"Anam-chara," he whispered. The term was an old one he'd learned in Ireland. It meant "soul friend."

"I'm truly beginning to believe there is something wrong with you, Kanakht," the young man said. "If you don't remember about the weapons and that you're supposed to keep your mouth shut about them, then—"

Kane turned to the young man, shutting him up with a steely gaze. "What's your name?"

The young man touched a hand to his chest in obvious disbelief. "I am Bakari. Surely you remember me. We grew up together. Remember that time when I fell in the river and you—"

A wave of nausea rolled over Kane. The incredible desert and its shimmering dunes faded from sight for a moment. He gasped and almost retched. "I need water." Maybe that would clear his head.

"Of course." Bakari bent and helped pull Kane to his feet. Taking Kane's arm across his shoulders, the young man helped him stumble across to the nearest tents where the overseers stood with their cruelly braided leather whips.

The sight of the whip reminded Kane of the young mother

he'd seen whipped in the clearing near Grande River. His fists clenched as two overseers turned to face them.

"What are you doing?" Bakari whispered desperately.

Kane didn't answer.

"You can't challenge these men," Bakari said. "They'll kill you for the slightest wrong look. They've already killed a number of men."

Somehow, Kane knew that was true. Stubbornly, knowing that living longer meant learning more, he lowered his eyes. There was no wind, only the dry, still heat that beat down from the cloudless sky and radiated up from the sand.

The two men stood side by side, stepping out of the shade of the tent.

"What do you want?" one of them snarled.

"Water," Bakari answered. "My friend Kanakht collapsed from heat exhaustion. Can't you see?"

The big man nodded into the tent. "Get some water. Not too much or he'll be throwing up and get even further dehydrated."

"Yes," Bakari replied. "Thank you. May Ra's blessings be forever on you and your get." He helped Kane stagger into the shade of the tent.

Huge clay pots sat in the center of the tent. Kane leaned on one of them and peered down into the tepid water it contained. His own features were reflected back at him, and he was surprised by the way he looked.

He was no more than a boy himself, perhaps not even as old as Bakari. Still, his eyes looked pale, though he knew the blue-gray color wouldn't be a normal occurrence in these surroundings.

"We're in Egypt," Kane said softly.

Bakari took a dipper from one of the clay urns and filled it. "Of course we're in Egypt. We've been in Egypt for years. Ever since our village was routed by Djoser's warriors and all the people enslaved." He paused, handing the dipper to Kane. Bakari lowered his voice. "Some days, even though I try to remain of good cheer, I think the dead ones were the lucky ones. At least they did not live to become slaves and die in this damned sun." He glanced skyward. "Ra forgive me if I have offended."

Kane drank the tepid water, finding it almost scalding to the taste and the smell atrocious. But at least it was wet. His stomach rumbled threateningly but held.

"C'mon out of there," one of the guards growled. "There's a lot of work to be done. If you don't hurry, I'll send you back out there with a bleeding back."

Swallowing his anger, Kane strode back out of the tent. Bakari walked at his side, thanking the guards profusely and ducking his head in subservience.

"I swear, Kanakht," Bakari said irritably, "one of these days that stiff-necked pride of yours is going to be the death of us."

Kane stared at the four-tiered pyramid sitting high on a gently rounded mountain of sand. He filed Djoser's name away for future reference. In case this didn't turn out to be just a dream of some kind—and in case he didn't wake up dead in the next couple minutes. "This is Djoser's pyramid?"

"Yes. Didn't the water help you?" Bakari asked.

"Not my memory." Kane joined a group of workmen at the bottom of the pyramid and seized a stone from the pile there. He fell into line with the men trudging up the pyramid's side, shifting the hot rock so he carried it over his right shoulder. He'd been shot in the chest with a heavy-caliber weapon; he remembered that. And even with the vest there should have been some damage. He should have felt something, but he didn't.

Bakari picked up a stone and followed Kane. His sandals slapped against the stone. "Can you believe the pharaoh is building this structure of stone? Stone!" His breath wheezed as he walked up the incline. "What is the purpose of building something of stone?"

At the top of the first mastaba, Kane halted and looked back. The view afforded him from that position looked out over a slow-moving river in the distance, as well as a tent city encamped on the banks of that river. Small boats trawled the waters, and men aboard them brought up nets of fish.

"You build a structure of stone," Kane said, "when you want to keep something locked away from other people."

"Well, since he means to bury himself here, I can understand that. With the way Djoser has been taking over villages here and taking over villages there, he's made a lot of enemies. Maybe they wouldn't be brave enough to stand up to all his soldiers, but I'll wager there would be more than a few that would be willing to piss on his grave. If I caught myself with a full bladder and no one looking, why you can bet I'd be tempted to—"

Kane ignored the rest of Bakari's tirade and watched as slaves carried a litter up one of the gentle hills leading down to the gray-green river. Wispy material shrouded the litter from the sun. Eight male slaves dressed in matching loincloths trudged through the burning sand with their burden.

"—probably write my whole name and the names of my family," Bakari declared proudly. "You know I have the bladder of a camel."

"Who's that man?" Kane asked.

"That's no man," Bakari said. Fear echoed in his voice.

Kane watched as the litter neared the pyramid. Slaves dropped immediately and placed their foreheads on the sand, their hands flat out beside their eyes. The overseers dropped to the ground, as well.

One old man, stumbling under the weight of a stone, didn't prostrate quickly enough to suit the overseer standing next to him. The overseer swept his metal-encased whip handle across the old man's face, drawing blood and knocking the old man unconscious on the ground.

"Get *down!*" Bakari knelt at Kane's side, then reached up and grabbed his wrist. He pulled fiercely. "Get down now or die!"

Giving in, Kane prostrated himself on the first level of the pyramid. But he still looked up and saw the figure shifting on the inside of the shrouded litter. "Who is that man, Bakari?"

"May the gods protect us, Kanakht, for surely the sun has addled your brains." The fear remained in Bakari's voice. "As I told you, as you *should* already know, that litter carries no man. It belongs to the god Set."

With the whole world still around him, the passenger pushed open the shrouds of the litter and stepped down onto a slave's back, then onto the sand. He was dressed in a hooded black robe that hid his face from view.

Kane watched with increased curiosity as the man reached up and pulled his hood back. When he saw the man's features, Kane's breath locked in the back of his throat. Although he had never seen the creature alive, Kane knew who he was.

There was no mistaking the narrow, elongated skull or the bony shape of a famine victim. The creature's long, skinny arms ended in hands that only had four fingers possessing razor-sharp claws. There was no opposable thumb. He was bald, and brownish-gray skin covered him. A central ridge of bone ran from the top of his head to the bridge of his flattened nose. Double rows of serrated teeth showed through the lipless mouth. More hard-edged bone protruded over his eyes. His cheekbones were so sharp they threatened to cut through the wrinkled skin. With the light gleaming down on him, his skin held a hint glistening scales.

His name was Enlil. From what Kane had learned over the past two years, Enlil was the last of the Annunaki, the alien race that had landed on Earth when humankind was in the early stages of development.

Kane knew Enlil was dead or at least in some form of suspended animation. He had seen the creature's body and Lord Strongbow's fortress, and Lakesh had only recently seen the corpse while a guest of the imperator.

Unable to help himself, Kane stared at the creature. What the hell was Enlil doing in ancient Egypt?

"Whatever you do," Bakari pleaded, "don't talk to Set. You probably wouldn't get the chance anyway, but *don't* try."

Before Kane could say anything, the wind shifted over the mastaba and brought with it whirling sands. And on that wind, Kane heard Brigid calling to him. The world darkened around him as Set started up the mastaba.

Chapter 5

Harry Lindstrohm sat at his desk in the old Spanish fort in the center of Campeche, which had been the capital of the state of the same name before the nukecaust. Only a few months after he'd set up shop in the Gulf area, he'd had the ancient desk brought up from one of the convents that had also survived that destruction.

Besides the desk, Lindstrohm had brought in huge, ornate pieces of furniture. Growing up, he'd lived in small dorms and had very little in the way of personal possessions. Books lined bookshelves, but most of them went unread. Many of them were in Spanish and he didn't read that language, but he liked the idea of possessing them.

A sophisticated communications relay and computer system filled half of the room. Alongside the books, the sophisticated technology blended the past and present, which he found fitting given all the dreams that had haunted him his entire life.

On the other side of the room, huge windows opened out onto a beautiful view of the sea and a particularly virulent bank of chem-storm clouds that was making its way north. By nightfall it would reach what had been Texas or Louisiana. He knew that for a certainty because he had worked as an archivist in Samariumville for almost twenty years before escaping and coming to Campeche.

That had not been so long ago if it was measured in years, but in reality—for Lindstrohm—it had been a lifetime ago. He'd gone from a life of servitude to that of an outlander. Now he was in the process of building yet another life.

Footsteps on the stone-tiled floor echoed in the empty halls of the old fort and drew him from his reverie. He rose up from the desk and prepared to greet his visitor.

Lindstrohm was a tall man, broadened by hard work and living well. Back in Samariumville, he'd always been fifteen to twenty pounds underweight. But here, working in the ocean and out in the sun nearly year-round, he'd reached his physical peak. His blond hair was bleached almost white by the sun, and the color was picked up in the goatee that jutted from his chin. Despite his tan, small freckles covered his face and arms.

He wore jeans and a lightweight red-and-gold plaid shirt that he left unbuttoned and untucked. A gold doubloon hung around his neck on chain. The Spanish coin had come from a shipwreck he'd found off the northern coast of the Yucatán Peninsula.

He also wore two Browning Hi-Power 9 mm pistols in shoulder rigs. When he had made his escape from Samariumville, he hadn't known much about weapons. He'd never been a Magistrate, nor had he ever spent time with Magistrates. He'd learned his weapon skills in the school of hard knocks. Since leaving the ville and becoming an outlander, there had been plenty of hard knocks along the way.

That wasn't the way it went anymore. Lindstrohm dealt hard knocks these days. He folded his arms and stood erect, knowing the impression that he wanted to make.

Narita Vasquez swept around the corner into the double-wide doors in a flourish, sending her skirt spinning and flashing black, red and green. She was a beautiful woman in her midtwenties, nearly twenty years younger than Lindstrohm and as tall. The dress, from one of the shops workers had only recently unearthed in the city, clung to every curve and revealed an ample amount of cleavage.

Lindstrohm grinned at her. Back in Samariumville, he'd never known women like Narita Vasquez.

She smiled back at him coquettishly, lights dancing in her dark eyes. She wore her long black hair down and had threaded tortoiseshell combs in it.

"You didn't have to get up," Vasquez said.

"It's a gesture of respect," Lindstrohm replied.

She smiled him again. "I've always thought you were respectful."

"As I recall, you weren't that convinced of my respectfulness in that New Orleans gaudy where we first met."

"That was a bad place you were in. And I was there on business. You know I always take care of business."

"Maybe. But you came close to chilling me when you chilled those other three men."

Vasquez stopped in front of him to take his face in one of her strong hands. "Yes, but I didn't." She paused, cocking her head to the left and looking at him with serious intent. "There are still a few days now and again that I regret not pulling that trigger."

"Only a few?" Lindstrohm reached for her and pulled her into his arms. She felt warm and soft and hard all at the same time, and she smelled of crisp, clean lemons. Some days it was vanilla but this day it was lemons. "I can remember a time not so long ago that you told me your regrets encompassed whole weeks."

"Maybe I'm just being generous today." Vasquez gripped the hair at the back of his head in one fist and pulled his face down to hers. She kissed him deep and slow, and her tongue plundered his mouth.

Lindstrohm's senses swam at the contact of her flesh. They had been together for years now, but the novelty never seemed to go away. Raised in Samariumville, he'd never dreamed such relationships existed. Still, he supposed, he was romantic at heart, and that was only one of the things the administrators and supervisors at Samariumville had never understood about him.

Without warning, Vasquez had a blade in her hand—obviously slipped from one of the sheaths she kept secreted about her body. The steel felt hot against his throat, and knowing that it had been so close to her body in some secret place made the experience even more exciting for Lindstrohm.

Vasquez leaned in close to him and brought her mouth to his ear. "As long as I live," she whispered, "I can always erase any mistakes I've made."

Despite the fact that he knew she wanted him to take her seriously, Lindstrohm couldn't help laughing.

And she was angry enough to cut him for it. The knife flashed in the afternoon light as she took it from his throat.

Lindstrohm felt the prick against his throat, followed by a slight burning sensation. He put his fingers to the cut. When he pulled them away, they were stained with crimson. Although he was fairly certain she would never seriously harm him without reasonable provocation, his stomach clenched until he realized he could still breathe and swallow without problem.

Vasquez stepped from his arms. The knife had already disappeared from her hand, back to wherever it had come from. "You shouldn't laugh at me," she said coldly.

"I wasn't laughing at you, Narita. I swear." Lindstrohm pressed his fingers against the cut on his throat to stanch the bleeding. In the heat given off from the Caribbean Sea, even a small wound could bleed for a long time and cause a considerable mess. "I was laughing *with* you."

She still didn't look at him, turned away from him and acted like a petulant child. "*I* was not laughing."

"I've hurt your feelings."

"Yes."

"I apologize. Really, Narita, I do." Lindstrohm didn't go after her even though every fiber in his being cried out for him to. One of the first lessons Vasquez had given him was to never pursue her. He'd nursed a broken arm and a concussion while learning that one.

She turned on him so quickly that his right hand went straight to the butt of the Browning tucked under his left arm.

Vasquez arched one eyebrow. "And you would shoot me to apologize?"

Lindstrohm kept a straight face. "Only if I apologized badly and you didn't take it well." It was a gamble, mixing threats and pleasure, but that made Vasquez even more exciting, as well.

For a moment, she held her distance. Then she laughed. "You have come such a long way, Harry."

Lindstrohm nodded. "That's right. I don't take shit off of nobody."

That was one of her favorite sayings. He rarely took anything from her like that.

"You can't afford to," Vasquez said. "You belong to Narita the Bleeder, pirate queen of the Ribbean Sea."

Maybe the title was a little self-aggrandizing, Lindstrohm thought, but she had done everything in her power to earn it. She had been one of the pirates that prowled the Caribbean Sea, and she had been feared in a number of ports.

Not long out of Samariumville, conscious of the Magistrates who were on his trail, Lindstrohm had stopped at one of the smaller ports along the Gulf in Louisiana territory, hoping for a bed and a meal. Besides being a pirate, Vasquez had been something of an entrepreneur. She provided protection for a floating gaudy that trolled the ports. The gaudy sluts that worked aboard the ship also acted as spies for Vasquez and her pirate crew. The gaudy sluts had literally pumped sailors and traders for information about their cargo, their destination and other ships they knew about.

Vasquez had gone into that Louisiana gaudy looking for four coldhearts who had killed two of the women working on the ship under her protection. The men had also robbed part of the jack onboard. Vasquez had followed them back to the Louisiana port the men worked out of.

Lindstrohm was talking to the men, knowing they had a small sailcraft and hoping to get a ride somewhere else in the morning. He wasn't naive about what the men were, but he was that desperate.

When Vasquez entered the gaudy, the four men sitting with Lindstrohm knew who she was and whom she was there for. The coldhearts had gone for their blasters, but Vasquez had her matched pair of Detonics .45s out first. Until that night, Lindstrohm hadn't known death could come so fast.

Except in his dreams.

Miraculously, Vasquez hadn't killed him, as well. But he did take a bullet through the left thigh while dodging from the table.

The other coldhearts gathered in the gaudy started to protest the killing of the four men they knew. Vasquez stood her ground, and in the next minute her crew stepped into the gaudy with weapons drawn. The protest died before taking real form.

Lindstrohm was lying on the floor bleeding, thinking he was going to bleed out, when Vasquez approached him and asked questions about who he was. Something, Lindstrohm knew, had drawn them together even then.

Of course, she didn't believe him about being an escapee from Samariumville. Especially not when he told her he was an archivist, one of the specialists who helped the barons rewrite history and search the records for things that might have been lost in the past.

She offered passage on her ship, and Lindstrohm was so desperate that he agreed without hesitation. As luck would have it, they ran into the two Magistrates looking for him while on their way out of the gaudy. The Magistrates hadn't been wearing the familiar black polycarbonate armor or the long dusters that were their badge of office in any of the baronies. As a result, they died quickly. When it came to killing, Narita Vasquez could do so in a heartbeat, and without compunction.

After that, she took him aboard her ship and saw to it that he was properly cared for.

The incredible chemistry between them kicked in after that. And he revealed to her all the plans he had for Campeche on the Yucatán Peninsula. Including the mat-trans unit he'd recently brought back on-line using his knowledge as an archivist and parts he'd finally been successful in trading for.

That chemistry was still kicking in, Lindstrohm realized as

Vasquez approached him. He dropped his hand from the Browning's butt and waited for her.

A mocking smile played on her lips as she wrapped her arms around his neck. Instinctively, his hands slid down her body, caressing the outsides of her breasts before finding a home on the flare of her hips. Her lemon scent filled his nostrils.

"Maybe we could have a glass of wine," she suggested.

"Only one," Lindstrohm agreed. "Wei Qiang's representatives should be here this evening. I don't want my mind clouded when I deal with them."

"Do you know who the representatives will be?"

Lindstrohm shook his head. He crossed the room and went down into the basement briefly to get a bottle of wine. The basement of the old Spanish fort had been constructed hundreds of years before, but it was still watertight despite the limestone foundation of the Yucatán Peninsula, which created numerous underground wells and even the world's largest underground river, undiscovered until 1982.

Returning to his office area, Lindstrohm took Vasquez by the arm and guided her out through the double-wide doors opening onto a generous balcony overlooking the Gulf of Mexico. The balcony had a patio table and chairs set up, and even had a huge umbrella over it that featured multicolored parrots.

A cool, gentle wind blew in from the Gulf, bringing a little respite from the baking heat of the Caribbean sun. Seagulls flew out over the ocean, gliding in on the winds and spying down into the city.

Although a number of buildings had survived the nukecaust and the rising sea, a third of the coastal city had vanished beneath the waves. Over the past two hundred years, the sea had receded somewhat, allowing some reclamation of the stone that had been used in the buildings and homes. Work crews, made up of slaves that Lindstrohm bartered for from the mainland to the north and south, toiled in the broken areas of the city. They cleared damage away, carting it to another area on the coastline farther south.

Eventually, Lindstrohm knew that the ville would fill up again. Perhaps Campeche would never be as it had been when Cortez and the Spaniards arrived to meet the Maya in 1517, but it would once more be a ville. The mark of the Spanish conquest still lay heavily on the ville, showing through in the architecture even more than the much fresher scars of skydark.

Lindstrohm pulled out a chair for Vasquez and seated her so that she could observe the city and the sea. Then he sat himself and opened the wine bottle. The wine was also exceptionally good in Campeche, though it was seldom found. After the nukecaust, the initial survivors had been very thorough in raiding for supplies. Two weeks ago, one of the work crews had found a buried cellar that had included the present wine stock.

Pouring the two glasses of wine, Lindstrohm observed how quickly the bottle emptied. He sat on the other side of her, sharing the shade given by the umbrella. Glancing out to sea, he spotted the patrol boats in the bay, and farther out, the salvage crews working on recovering oil from sunken freighters and floating oil rigs that had been lost during the nukecaust.

That had been the secret he had learned while in Samariumville as an archivist. Only shortly before skydark, Campeche had been the sixth largest producer of oil from underwater fields in the world. Drillers had tapped those fields for years, but all the indices that Lindstrohm had researched seemed to bear out that a lot of oil remained in those fields—if a person knew how to get to it.

Before he had left Samariumville, Lindstrohm had made it a goal to learn how. While with Vasquez on the pirate ship, he'd make contacts with different small groups along the southeastern coastline. He'd recruited from those men, finding men he could lead and men who would be loyal.

Lindstrohm had also cultivated buyers, such as Wei Qiang of the Western Isles, who had goods they could exchange for the crude oil he could pump from the lost ships and underwater fields. In only a few years, the empire he had envisioned while still at Samariumville had begun to take shape.

"Have you given any thought to what you are going to do if Wei Qiang wants more time to think about your offer?" Vasquez asked.

Lindstrohm sipped at his glass of wine. "He won't turn this offer down," he said. "Wei Qiang can't. He needs the crude oil I can give him to maintain his armies."

Vasquez made a face, and the wind pulled at her hair. "I don't trust him."

"You don't have to." Lindstrohm had only met the Tong warlord once, and that had been at the Dai Jia Lou gaudy in Autarkic, a small island that allowed free trade in the Western Isles.

"Wei Qiang is a walking dead man," she declared. "And he has no blood heir to leave his kingdom to. One day he'll wake up and realize that, and he'll throw his Tong hatchet men against those other islands."

Her comment made Lindstrohm curious. "Why do you say that?"

"Because power is what makes Qiang tick." Vasquez brushed hair from her face. "He lives, partially content now, because he still thinks he can have it all before he dies."

"Maybe he can," Lindstrohm commented.

"He's in his eighties," the woman said. "That's bastard old by anybody's counting. He had a son—"

"He still does."

"Not in Qiang's eyes. His son likes other men, and Qiang knows that. Qiang wouldn't leave a dynasty to a man like that. He'd see it destroyed before he did that."

Lindstrohm didn't disagree. He'd carefully researched the Tong warlord, and many of the people who'd had dealings with Qiang were voicing similar concerns.

When the nukecaust had ripped across the Pacific Ocean, changing so much of the eastern coastline of Asia and drinking most of California down into the boiling waters, a fleet of Chinese ships had abandoned its homeland and sailed across the ocean toward California. Lindstrohm had never discovered to his satisfaction what had sent those people running to the Deathlands. Maybe it was because so much damage had been done to the coastline and they'd known there was no way what was left would support a population, or maybe they'd been drawn to America, thinking that when the war broke out between the United States and Russia that America hadn't been as devastated as it was.

What had they thought, Lindstrohm mused, when they'd seen the jagged hunks of rocks that took years to become proper islands where California had once been? The huge earthshaker bombs secretly planted along the Pacific coastline had triggered massive earthquakes that triggered tectonic plate shifting even out in the middle of the ocean. There had been nothing for the Chinese immigrants when they'd arrived in their new homes, but they had survived. Wei Qiang had founded an empire on what had once been barren rock.

"Then what do you think he would do, Narita?" Lindstrohm asked. As always, he valued her opinion regarding dangerous men because she had insights into them that bordered on the fantastic. It was those innate skills that had allowed her to become what she had become.

"When Wei Qiang realizes he's not going to live forever," Vasquez said, "he'll make one last bid to take it all." She smiled. "Hell, maybe he'll even be able to." She glanced at Lindstrohm meaningfully. "Some men are born to live lives of danger and die big deaths."

Gazing at her, Lindstrohm couldn't help smiling and feeling his heart swell within him. Tenderly, he took her fingers in his hand and brushed his lips against them in a gesture that he had never learned but remembered from the dreams that had driven him all his life. "Truly, my beloved," he said in a thick voice, "you honor me."

"I recognize the difference in you," she said sadly.

Noticing the difference in her demeanor, Lindstrohm held

her hand. "What are you thinking about that makes you so sad?"

She shook her head and gave him a small smile. "It's nothing."

Lindstrohm knew that wasn't so, and despite the fact that he knew Vasquez did not like him to press, he started to ask further questions.

Then a voice shouted up from below. "Hey, Lindstrohm! Where are you, you fucking dog?"

Chapter 6

"Kane."

Struggling against the lethargy that filled him, Kane grew aware of someone's arms cradling him. Then he sensed a mouth descend on his, and the lips felt warm and inviting.

Surprised, he opened his eyes and found Brigid's face pressed next to his. For a moment, he was disoriented. Only a moment ago he had stood in the baking desert heat of ancient Egypt and gazed at a living Enlil. Now he lay in the shadowed embrace of the swamps. The ground was cool beneath him.

Kane blinked his eyes.

Beside him, a worried look on his big face, Grant smiled in relief. "You got him back, Brigid. You did it."

Brigid pulled back from Kane, and he had to squelch an immediate impulse to hold her next to him for a little longer.

"Are you all right?" Brigid peered at him, then reached forward and opened one of his eyelids a little wider.

"I was shot," Kane croaked. His voice sounded thick and phlegmy, and it hurt to talk because his chest felt as if it were on fire.

"Kevlar stopped the bullet," Grant told him, "but the bullet stopped your heart. Brigid had to administer CPR to get you going again."

Kane looked at her, but part of his mind was still back in ancient Egypt. Had the experience been real, one of the buried memories that sometimes revealed itself to him? Or had it all been a hallucination triggered by the stress his body had been under?

"Thanks, Baptiste."

She acknowledged him with a nod.

"I see you got out of it with a whole skin, too." Kane glanced around the forest, but found the brush obscured his vision of the clearing. "What about the slaves?"

"They got away," Grant said.

"The slavers?" Kane shoved a hand out to Grant.

Grant took Kane's hand and helped him to his feet. "Some of them got away."

"Guy who shot me was new." Kane took most of a deep breath and instantly regretted it. His chest felt as if it were filled with broken glass. He held a hand up in front of his face and breathed out onto it forcefully. He was relieved to see no blood.

"I don't think anything is broken," Brigid said as she picked up her Copperhead from the ground. "But you are going to be sore for a few days. We might even want to reconsider this trip."

Kane shook his head and instantly regretted it as his senses spun. A headache dawned behind his left eye, and from the feel of it he knew it wouldn't be leaving anytime soon. Moving cautiously, he checked his gear and found everything in place. He picked up the Kevlar vest and slipped it back on. Someone had sliced his shirt to ribbons, so he didn't worry about putting it back on.

"We're here, Baptiste. We might as well make the most of it."

"You might feel badly now, but you are going to feel a lot worse tomorrow."

"We're still two days out from the site. The least we can do is a recon of the area. I'll know then if I'm not ready to go any farther."

"All right," she conceded.

Still, Kane knew his decision bothered Brigid. She had only been thinking of his welfare. "I appreciate the thought, Baptiste, but hiking through wilderness for a couple of days sounds a whole hell a lot better than making another mat-trans jump." Even healthy, a mat-trans jump wasn't an entertaining prospect. He gazed meaningfully around the forest. "And staying here definitely isn't an option."

"Too much talk," Domi complained from a short distance away. Her ruby eyes scanned the forest restlessly. "Gonna be dark soon." She pointed south. "Storms come tonight. We need shelter, warm dry place to sleep."

Glancing up at the southern sky, Kane discovered Domi was right. A storm was blowing in from the Gulf.

Nearly ten yards away, a twig snapped.

Kane shouldered the M-14 immediately and peered down the open sights at the young mother standing in the brush.

She held her hands before her defensively. "Please don't shoot," she said. "I don't mean you all any harm."

Kane lowered the M-14 but kept it alongside his leg so he could bring it up easily.

"What do you want?" he asked.

The woman stepped away from the brush and held her hands out at her sides. The small boy still clung to her leg. The welt from the slaver's whip stood out starkly across his thin shoulders. He flinched instinctively as flying insects landed on the wound.

"I just wanted to thank you, that's all," the woman said. "If you hadn't stopped him, he would have chilled my boy."

Kane nodded.

A momentary look of fear flashed across the woman's face. "Most folks wouldn't have done something like that. Unless they was slavers themselves looking for easy jack." She glanced around at the corpses. "Like mebbe that other group was."

"We're not slavers," Kane assured her.

The woman smiled a little and brushed tangled hair from her face. "Then mebbe you're angels."

Grant grinned but quickly hid the expression behind his hand and looked away. Neither he nor Kane had ever been accused of being an angel.

"My mama always swore by angels," the woman went on, talking a little faster as she relaxed. "That's how come she named me what she did. You see, she named me Angel. This here's my boy, and I named him Cherub. That's what baby angels are called. On account of they're so little.''

''I've got some salve in my pack for the cuts on your son's back and face,'' Brigid offered.

Angel nodded. ''I'll take it if you got it to spare. I wouldn't want to put you folks out none.''

''It's no problem.'' Brigid dug in the war bag and took out a packet of antiseptic.

Angel took the antiseptic from Brigid, opened it and smeared it across her son's back. The boy whimpered and held tightly around her neck.

''Thank you,'' Angel told Brigid when she'd finished attending to her son. ''Where are you folks going?''

Kane hesitated, and the others took their cue from him.

Angel looked embarrassed. ''Oh, I'm sorry. That's probably not a question you want to answer. I know you all aren't from around here.'' She paused. ''The reason I was asking is because if we can share the road, I'd appreciate it.''

''Where are you headed?'' Kane asked.

''South to Fiddlerville,'' Angel answered.

''Dammit, Angel!'' said a big, moon-faced man with scraggly whiskers and wearing orange coveralls that had Property Of Louisiana County Jail stenciled on the back. ''You aren't supposed to be blabbing that to everybody you meet.''

Grant shifted slightly, but his body language instantly backed the moon-faced man down. The slave collar around the big man's neck was almost covered by the beard and sweaty rolls of fat. The big man glanced at the pistol in his manacled hands stubbornly.

A cold smile twitched at Grant's mouth. ''No chance at all, fat man.''

The big man's lower lip stuck out, and he turned away from Grant.

Intrigued, Kane asked, ''What's Fiddlerville?''

Angel smiled and hugged her child tightly. ''Freedom.

Freedom, and plenty of it. They say you ain't gotta worry about no slavers down in Campeche."

Campeche, Kane recalled, was where the dead mat-trans unit had suddenly gone back on line. "What's Campeche?"

"Campeche is a ville down in South America," Angel replied. "I always thought South America was really far away, 'cause most folks always talked like it was. But now they tell me it's not so far when you go by boat."

"So what's down in Fiddlerville?" Kane asked.

"Why, a boat, of course. There's this man, you see, named Lindstrohm. Supposed to be some kind of rich man. He's got a lot of jack, and there's traders in this area to do business with him."

"What kind of business?" Bridget asked.

"Lindstrohm has got himself an oil well. He produces fuel and sells it."

Kane thought about that, turning it over in his mind and wondering what he was supposed to make of it. Gasoline, or oil in any form, was an important resource. It was also a resource the barons wouldn't ignore.

"It can't be that much oil," Kane said. "If it was, Baron Samarium would take it over."

Angel looked a little disappointed, but held on to her child, who was already closing his eyes and drifting off to sleep. "Rayland over there—" she nodded toward the big man in orange coveralls "—he says we're all being a bunch of damn fools. He says there can't be no place where folks can live free."

"You're fucking right about that," Rayland snarled. "What kind of man is just going to open his doors and let everybody in for free? I'm telling you, that makes no fucking sense." His expression challenged Kane to disagree with him.

Kane didn't say anything, but it appeared that there were a lot of things going on in Campeche that the Cerberus personnel didn't know about.

"You can't believe that, Rayland Starns," the woman told

him haughtily, "because your mama didn't teach you to believe in angels."

"I didn't even know my mama," the big man retorted. "And probably my daddy, he didn't know her, neither."

"Well," Angel said, "when we get down to Fiddlerville and we catch that boat that's going to take us to Campeche, you're going to believe in angels. You'll see. I ain't never heard nobody say nothing bad about Harry Lindstrohm."

"LINDSTROHM, you bastard, do you fucking hear me? I know you're up there spying on people the way you do."

Instantly outraged, Lindstrohm stood and walked to the balcony railing. Narita Vasquez followed him one step behind and to his left.

A group of perhaps twenty ragged men stood in the Spanish fort's carefully restored courtyard below. All of them were armed. The leader was a rawboned man with a shock of fiery red hair that looked as if it had never been combed. Beard stubble covered his face, and scars from old rad burns showed on his arms and face. He carried an M-16 in one hand nonchalantly, the barrel tilted up to touch one shoulder.

"What do you want, Reynolds?" Lindstrohm demanded.

"I want more jack for the fuel runs me and my crew are making for you." Reynolds's tone was belligerent.

"I'm paying you all you're going to get," Lindstrohm said.

"That's not how I see it." Reynolds grinned and shook his head. "Way I see it, me and the ships' captains are taking all the risks. Every time we put out to sea, we could be taking a seat on the last train headed west. In the meantime, here you sit on your ass making money off of us taking risks."

"That's not how it is." Lindstrohm surveyed the crowd, realizing that at least thirty percent of the ships' captains were represented in Reynolds's group. The man had only been part of the fuel reclamation project the past eight months, but he had been a problem during most of that.

There were very few shipments that went out on Reynolds's ship that made it to the delivery point without suffering "losses." Although Lindstrohm hadn't taken the time to prove that Reynolds was scabbing from the shipment and selling to traders along the southeastern coastline, he knew it was happening. So far, Reynolds's pilfering had remained within tolerable limits.

"They've all been drinking," Vasquez advised quietly. She didn't look at Lindstrohm. Instead, she kept her eyes on the group of men. "You won't be able to talk reason with them."

"I will," Lindstrohm responded just as quietly. "Leave it alone, Narita."

"You're making a mistake," the woman told them.

Despite his love for her, her words roused an anger inside him that made him shake inside. Very seldom had he let himself get completely out of control, but when it happened, only bad things followed.

"Fuck you, Lindstrohm! It ain't your ass out there hauling on lines in chem storms and dodging fucking pirates."

"It wasn't that long ago," Vasquez commented, "that he was one of those selfsame pirates he speaks badly of today."

Lindstrohm knew that. All of the captains he had sailing for him now had once been pirates in the Caribbean Sea. Most of them lived off scavenging the coastline and demanding tribute from coastal villes. But there were several others who took down other ships for their cargoes. Many of the more recent pirates had come from the Western Isles and northern Mexico.

Until only a few months ago, Ambika—called the Lioness of the Isles—had operated a fuel-reclamation operation in Mexico that had done well for her. Then she had been killed in some kind of firefight against some of Baron Cobalt's Magistrates. Lindstrohm still hadn't managed to find out all the specifics of that story. But the passing of the Lioness had opened many of the opportunities for Lindstrohm.

The Western Isles pirates had hunted Ambika's ships, as well, and her vessels had sailed under Wei Qiang's blessings. He had been one of her main trade partners, as Lindstrohm now hoped the Tong warlord would be his.

"You and those men with you aren't working in the fuel-recovery stations, either," Lindstrohm accused. "And they're the ones making the dives into that sea to bring the oil up."

"Fuck them," Reynolds said. "Let them ask for their own damn increase. Or better yet, just give them an increase, too. As long as it ain't any bigger than ours."

The comment drew some nervous laughter from the crowd around Reynolds.

Lindstrohm wondered how long they'd had to drink before they'd gotten the courage to come to face him. He didn't have a reputation as being a tolerant man.

Plus, they had known that Vasquez was with him, since she was currently on the island. The captains had gotten very brave or very drunk.

"What if I told you there was no more money to share out?" Lindstrohm asked, struggling to be patient. As with the ships themselves, captains were hard to find. Losing these men would hurt the operation.

"Well, I wouldn't fucking believe you, is what." Reynolds spit in the street and dragged an arm across his sweating brow. "I was down at the docks only a little while ago when another one of them slave ships—"

"They're not slaves," Lindstrohm interrupted heatedly. "They're going to inhabit this place and become a ville." He'd been very clear about that from the beginning so there would be no mistakes.

Reynolds shrugged expansively. "They're rooting around in the ruins of this ville, looking for things you want them to look for, building the things you want them to build, and they can't go anywhere else." He shook his head. "Call 'em the fuck whatever you want to. Me, I call a spade a spade."

"We need workers to build this ville," Lindstrohm said.

"The hell you do. You got a sweet thing going on here, Lindstrohm, but you're taking on too many mouths to feed. Way I see it, most of your profits are going back out for the food the ships are bringing back in."

"That's how trade works, Reynolds. A lot of the people

we do business with don't have anything but the things they make to trade with."

"Then trade with them that have a little more jack. If they don't have it now, they'll come up with it. If they want the damn oil bad enough, you can bet your ass they'll come up with it quick. Nukeshit, me and some of the other captains were just talking how you could probably do business with Baron Samarium."

The suggestion triggered a sour bubble in Lindstrohm's stomach. He didn't doubt that Baron Samarium's Magistrates would still recognize him if they saw him, and the only reason they hadn't found him out now was because he'd changed his name. There were Mags who would remember his face.

"The barons are too big to deal with," Lindstrohm replied.

"They've been at war with each other," Reynolds pointed out. "It's one thing for them to make war on outlanders what ain't got much, but them going at each other hammer and tong had to have exhausted some of their stockpiles. I got word a couple weeks ago that Baron Cobalt has got mining prospects out in the Utah Territories. They'll be needing fuel to move those men and machines, not to mention the loads."

"I won't deal with the barons," Lindstrohm said. "Not yet." In fact, it was surprising that *they* hadn't encroached onto his territory, but the baronies had been rife with their own problems.

"Why?"

"Because barons don't buy what they can take."

Reynolds shook his head. "That's fear talking in you, Lindstrohm."

The anger burned so brightly inside Lindstrohm that he almost reacted. "If you don't like what you're getting here, Reynolds, weigh anchor and leave."

"Don't see how I can do that," Reynolds said. "You see, I know how your operation works down here, and I'll bet there are people who would like to know how many people you actually got in here, and that most of them aren't trained warriors."

The anger burned cold in Lindstrohm now.

"Mebbe you got them wells out there in that bay all boob-ied up so they'll explode if somebody else tries to take them," Reynolds said, "which I thought was pretty slick, but it works against you, too."

"What do you mean?"

"I mean them boobies could work against you," Reynolds said. "Say a man come into the bay and intentionally blew them recovery sites you're working on all to hell and gone. How are you gonna meet the demand you already got stirred up?"

As the men in the crowd talked quietly among themselves, their voices became stronger and more confident.

Reynolds grew cockier, aware that he was putting on a show. He looked back up at Lindstrohm, another comment already on its way.

Smoothly, with no hurry at all, Narita Vasquez brought up a compact .38 Chief's Special revolver that Lindstrohm had only seen twice before in all the time that he had known her. Her arm drew level just as the conversations below died in their tracks.

Maybe the men below expected Vasquez to issue a warn-ing. Lindstrohm didn't know. But it only went to show that whatever they had heard about her, it wasn't enough. She thumbed back the .38 hammer and squeezed off a round.

The bullet caught Reynolds between his widened, staring eyes. A shudder passed through him, then he took a half step back as he tried to point his assault rifle in her direction. Blood trickled from the bridge of his nose down across his lips. His mouth opened in a wordless cry.

Vasquez pulled the hammer back and fired again. This time the bullet slammed against the top of Reynolds's head and snapped it back. He tumbled backward and lay twitching on the ground.

The ships' captains and crew around Reynolds stared down at the man, then quickly dragged their gazes back up at the balcony of the fort's main building when they heard the menacing cocking of the pistol for a third time.

She squeezed the trigger again and put another bullet into Reynolds's face that broke his teeth and tore his jaw open. The fourth shot splintered a cheekbone and jerked the dead man's head. Her fifth and final round smacked into Reynold's left eye.

Calmly, as if the chance of the men below drawing their weapons and firing back with any degree of success didn't even enter her mind, Vasquez broke open the revolver and dumped the empty shell casings. The tinkle of the brass striking the stone tiles rolled over the immediate area.

"Johnson," she called as she lifted her dress and removed rounds from a bandolier wrapped around one tanned and shapely thigh without managing to reveal her undergarments.

"Yeah," Johnson growled, but his voice broke and revealed the tension he was feeling.

Vasquez dropped rounds into the cylinder in full view of the men. "When you get back down to the docks, tell Charley One-thumb that he's now in command of *Scarlet Witch*."

"That's not his ship," another man protested. "He's never even been part of the crew under—"

The group stepped away from the protestor just in time. Vasquez's bullet caught him in the shoulder and spun him halfway around, almost knocking him from his feet.

"It's Charley's ship now," she said evenly. "If we're done arguing."

Groaning quietly, the man clutched his wounded shoulder and nodded.

"Good," Vasquez said. "Then you men move out. There are barrels coming in by boat even as you're standing here wasting time. They're not going to ship themselves."

The men nodded and moved back cautiously, staying away from the wounded man.

"And don't make me step in again to save your jobs here," she warned. "Otherwise I'm going to promote a few more captains. You fucks are standing around talking about taking

Harry's ville away from him, and you got men aboard your own ships that would step right into your boots for the cut of the cargo that you get.''

Without another word, the members of the once surly group turned and tucked their tails between their legs and meekly made their way back down the hill to the docks. In the distance, a bell clanged to signal the arrival of another barge loaded with fifty-five-gallon drums. Dockworkers moved forward to unload the barges and ready the shipments.

"You couldn't let them get away with that," Vasquez told Lindstrohm without looking at him. The pistol had already disappeared, back wherever she'd taken it from.

"No."

"And you can't let them talk to you like that, Harry. Someone somewhere will get the idea that you're too soft." she looked out over the city. "You'll never be able to survive here with that kind of rep. It's bad enough you're taking in all these slaves and taking on the burden of feeding them."

"I'm building an empire," Lindstrohm argued. "You can't have an empire without a people to lead."

"You could have a good life here."

"I already do," Lindstrohm said.

"Sometimes," she said, shaking her head, "you say the strangest things."

A droning noise rattled through the sky and echoed inside Lindstrohm's office in the Spanish fort. Far out into the blue western sky, he spotted a moving object. He retreated into the office and took a pair of high-powered Zeiss binoculars from a desk drawer, then returned to the balcony.

Training the binoculars on the object in the sky, Lindstrohm focused the lenses and barely made out the crimson single-winged air wag floating lazily between wispy clouds. The air wag was of primitive design, merely lacquered and painted canvas stretched tight over the wooden frame. At most, the air wag carried two passengers. The air wag proved to be amazingly resilient, though, as Lindstrohm had seen. Once a machine gunner or a bombardier was added to the air wag, it became a fierce weapon of destruction.

Every year Wei Qiang produced several of the air wags from small factories he had on his islands. And every year, several of those air wags were shot down or plummeted into the ocean or the side of a mountain when they were betrayed by the fickle winds. They were nothing at all like the Death-birds flown by the Magistrates in the service of the baronies, but the Tong air wags could be built cheaply and the Death-birds were hard to replace.

"Is it the Tong?" Vasquez shielded her eyes with a hand as she peered into the sky.

"Yes," Lindstrohm replied, lowering the binoculars. "That's an advance scout. They're supposed to meet with us tomorrow morning. But I don't blame them for looking things over first." A smile was on his face. Even given the circumstances regarding Reynolds, there was nothing that could go wrong. He felt certain of that.

Slowly, the little red plane coasted over the ville that Lindstrohm's volunteers worked so diligently to restore.

Chapter 7

"How did you hear of Lindstrohm?" Kane asked. He walked point on the ragtag line that marched steadily south through the increasingly swampy land.

Sundown was nearing, purpling the eastern skies into a huge bruise and making the trees in that direction stand out as two-dimensional cutouts. Farther south, lightning flickered in virulent green clouds that moved rapidly and twisted in on themselves violently as if they were being pulled at by a strong current.

"Don't worry about the storm," Angel said, hitching her sleeping son up a little farther on her hip. "It's still at least two hours out. We'll come up on Fiddlerville before that."

Kane nodded, accepting the young woman's prediction, assuming she had a good idea about the local weather conditions. It would be bad to be caught out in the forest during a chem storm, but the trees and brush were thick enough to provide partial cover.

"Lindstrohm," he reminded quietly. He carried the M-14 in his arms, his finger resting on the trigger guard.

"Oh," Angel said, "I heard about him from Luther."

"The slaver back in the clearing?" Kane asked.

Angel nodded.

"Why did Luther tell you about Lindstrohm?"

"To devil me, of course. He knew I wanted Cherub to grow up free more than anything else in the world."

"He told you this after he'd captured you?"

"No. Before."

Kane looked the question at her. Angel had an irritating habit of only answering half the question she was asked.

"See, before he up and decided he wanted to be a slaver," Angel stated simply, "Luther was my man and I was his woman. And, of course, Luther was Cherub's daddy. He fathered him and everything."

"He was going to kill his own son?" Kane asked.

"Sure. He'd do whatever it took for him to get by. That's the kind of man Luther was before you chilled him." Angel seemed a little proud because she smiled. "That's the kind of man my mama told me to get with—a strong man, a hard man willing to do what it took to survive. And Luther was always good at that. Whatever he had to do to see that he survived, he just up and did. That's why I stayed with him, you see. Me and Cherub, we had an easy time living off of what he left over."

The Outlands were harsh, and survival of any degree there was something of a miracle. Domi had entered into the same kind of pact when she'd agreed to stay with Guana Teague in order to get a bogus identity chip so she could enter Cobaltville. Of course, later on the little albino had slit Teague's throat.

"Luther becoming a slaver wasn't no real surprise to me," Angel admitted. "Cherub's almost five now, and I guess he decided it was time to move on." She flicked a brief glance at Kane. "It wasn't no other woman, if that's what you're thinking. I'm good at sex, Mr. Kane," she said. "That's another thing my mama always told me to spend time at. And to be willing to share a man, 'cause sometimes you had to do that to hold on to them. Luther liked to have a strange woman now and again, and I didn't mind at all. I always found that interesting. You sort of got to rest and watch things a little, you know. I mean, while you're doing it, you don't always see what's going on because of where all the equipment's situated."

Kane felt more than a little uncomfortable with the conversation. It wasn't the talk about sex that bothered him, or the fact that they were discussing it over the head of the woman's sleeping child, but he got the feeling she was speaking so frankly in an effort to get him interested in the idea of it.

And Brigid was walking only a few steps behind him, probably hearing every word of the discussion.

"Nope, Luther just got interested in all that jack the barons are paying out to get new slaves for their Tartarus Pits," Angel went on.

The group followed a trail that was almost a road. Ruts from passing wagons stood out in sharp relief from the ground. Angel stumbled over one of them and Kane had to reach out quickly to steady her. She took that as an excuse to walk even closer to him, not stepping away so that he could drop his arm from her shoulders.

Kane felt the heat of her body pressed up against him and was suddenly aware of the sexual electricity pinging between them. Still, it was solely based in creature comfort. Angel wasn't a woman he'd be interested in.

"You know," the young woman said, glancing up at him, "you strike me as an uncommonly strong man, Mr. Kane."

As it turned out, the chem storm broke before the group reached Fiddlerville.

Luckily, the first few minutes of the storm consisted of a stinging mist that was only a little caustic and tightened up a man's lungs if he took a deep breath. Kane led the way off the trail into a clearing that had obviously been used as a campsite often in the past. It was mostly circular and located on a flat hill of hardpan that wasn't covered over with the thick loam like most of the rest of the forest.

By tucking in close to the hills that fronted the campsite on the far side, the group was able to keep out of most of the rain. Kane, Grant, Domi, Brigid and a few of the men used knives to hack large branches from the surrounding trees and fashion a shelter.

When they'd finished, little of the rain got in, but the closed-in area stank from all the unwashed flesh present. The men and women had been in the chains for four days. Creature comforts hadn't been a big issue with the slavers.

"Mama, I'm hungry," Cherub called out a few minutes later.

"Shh, baby," Angel whispered. "Mama ain't got nothing for you now, but I will soon. I promise."

Without a word being spoken, Grant and Brigid reached into their war bags. In short order, they'd passed out all the food they had, and it was gone in minutes.

Kane sat with his back against the hillside and peered out through the branches they'd laced together over the hillside. He tried in vain to find a comfortable position that didn't compress his bruised chest painfully.

Brigid sat next to him, their shoulders touching because there wasn't much room in front of the hillside by the time everyone crowded in. Kane sat quietly, not wanting to break the moment, feeling her body weight slump a little heavier on him as she involuntarily relaxed.

Seated next to her, Kane took some comfort in her presence. It was one of those rare times when the silence between them was comfortable and good. So often, on one of the missions away from Cerberus, they were at loggerheads over which course to follow. Having Brigid worry about him was pleasant, but he didn't make too much of it.

The rain came down in sheets now, pounding against the leaves and the trees and the ground. Kane had chosen the location against the hillside because of the boulders that stuck out like a shelf above. Acid rain collected higher on the hillside and came down in gushing torrents, which ran like black oil under the clouded sky.

Some of the ex-slaves talked quietly among themselves. Fear stood out as the prevalent emotion. None of them knew what Fiddlerville was actually going to deliver when they reached it.

Grant sat at the other end of the makeshift shelter. His Copperhead rested easily on his knees, ready to be brought into play at a moment's notice. Although they had saved the men and women in the shelter with them, Kane knew those people would turn on them in a heartbeat if it meant their own continued survival.

And those people knew that the two war bags the Cerberus team carried were filled with weapons.

Back at the clearing, Kane and Grant had gone through the fallen slavers and taken most of the weapons and ordnance. They knew they would be able to trade the weapons and extra ammo for other necessary provisions throughout the small villes that surrounded the slave block to the east. But when they'd checked the bodies, they noticed that some of them had already been stripped.

They knew some of the men, like Rayland, were armed, but they didn't know all of them who were. Without speaking, Kane and Grant knew they would be standing watch during the night. It was a pitiful thing to think that a man could save another man's life only to have that man kill him as soon as possible. But that's how life was in the Outlands.

Grant surreptitiously waggled a forefinger on the Copperhead's buttstock, indicating that he would take the first watch.

Kane nodded imperceptibly. He laid his head back against the hillside and tried to relax. As soon as he breathed out deeply, the pain from his bruised chest hit him again. The muscles cramped and almost took his breath away.

Brigid stirred beside him, then came awake. She looked at him. "Are you okay?"

"I'm hanging in there, Baptiste," Kane said quietly. Showing too much discomfort in front of the ex-slaves wasn't a good idea, either.

"There's a tranquilizer tab in the med kit," Brigid offered.

Kane shook his head, then stopped himself because it hurt so damn much. "If I get tranked, we may not wake up in the morning."

"Grant and I can keep watch."

"You need your rest, Baptiste. You've put in some hard days."

"*We've* put in some hard days getting here," Brigid agreed.

"But you were the one who got shot." She nodded toward Grant. "Stand down tonight, Kane. We'll handle the night watches." She nodded out at the rainstorm. "With that going on, nobody wants a problem in here. If something happens, there's nowhere to go."

Kane knew that she was right, and he also knew if there was any way he could get some sleep tonight, it would help heal the damage he'd be facing tomorrow. Still, he couldn't let go of the day that easily. The dream he'd had of Egypt still lurked at the front of his mind. It had been *too* real to be only a dream. Of that much, he was certain.

"Hey, Brigid," Kane said softly.

"You need to sleep."

Kane ignored her statement. "Tell me about the Egyptian god Set."

Brigid turned to look at him. A sudden lightning barrage turned the sky above the forest a gangrenous emerald shot through with white-purplish threads. The thunder sounded a split second later, letting Kane know that the storm was now right over the top of them. Concern showed on Brigid's beautiful face.

"What brought that up?" she asked.

Kane shrugged out of habit and instantly regretted it when iron bands of pain seized around his chest. They felt fresh out of the furnace. His breath locked in his throat for a minute, then he forced it out.

"You should take something," Brigid said. "And I'd feel better if we went back and DeFore had a chance to look at you. That bullet's impact could have broken or fractured your sternum. There could be bone splinters waiting to shred your lungs."

Kane grinned laconically. "That's one of the things I like about you, Baptiste—that ever-present ray of sunshine." He paused, knowing she was upset at him. "I can't take the trank. If I do in the situation that we're in, I'll be fighting the pain and the narcotic. If I'm going to sleep, it's going to be on my own."

Brigid let out a breath, and he knew she had accepted his terms. "Why Set?"

"In the forest earlier, I dreamed about him."

"You dreamed about Set?" Brigid hesitated. "Have you ever dreamed about Set before?"

"Not that I know of, Baptiste." Kane let a little of the impatience he was feeling show in his voice. "I don't keep track of all my dreams." He worked hard not to remember most of them.

"What do you know about Set?"

"Evidently, not a hell of a lot if I'm asking you."

"How can you have a dream about someone you've never met and aren't familiar with?"

"Damn, Baptiste, that will be my second question."

The concern in Brigid's emerald eyes deepened.

"Look," Kane said, "in my dream Set looked like Enlil."

Brigid considered that for a moment. "Okay, I can see that. But why would you dream about Enlil?"

"Baptiste, I was shot. Maybe everybody dreams about Enlil when they're shot." Maybe, Kane told himself, it would have been easier to just try to go to sleep.

"Actually, given the description of Set, Enlil is not a bad match," Brigid admitted. "Set was described as a man with a jackal's head. In other drawings, Set had a crocodile's head. And there were other depictions of him, as well, that showed him as a black pig and a hippopotamus during his battle with Horus." She looked at him. "Did you dream about Horus?"

"I don't even know who that is, Baptiste."

Brigid shook her head. "It makes no sense that you would dream about Set and not Horus. In the Egyptian mythologies, those two are closely linked."

Kane waited. Part of Brigid's methodology he could do without. Most of the time she was so busy trying to organize her thoughts that she didn't simply let the information flow. She forgot that Kane was not an archivist, and that most of the time he was looking for a simple answer, or part of a simple answer that would lead him to the rest.

"Set was also known as Sutekh," Brigid said. "Egypt was basically divided into two lands, the upper and lower. Set was one of the more important gods of Upper Egypt. He represented the winds, storms—"

Lightning flashed again and made Cherub cry out while he lay sleeping in Angel's arms. The rolling cannonade of thunder shuddered through the branches interlaced over the hillside.

"—war and, eventually, evil," Brigid went on.

"The Egyptians didn't think of Set as evil in the beginning?" Kane asked.

"No. In the beginning, Set was simply one of the other gods. He was the moodiest of the gods, and was believed to be a friend of Osiris and Isis. He was also a staunch defender of Ra, who was his father and the Egyptian sun god. Somewhere through the mythology, Set changed. He no longer aligned himself with the gods of light, and chose to become the god of darkness instead."

"Why?" Kane asked.

"The Egyptian mythology doesn't say," Brigid answered. "There was another god named Apep, who was the original god of evil. Apep disappeared at some point, as well. Apep was a serpent-looking god, which could coincide with the crocodile look that is credited to Set."

Sorting through what the archivist was telling him, Kane found nothing to indicate why he dreamed about an Egyptian god that happened to look like Enlil. He supposed that the accident was claiming too much of his attention, but he could let it go. He watched the acid rain sluicing across the swampland outside the shelter.

"By the XXVI Dynasty, Set was acknowledged by all the Egyptians as the god of evil. He fell out of favor with the Egyptian people, and he made war against Horus, who was a son of Osiris, his brother." Brigid paused and frowned in thought. "You know, Enlil was around during that time. We've learned from Balam that the Annunaki were on earth at that point. Maybe he *was* the god Set. Or maybe he only played Set for a time.''

''The evil time,'' Kane said. The information they had finally ferreted out about the Annunaki revealed that the alien race had viewed Earth as a combination industrial dream-come-true and an experimental lab. The Annunaki immediately set out to restructure Earth's human inhabitants into a race of slaves that would be smarter and faster with each successive generation. When they found that their slave race had grown largely intractable, they wiped out their slave race in an event that came to be known as simply the Flood, the Annunaki left again.

During their absence, another alien race visited Earth. This group became known as the Sidhe, the Faylinn, the Dei Terreni and the Tuatha de Danaan. They settled in isolated Ireland, and spent their lives teaching the wild Irish clans about art, architecture, mathematics and the science they had built based on the controlled manipulation of sound waves.

When the Annunaki returned, they convinced the humans that the Tuatha de Danaan were their mortal enemies and set up wars that nearly devastated Ireland, as well as the earth. Realizing that they'd nearly destroyed each other, the two races chose to unite and try to build one combined race that would control the future of the earth. That hybrid race became the Archons. Enlil, the last of the Annunaki, had chosen not to go along with the agreement.

''Set fought a war against Pharaoh Menes, who had unified Egypt,'' Brigid said. ''When Set killed Osiris, his brother, the mythology indicates that he scattered Osiris's body.''

''To where?''

''It doesn't say.''

Kane quietly considered that, finding the lack of detail uncomfortable. He turned his attention back to his original objective. ''What happened to Set?''

''According to legend, Set and Horus continue battling for control of the world.''

"There are a lot of parallels between Set and Enlil," Kane observed.

Brigid nodded. "I noticed that. I hadn't looked at the legend that way. The puzzling part is why you dreamed about it."

"Yeah." Kane closed his eyes, feeling the fatigue settle on him. His mind spun, fitting all the pieces together and trying to make sense of it all.

He remembered the dream vividly, and he recalled that Kanakht had somehow known the pyramid was being built to house something important. Maybe the fact had been whispered about by the slaves, or perhaps they had merely conjectured it on their own.

Adjusting against the hillside, Kane listened to the storm and knew when lightning struck because the blaze of illumination painted his eyelids the color of blood. He smelled the ozone, as well as the sour stench of the acid raid.

He slipped in and out of sleep for a moment, clutching fitfully at memories of the battle fought with the slavers in the clearing. Images of the rider breaking free of the tree line and galloping toward Brigid again—and this time he had no voice to warn her—jerked him awake, panting as if he just finished a long, hard run.

Heart beating frantically, he gazed around the shelter. Grant was asleep, but Brigid sat on her haunches just in front of him. Her attention remained on the swampland outside.

The rain had slowed, but Kane heard the distant blat of a combustion engine drawing nearer, buzzing like a bee. He barely kept his eyes open as some kind of motorcycle raced by the clearing on the rutted wagon trail. He had a brief glimpse of a rider clinging desperately to the vehicle as it jounced down the uneven trail. The single hazy headlight splattered against the trees, and it was gone a moment later.

Brigid glanced at him, then noticed that he was awake. The silver moonlight finally making its way through the storm clouds outside the shelter turned the black mud pale and added platinum highlights to Brigid's face and red-gold hair.

She placed a palm against his head, and then frowned worriedly. "You're burning up, Kane."

He could feel it then, the sickness that was upon him. But he didn't know where it could have come from. Even though the bruising on his chest had been extensive, there had been nothing infectious about it.

Brigid rummaged in the war bag and brought out the compact but complete med kit DeFore had bundled up for them. She took out two tabs and put them in Kane's mouth.

He tasted the bitter powder of them and wanted to spit them out, but he lacked the strength. A moment later, Brigid held a canteen to his lips. He drank thirstily, feeling the coolness of her body next to his. The tabs went down.

Head spinning, Kane closed his eyes and tried to remain awake. But his consciousness skittered away from him, as slippery as a greased pig. He heard a girl's voice calling to him. For a moment he thought it was Angel, then he realized this was another voice with a different accent. The name she called him was not his own. At least, he believed it wasn't.

Kanakht. Kanakht...

Fatigue pulled Kane back into slumber, and when he dreamed, it was of Egypt.

Chapter 8

"Kanakht! Kanakht!" a young woman's voice pleaded. "Come on. Don't sleep. We don't have much time."

Wearily, still feeling feverish even though his body no longer radiated the uncomfortable heat, Kane forced his eyes open. He knew at once from the loose wrap the young woman in front of him wore that he was back in Egypt.

"Are you awake?" the young woman asked impatiently. She was lithe and supple, dark skinned, dark haired and sloe-eyed.

Kane gazed around the small room that they were in, guessing that it was a stockroom. Shelves filled with clay tablets lined the walls. He stared at them but couldn't read them. Maybe he was looking with his own eyes, or the young man whose body he now wore didn't know how to read.

The young woman grabbed him by the hair of the head. "Kanakht! Come on! We don't have time to dawdle." She glanced around quickly, her eyes lighting on a small table in the center of the room. "Over here. We can do it over here." She grabbed Kane's hand and pulled him along.

"What?" Kane asked.

The young woman grabbed Kane by both shoulders, spun him and put his back to the table. The table's edge slammed against the backs of his thighs.

Kane looked at her in puzzlement. Facing this way, he could see the doorway behind her that let out into a narrow passageway. Were they in the pyramid, then? The possibility excited him. He started to take a step toward the door.

"What are you doing?" the young woman asked.

He looked at her, trying to figure out what he'd done wrong. "Where's Bakari?"

"Watching the passageway, of course." The young woman slid the wrap from her nubile body, revealing her breasts and slim, rounded hips. Her nipples were turgid and dark, and the black fleece between her thighs glistened damply. "I don't want to get caught."

"Get caught?" Kane asked, not understanding.

"The other women say you're really bright, Kanakht," the young woman said. "But you couldn't prove it by me." She put a hand in the center of his chest and pushed him backward. The table's edge caught him behind the thighs and he fell.

Thankfully, the fall was short. He landed on the tabletop with a thump and banged the back of his head. Before he could get up, she yanked the thin cloth from his loins and left him naked. Incredibly, his body was already responding and he had an erection. She grabbed him with one hand and climbed on top. She placed him at her wet entrance and settled into position with a harsh bounce.

Kane's mind reacted instantly and he reached out to shove her off of him—only instead of pushing her, he cupped her slim ass in both hands and pulled her to him, driving himself deeply into her. He tried to move his hands and couldn't do that, either. Realizing he was trapped in the dream—or the memory, if that's what it was—he let go trying to control the situation. He felt the rough grit clinging to the tabletop beneath him as it bit into his back and buttocks.

The young woman's mouth hungrily sought his. "Kiss me, Kanakht," she whispered fiercely. "Kiss me and call me by name." Her mouth descended on his, and just for a moment Kane was reminded of Brigid earlier in the day when she had covered his mouth with hers.

Kane kissed her, but the attempt was sloppy and mistimed. Their flesh barely touched, but she kept settling onto him harder and harder. Her juices drenched him, covering his loins as she sought her release.

"I don't know your name," Kane said, and he didn't know if that came from now or from the experience he was trapped in. He craned his head, glancing swiftly into the passageway on the other side of the small room's open doorway. Torchlight flickered in the hallway and he thought he could hear voices in the distance. What would happen if they were caught?

"Come on, Kanakht," the young woman whispered. "Make it good for me. The overseers take me whenever they want, and I have nothing to say about it. If I'm going to do this thing for you, at least make it good for me."

Kane only had an instant to wonder what she was supposed to be doing for him. It obviously wasn't the physical encounter; that was her payoff. Before his mind could wander too far, he grabbed her by the shoulders and rolled her over. He was amazed at his own show of skill atop the table.

The young woman flipped easily, sliding beneath him as if she'd been doing it all her life. "Yes," she whispered eagerly. He gripped the sides of the narrow table as he pushed himself up above her. She drew her knees back to her chest and allowed him to thrust as deeply as he could. The whole table shook and Kane worried that it might collapse beneath them.

Her eyes widened as the first of the tremors took her. He felt the walls of her sex clenching around his erection, trying to milk him. She reached up and wrapped her arms around his waist, pulling him close as the sounds of their wet lovemaking echoed in the small chamber around them.

"My name," she said, gasping as he drove himself against her, "my name is Pasht."

"Pasht," he said, but to Kane's ears it sounded as if he were trying to remember the name, not trying to say it with any passion.

"Yes," she whispered, smiling. She closed her eyes in bliss as a deep flush ran through her neck and breasts. Her nipples stabbed into his chest repeatedly, scraping against his sweaty skin. "Say it again, Kanakht."

He whispered her name again, then leaned down and nuzzled her neck, obviously seeking his own pleasure, as well. Metal clanked out in the passageway. He and the young woman both glanced in that direction, but neither of them stopped what they were doing.

In another moment, it was over. He pulled himself out and came over her smooth belly.

She looked up at him with a little frustration in her eyes. "Why did you do that?"

"I didn't want to make a child," he whispered to her apologetically.

Pasht's grimace softened a little and she reached up to touch his face. "That is very thoughtful, Kanakht. Olabisi never mentioned that about you when she described this to me."

Kane didn't know who Olabisi was, either. More voices sounded out in the passageway, then footsteps. There were a lot of people out there, he realized. Some of them were coming toward this place while others were walking away from it.

"You didn't have to worry about making a child," Pasht said, tracing her fingers lightly over his chest. "The overseers have one of Set's magical elixirs, one that doesn't allow children to be born unless they are wished."

"Set?" Kane grew slightly chilled in his own mind. Set or Enlil? Which it was, remained to be seen.

"Yes. Set is helping Imhotep, Djoser's vizier, with the construction of the mastaba. While he is here, Set is also overseeing all the births." Pasht smiled beatifically. "This is going to be a very special place, Kanakht. When it is my turn to have a child, which I hope will be soon because when I am pregnant the overseers won't be allowed to touch me. That will be a relief." She pushed both hands against his chest regretfully.

Taking the hint, Kane climbed off her and the table. He stood naked and watched her step down. She found the wrap she'd been wearing and quickly pulled it back into place. The flickering torchlight outside the darkened room played over her sweat-drenched body. She smiled at him. "Get dressed, Kanakht. Anyone who passes by is going to know from the way that you're dressed that you're no pharaoh's scribe." She glanced down. "But you have a most attractive stylus."

Flushing with embarrassment, Kane found his loincloth and wrapped his nakedness again. "What about what you were supposed to do for me?"

"Set's hidden area is in the South Tomb," she replied.

Kane wondered what hidden area the young woman was talking about, but his words betrayed him. "Where in the South Tomb?"

Pasht looked worried. "I don't have time to take you there."

Reaching out, Kane caught up one of her wrists. "I have done this thing for you, Pasht," he stated fiercely. Kane felt guilt at the words, harsh because of their baldness. He understood then what Pasht had asked for by asking for the encounter with him. As a slave, she was property of the overseers to use as they saw fit. Probably she didn't work on any of the construction, but she would ferry materials and at least food back and forth to the construction site.

And she was there for the pleasures of the overseers, as well. By agreeing to do whatever Kanakht had demanded, she had placed herself in control of that sex life—reached out and taken something she'd wanted for herself—instead of having it forced on her. Kane couldn't help wondering if Kanakht knew that, or if the young man simply thought it was because he was so well equipped or good at sex.

Despite being in Kanakht's mind, Kane didn't know if he knew the young man at all.

"All right," Pasht breathed out a moment later. "But we'll have to hurry. I will be missed soon."

"So will I," Kane said. The overseers, he remembered, were very good at keeping track of all the slaves they guarded.

"Come on," she urged as she walked out into the passageway.

Kane followed. The heat of the structure pushed into him,

going bone-deep. His hair lay plastered against his scalp and perspiration dripped from his body. Not all of that came from his recent exertions.

The passageway outside the scribe's room doglegged at either end. It was so short in height that Kane had to walk stooped, and it was so narrow that two people could not have walked abreast of each other. Powdery sand dusted the floor, and it crunched beneath Kane's sandals as he moved.

Bakari was at the end of the passageway to the left. He turned at the sound of them moving out into the passageway, a fearful look on his face. "Thank Ra, there you are. I was beginning to believe that the two of you had been swallowed up in this place." He frowned and shook his head. "How can something like that take so long? Why, myself, I never—"

"Quiet," Pasht snapped imperiously.

Obviously, her ranking stood her somewhere above Bakari, because the young man shut up immediately and bowed his head. "Of course, mistress."

Pasht turned to the right, walked down the passageway and took one of the wrapped rush torches from a pile at the corner. She paused to light it from the flaming oil torch burning in the wall sconce there. She turned to Kane. "Quickly," she urged.

Kane fell in behind her and took up one of the torches himself. He lit it and watched the flames mushroom up as they started consuming the rushes. The heat washed over him.

"Where are we going?" Bakari asked nervously.

"To the South Tomb," Kane whispered.

"What?"

Kane followed the young woman, surprised at the length of her stride when she moved. He left Bakari standing behind him, but knew immediately when he heard the other man's sandals slapping and skidding across the sand-covered stone that Bakari hadn't remained behind.

"Do you want to be killed?" Bakari demanded.

"No," Kane growled.

"Then why are we doing this?"

"Because I want to," Kane replied. Though he felt certain the words had been Kanakht's all those years ago, Kane felt that he was bound to the course of action as well. This was similar to the memories he sometimes got of Brigid and himself—*if* those were memories even—but he knew it was different, too.

Why now? he wondered. Was this dream inspired by the fever that coursed through him while he lay sleeping in the shelter, a tangent taken from his earlier dream while lying between life and death? Or could it be something else?

Kane didn't know. He pushed the questions from his mind as he followed Pasht through the swiftly turning passageways.

"We're never going to find our way out of here if we get lost," Bakari whispered fretfully.

"Yes, we will," Kane assured him.

"Do you know your way out of here?" Bakari demanded. "This place is a maze."

"Mazes can be defeated," Kane said. "It's the other tricks and traps that the pharaohs place in their tombs that are the true dangers."

"What tricks and traps?" Bakari asked. "You didn't say anything about tricks and traps."

Kane wheeled suddenly, stopping in front of Bakari so quickly that the man bumped into him before he could stop himself. Kane drove a stiff forefinger into Bakari's thin chest. "Be quiet or go back."

Bakari glanced fearfully back the way they'd come. He swallowed hard, then nodded. "I'll be quiet."

When Kane turned back around, he saw Pasht glaring at him. He nodded and caught up.

"The underground mazes are going to be the actual resting places of the pharaoh and his family," Pasht explained. "When it's completed, the pyramid will have six mastabas, each smaller than the other, stacked on top of each other."

"Are there any rooms above?" Kane asked.

"You helped build those mastabas. Don't you know?"

"No," Kane replied.

Pasht drew up suddenly around another corner. She stood in front of a T-intersection. Shoving her torch forward, she cast the light into each passageway. The passageway to the right went up, and the passageway to the left descended at a steep decline.

"This way," the young woman said, swinging her torch in that direction.

"You're sure?" Bakari asked from behind.

Pasht went forward without a word, and Kane followed. He felt a sudden, sharp pain in his chest and thought for just a moment that he had tripped one of the deadly traps the young woman had mentioned. Then he realized he had to have shifted in his sleep back in the shelter and aggravated the bruising.

As he followed Pasht down into the underground labyrinth beneath the pyramid, Kane noted that the temperature dropped quickly. The flames of their torches cut through the darkness and guttered slightly as they moved.

"The pharaoh plans to have his mummy buried in the pyramid," Pasht said, "but his viscera will be buried in the South Tomb."

"Why?" Kane asked.

"As he and Set work to unify the Egyptian lands and make the people better understand the importance of the god-kings," Pasht said, "they have decided there must also be a unification of the two lands of Upper and Lower Egypt. Having tombs representing both places will satisfy those separate interests."

Suspicion darkened Kane's thoughts when he considered Djoser's decision about the viscera. Was it as simple as satisfying the issue of political boundaries? Or—with Enlil involved—was there something more sinister involved?

Twice, Pasht led them into side rooms while architects and overseers walked past. Even with the torches burning, those people never looked twice. Security was lax.

After a few more minutes of traveling through the passageways, Pasht found one that led up again. At the top of the incline, they stepped out into another passageway. Without hesitation, the young woman led the way into a large room.

"This is the chapel," Pasht whispered, stopping long enough to get her bearings. "The overseers bring the women here for sex when they can get away with it. Set and Djoser visit here only occasionally."

"Show me where the hidden door is," Kane said, but he knew it was Kanakht speaking, not him.

Pasht moved forward as footsteps echoed out in the hall. She never even looked back.

Bakari caught Kane's arm. "We should get out of here. If the overseers find us here, they'll kill us all."

"I need to know," Kane replied.

Shaking his head, Bakari asked, "Why do you think you always need to know? Ever since Set first came to visit the pharaoh you've been like this. You're not on their level, Kanakht. They would destroy you with one look."

"Because," Kane said, "I don't trust Set."

"You're a slave!" Bakari whispered in frantic frustration. "You're in no position to trust anyone!"

Kane clapped the smaller man on the shoulder. "I trust you." Then he followed Pasht.

She led the way into a room to the left. It was long and narrow. "This is the room where Djoser's viscera will be laid to rest in canopic jars."

At present, the room was empty.

"What about the hidden room?" Kane asked.

Pasht hesitated a moment, then walked to the wall on the right. She began at the right side where the wall butted into the next. Kneeling, she counted rows of stones. "The release is eight stones up," she said, then moved to her left along the row of stones, "and thirty-three stones over." She used both hands to push the stone she isolated from all the rest.

A click echoed throughout the burial chamber.

"Ra preserve us," Bakari whispered.

Suddenly, a section of the wall folded back, revealing a chamber within.

"There," Pasht said, moving forward cautiously. Her torch illuminated the room and glittered against metal-and-glass surfaces. Surprise showed on her face.

"What is it?" Kane asked. He stepped in behind her and raised his own torch until the flames touched the ceiling.

The device sat on a flat table. It was something less than three feet tall and no more than two feet deep and two feet wide. A curved metal surface shaped like an upside-down bowl covered the top of the machine. Two smaller bowls, these right-side up, occupied space under the much larger bowl on top. Glass tubing connected all the bowls, then ran down into a basket below. The device looked incredibly simple, but the tubing was twisted into arcane shapes.

Pasht shook her head. "I don't know. This has never been here before." Suddenly, she froze, her mouth halfway open as if to say something else.

"Pasht," Kane called softly.

The young woman didn't answer.

Kane stepped closer to her and put an arm out to touch her. "Pasht."

Her flesh felt cool and dry to his touch despite the fact that he could see perspiration gleaming on her. She also felt as stiff and as immobile as a statue.

The skin at the back of Kane's neck tightened. He looked at her torch and saw that even the flames had stopped moving, though they remained as bright as ever. He looked to his own torch and saw the same thing had happened. Cautiously, he reached up and touched the torch flames. The light in the room remained but only some of the heat.

"Kane."

Recognizing the voice, Kane turned swiftly.

A strange figure stood in the doorway leading to the tomb proper. He stood less than five feet tall and possessed a slender build. His head was a round, bald dome, but his features were sharp, primarily all cheek and forehead, with pale gray-

ish-pink skin stretched tightly over them. His eyes were two
great hollows in his face, seemingly depthless. His mouth was
a slit over a weak-looking chin. He wore gray robes and knit-
ted his six-fingered hands before him.

"Balam," Kane breathed, calling the creature by name.

Balam was the last of the Archons, the last of the children
Enlil had created from the two alien races that had come to
Earth and turned it into a battleground until they had almost
wiped each other out.

"Do you remember this place?" Balam asked quietly, waving his hands at the room.

"No," Kane answered.

"But you are here now," Balam said. "So if you are here
now, then you must have been there then."

The logic was confusing, but Kane knew better than to
argue with it. "Where am I?"

"In the past," Balam said. "In Egypt, land of the pyramid
builders. It looks as though it was a very interesting period in
your culture's history."

"I wouldn't know," Kane said. He tossed the torch away
to free his hands and wished that he had a weapon. He didn't
fear Balam because the Archon had never tried to injure him,
and had even helped him on occasion. But wherever Balam
turned up, danger seemed to follow.

Did that hold true if Balam turned up in the past? Kane
wondered. He glanced down at the frozen flames of the rush
torch and guessed that it was entirely possible. As he turned
back to Balam, he saw the Archon waver out of sight for a
moment, then pop back and become clear again.

"You should know," Balam said, "since you were here."

"I was never here," Kane said. "I'm not sure I'm here
now. This could be a fever dream." And if it is, he thought,
I'm talking to myself.

"Don't overly concern yourself about the fever, Kane,"
Balam replied, approaching the machine in the center of the
room. He stepped around Bakari, who also stood frozen, to
get there. "The fever is merely your body's reaction to the

stress I'm putting your mind under to remember these things.''

''What things?'' Kane demanded.

''This machine,'' Balam answered. ''For one.''

Kane looked at the dormant machine. ''Why should I be interested in this machine?''

''Because later, Kane,'' the Archon said, ''you will make a promise about this machine, and you will make an enemy.'' He touched the machine, but his hand passed through it, not capable of physical contact. ''I'm not here, but I have a connectivity to this place through you. And through others.''

''What is this machine?'' Kane asked. Looking at it, the machine didn't appear to be much. But anything the Archons were involved with was always much more than it appeared to be. His experiences with the Chintamani Stone were proof enough of that.

''It is,'' Balam said, ''a machine of great power.''

Kane felt himself growing irritated at the response. ''That's not an answer.''

''Now is not the time for all answers, Kane,'' Balam said. ''You will be shown the things you need to know as you need to know them. Rest assured of that. This journey that you're on has been predetermined by your promise, and by who you are.''

''Is Enlil here?'' Kane asked. ''Is he Set?''

Balam hesitated for a moment. Enlil's hand had guided the birth of the Archons, and Balam still had ties to that, as well as emotional complexities of his own. ''The Enlil that was,'' he stated slowly, as if wanting to be certain he was understood, ''is the Enlil that you have seen here. But he is not the Enlil that now is.''

''I don't understand.''

''You will, Kane, in time.'' Balam stretched out a hand, and light seemed to radiate in his palm. ''You can find all the answers—in time.''

Kane reached for Balam's hand, meaning to brush it aside

and keep the bright light from burning into his eyes. Only his hand passed through the Archon's.

Balam faded before him and the torch in Pasht's hand suddenly wavered again. The young woman turned to him with a worried look. "Kanakht? Are you all right?"

Kane tried to answer, though he didn't know what he was going to say. But Bakari interrupted. "Someone's coming!" the man hissed fearfully. "I hear them."

Turning, Kane heard them, too. Besides the scuffing footsteps dragging across the sand-covered floor, there were also muted voices. "Douse the torches," he ordered, moving quickly to step on the one he'd carried in. The flames went out reluctantly and embers flew into the air. Thankfully, they quickly extinguished.

Pasht wrapped her own torch in her shift and extinguished it with the sweat-soaked material.

Kane grabbed both extinguished torches and followed Pasht out of the room. She tapped the recessed stone again, and the hidden door swung closed.

"There's another way," she whispered.

Kane reached back for Bakari, grabbing him by the shoulder and yanking him from the hidden room with only inches to spare.

Pasht led them to the other side of the temple area as the footsteps continued to come closer and the voices grew louder. She knelt on the floor and pulled at one of the large stones. "Here," she said frantically. "The overseers know about this place. Imhotep and Djoser and even Set think they have secrets in these places, but there are few that the overseers don't know."

Kane joined her and had trouble jamming his fingers into the small crevice that separated the stone from the others. Even when he had managed a grip, he found the stone was incredibly heavy. When he shoved it aside, he could barely make out the round entrance to a passageway.

"What is this?" Kane asked.

"An escape route," Pasht said.

"Where does it go?"

"Out. Does it matter?" Pasht's voice held fear. "If we get caught, they'll kill us." She slid over the edge and dropped down. Kane followed her and found a ledge at the passageway's edge that allowed him to stand and reach the stone overhead.

Bakari hesitated above.

Kane reached up and grabbed the man by the hair and yanked him down into the escape tunnel, clapping his other hand over Bakari's mouth. "Quiet!" Kane barked. "Or you'll get us all killed!"

Bakari nodded.

Kane released the man, then quickly stood and replaced the stone over the passageway entrance. They were sealed in utter darkness as footsteps resonated in the temple above.

Then a light flared in the darkness, revealing a middle-aged man holding a small torch in one hand and a curved dagger in the other. A young woman lay in the passageway behind him, hurriedly putting her clothing back on.

The man was dressed in the uniform of an overseer. A whip lay coiled on the ground next to him. He smiled as he looked at the three new arrivals. "You three are surely in trouble," he promised. Then he looked at Kane and some of the arrogant demeanor slipped. He peered more closely.

The torchlight glared into Kane's eyes. He held up a palm to shield it from his face, but somehow the harsh light seemed to bend around his hand, growing brighter and brighter.

"Do I know you?" the overseer demanded.

Kane's eyes teared and his vision misted as the light continued increasing. In a heartbeat he couldn't see anything but the light, and pain exploded in his head.

"Ka'in?" the overseer's voice thundered. "Is that you? *Ka'in?*"

Chapter 9

"Ka'in?" The name came to Harry Lindstrohm's lips unbidden as he stared at the young slave illuminated by the torch in front of him. A wave of nausea swept through him as he settled more firmly into the dream, but he kept focused on the young slave. Did dark recognition spark in those eyes?

The young woman with the slave quickly stepped behind him. Obviously, she was afraid of being recognized. It could only mean that whoever Lindstrohm was in this life had known her. But from the look he'd gotten of her, he would have sworn he'd never seen her in his life.

"Ka'in," Lindstrohm said again. He peered around quickly, not wanting to take his eyes from the young slave in front of him. They were in a passageway, and it was one of the smallest ones he'd seen in the pyramids. That meant it was probably one of the secret tunnels under the lowest mastaba.

The thinner man of the two threw himself to the floor. "Oh, please, I ask your forgiveness, Overseer. We were traveling through the passageways doing our work and became lost."

Lindstrohm ignored the scared slave and kept his eyes on the other man. The glacial and predatory set of the man's features was warning enough that he was capable of immediate violent behavior. A thought stirred in the back of Lindstrohm's mind, letting him know that if the slave did take such action, it was punishable by death.

Would Ka'in know that? Lindstrohm wondered. Or would the man care? He wasn't certain. He'd only met Ka'in a time or two in his dreams, and he'd never really learned much about the man. However, Lindstrohm was certain that Ka'in was real, because the Holy Grail was real.

"Ka'in," Lindstrohm tried again.

The young man shook his head. "My name is Kanakht."

Lindstrohm moved closer, pushing his torch toward the young man. The spark of recognition he'd seen in the man's eyes had disappeared. "What were you doing here?" Lindstrohm demanded.

"Overseer," the prostrate man on the floor of the passageway said, "we were lost."

"No," Lindstrohm said. "I don't believe you."

Kanakht didn't reply.

"Honestly, Overseer," the prostrate man said. "It was a mistake. We—"

"You were here to look at the machine, weren't you?" Lindstrohm demanded.

Kanakht shook his head. "I don't know what you're talking about."

Lindstrohm gripped his knife more tightly and felt the black rage that often overcame him in the dreams seethe through him. Vasquez had accused him of not acting quickly enough earlier in the day, but in his dreams he always acted immediately. "Yes, you do."

Kanakht's eyes slitted. "No. I came here with a woman." He nodded toward the woman seated behind Lindstrohm. "The same as you did. It was hot outside, and I've been worked too hard lately."

It was no use, Lindstrohm realized. Ka'in, if he'd ever truly been there, was gone. He blew his breath out in a great gust that echoed through the passageway. "Get out of here," he commanded.

The skinny slave pushed himself to his feet in a heartbeat. "Which way is the quickest?"

Lindstrohm pointed his torch at the other end of the passageway.

The skinny man started down it immediately, catching the young woman's hand in his and pulling her along into the darkness. The other young man backed away, keeping his eyes on Lindstrohm and his hands out to his sides. That way he remained ready. He didn't trust Lindstrohm.

Ka'in doppelgängers always exhibited such control and awareness.

Lindstrohm held his torch high for a time, watching them go until they disappeared from the light. Embers flew from the rush torch he carried, spiraling down and extinguishing before they touched the ground. He felt the loneliness and loss as he always did when such a close encounter with Ka'in happened in the dreams and ended so unsatisfactorily.

"Heqaib."

Slowly, Lindstrohm turned to the slave woman he'd brought down into the secret tunnel with him.

She was young and lovely, as were nearly all of the women that he brought inside the pyramid with him. Her mouth was a little large perhaps, but that had been diverting, he well recalled. Even though she had wrapped herself and covered her nudity, the torchlight revealed the small, sleekly rounded flesh of her thighs and calves.

"What are you going to do about them, Heqaib?" the woman asked.

Lindstrohm tried to recall her name. Sometimes he could remember things from the memory of who he had been at that time. But he couldn't recall the woman's. And it didn't matter.

"I'm not going to do anything about them," Lindstrohm said. He took a firmer grip on the knife and started toward her. He held the torch to the side so her eyes were focused on it instead of the knife.

"You're going to let them sneak around the pharaoh's secrets and let them go unpunished?" The woman sounded as if she couldn't believe that. "They're common slaves, Heqaib. They'll tell everyone what they've done, and then the pharaoh will have no secrets left."

Lindstrohm knew that wasn't true. Ka'in and whoever the other man had been wouldn't tell anyone anything. Ka'in never did, no matter where the dreams in time took them. And the woman already knew about the secret chamber.

The only real danger lay in the woman at his feet. She would tell others that he had let Ka'in and his companions go, and that would be dangerous to him. He hung the torch on the sconce on the wall.

"Come," he told her, smiling a little and holding his hand out. "We can't spend any more time here. In case they get caught."

"I still don't understand why you didn't kill them," the woman said. "You had a knife—they didn't. I know you weren't afraid of Kanakht." But her tone implied that she thought that exactly.

"No," Lindstrohm replied. "I wasn't afraid of him." He drew her close to him, and she came a little timidly. Although he couldn't remember their encounter in the passageway because his arrival in the memory had started too late in his dream, he knew they'd been having sex.

At Samariumville he hadn't been able to find someone else who drew out his baser side. His occasional flings with other archivists were extremely limited and less than fulfilling. It hadn't been until he encountered Narita Vasquez that he had found someone who could meet him desire for desire. Still, he enjoyed the dreams he had of past women he'd slept with.

But he never told Vasquez.

"Let's get out of here," Lindstrohm said, pulling her forward with his left hand so he could fall in behind her.

She glanced at him nervously as she walked, as if she might have known what was on his mind.

Lindstrohm only smiled reassuringly at her, then tightened his grip on the knife. When she turned to look forward again, he stepped forward hurriedly and clapped his hand over her mouth. She grabbed his restraining hand with both of hers, and he had to knock them out of the way when he used the knife to slash her throat.

The woman kicked and fought as she struggled to free herself, but that only added to the way her heart frantically pumped her lifeblood from her. In less than a minute, she'd bled out and lay lifeless in his arms.

Lindstrohm cleaned himself up with her clothing, wiping the blood from both arms as he squatted beside her. He cleaned his knife off, as well, listening intently as the torch guttered and popped behind him.

This was one thing Vasquez didn't know about him, and Lindstrohm had taken pains to see that she didn't. Killing was easy for him. He'd spent decades and centuries at it, if he was to believe the dreams he'd had all his life. When he practiced with Vasquez, when he killed with her, it was only working to remember an acquired skill.

The passion *to* kill had always been there.

He remained in the passageway for a time and knew that this dream sequence was going to be an important one. There was going to be something more for him here than normal. Seeing Ka'in here—even for only that brief, flickering moment—had guaranteed that.

The torch finally guttered a last time and went out, leaving him in the darkness. Lindstrohm thought that he might leave the dream then, because there were a number of places to hide the woman's body and he knew he probably wouldn't get named as her killer anyway.

He listened to the sound of his own breathing intermingling with the sharp, muffled voices coming from above. He recognized Djoser's voice easily, but he also recognized Set's. *Enlil's,* he told himself. He knew that his past was inextricably linked with Enlil's, although he couldn't remember why.

Finally, when the voices faded and disappeared, Lindstrohm put a hand out and dragged his fingertips along the ceiling of the passageway. He located the trapdoor by touch, stepped up onto the ledge and shoved the heavy stone from the passageway's mouth.

His breath quickened when he hauled himself up into the temple, and his heart thudded rapidly in his chest. He wondered how long it had been since he'd seen the complete machine in a dream. Months, at the very least, had passed.

He studied the temple, remembering now how he'd been there when the secret room had been built. He also remembered how it was opened.

Quietly, conscious of other voices still drifting through Djoser's pyramid, Lindstrohm made his way to the wall on the opposite side of the room. He counted the stones, quickly finding the one that triggered the door.

Silently, the door opened.

Lindstrohm searched along the wall until he found the pile of rush torches that he knew would be there. With all the construction going on inside and below the pyramid, torches were replenished by slaves daily. He retreated down the hallway leading to the temple until he found the short remains of the torch the last visitor had used hanging in the wall sconce. He lit his own torch from that and returned to the hidden room.

He stared at the machine, and its otherworldly beauty took his breath away. He surveyed the bowls and the tubing, remembering every curving line and feature.

So much power was contained within the device. And it was all power that he was determined to have.

Hesitantly, Lindstrohm walked toward the machine, breathing shallowly in his excitement now. He stretched out a hand toward the top bowl of the machine, his fingers trembling in anticipation.

"Grail," he whispered, not even knowing he was going to speak. "Food of the gods. Ambrosia."

When the machine had been hidden from human hands and scattered across the earth much later, it had been taken apart in three pieces. The top section, the large bowl that sat over the other two bowls, had been the hardest to find throughout the history open to Lindstrohm.

He touched the top bowl, seeking the resonance he hoped to find within it. His fingertips registered the humming vibration within the strange silvery metal-glass that was like nothing else on the earth.

In some of the moments in the pasts he'd visited, he'd

talked with people who thought the machine was of divine origin if not extraterrestrial. There were also some who believed it had been smithed by a process that had been forgotten, and others swore the unknown metal had come from the meteor that had smacked into the earth millions of years ago and killed off all the dinosaurs.

Lindstrohm didn't know and didn't care. All that mattered was that the machine worked. His fingertips grazed the cool metal surface that oozed and shifted beneath them. The metal was hard, nearly indestructible, yet it gave at his touch.

Without warning, electricity flared from the metal bowl and arched to his fingers.

The spark lit up the whole room and knocked Lindstrohm backward. He stumbled for five or six steps, then caught his balance.

Fiery comets, blazing golden and blue, orbited within the metal for a moment. He gazed at them, and suddenly the world he perceived around him shifted and took a sudden, hard turn to the left.

BLACK-CLAD MEN RAN everywhere in front of Lindstrohm. He stood transfixed in a narrow metal corridor looking at an elliptical door. Water swirled around his ankles, cold and smelling of the salty sea.

"Get out!" an officer yelled, waving his hand for effect. He was clad in black, as well, but the cut of his clothing denoted his station.

Lindstrohm concentrated. Usually, a dream-within-a-dream meant something, brought special knowledge of the machine that he wanted. Men yelled and ran around him. He was nearly knocked down twice.

He turned, trying to figure out where he was, trying to figure out who the men were. Before he could guess, one of the men grabbed him by the front of the black uniform he wore. His, he noticed then, was different from the uniforms of the other men. Where they wore common blouses and baggy pants, his uniform was crisp and clean. There was a scarlet band around his left upper arm. There, on a field of white, the right-angled arms of a swastika stood out boldly.

The Germans, Lindstrohm thought, I'm with the Germans. He stumbled through the narrow corridor after the man who pulled him. However, the man's actions caused the person Lindstrohm visited mentally to draw his side arm. He wasn't surprised to see the Luger clenched in his fist. He'd dreamed of the German Nazis before.

The man grew wide-eyed looking at the pistol suddenly thrust into his face. He released Lindstrohm and held up his hands. "No," the man said fearfully.

"Never," Lindstrohm ordered, "dare touch me again. I am one of the Führer's select men."

"I'm sorry, Captain," the man said. "But we must hurry to other parts of the boat. With this section taking on water as it is, the crew will shut it off from the rest of the boat. I don't know how extensive the damage is."

Boat? Lindstrohm glanced around. For all intents and purposes, he was in a long, narrow corridor. Great engines on either side of him filled the walls. Steel encased him like a tomb, and the realization sent a sudden stab of fear shooting through him.

He had been here before. Perhaps this was the first time in a dream, but he had been there before.

"Captain," the other man urged. "I beg you. This is no time to stand and do nothing. The commander of this boat will not hesitate to save this vessel or his men no matter who you are." He paused. "Even at the cost of our own lives."

Lindstrohm knew the man spoke the truth. He holstered his pistol as Klaxons sounded around him. Had they already been blaring? He suddenly wasn't sure. Red lights flickered on the narrow walls, flooding the narrow corridor with crimson light. The water at his ankles suddenly surged, rising nearly to his knees. The cold bit deeply into his flesh.

"We're sinking," Lindstrohm said.

The other man glanced at the water worriedly. "We're taking on water. It may only be this compartment, or one or two compartments next to it. But the boat commander has given the order to clear this one. We must go.''

Lindstrohm nodded, suddenly afraid of the water. He had died in the dreams before, and those memories remained some of the strongest within him. He had been shot and slashed with a sword, had his head burst open like an overripe melon with a cudgel, but he had never before drowned.

He followed the man forward, slogging through the water. Something bumped into him. When he turned, he found himself staring down at a dead man.

The seaman's face and upper body were badly burned, and one of his eyes had filmed over and bubbled up like an egg white on a sunny-side-up order. A jagged piece of metal protruded from his throat.

A barrage of explosions suddenly sounded muffled and far away, but the boat jerked in response.

Lindstrohm fell, submerging for a moment before he was able to find solid footing and push himself back up. He gasped. The shock of the cold water in his face had seized up his lungs. The man in front of him struggled, trying to push the floating corpse from him.

Grimly aware that he didn't know his way through the vessel, Lindstrohm reached down and plucked the other man from beneath the corpse.

The man spluttered, and water—painted the color of blood by the flashing red light—cascaded down his face. He pointed ahead. ''The control room! We have to get to the control room!''

Metal clanged behind Lindstrohm and echoed through the boat.

Turning, Lindstrohm glanced at two men sealing a compartment door behind him.

''It's the electric motor room,'' the man beside him said. ''They have to seal it off. Otherwise the salt water from the sea will hit the batteries' acid and create chlorine gas. If the boat fills with the gas, we're all dead.''

Lindstrohm nodded and shoved the man forward. They ran

through the deepening water. The heat of the great engines laboring on either side of him basted him, and their throbbing beat a dizzying crescendo into his head. How could men live like this?

Another salvo of explosions sounded, and the resulting shock wave knocked them from their feet again.

"The damned British are getting closer with their depth charges again," the other man swore. "They have found us now." He pushed himself forward again, moving toward the compartment hatch.

Just before they reached the hatch, someone closed it.

"No!" the man screamed, throwing himself at the door. "We are in here! Let us out! You will kill us."

Panicked now, Lindstrohm shoved the man out of the way and seized the great wheel on the door himself. He threw his weight into the effort of turning it, but got nowhere. The door had been locked down from the other side.

The boat rocked again, nearly twisting on its side this time. The water level rose even more dramatically.

When Lindstrohm turned to gaze back at the giant diesel engines, the flickering red lights showed a half-dozen new leaks that jetted water into the compartment from the walls and the ceiling. The cold seawater roiled and rushed in.

"Plug the leaks! Plug the leaks!" a seaman cried immediately.

Lindstrohm watched seven other men in the compartment, hardly more than shadows in the uncertain red light, stagger through the rising water and begin working on the leaks. All their efforts, he knew, were doomed to failure. Every man in that compartment was a dead man, unable to halt the encroachment of the sea.

"Help me!" a man yelled. "Help me!"

Lindstrohm wondered how he knew for a certainty that they were all going to die. Perhaps he had dreamed the dream before, or perhaps he had dreamed similar circumstances. In other dreams, he had walked through different parts of World War II, but it had always pertained to the recovery of the machine. Until the nukecaust that caused skydark, that war had been the worst ever fought.

He knew the machine had to have been the reason he was there on that boat now. There'd been a reason back then, and there was a reason now.

The water continued to rise, growing deeper and colder. He felt his body begin to grow numb. His teeth chattered, and he started gasping for his breath. Perhaps some of the chlorine gas created by the salt water reaching the battery acid had invaded the room. Chlorine gas, he knew, was heavier than air and would lie along the floor. However, the rising water would push it up.

In long minutes, the water rose to his midchest, then began creeping up, crawling up across his shoulders and up to his chin. The other men panicked around him. They cursed and screamed and cried, calling on God to spare them.

Lindstrohm tried to keep himself calm. He had died before. This time would be no different. Only a little longer in the coming, perhaps.

That was another thing that Narita Vasquez didn't understand about him. He didn't fear death. Sometimes he wondered if the life he was living with her now was only one more memory, one more dream.

A short time later, the boat—he still wasn't sure what boat it was—shifted again, settling on its side. The booming depth charges sounded farther off, and though the concussive waves slammed into the boat, there was less reaction aboard it.

The boat was sinking, Lindstrohm realized. Then the water closed over his head. He tried to hold his breath, and did for a while, but in the end there was no way he could survive. He kept hoping that he would fade from the dream. Then he took his first deep breath and the cold salt water invaded his body, burning his nose and the back of his throat. He coughed, then threw up, vomiting out into the invading ocean. Despite himself and the calmness he tried to hang on to, he opened his mouth to scream—

AND FOUND HIMSELF panting weakly in the secret room in the pharaoh's temple.

Lindstrohm stared at the machine in front of him. The blue-and-gold comets whirling within the otherworldly glass-metal dimmed, then finally faded entirely. He panted, feeling his thundering heart finally starting to slow.

Only then did he realize that he no longer felt that he was alone. He spotted his own shadow, stretched long and lean before him, draped across the machine. The only way, he realized, that he could see his shadow before him while he held the torch in one hand was if someone was standing behind him.

He turned slowly, the skin at the base of his skull tightening and burning.

Enlil stood there, in his guise as Set, and pyramid guards flanked him, their weapons drawn.

"What are you doing?" Enlil asked. His reptilian gaze was cold and forceful.

Lindstrohm said nothing. There was nothing he could say after being caught so red-handed. And what had he learned? He took a step back instinctively, looking for a way out. His free hand fell to the knife at his waist.

Enlil waved for the guard to stay put, then walked into the secret chamber. "What are you doing?" he repeated.

Before he knew it, Lindstrohm's back was against the wall. He set himself, then tossed the torch aside because he no longer needed it with all the other torches in the room. The light flickered along the knife blade. "Stay back," he whispered.

Enlil cocked his elongated head to the left and gazed into Lindstrohm's eyes. "What do you know about the machine?"

"Nothing," Lindstrohm replied.

"You lie," Enlil stated flatly. "And you don't lie very well." He snapped his arm out without warning, blocking Lindstrohm's knife to one side so that he could strike with his other hand. The talons at the end of his fingers drove deeply into Lindstrohm's skull.

Lindstrohm felt the talons cleave his skull, feeling like daggers wedging their way through the bone and into the brain behind. A heated paralysis filled him, but he didn't know if it was from the wound to his brain or if it was some power of Enlil's.

"Who sent you?" Enlil demanded, tearing his bloody hand back.

Lindstrohm tried to answer but couldn't. He wasn't even sure if his mouth had opened. A bloody flap of skin hung down into his left eye and obscured his vision.

Enlil drew his other hand back to strike.

Helplessly, Lindstrohm watched the blow approaching. He heard himself screaming in his own mind—

THEN SUDDENLY his arms worked again and he lashed out. His fist caught flesh in the sudden darkness. He drew back his fist to strike again, his breath exploding in his lungs. He was suddenly aware that he was lying on his back, and that someone else was atop him.

He punched again, but this time the blow was painfully blocked outward, causing his wrist to go numb instantly. Before he could recover, a revolver barrel pressed against his face, digging into his left cheekbone.

"You stupe bastard! Hit me again and I'll fucking chill you!"

Heart pounding frantically, Lindstrohm lay back on the bed. He was tense, only then realizing he was in the middle of having sex.

Vasquez sat atop him, her thighs on either side of his hips as she took him deeply inside her. Her juices cooled across his lower stomach and loins as she remained motionless—except for the slight quivering of the blaster barrel against his cheekbone.

"I didn't mean to hit you," Lindstrohm said. "I thought you were someone else." His eyesight adjusted, making the most of the lit candles sitting on the windowsills.

Her face was cold and devoid of softness, looking hard and

merciless as brass in the candlelight. Her arm was steady. Only the barrel shook softly.

Lindstrohm tasted blood inside his cheek. The pain there became a dull ache, blasting into his face bones. She knew about his dreams; he'd told her about them.

But he also knew there'd be no excuse for hitting her. The Outlands were harsh and fierce. And the way she'd been raised and treated as a young girl in Louisiana would have killed most children.

"No one hits me," Vasquez whispered in a voice that was as smooth as silk. "Every man that ever hit me has died. I started that tradition with my father." Rage glimmered in her eyes for a moment.

"I'm sorry," Lindstrohm said.

"You're a dead man, Harry," she whispered. "All I have to do is squeeze this trigger to make it happen."

Lindstrohm swallowed hard, knowing there was no argument he could offer that would stay her hand if she chose to pursue that course of action. He resisted the impulse to ball a fist, knowing it would have alerted her and probably made the decision for her.

Silently, still holding the .38 Chief's Special against his face, Vasquez pulled up and disengaged their sexes. The suction noise was loud in the big bedroom. She threw a leg over the side of the bed and got to her feet, keeping the blaster shoved against his face.

"This is one of those times, Harry," she said, "that I regret letting you live."

Lindstrohm waited, remembering how coldly and dispassionately he'd killed the young woman in the passageway beneath Djoser's pyramid. Maybe he should have never become involved with Vasquez. Yet at the same time, he realized that without her he would have never gotten the two pieces of the machine that he had, nor would he have been able to organize Campecheville as he had.

He waited, as tensely as a coiled spring.

"I hate you, Harry Lindstrohm," Vasquez whispered. "I

hate you with everything that I am. Not for hitting me, but for making me live with what I'm about to do."

Lindstrohm considered his chances, knowing it was only slightly possible that he could knock the pistol away before she shot him. A thousand things went through his mind in that moment. Images from past dreams of what had possibly been past lives trickled through his mind.

There was also a lot of pleading for his life. But in the end he trusted what he knew to be true about her. There was no other choice. Even if he knocked the pistol away, there was a good chance she would kill him anyway with some other weapon she had. Or he would have to kill her and explain her absence to Wei Qiang's men, who had come in late last night.

Despite everything else he knew to be true about her, she loved him.

He stared into her eyes, willing her to put down the pistol.

"And I hate myself a little, too," she said, "because I put myself into this position."

Lindstrohm forced his breath out.

Slowly, as if not trusting him and not happy with herself, Vasquez pulled the .38's muzzle away. Then she eased the hammer back down and lowered the pistol to her side.

Lindstrohm gazed at her, seeing her lithe body, the high, conical breasts and the generous flare of her hips. She kept her pubic thatch neatly trimmed so that the lips of her sex could be seen clearly. The glistening there revealed how much she had wanted him. Her perspiration-streaked body glimmered in the candlelight.

"Good night, Harry," she said coolly. She backed out of the door and stepped out of sight through the doorway. He didn't even hear the padding of her feet as she walked down the hallway. "Don't come after me."

Lying in the bed, Lindstrohm became aware of the aching need he had for her. And he became aware of the black anger that filled him at the thought of her pinning him to the bed and threatening to kill him.

He rose from the sweat-dampened sheets they had twisted about themselves. He tried to remember the physical encounter that had been going on before the dream. Maybe there hadn't been one. Maybe Vasquez had simply crawled on top of him while he slept. It wouldn't have been the first time.

Sex with him was different for her. She'd told him that. And he suspected it was because she came closer to giving something of herself away that she'd fought for and protected for years.

Nude, he walked out onto the small balcony and stood in the cool wind sweeping in from the Bay of Campecheville. Farther out into the bay, boats marked with lanterns moved back and forth across the gentle waves rolling into land. Bells echoed, rolling over the ville.

Farther inland, protected by a sand and rock bar that the ville's inhabitants had made at his instruction, was a small lagoon that held fishing boats, as well as the tugs that toiled night and day. This night it also held the Tong's two prop-driven air wags that looked like fragile, crimson dragonflies and rocked on long, narrow pontoons.

The Tong advance representatives had easily acquiesced to his invitation to spend the night at the ville. Their reluctance had been carefully weighed, and they made just enough noise that it hadn't seemed too easy. Lindstrohm had no doubts that the men would scout around the ville. Despite Vasquez's suggestion to keep the Tong men confined and under guard, Lindstrohm had posted no such orders.

There was nothing to hide at Campecheville except what he chose to hide. And that stayed very well hidden. Only Vasquez knew.

Moonlight streaked the partially cleared streets, and he watched cats chasing rats near piles of rubble that had to be hauled off to dump sites in the next few days. There were, he noticed with satisfaction, more lights in the windows of the buildings that had survived the nukecaust now than there had been even a month ago.

Vasquez was right, and Reynolds had been right, as well:

feeding all the slaves he was buying or accepting immigrants from the American coastline had always been hard. Now the expanding numbers were making that even more impossible.

But he believed he could do it. Nothing else was acceptable. All he needed was the third part of the machine. Over the past few years, he'd found two of them and he'd gotten them through the mat-trans unit he'd discovered in Campecheville and brought back on-line.

Timing was becoming critical, but he was certain he was closer to the revelation of the third piece of the machine. When he had found the earlier two pieces, the dreams had increased frequency and intensity—just as they were doing now.

And now, just as then, he'd found Ka'in in his dreams. But would he be a friend or a foe? That remained to be seen. It always did.

Chapter 10

Harsh sunlight struck Kane when he woke, burning through his eyelids in violent reds. He felt the dull remnants of a headache, and his throat was parched. Voices, grumbling and tired, created an undercurrent of noise around him, and the smell of cooking meat filled his nose.

He opened his eyes slowly, slitting them so he could ascertain where he was. It was an old Magistrate practice that he knew he'd never get over.

Everything looked normal, though. The people they'd rescued were huddled around small cook fires. Early dawn stained the eastern skies, barely lightening the thick fog bank that had settled over the area. The previous night's acid rain storm lingered in the stench that filled the air and the occasional sting of drops that landed on the people hunkered below.

"Are you awake?"

Lifting his head from the hillside, feeling how stiff and achy he was from the position he'd been forced into during the night, Kane looked over to his left at Brigid.

She sat cross-legged only a few feet away. "Feeling better?"

"Yeah."

"You ran fever most of the night."

Kane nodded carefully, feeling the pain still throbbing in his temples. "I don't think I have it now, Baptiste."

"No. It broke about an hour ago."

"You've been watching over me."

Brigid didn't say anything.

"Did you get any sleep, Baptiste?" Kane asked. He forced himself to his feet.

"Some. Enough. Watch out for the branches above your head. They collected a lot of acid-rain water last night that hasn't dried out yet. A couple of people got burns from it this morning when they weren't paying attention to what they were doing."

Kane stayed low enough to avoid contact with the sheltering barrier. "What's the sitrep, Baptiste?"

Brigid nodded out toward the cook fires. "Grant and Domi found a nest of squirrels about a hundred yards away on the other side of this hill. The two young boys in the group went with them when they found out they were going hunting. They've been bringing back the kills."

"Nobody else is in the area with us, then?"

"Everybody last night would have had sense to get in out of the rain," Brigid commented.

"Except the rider on the motorcycle," Kane stated. "Unless I hallucinated that." He thought about the dream he'd had, realizing that a hallucination might have covered all of it. But it was strange that there appeared to be no aftereffects of the fever, and no other symptoms of sickness, either.

"No. That was real."

"Where did the rider go?"

"Down the road."

"Alone?"

"I think so," Brigid said. "If the rider was an advance scout for a group, Grant or Domi would have seen them. They went out looking for them this morning, which is how we ended up with the squirrel feast. We've got breakfast for the morning, Kane, but we're out of food. The slavers' packs had some, the ones that were recovered, but those people ate it. And I wouldn't have tried to take it away from them yesterday."

"It would have caused a fight. Someone might have been killed."

"I know, but now that I'm looking at those people, I realize we've taken on a lot of responsibility.'' Brigid sounded resigned.

Kane almost grinned at her, but knew better. He looked away, watching the ex-slaves gather around the cook fires and prepare their own meals. ''Freeing them yesterday was a good idea.''

''I know, but now I understand a little better why you and Grant are a little more reluctant to get involved in other peoples' problems. The next problem is to figure out when to let go.''

''There's only two decisions regarding that, Baptiste,'' Kane assured her. ''You let them go when they're able to handle being on their own, or you let them go when you have to.''

Brigid handed a sharpened stick and several squirrels to Kane. ''You can skin and roast your breakfast. If it hadn't rained last night, we could have gathered berries and nuts from the bushes and trees. A lot grows around here, foraging materials mostly, but the acid rain from last night will make them inedible for a while. We're going to have problems with a water supply, though. Whatever natural water was in the area will be contaminated after last night's rain. The last of what we've had has already been used this morning.''

''Does anyone know how far it is to Fiddlerville?''

''I've asked a couple of others, but they all say the same thing.''

''That Fiddlerville isn't far?'' Kane asked.

''Right.'' Brigid looked out at the people. ''None of them have even been there, Kane. Maybe it doesn't even exist.''

''Did you read any records at Cerberus about Fiddlerville?'' Kane knew all about Brigid's memory, and he knew if the ville had been mentioned she would remember it. Added to that was Lakesh's own driving need to know more about everything.

So it was surprising when Brigid shook her head. ''For all we know, it's a myth. Something to give these people hope.''

Kane looked to the south, following the curve of the rutted

road they had been following. "We'll know soon enough,
Baptiste."

"There're going to be other slavers. In fact, the whole myth
of Fiddlerville could be a trap."

Kane nodded. "I know, Baptiste, but we can't stay here,
and going back isn't any more attractive than going forward.
We'll keep going. We haven't been that way yet."

KANE SAT on his haunches and pinched meat from the roasted
squirrel while he held the spit he had cooked it on. The flavor
was slightly gamy, but the meat helped fill his belly.

Metal clanked around him as two of the men used hammers
they had taken from the dead slavers to remove the iron slave
collars from the others. Counting Angel and Cherub, there
were sixteen ex-prisoners in the group. The five children
among them, including Cherub, were restless and anxious to
go. All of them were thirsty.

Glancing up to the right, Kane spotted Brigid keeping
watch high on the hillside next to a gnarled sycamore tree.
She had gotten good at keeping herself concealed. Finished
with the squirrel, Kane used his M-14 to push himself to his
feet, then made his way up the hill to join Brigid.

When she looked at him, wary hostility was evident in her
emerald-green eyes. "Did you come up here to take over
watch?"

Kane subdued the immediate feelings of irritation that
swelled within him. There were times when the chemistry
between himself and Brigid Baptiste was difficult to handle.
Both of them were too independent to get along easily much
of the time.

"No, Baptiste, I didn't." Kane sat gingerly, mindful of the
throbbing ache that had ballooned up inside his chest after
he'd gotten up and started moving around. A brief inspection
of his chest earlier had shown that his whole upper body was
covered in deep purple bruising. "I came up to talk."

Grant and Domi were on the other side of the trail. If anyone approached, they would have a chance to put him or her

into a cross fire. Kane and Grant had talked briefly and decided that it was in their best interests for the slaves to remove their collars. That way maybe they wouldn't be an open invitation to the next slavers that came along.

Brigid seemed surprised. "What do you want to talk about?"

After only a moment's hesitation, Kane told Brigid about his two dreams of Egypt.

"DJOSER WAS an important pharaoh," Brigid Baptiste said after Kane had finished. "He was part of what scholars termed the Third Dynasty. There were actually four dynasties during the time of Egypt's Old Kingdom. During that period, governments became centralized and administrative systems came into being. There were also dramatic increases in technology, building, hieroglyphic writing and art."

"Like someone was guiding them along," Kane said, thinking of Enlil. The campsite was ten minutes back along the rutted road they followed south. The forest stayed thick on either side of the road, which was why Grant and Domi walked the wing positions. No one would able to slip up on the group with them watching, and they could range ahead to scout out the new territory. Kane walked point with Brigid.

"Back before skydark," Brigid went on, "there were many archaeologists and other historians who believed the ancient Egyptians had contact with aliens. The Maya, as well as Native Americans, were thought to have traveled across the Bering Strait and settled into North and South America. Those people believed that the extraterrestrials—what they called grays, like Balam or Enlil—had guided civilization in those days."

"Well," Kane said dryly, "we know those people were right. So why was Djoser important?"

"He was the first pharaoh to unite Upper and Lower Egypt. When he had his pyramid built, he—"

"It was six mastabas tall," Kane said, musing over the images still strong in his head. "Did I tell you that already?"

"No," Brigid replied, "you didn't tell me that. How could you know that? Only four of the mastabas were surviving at the end of the twentieth century."

"Because I saw it in the damn dream." Kane swallowed reflexively, finding it harder to do since they'd been without water all morning long. Adults had to watch their children to make sure they didn't try to drink from the pools of acid rain that occupied the hollows of the land.

"Are you sure you've never seen the pyramid anywhere before?" Brigid asked.

Kane struggled to keep the irritation from his voice. If he hadn't been sure that he had never seen the pyramid before yesterday, he would have said so. "Baptiste, I'm not an archivist. All the material I've been exposed to regarding pyramids has been while I was with you. Back in Cobaltville, reading about pyramids never happened. I was a Magistrate—I wasn't there to read. I don't think even Lakesh has droned on about anyone named Djoser."

"I just thought maybe you had seen a book on Egyptology while you were at Cerberus."

"No."

Brigid nodded. "Djoser wasn't the name scholars knew this pharaoh by. He was also called Netjerikhet, and that is the name he is best known by. It wasn't uncommon for a pharaoh to have five or more names."

"I haven't heard anything about that name, either."

A crow started cawing ahead of them. The big black bird sat at the top of a towering oak tree that overlooked the road and shallow valley it descended into. The Grande River ran narrow and shallow farther ahead and to the west, like a bright ribbon laid through the overgrown forest. The road meandered down the side of the valley and disappeared into the trees when it hit level ground. There were no villes and no one else moving on the road as far as Kane could see.

"Was there anything in the materials that you have read about some kind of machine that Djoser had?" Kane asked.

"What kind of machine?" Brigid asked.

"I don't know what kind of machine, Baptiste," Kane retorted. "If I knew already, I wouldn't have all these questions."

"Even given your description of the machine, I can't place it."

Kane had drawn it out for her, as best as he remembered from the dream, in a smoothed-over patch of ground near the gnarled sycamore tree they'd kept watch by. Brigid had confirmed that she had never seen anything like the machine.

"Balam was there in your dream," Brigid said.

"Yes."

"But you said that you had the impression that Balam didn't belong there."

"He didn't," Kane stated.

"Because he knew you weren't Kanakht?"

"Yeah. And because of how the whole situation felt, Baptiste." They were quiet for a moment, and Kane listened to the wet mud of the rutted road sucking at his boots.

"You don't think it was a dream, do you?"

Kane hesitated a moment, then shook his head. Analgesics had dimmed the pounding in his head somewhat, but the unexplained fever from the previous night had left him incredibly thirsty. "No, I don't."

"Then what was it?"

"I have no idea, Baptiste."

"WELL, NOW WE KNOW what happened to the motorcyclist." Grant stood near the body, his Copperhead canted over one broad shoulder. "Poor bastard never made it in out of the rain."

Kane peered down at the corpse. She had been a young woman with mousy brown hair, but he had no idea what she had looked like or what age she'd been. The acid rain had burned and seared her flesh, bubbling it up in places. It also ate holes through her clothing.

"You think she was lost?" Domi asked. She knelt quickly and started going through the dead woman's clothing. She found a necklace that featured a beaten silver heart wrapped over a blue stone. Without any hesitation in the slightest, the albino took the necklace and placed the jewelry around her own neck. The blue stone glittered at the hollow of her throat.

Kane witnessed the pilfering but didn't say anything. To Domi's mind, the small theft from the dead woman wasn't a theft at all. It was accepting a legacy and a piece of good fortune.

"Lost," Grant replied. "Or running. Judging by the jewelry, I'd say she was running." He knelt and slipped his combat knife from his boot. He pushed the sleeve of the jacket the dead woman was wearing back to reveal the iron band around her left wrist.

Domi pushed the sleeve back on the other arm and exposed the iron bracelet there, too. "Slave. Must have broke free and stole motorcycle."

"Mebbe she was running for Fiddlerville," one of the men in the group volunteered. "Everybody around these parts has heard about Fiddlerville and how you can catch a ship to Campecheville from there."

Kane stared at the dead woman, thinking if everybody knew about a mass escape route in a land full of slavers, it probably wasn't a good thing. Slavers would view an escaped slave as lost profits, while the barons would view an escaped slave as a reduction in the potential labor force to aid in rebuilding and refortifying their villes. And everybody seemed to know about the enemy camp that lay at the end of the path they currently followed.

"She not running," Domi announced. "She hunting." The albino opened the scarred leather saddlebags tied down to the motorcycle. Inside the saddlebags were boxes of ammo and three handblasters.

"Must have been in a hurry if she didn't bother to lose the bracelets," Grant observed. "They would have marked her to anyone who saw them."

"She was out in the storm," Brigid said. "She must have thought what she was doing was important, and she had little time to do it."

Grant nodded, then looked down the muddy, rutted road. "Makes you wonder what we've got waiting up ahead."

"Mebbe we should take a look first," Kane said. He looked down at the motorcycle. The old, military-equipped Enduro had a high chassis set inches above the ground. The exhaust pipes ran along the left side. "The motorcycle looks like it's all in one piece."

"Handlebars look a little crooked," Grant agreed. He turned and looked back at the skid marks that led up to the motorcycle. "It looks like she rode it as far she could go, then the acid rain got to be too much and she rode it down to the ground."

After a few minutes of cleaning the carburetor using tools they found under the motorcycle's seat, Kane threw a leg over the motorcycle and pumped the kick start up to full prime. Then he kicked again, turning the engine over. Three kicks later, the motorcycle started with a hearty roar. Black smoke poured from the exhaust and created a minor smoke screen.

Kane checked the fuel tank and found it half-full. From the smell, he guessed that the fuel was homegrown and alcohol-based. That kind of fuel was hard on engines, but it would get the job done as long as proper maintenance was conducted.

Grant stood in front of the motorcycle and grabbed the handlebars. Kane loosened the handlebar retaining screw, let Grant realign the handlebars and tightened it back down.

"I'll go ahead," Kane said. "I'll go see how far Fiddlerville is and find out what's waiting up ahead."

"Might be better if you had some company," Grant suggested.

"I'll go," Brigid offered.

Kane hesitated, not knowing what to say and not knowing what would set off an argument between them.

Grant came to his rescue. "Brigid, it would be better if you stayed with me and let Domi go."

"Why?" Brigid asked.

"Because if someone in the ville is keeping watch on people, I fit in better than you.'' The albino crossed her arms over her breasts.

For a moment, Kane thought Brigid was going to put up an argument.

Then Brigid shook her head. ''You're right.''

Kane secured the M-14 across the motorcycle's handlebars with leather straps, tied for quick release so he could get the rifle loose quickly if he needed it. He wore the .45 on his hip openly. None of the people in the group with them had ever been to Fiddlerville, and he wanted to be prepared for anything. Having Domi, who had been raised in the Outlands, along also increased his chances.

He held the motorcycle steady while Domi climbed on. The albino wrapped her arms around Kane and leaned her body against his. She also insisted on carrying the .357 Magnum pistol in one hand so it would be ready. The presence of the big pistol pointed in the region of his groin was somewhat disconcerting to Kane, but having the weapon ready might prove handy.

Kane twisted the accelerator and released the clutch. The motorcycle's rear tire bit into the loose mud of the road and shot forward. Although he didn't prefer travel by motorcycle, Kane was adept at driving them. He ran the gearbox quickly and efficiently, getting the feel for the powerful Enduro.

He kept his mind on the road, aware that the noise of the motorcycle engine would alert other people they were in the area, and also that game could run out into the road before him. But part of his thoughts replayed the dreams he had had of Egypt, and of Balam.

Chapter 11

Kane came upon Fiddlerville almost unexpectedly even though he had been looking for it. The ville was located at the base of red clay foothills scarred by dozens of years of runoff water. Deep trenches looked as if they had been hacked into the land with a dull ax.

Spotting the ville spread out across the harsh, broken terrain below, Kane pulled the motorcycle to the side of the road and kept driving through the underbrush until he reached a copse of trees that provided shelter, as well as cover.

He knew there was a chance that the motorcycle had already been overheard, but he didn't want to go down into Fiddlerville without doing at least some recon. He took the minibinoculars from inside the war bag he and Domi had brought with them.

With the albino drifting behind him as silently as a ghost and totally at home in the forest, Kane made his way farther up into the foothills. The sun was starting to descend in the west now, and he knew there was almost no chance at all of accidentally catching a reflection from the binocular's lenses.

He hunkered down, and the loudest thing in the forest was the ticking of the motorcycle's cooling engine. Focusing the binoculars, he scanned the ville, working patiently and thoroughly.

Fiddlerville was a hodgepodge of broken and tumbledown buildings. Rubble lay scattered across cracked and buckled streets, and even though there were dozens of wags on those streets, none of them remained intact. All of them had been stripped over the years, and the salty mist that rolled in from the Gulf had ground them down to rusting heaps.

The few people who moved through the ville were all armed. Scanning the buildings, Kane spotted three machine-gun nests that roughly triangulated the central area of the buildings that had been restored enough for people to live in.

"Some people look like slaves, mebbe," Domi said quietly.

Kane agreed. "Mebbe they're there waiting on the next ship." He trained the binoculars on the natural harbor that lay just south of Fiddlerville.

Whitecapped waves rolled in from the Gulf as smooth as spun glass. Eight fishing vessels sat at anchor, but the crews aboard the ships stayed busy cleaning the day's catch. Once they were clean, children carried fillets to the shore where they were smoked and could be later used to trade and barter with. There were no big ships in the harbor, but ironworks towers stood along the beach. More machine gunners occupied the towers and had overlapping fields of fire.

"Machine-gun nests on beach," Domi said. "Not just for protecting fishermen."

Kane didn't believe so, either. The ragged line of towers formed a shore-defense zone. He glanced at the open beach at either end of the docks. The sea encroached deeply into the land, and the beach was rough, laced with craggy earth and broken rocks. A pile of wags lay halfway submerged to the east, probably towed there by the people who cleaned the ville.

As Kane watched, a man hitched a team of mules to one of the wags on a street that was partially cleared. The mules dug in and pulled the broken-down wag into motion. The tires had been gone for years, leaving only rusty metal rims that had frozen up and wouldn't turn. Screeching metal filled the air and reached Kane's ears.

"What we do?" Domi asked impatiently. "Getting tired standing around here. I'm thirsty. They got gaudy down there. We go down. Look around closer."

Kane nodded. At the very least, they needed water. And if the ville proved safe enough, they could drop the group off there and go on about the business of finding the way into Campecheville.

KANE STAYED AWARE of the stares he and Domi drew as he drove the motorcycle through Fiddlerville's streets. He was also aware that he was never out the field of fire of one of the machine-gun nests that overlooked the ville itself. One wrong move and there would be no safety in those streets.

He brought the motorcycle to a stop in front of the gaudy. It was a three-story red brick structure with cracked walls and broken windows covered with plywood. The double front doors yawned invitingly, and throbbing music echoed from inside.

The sign over the double doors proudly proclaimed Chantilly Lacey's. The picture on the sign was faded, but it still showed the picture of a masked woman dressed in a silver-and-purple bikini. The masked woman held a futuristic handblaster with telescopic sights in a two-handed, ready stance.

Kane nodded to Domi, signaling her to get off the motorcycle. When she did, he rolled the motorcycle backward and parked it so that it faced out into the street for a quick getaway—if one became necessary. He also chose to place the bike between two tall four-wheel-drive wags that would provide temporary cover.

Glancing around, even making sure to look up directly at the machine-gun nest that covered the front of Chantilly Lacey's, Kane let everyone watching him know that he was aware of the stakes. He switched off the engine, swung out the kickstand, leaned the motorcycle over and got off.

Domi waited on the cracked and buckled sidewalk in front of the gaudy. The anticipatory smile on her face was real. The albino loved the comfortable accommodations available at the Cerberus redoubt, but she was best in her element when she was in the Outlands. She holstered her .357 Magnum pistol with a spinning flourish that was straight out of the old West gunfighters that Grant had taught her about.

The obvious experience with the weapon was not lost on the spectators.

Kane took a moment and untied the M-14. He rested his finger alongside the trigger guard and walked with the rifle pointing toward the ground. He nodded to Domi, signaling her to go ahead. Men's eyes would linger on her before they moved on to Kane, and it would give him a little more time to size up them and the situation.

Inside the gaudy, oil lanterns fought back the gloom fostered by the covered windows. The smell of unwashed flesh lingered amid the scents of homemade lye soap and malt liquors and beers. Cheap homegrown tobacco also filled the air, and smoky clouds wreathed the gaudy's interior.

Conversations quieted or stopped as Kane stepped into the gaudy. He swept the room with a glance that was pure Magistrate. He had worn the look often while dressed in the black polycarbonate armor. It was both challenge and warning.

Domi made her way to the bar.

The bartender was a broad, squared-off man with a shaved head and a fierce red goatee. Savage tattoos of green-and-purple geckos twined together in various sexual positions covered his face and arms. Silver earrings and his nose ring caught the light of the lanterns hanging over the bar. Bottles lined the shelves behind the bartender and were reflected in the mirrored tiles that covered the walls.

"What'll you have, pretty lady?" the bartender rumbled in a deep voice.

Domi leaned on to the bar, resting on her elbows and getting close to the bartender.

Kane knew she was aware that she had the attention of nearly every man in the gaudy. He raked the establishment with an experienced eye, knowing no place like this existed without someone who was in charge.

"Where you get water?" Domi asked.

The bartender reached for a glass mug from a stack at the end of the bar. He took it down and wiped it with a bar towel.

"Got wells. Natural wells. About ten klicks north of the ville."

"Storm brought acid rain last night," Domi pointed out. "Wells mebbe not so healthy."

"This one is, pretty lady. I promise." The bartender gave Domi a wink, then reached under the bar and brought out a five-gallon see-through glass container. "Don't understand everything that was explained to me, but I know that we have limestone over that well. Rain comes down, but it filters through that limestone. Leaves all the bad stuff behind. Time the water reaches the well a hundred feet down, it's as pure as water gets." He poured, then pushed the filled mug over to Domi.

Domi glance into the mirrored tiles behind the bartender and locked eyes with Kane. "If this stuff makes me sick, chill this stupe bastard."

"Consider it done," Kane said. He lifted the M-14 in one hand and pointed it at the bartender's head.

The bartender held his hands up in consternation. "Hey! Now wait a damn minute! There's a nothing wrong with—"

Domi lifted the mug and drank until it was empty. She set the mug back on the wooden bar with a loud bang that echoed over the gaudy, then wiped her lips with the back of her sleeve. "Water's fine. Could be colder."

The bartender mopped his face with his bar towel in relief. "Fuck, mister," he said, looking at Kane, "I thought you was gonna blow my damn head off."

"I still might," Kane promised softly. "The water hasn't made it through her system yet."

Domi grinned. "I let you know when it does."

Suddenly, three men appeared along the catwalk that ringed the second floor and peered down onto the first floor. All of the men had Ingram submachine guns cradled in their hands and wore Kevlar vests.

"That," a calm feminine voice said, "will be enough of that."

Kane glanced up at the speaker.

The woman looked to be in her early thirties. She was petite and svelte, and her hair was striped in pale green and frost. She wore lime-green vinyl pants that looked painted on, and a dark blue crop top left her flat belly exposed. A jade gem gleamed in her belly button.

"Are you trying to get yourself chilled?" the woman demanded.

"No," Kane said. "I just wanted to meet the man in charge."

Domi calmly drank the second mug of water and watched the action unfold as though it were something she did every day.

"It's not a man," the woman replied, grabbing hold of the railing in front of her and leaning forward. She wore a big pistol in a cross-draw flap holster on her left hip. "It's a lady in charge of this gaudy."

"Chantilly Lacey?" Kane asked.

The woman smiled. "Not hardly. You can call me Fiddler."

Kane grinned and slowly pulled the M-14 back over his shoulder so the men watching him could clearly see that his finger wasn't inside the trigger guard. "It's not the gaudy named after you—it's the whole ville."

Fiddler shrugged. "I built the ville, so I felt obliged to name the ville. I wanted to name it something that I could remember." She gazed at Kane with open interest. "I end up meeting most folks who travel through this ville. I especially get to know the ones who are trouble or who pass through here more than once. We're not exactly on the beaten path."

"That's not what I hear," Kane responded. "I've been told that if I want to escape slavers I can come to Fiddlerville and catch a ship to a place called Campecheville."

"You don't look like an escaped slave," Fiddler said.

"Not me," Kane said. "But I do have sixteen people who are thinking they can get a ship out of here. Mebbe I should go back to them and tell them they're wrong."

The woman pushed off the railing and stood on her own

two feet as she gazed down at Kane. It took her a moment to reach what she evidently considered to be an important decision. "Sixteen people?"

Kane nodded. "Five of them are children."

"Did they have something set up before now?" Fiddler asked.

"With who?" Kane asked.

"Me and the captain of the ship that's going to take them out of here."

Kane shook his head. "No. They were coming because they had heard about Campecheville. Slavers took them a few days back."

"How did they get free?"

"They had help."

Fiddler raised an arched brow. "You?"

"And some friends," Kane replied.

The woman turned her direct gaze onto Domi.

The albino raised her mug of water in a silent toast.

Glancing back at Kane, Fiddler asked, "What made you become involved in the plight of the few slaves?"

"I've never much cared for slavery."

Fiddler waved at the three men with Ingram submachine guns. The three men stepped back from the railing and turned their weapons away.

"Join me," Fiddler called down. "I've got a suite of rooms on this floor. We can talk."

"I can't."

Anger flickered across the woman's face. "It's my ville. You can believe me when I say I don't often get turned down. I've never learned to like it."

"I appreciate the hospitality," Kane said. "But those people out there have been out of water since last night. The least I can do is take some back to them."

"I'll send someone with a wag," Fiddler offered. "They can take water out and bring those people back in. Riding that motorcycle, you're not going to be able to take much water with you, and those people are still going to have a long walk into this ville.''

"Fair enough. I can talk to you when I get back.''

"I'd rather you stayed.'' Fiddler's voice was soft and low, but there was no mistaking the steel in it. "After all, I'm sending a wag out to meet this party you say is walking toward Fiddlerville. I'm also risking the lives of the man I ask to go. If it turns out that you're all coldhearts just looking for a wag to transport those people to the Grande River slave auctions, then you're going to lose, too.''

Kane curbed the anger that rose within him. Relinquishing control of a situation was never easy for him. But he factored in the use of the wag, which meant the five children with the group would no longer have to walk or be carried the seven miles into the town. Wag transport also meant Brigid and Grant would rejoin Domi and him in Fiddlerville in less than an hour instead of taking hours to get there. All of them were more vulnerable on the rutted road they were following into Fiddlerville.

Moving easily, offering no outward threat, Kane turned and walked up the zigzag stairway to the second floor. Domi fell in behind him. All eyes in the gaudy followed them.

Kane switched the M-14 over to his left hand but kept it ready to pull up. His right hand stayed loose near the .45 on his hip. He looked up at Fiddler as he took the last few steps.

"It might be more dangerous for you if I stayed," Kane promised.

"What do you mean?''

Kane stopped in front of the woman, just out of arm's reach. "I mean that if anything happens to those people I've brought this far, or to my friends, they're going to have to rename this ville.''

Fiddler's eyes narrowed. "I don't take threats kindly.''

"I don't offer them with any kindness," Kane said. He saw the bright spots of color on her cheeks and forehead, and thought that quite possibly he had pushed her too far too hard.

"You're an interesting man," Fiddler observed. "You

walk into this gaudy bold as brass and threaten one of my people, knowing that I'm going to get involved.''

"I didn't know it was you," Kane said. "But I figured it would break the ice and move me on up the ladder to whoever was in charge.''

"You're not big on patience.''

"No. Not when it gets in the way of something I need to do.''

"Have you eaten?''

"Some,'' Kane said. "But I'd be more interested in knowing that wag has been sent. They're seven miles back. A lot can happen in seven miles.''

Fiddler leaned back over the railing and called down. "Pilgrim, want to earn a little extra jack?''

Kane gazed down at the room below and watched as a giant of a man pushed himself erect and took off his hat.

"Hell, yes, Miss Fiddler.'' Pilgrim had a moon face with a narrow, lipless mouth and eyes set so deeply that he looked like a jack-o'-lantern from a picture in a book Kane had seen a long time ago. His wispy blond hair showed a lot of pink scalp, and his china-blue eyes made him look like a child. He stood nearly seven feet tall and was built as solid as an oak tree trunk. As he stood waiting expectedly, he rolled his hat brim nervously in his huge hands. Judging from the pistol at his hip, the one snugged into shoulder leather beneath his left arm and the shotgun sheathed down his back between his shoulders, Pilgrim was a walking arsenal.

"Did you hear this man say where his friends were?'' Fiddler asked.

"Oh, yes, ma'am. Out on the north road. Don't hardly nobody use that road anymore, but I know it well enough.''

"Go get them for me.''

"Yes, ma'am.'' The big man clapped his hat back onto his head.

"And take Ernie and Frogger with you.''

"Yes, ma'am. Will do.''

The big man turned and headed for the double doors at the front of the gaudy with all due haste.

"Hey, Pilgrim," Kane called.

Pilgrim halted near the door and glanced back up with an unmistakable hardness in the china-blue eyes.

"Be careful approaching that group," Kane advised. "When you get close enough, yell for Grant and tell him Kane said this was no one-percenter. If you don't, he may chill you. And if he doesn't, one of those people may open fire and you'll never get it all sorted out."

"I'll do 'er," Pilgrim replied. Then he vanished through the double doors.

Kane turned back to the woman.

"Most people never hear Pilgrim coming," Fiddler advised.

"Grant not most people," Domi said, bridling up to defend Grant.

"He'd chill somebody that quick?" Fiddler asked.

"When it's not just his ass on the line?" Kane nodded. "He'd do it, and never even blink."

"He'd chill an innocent man?"

"Not as long as he was wearing a sign that Grant believed. Otherwise, Pilgrim might as well tie a bull's-eye mask over his face."

Fiddler raised an eyebrow. "He chills that quickly, and you offer to shoot up bartenders in order to get attention. You pair are probably really big at social events."

Kane let the comment pass.

"My suite is this way."

Chapter 12

Fiddler led the way across the second floor and walked through double doors that opened onto a large room containing comfortable furniture. Pictures of clowns in white faces covered the walls. An attached balcony peering out over the ville's main street was covered in afternoon sunlight.

Kane strode to the balcony area and glanced out. He was instantly aware that the balcony was almost directly across from the machine-gun nest overlooking the front of Chantilly Lacey's.

Domi automatically took up a position on the other side of the room. That way, if anything untoward happened, nothing less than a gren would take them both out at the same time.

"You like clowns?" Domi asked, picking up a small porcelain clown from the coffee table in front of the L-shaped couch. The porcelain clown held a frayed and tattered parasol and looked up sadly as if he were standing in the rain.

"My father was a clown," Fiddler said. She walked behind a small wet bar tucked into one corner of the room. "Can I get you something to drink?"

"Water," Kane answered.

"I've got a selection of liquors," Fiddler offered. "Scavenging this ville has been good for us."

Kane shook his head. "Water. I'm too dehydrated for alcohol."

Fiddler smiled. "Of course. I should have remembered." She took out a clear gallon jug and poured water into a large glass that looked like a fishbowl on a stem. She crossed the room and handed the glass to Kane.

"Thank you," Kane said.

Fiddler turned and went back to the wet bar.

Kane sniffed the water, searching for any traces of chemicals.

"You don't trust me very much, do you?" Fiddler asked. She stared at the small oval mirror behind the bar.

"I don't trust anybody very much," Kane replied. He sipped the water. The mineral taste was strong and almost gagged him at first.

"I apologize about the water," Fiddler said. "The limestone leaches out the acid rain, but the downside is the mineral taste. It goes down easier when you put some whiskey into it."

Kane drank more, taking it easy because he didn't want to make himself sick. He still felt the ravages of the fever within him, and the headache still echoed within his head.

"What can I get you?" Fiddler asked Domi.

"I'll take more water," Domi answered.

"You people are no fun," Fiddler said. "You've been living too hard." She poured Domi a glass of water as big as the one she had given Kane. Then she poured herself a small glass of amber liquid. Evidently knowing that the albino wasn't going to give up her position in the room, Fiddler took the glass to Domi.

"From what I see," Kane replied, "nobody lives easy around here."

"Excluding me?" Fiddler lifted a mocking, arched eyebrow.

"Mebbe," Kane responded.

"And those who live well are suspect."

"Something like that."

Fiddler glanced at the porcelain clown Domi still held. "As I said, my father was a clown. He saw a vid somewhere, in some ville he was at while he was a kid. It was all about clowns. My father chose to become a clown, and he traveled from ville to ville with traders. He would tell jokes and sing and do ridiculous pratfalls to attract the attention of a crowd. Not that the arrival of a trader wouldn't already attract a lot of attention. But my father somehow turned a fierce bargaining session into entertainment. The trader gave him a piece of the action at every ville. He did that for more than twenty years. Then he was killed by a coldheart stoned on jolt.''

Domi carefully placed the porcelain figure back onto the coffee table.

"After that, I worked for the trader for a while," Fiddler continued. "When the trader died, his son took over the wags. We didn't get along. Then the trader's son started running slaves. I got out. Pilgrim and a few of the others got out, as well. They came with me and we set up Fiddlerville."

"So why help the slaves?" Kane asked.

"Because I was a slave." Fiddler sipped her drink. "My father found me in a coldheart ville. The trader didn't know the ville had fallen into their hands until the wags were inside the walls. For a while, it looked like the coldhearts were going to make a try at the wags."

"They didn't," Domi said.

"No, but it wasn't until after the trader proved to the coldhearts that the wags were set to self-destruct and carried enough explosives to take out the whole ville if it came to it. The coldhearts backed down. My father saw me peeking out a second-story window of the ville's gaudy house. He used to tell me that looking at my face that day broke the heart of a clown. He made a trade for me and took me away from there. The trader backed his play, and the coldhearts couldn't refuse. From that day onward, I was his daughter. But I've never forgotten what it was like to be owned."

"So you operate slave ships out of goodness of heart?" Domi asked, and there was only a little sarcasm in her voice.

Fiddler took another sip of her drink and gazed frankly at the albino. "My, my, someone certainly is suspicious."

"Stay alive longer that way," Domi said.

"Yet you came here for help."

"I don't see any ships out in the harbor," Kane said.

"Come out onto the balcony with me," Fiddler suggested.

"So the guys in the machine-gun nest have a clearer field of fire?" Kane asked.

"Those machine guns are loaded with steel-jacketed .50-caliber rounds that will have no problem punching through this wall," Fiddler said. "And you'll never make it past the men standing outside the double doors. If you do, you'll have to make it through the machine gunner again." She paused, then smiled. "I thought we might enjoy the sun. After the cloud cover we had this morning and the storm last night, I thought it would be nice to sit out on the balcony. Plus, I can show you what we've been doing here."

After only a moment's hesitation, Kane nodded and followed her out onto the balcony.

A white wrought-iron table with matching chairs sat on the balcony. Fiddler sat on one side and Kane sat on the other. Domi folded her arms and stood in the double doorway, leaning a slim hip against the frame. She gazed up at the machine-gun nest and waved.

None of the machine-gun crew felt inclined to wave back, but sunlight gleamed along the blaster's long snout.

"Welcome to Fiddlerville," Fiddler announced extravagantly. "Temporary land of those who would be free and temporary home of those who are brave enough."

Kane sipped his water, conscious of the machine gun pointed in his direction. The Kevlar vest would offer no protection at all from the steel-jacketed bullets. However, they did have to hit him first. And instead of retreating back inside the building, he knew his first move would be over the balcony railing and into the street below. Maybe the surprise would buy him some time.

"This is the third Fiddlerville in the past two and a half years," Fiddler said. "The first ville I set up to shelter slaves didn't last more than a few weeks. I didn't have enough people convinced to take me seriously. There were only eleven of us. When we fought clear of the ville after being there less than three months, there were only seven of us. I lost some good friends."

"What's in it for you?" Kane asked.

Fiddler looked at him and smiled. "When you set your mind to it, you're bald-faced enough about it."

Kane remained silent. So far, he didn't get any bad feelings from the woman, but those didn't always come before it was too late.

Fiddler stood and waved out at the ruins of the ville. "What I get out of this, besides the feeling that I've helped someone, is pure profit. I'm hooked in really tight with the traders who move throughout the southeast and southwest Outlands. Some of them trade with the baronies." She turned and placed her hips against the balcony railing overlooking the street. She gripped the railing on either side of her. "Ironic, isn't it? That the baronies buy slaves, yet they help finance my operation to keep those slaves free."

"The baronies are allowing you to stay in operation?" Kane asked.

"Hell, no." Fiddler laughed, and the amusement was genuine. "It was Baron Samarium's Magistrates who drove me out of the second Fiddlerville. We were more prepared for them then."

"Then?"

Fiddler nodded. "It was Magistrates who drove us out of the first Fiddlerville. They were protecting the interests of the Grande River slave markets."

"Because having slavers operating is easier and safer than pursuing slaves into the brush and forests," Kane said.

"Exactly. And the slavers are eager to trade with the baronies. Where else can they get top-of-the-line weapons and what appears to be an inexhaustible supply of ammunition?"

Kane sipped his water. The sun burning down on him carried a tropical heat in the dense humidity. He was covered with perspiration. "I know what they get out of it, but what do you get from the slaves?"

"I get scavengers who work through the two villes that I've been at until now." Fiddler nodded toward the north and east. "A lot of the smaller villes that existed before skydark were looted by scavengers. However, most of the people living in small villes moved on quickly. There was safety in numbers and most of them had family in the metropolitan areas. They went there seeking the families, and security put up by men who stepped in as barons. Those small villes that got left behind often had a lot of things worth scavenging."

Kane listened, knowing Fiddler's argument made sense.

"Villes down in this part of what had been Texas and Louisiana," Fiddler said, "had been hot spots for a time. There were a lot of muties and swampies. Now it's not so bad. Before those people load onto a ship bound for Campecheville, they generally have to spend a week to ten days scavenging through Fiddlerville. Whatever they find during that time is mine."

"And you trade traders?" Domi asked.

Fiddler nodded. "Yes."

"What about the ships?" Kane asked.

"The ships' captains are paid by Harry Lindstrohm. He's in charge of Campecheville."

"Have you ever met him?" Kane asked.

"Yes. When I first got into this business, Lindstrohm met with me."

"Did you find out about him, or did he find out about you?"

"I think we sort of found out about each other. Lindstrohm is involved with a woman named Narita Vasquez. Maybe you've heard of her? She's also called Narita the Bleeder."

Kane shook his head.

More suspicion darkened Fiddler's face. "You've never even given me your name."

"Kane."

"Domi," Domi said from the double doorway.

"I've never heard of either of you," Fiddler stated. "And that bothers me. Baron Samarium has been sending spies into this area. They infiltrate a slave-rescue operation, then call in the Mag force that camps out in the forest. A lot of those operations have been exterminated down to the last person these past two months. That's why everyone downstairs regarded you with so much suspicion."

"Those men are involved in freeing the slaves?" Kane asked.

"Yes. Most of them are guides and trained sec men from traders in the area that believe in what we're doing. I pay them out of the jack I get paid from Lindstrohm."

"Lindstrohm must have deep pockets," Kane commented.

"He does," Fiddler agreed. "During the past three years, he's worked at setting up and establishing an oil reclamation depot. Before skydark, there was a lot of oil down in Campecheville. And since skydark, that oil has been down there and no one knew enough to get it."

"How Lindstrohm know?" Domi asked.

Shaking her head, Fiddler said, "I don't know. Narita said that Lindstrohm is different from anyone she's ever met."

That, Kane knew, was no answer. The kind of operation Fiddler was talking about required a lot of specialized knowledge. And knowledge of the fact that oil had existed in the undersea fields near Campecheville.

Fiddler pointed to a wag slowly grinding through the ville. The wag pulled a long flatbed filled with pipes and drilling equipment. "Lindstrohm also pays for any oil field parts and supplies that we recover. As long as they're in good condition. When the nukecaust hit, a lot of drilling rigs out in the Gulf got busted up. Every so often, the sea pushes those parts into the beach or shallow water where scavenger boats can get at them."

Kane thought about what the woman had told them, and he thought about the mat-trans unit that Lakesh and Bry had told him had gone mysteriously on-line. Memory of the sec probe that had been destroyed at the other end of a jump from Cerberus redoubt stayed sharp, as well. Whoever had brought that mat-trans unit on-line also knew someone had tried to access it.

Was it Harry Lindstrohm, or was it someone else?

Fiddler folded her arms across her breasts and looked at

Kane directly. "So I've answered all of your questions. Maybe it's time you answered mine."

Kane made no comment.

"Where are you from?" Fiddler asked. "I might believe your little friend was from around here, but there's no way you are."

"I'm just passing through," Kane said. "I never meant to get involved with those sixteen people, but once I found them, I couldn't just abandon them."

"You see?" Fiddler said. "That kind of mentality is usually found in someone who has a home. You're not a drifter, and this isn't your home."

Kane considered his options. There was no way he could tell the truth. So which lie would best serve him? He looked at Fiddler, wondering how good she was at discerning the truth from a falsehood. "I came down hoping to see Lindstrohm."

"Why?"

"To see about getting an oil supply," Kane said. "I'm interested in setting up a fuel-supply depot in the Utah Territories."

"Because of all the mining going on in that area." Fiddler nodded her understanding.

"From what I hear, Lindstrohm sells crude oil. I've got a small refinery set up that we've been using to manufacture grain-based alcohol fuel. The grain is hard to come by these days because Baron Cobalt has been annexing several outlander farms in the area. There weren't many farmers found in those areas anyway, and now they're becoming a lot more scarce."

Mostly, Kane knew what he said was the truth. The Utah Territories had become a mining district once more, and the buyers ranged from the Western Isles to all of the baronies west of the Mississippi River. Although, a man could earn a decent amount of jack with just a pickax and a mule, the operations in the area were growing larger. In order to sustain that growth, new fuel sources had to be found.

If Kane *had* been in the fuel-supply business, Harry Lindstrohm's underwater oilfields could have been a gold mine.

"How are you planning to transport the oil into the Utah Territories?" Fiddler asked.

"Overland wag caravan," Kane answered.

"That's a lot of unprotected territory to cover by wag," Fiddler commented.

"Mebbe, but I don't see another way to do it."

"More than likely, you're going to lose a few caravans. That amount of distance will wear hard on a wag."

"Losing caravans also means the price will go up," Kane said.

"You're ambitious," Fiddler said, nodding. "That's a quality I find attractive in a man or a woman."

"When does the next ship arrive?" Kane asked.

"Before nightfall," Fiddler replied. "At least, that's according to schedule, but that also depends on whether Blakeney made it across the Gulf. Besides the storms and mutie sharks that are sixty feet long, there are also pirates."

Domi stirred in the door frame. Her body language told Kane she was getting bored. "What happens to people who go to Campecheville?" she asked.

"The ship captains I've talked to say those people are put to work in Campecheville," Fiddler answered.

"Working on the oil-reclamation project?" Kane asked.

Fiddler shook her head. "The ones that know how, and the ones that are willing to learn, go to work on the drilling rigs. The rest work at clearing the ville and scavenging."

"That's a lot of mouths to feed."

"But that's what Lindstrohm does," Fiddler said.

"Sounds like Lindstrohm's building a barony," Domi suggested.

"Or," Kane said softly, not understanding completely where the thought came from, "an empire."

GRANT MOVED as silently as a wraith through the forest, taking advantage of every scrap of cover afforded by the thick trees and dense underbrush. His combat senses screamed an alert, and told him that he was not alone.

He cradled the Copperhead in both hands before him, canting the assault rifle so that the buttstock pulled in close to his right shoulder and the muzzle pointed down and slightly ahead. That way he could bring the Copperhead into play quickly and fire without worrying about the weapon's tendency to rise on the recoil.

Now that the cloud cover had burned off, bright shafts of sunlight pierced the leafy canopy like sec beams guarding a sensitive area. The birds had grown quiet in the immediate area, as well, which told Grant that he was close to whoever else was in the forest.

Quietly, slowly, Grant eased into position beside a cypress tree. He breathed calmly, inhaling through his nose and exhaling through his mouth. The humidity had left him drenched, and his clothing stuck to him uncomfortably.

Grant wondered about Kane, very aware of his friend's absence in light of the present situation. That continued absence concerned Grant. Knowing that they were there without water, Grant was convinced that Kane would have returned immediately if something hadn't held him up.

After getting an uncomfortable itch across the back of shoulders for too long, Grant had told Brigid he was going to take a quick recon of their back trail. He'd left the archivist in charge of the group and told Brigid to keep them moving.

From his position on the hillside overlooking the rutted road, Grant could see Brigid and the group. He was also aware that anyone on the hillside with him would be able to see them, as well.

They looked vulnerable in spite of the weapons they carried. The past few days, coupled with the lack of water that morning, had nearly exhausted their reserves. Even Brigid looked to be slowing.

Five minutes dragged by. Then another five minutes passed.

Grant's indomitable confidence dipped a little. He started reconsidering the possibility that whoever had been following them had circled around to the front and was preparing an ambush there.

If that was true, Grant was going to be too damn late to get there in time.

Then a shadow stepped away from a tree farther down the hillside and became a man. The man held a lever-action rifle and walked half bent over to present a lower profile against the trees.

The man looked rough and hard, as if he were used to living outdoors. A fierce, unkempt beard covered his lower face. He stopped beside a tree and gazed at the group making its way along the rutted trail. His interest was obvious, but what he chose to do with it remained to be seen.

A moment later, two other shadows stepped from the trees. They stayed slightly behind the lead man, flaring out in a conventional two-wing follow-up to a point man.

The fact that the man showed some experience with military maneuvers didn't surprise Grant. A lot of coldhearts and slavers learned some of those moves or died early. The problem was, a point man and two wings generally worked as the advance guard for a much larger group.

Grant glanced back to the north, turning his head to the left. He was content for the moment to let the three men continue trailing Brigid and the group of ex-slaves. However, the longer he stayed in position, the deeper he was going to be inside the enemy field of fire.

Dust swirled into the air to his right, coming up the rutted trail from the south.

Grant watched in puzzlement as the dust cloud came closer to the group. He immediately realized that the dust cloud was too large for the motorcycle Kane and Domi had driven off on.

He watched in pride as Brigid immediately sized up the situation and ordered the group off the trail. She even split them in two so they would have overlapping fields of fire if they needed it.

The three men went to ground, disappearing almost at once in the leafy foliage.

Grant marked their positions mentally, then turned his attention to the arriving lag.

The wag was an old truck with a large bed. It traveled slowly, and Grant could see the men inside glancing around on both sides of the trail. One of the men riding in the back slapped a palm against the wag's cab and evidently called out.

The driver pulled the wag to a stop. Dust roiled over the vehicle. Once the sun had broken through the cloud cover, the ground had dried out surprisingly quickly. Since starting out that morning, they had left the swamplands behind.

A huge man wearing a cowboy hat that almost looked too small for him got out on the passenger side of the wag. He was armed to the teeth. He looked as if he were talking, but Grant couldn't hear over the wag's unmuffled engine.

A moment later, Brigid Baptiste stepped out into the open.

Then the feeling of being watched returned to Grant at full intensity. Red-hot prickles chewed into the back his neck. He turned, shifting slightly, and that saved his life.

The man behind Grant was of average size and lanky. However, he put everything he had into the machete blow that would have decapitated his intended target. The heavy blade cut the air and sheared finger-thick saplings growing beside the cypress Grant had chosen for cover.

The former Mag rolled away as the man pulled the machete back for another slash. Raising the Copperhead, Grant aimed at the center of the man's chest. His finger slid over the trigger guard, then over the trigger.

And he knew that when he fired the assault rifle, the entire group in the forest would know he was among them.

Chapter 13

Harry Lindstrohm stood at the docks and watched the Tong ship come about smartly and drop anchor. The wind had favored the crew so docking wasn't difficult, but the maneuver showed the readiness of the men aboard.

The four Tong men who had landed the two air wags in the harbor the previous evening stood only a short distance away on the docks. They wore black homespun clothing with white detailing. The clothing fit loosely, making it easy to conceal and get to the weapons they carried strapped to their bodies. Chinese-made handblasters were strapped to their sides, and AK-74s were slung over their shoulders.

None of the men looked older than twenty-five, but they all stood at attention. Their eyes were locked on the Chinese junk that stood out among the other ships in the bay.

Crews aboard the other ships stood on deck and stared at the newcomer with obvious fascination. Even the tugboat crews took time out from their work to watch the Tong ship.

The wood had been heavily varnished and lacquered to the bright red color of fresh-spilled blood. Narrow black lines defined the intricate planks. The ship was crafted so that it looked to be all angles and arches. Three masts held sheets of sailcloth that folded as neatly as a paper fan. Chinese characters marked her stern, but Lindstrohm couldn't read them.

Red-lacquered panels also covered the gun ports where cannons could be rolled through and readied for action. The way the ship docked left Lindstrohm open to a full salvo of cannon fire if the ship's captain chose to.

Lindstrohm was acutely conscious of standing there alone; he had planned on having Narita Vasquez at his side. There had been no more dreams during the night. But Vasquez hadn't come looking for him.

Hunting for her, he had decided, wasn't a good idea. Instead, he'd gone to his office and sat at the desk, gazing out at the sea over the balcony railing. Surprisingly, it was hours before the Tong ship blew into the harbor. During that time, Vasquez remained missing.

That morning, Lindstrohm took time to make sure her ship still lay at anchor in the bay. Because he had never before struck her, he believed it possible that she might leave him. The thought filled his stomach with knots of anxiety.

He had come too far to fail now.

The Tong crew aboard the junk ran a longboat down the falls. The ropes sang as they shot through the block and tackles, then the longboat smashed against the rolling surface of the harbor.

Six men slid down the falls in quick hand-over-hand motions. By the time they took up oars, two more men in flashier dress slid down and joined them. The respect from the rowing crew was immediately obvious. The two men sat easily in the stern of the longboat and gazed at the docks in the ville beyond.

Lindstrohm watched the longboat approach, conscious of the deck crews aboard the Tong ship that stayed conspicuously near the gun ports. He had no doubt that the cannon were loaded and ready to fire.

Taking a deep breath, Lindstrohm strode to the end of the dock, stepping right at them. He wore black slacks, boots and a bright red dress shirt that had come from one of the recently unearthed basements of a clothing apparel shop. He also wore the double shoulder holsters.

He reached the end of the dock at about the same time as the longboat. "Toss me the rope," he called down.

The crewman kneeling in the longboat's prow unfurled the coil of rope and tossed it up.

Lindstrohm caught the rope easily, then knelt and secured it around the dock cleat. He called for the stern rope, as well, caught it and pulled the longboat close to the dock. By the time he had secured the stern rope to the second docking cleat, the first man was already scaling the wooden ladder attached to the side of the dock.

Once he was on the dock, the man glanced at the four Tong airmen. All of them nodded at Lindstrohm. The man turned his attention fully to Lindstrohm. "Mr. Lindstrohm," the man said in perfect English, "I bring you greetings from Wei Qiang, lord of the Celestial Isles, in hopes that good fortune has prevailed and you have known only victories since last you spoke with Lord Qiang." He bowed slightly as he finished the speech.

"When you return to the Celestial Isles, please inform Lord Qiang of my expressed gratitude regarding his wishes," Lindstrohm said. "May I have your name, Captain?"

The man smiled slightly. "Forgive me, Baron Lindstrohm, but I am not the captain of the ship. I am what you would call a first officer."

Lindstrohm looked at the second man, but realized he looked even younger than the first.

"I am Kyung-Bae Ren. Captain Zhao regrets that he cannot join you on shore. He has been at sea so long that his stomach no longer deals comfortably with being on land."

Looking back at the Tong ship, Lindstrohm saw an old, gray-haired man dressed much the same as Ren standing on the stern castle deck. The old captain did nothing except stare back blankly.

"Very well," Lindstrohm said, trying hard not to show his disappointment.

"But you should be glad to know that my companion is Ong-Yai Yip, Lord Qiang's handpicked trade adviser. He will be the one preparing the reports regarding the business Lord Qiang is interested in."

Yip bowed deeply, his eyes never leaving Lindstrohm's. "I am pleased to make your acquaintance, Mr. Lindstrohm, and I look forward to doing business with you."

"Of course," Lindstrohm replied. He felt certain that Yip

had a senior that he reported to, as well—and that the man was probably on the Tong ship. "I've set aside today to make myself available to you. Would you like to freshen up first in the rooms I've prepared for you?"

"My companion and I are quite well rested," Ren replied. "Our journey from the Western Isles was actually quite enjoyable."

"You didn't encounter any of the pirates that are in those waters?" Lindstrohm asked.

"Only once," Ren stated. "The gun battle lasted only minutes, then the pirate ship went down. There were no survivors."

"Good," Lindstrohm said, raking the Tong ship with his gaze. The crew was either really good at repair and maintenance, or the pirate ship had never touched them. It was also possible, he supposed, that the air wags had been used in the encounter. He had heard reports from other ships that the Tong air wags often threw bombs from the cockpits onto land-based opponents, as well as those on ships at sea. "Is there anything your captain or the ship needs?"

"Fresh water, if possible. And perhaps Cook would be interested in trading for food. *Green Lady* has several spices aboard."

"We can definitely make a trade for the spices," Lindstrohm confirmed. Wei Qiang's Tong traded extensively among the recovering Isles of Spice that were remnants of the southeastern China coastline. Although those lands had broken off from the mainland during skydark, they'd remained arable and productive after a time.

Every trader that Lindstrohm knew would barter for spices because every ville along their routes would take them.

A warning bell clanged aboard one of the tugs as it chugged into the dock area. The tug was a simple flat-bottomed boat with a large cargo area surrounded by railing. The gasoline engine wheezed asthmatically and thundered with the consistency of a smith's hammer banging an anvil.

Dockworkers surged out of the warehouse to meet the tug.

Boatmen threw lines to the dockworkers, who tied off the tug. The dock landing had been constructed at the right height to lead directly onto the boat. During high tide, the arriving filled barrels had to be handed down a foot or more, but it was better than trying to pass them up.

In short order, the freshly pumped barrels of oil were exchanged for empty barrels. The lines were thrown clear and the tug turned and chugged back out to the distant drilling rigs.

"I must congratulate you on a very efficient operation," Ren acknowledged. "And on your ability to create such an operation. As you know, Lord Qiang is very interested in how much oil you can produce."

"At the present rate of production," Lindstrohm said, "I can produce more than he can use in a year."

An uncomfortable look passed across Ren's face. His eyes narrowed. "How much do you know about Lord Qiang's business?"

The unexpectedness of the question caught Lindstrohm off guard. "Only the little I've gleaned about Lord Qiang from ships' captains that deal with him or others in the Western Isles. I know that Ambika's death and the subsequent loss of the oil fields she had set up has left Lord Qiang possibly short of fuel."

"Other resources are being investigated even now," Yip interjected. "The supply you offer is not the only one being considered, Mr. Lindstrohm."

Hostility rose within Lindstrohm before he could cap it. "Perhaps we're wasting each other's time."

Yip blinked, as if not knowing what to say.

Ren stepped in smoothly and adroitly, showing years of experience at diplomacy where Yip was still lacking. "I fear my companion has spoken too quickly, Mr. Lindstrohm. I think he has come across sounding much...*fiercer* than he had intended."

"And maybe he came across truthfully," Lindstrohm responded.

"No," Ren said calmly. "One thing I am certain of, Lord Qiang would like to do business with you if at all possible."

Lindstrohm remained quiet, but looked pointedly at Yip.

The younger Tong man dropped his gaze self-consciously.

"Other markets," Lindstrohm said in a voice filled with calm control, "have approached me. Markets that I have *not* had to curry favor with."

"Those markets," Yip said, "are also with pirates who would—"

Ren spoke harshly in his tongue, taking a threatening step toward the younger man.

Yip subsided, but not until Lindstrohm saw a hidden blade gleam in Ren's hand.

Lindstrohm filed the presence of the blade away. The years he'd spent with Narita had sharpened him to such things. Or, at least, reawakened his eyes to them. He wouldn't let Ren easily step inside his private space again without being prepared.

Yip raised a hand quickly to his throat as Ren stepped back. Yip covered the slight wound to his throat with a hand and unshed, fearful tears pooled in his eyes. But even his movement wasn't quick enough to hide the crimson line marring his neck. His mouth trembled.

Clearing his throat, making the knife disappear back up his sleeve, Ren faced Lindstrohm again and smiled slightly. "Adviser Yip is a cousin of Lord Qiang's. Sometimes he forgets himself and thinks that such a position matters to Lord Qiang. He doesn't yet know that Lord Qiang allows nothing to interfere with the business of the Tong."

"Nor do I allow anything to interfere with my business," Lindstrohm said, thinking briefly of Vasquez and trying not to feel how much he missed her at his side.

"I feel certain that Lord Qiang has noticed that quality in you," Ren said.

Lindstrohm looked at Yip, but the other man didn't acknowledge him.

"Perhaps we could see your operation in action," Ren suggested.

Glancing back at the man, Lindstrohm nodded. "Of course." He looked around at the people ferrying the oil back and forth from the offshore drilling platforms and knew they were all thinking that he'd brought a host of predators into their midst.

And they were right, but it remained to be seen who preyed on whom.

GRANT SLID his finger from the trigger at the last moment, then turned the Copperhead to block the descending machete. Sparks flew as steel rasped against steel, but the sound didn't carry over the rumbling engine noises of the wag on the rutted road where Brigid and the ex-slaves hid in the brush.

Regaining his balance quickly, Grant blocked the machete to his left, leaving the man open to his attack. He rammed an elbow into his adversary's face. Blood spewed as the man's nose broke. Taking a step forward, slamming into his opponent with his right hip, Grant brought the Copperhead's butt into the man's temple.

The impact turned the attacker's head so viciously it snapped his skull from his spine. Eyes wide in disbelief but quickly glazing over, the dead man's knees buckled and he fell to the ground.

Breathing harder but nowhere near winded, Grant reached down and caught the corpse by the shirtfront. He dragged the body into a stand of brush where it wouldn't be easily found.

Farther down the hill, one of the men tracking the group walking toward Fiddlerville went to ground beside a tall tree. A squirrel darted through the limbs above and took cover from the intruders.

Patiently, Grant watched as other hunters locked down into position and observed what was taking place in the road. Evidently, the arrival of the wag and the man in the big cowboy hat hadn't been part of the plan. Grant took heart in that, but that was partially lost immediately when he saw how many men were skulking in the forest.

"We wait too long," one of the men below Grant's position said in a low voice, "and we are gonna have trouble collectin' them fuckers."

"Our best bet is to take them here and now," another man said. "We get more jack for them that we bring in on chains ourselves. Otherwise, Baron Samarium ain't quite so generous."

"Talbot's got the right of it," another man said. "Them that we herd on into Fiddlerville ain't going to bring the same price as ones we can take out here."

Grant's stomach clenched at the mention of Baron Samarium. Anything having to do with the barons was bad. He had no doubts that the men were part of a Magistrate action. Cautiously, knowing a trained Magistrate might be overseeing this part of the op now, he checked the skyline above him.

Nothing was moving.

Back on the rutted road, the man in the big cowboy hat stood his ground and talked. Neither he nor his crew reached for a weapon.

Grant decided to take that as a good sign. Knowing that he didn't have a chance of cutting through the line of hunters scattered across the hillside between Brigid Baptiste and him, Grant crept up the hill silently.

Once he was over the crest of the hill, Grant took a moment to do a quick recon and make sure he was alone. From the top of the hill, he could peer down into the valley ahead. He removed a pair of binoculars from the war bag he carried and trained them on the valley.

Carefully, keeping the sun behind him and to his right, Grant surveyed the valley ahead. He hadn't checked the view for the past two miles. Now, he could barely make out building rooftops ahead.

They were close. Knowing that gave him hope, but that was also assuming that the wag below was there to help. He still didn't know that.

Grant put the binoculars away and took up the war bag. He managed the Copperhead in one fist and started out in a long, loping stride that quickly ate ground. He remained behind the sheltering hillside, certain that the hunters had somewhere posted a sniper along the hillside because it was something Kane and he would have thought of doing.

BRIGID BAPTISTE STARED at the giant of a man wearing the big cowboy hat. She kept the sights of her Copperhead squarely centered over the man's broad face.

"Y'all come on out of there," the big man said. "You ain't foolin' nobody nohow. I know y'all are in there." He took another step forward.

"Don't come any closer," Brigid warned.

The big man squinted his eyes and peered more intently into the brush. "Come on out of there."

"If you take another step," Brigid promised, "I'm going to shoot you through the head."

The big man halted and his face wrinkled with mirth. "Lady, if you're as tough as you think you are, I don't know why Kane sent me out here to fetch you all."

Keeping her sights over the big man's face, Brigid asked, "Where do you know Kane from?"

"Fiddlerville," the big man said. "He sent me out to get you folks. Said I was to ask for a man named Grant." He looked around the brush. "Is there a man named Grant here?"

"Grant ain't here now," one of the men in Brigid's group replied.

The announcement, Brigid knew, was not good. If Grant had been right about the group being followed and if they were close enough to be overheard, then the people following them knew Grant was missing. She resisted the impulse to look back along the road.

"Kane told me to talk to Grant," the big man insisted.

"What did he want you to tell Grant?" Brigid asked.

"Said tell Grant this was no one-percenter." As if suddenly

remembering himself, the big man swept his hat off his head. "Excuse me. Forgot my manners. My name's Pilgrim."

Brigid thought about the big man's words. Only Kane and Grant would know about the one-percenter reference, and Kane wouldn't have given it if things in Fiddlerville hadn't been safe.

"What do you want, Pilgrim?" Brigid asked.

"Miss Fiddler," Pilgrim said, "She sent us out here to make sure you folks got to the ville all right. She knew you had kids among you and didn't want y'all to suffer any more hardships than you had to."

"Where's Kane?"

"I suppose he's talking to Miss Fiddler. You have to go through her to get a ship to Campecheville."

"Is there one going to Campecheville?"

"Yeah, but I couldn't rightly tell you when. Miss Fiddler, she keeps up with that sort of thing more than I do." He clapped his cowboy hat back on and gazed around the brush, ignoring the blasters that were obviously pointed in his direction. "We got water on the wag. Kane said you folks had gone dry for a while. I suppose them kids you got with you would like a drink."

"How do we know we can trust you?" Angel demanded. She stood only a few feet from Brigid and held Cherub close to her, one hand over the small boy's mouth.

"I don't suppose you will," Pilgrim told her, turning toward the sound of her voice, "until after you already do. But I'm trusting you folks not to shoot me right now. Mebbe that means something—mebbe it don't. I expect that's up to you to figure out."

Brigid was acutely aware that the other people in her group were looking to her for guidance. She wished that Grant were back or that Kane were there. Decisions like the one facing her seemed to be made much easier by either of them. She was tired and hungry, and her throat was so swollen from thirst that it hurt. She knew the children among the group had to be faring even worse.

Still, it was hard stepping off into the unknown and being responsible for so many other people. Brigid let out a tense breath, then lowered the Copperhead. The wag had obviously come from farther down the rutted road, which was the direction they were headed in. If they didn't deal with Pilgrim and his crew there, she had no doubt that they would have to later.

"All right, Pilgrim," she said.

A beatific smile carved the big man's cruel lips. "Well, y'all come on out of there, you hear? Fiddlerville ain't but a few more minutes up ahead. We got water for you here, but Miss Fiddler, why she'll have food a-waitin' at her place. There's plenty to eat for everybody."

A low rumble of conversation buzzed through the group in the woods, barely rising above the tick of the wag's cooling engine.

"Do you think it's really okay?" Angel asked, looking at Brigid.

"I think Kane sent him," Brigid answered.

The woman nodded and raked her fingers through her tangled hair. The whip lashes across Cherub's shoulders stood out as livid bruises that showed signs of infection.

"I wish Kane was here now," Angel said.

Brigid stepped out of the trees and brush toward the road, avoiding the deep ruts where other wags had toiled through in past weeks. As she gazed at the ruts, she knew that they presented a trail for any slaver to follow.

Pilgrim walked to the rear of the wag and unlatched a heavy gate that allowed access to the wag bed surrounded by an iron railing four feet tall. The rear section reminded Brigid of a cattle car she'd seen in a picture in a book at the Cobaltville archives.

Two armed men rode in the wag bed. They slung their weapons and started doling out water in tin cups as the group climbed wearily into the wag.

"Just take your time," Pilgrim coaxed. "There's plenty for everybody, and there's gonna be more in just minutes if that ain't enough." The big man turned to face Brigid and touched his hat with one hand. His other hand rested on the gunbelt strapping his hips. "Ma'am."

"Brigid," she replied. "Thank you for doing this."

Pilgrim nodded. "Yes, ma'am. Happy to oblige. But I'd appreciate it if you'd thank Miss Fiddler proper, as well."

"I will," Brigid replied.

The freed slaves sat tiredly in the back of the wag, talking more animatedly now that escape finally seemed at hand. The conversations immediately steered toward Campecheville and the easy life that was surely waiting there.

Brigid glanced at the tree line to the north. If they were being spied on, she knew the slavers gathered there would realize they had little time in which to act. Her scalp prickled. No matter how hard she stared into the shadowy depths beneath the trees, she saw nothing.

She also saw no sign of Grant, and that bothered her. He had to have seen that they were loading up, as well, which meant that he was reluctant to show himself. Or something had already happened to him. She pulled her mind away from that line of thinking quickly. Nothing, she knew, would ever happen quietly to Grant—or to Kane, for that matter.

"Something wrong?" Pilgrim came up to stand by Brigid.

"Grant's out there," Brigid said.

"Why?"

"He thought we were being followed."

Pilgrim was silent for a moment. "If he's as good as Kane appears to be, Grant's probably right. Got any idea who it might be?"

"Slavers."

"Did you cut sign on any of them?"

"Grant doubled back to check while the group rested."

"How long ago?"

"Only minutes," Brigid answered, but she'd learned from her experiences with Kane and Grant that a lot of things could happen in minutes.

Pilgrim reached out and slapped the wag's hood. The metallic pounding echoed over the quiet of the forest. "Jojo," Pilgrim called out.

Obediently, the small, carroty-haired man behind the steering wheel switched over the wag's engine. The starter ground and the engine turned sluggishly, catching after a long moment then roaring powerfully.

All of the group was aboard the wag.

"We can't wait on Grant," Pilgrim said apologetically, turning to face Brigid. "If he's up there, he's seen us. Same as them. If he ain't showed up, there's a reason."

"He's not dead," Brigid said, and she was surprised to find how she'd said that partially to reassure herself.

"No, ma'am," Pilgrim agreed. "But it's probably best if we pushed on. If he's good enough, he'll catch up or follow us on into Fiddlerville."

Brigid nodded.

Pilgrim stood up on the wag's running board, remaining outside the vehicle. Beneath the big cowboy hat, his gaze searched the northern tree line restlessly. He reached into the wag's cab and took out a SG 552 Sturmgewehr assault rifle that Brigid recognized from specs she'd seen at Cerberus redoubt. Pilgrim's weapon came equipped with a folding buttstock and multipack magazine capability. Three ammunition clips were secured side by side beneath the assault rifle.

Brigid retreated to the rear of the wag. One of the armed men shoved the gate open and offered to let her in. She shook her head and stepped up onto the rear bumper, holding on to the rails with one hand while she kept the Copperhead ready in the other.

Jojo ground the transmission gears as he started out. The four-wheel-drive's big tires chewed into the mud and splashed through water puddles as the man pulled the wag around in a tight circle. The rutted road wasn't big enough for the wag to turn completely around, though. Jojo pulled it into the trees on the west side of the road, mowing down the smaller ones and stopping only when he reached trees too tall to push over.

Brigid watched the man fighting the wag's wheel through

the cab's back glass above the heads of the seated men and women in the bed. Jojo thrust the transmission into reverse. The transmission whined, then bucked when it caught. The wag started bouncing over the rutted road, backing in another circle designed to leave it facing back the way it had come.

Suddenly, the wag's fractured windshield shattered, chunks of safety glass pouring into the cab. Jojo jerked violently, like a puppet getting yanked by its strings in a half-dozen different directions. Then a bullet cored into his head and sprayed blood and brain matter across the back of the cab, including the window that Brigid was watching through.

Brigid threw herself from the wag's bumper, in motion even as the sound of the first shots rolled over her.

Chapter 14

Kane sat at an imposing table in the gaudy's main room. The table was littered with food that servers had brought out only moments ago. The menu seemed to be mostly Tex-Mex. The aroma of spicy meat laced with peppers and onions opened his sinuses and took some of the pressure of the constant headache thumping his temples.

Fiddler sat next to him. "Have you eaten this kind of food before?" she asked.

"Sure," Kane said. "But I haven't seen so much of it all in one place." The food at Cerberus was blander, and in Cobaltville Magistrates ate more simply. The only times he'd encountered such food had been in the Outlands.

Domi sat at the table across from them and had no problem at all about getting started. Her pale hands flashed across the table and quickly filled her plate.

Kane took taco shells and tortillas, then covered them with meat and vegetable relish that consisted of jalapeno peppers, onions and carrots. There were even thick logs of cheese.

"Do you like cheese?" Fiddler asked.

Kane nodded, his mouth full of taco. The taste, combined with the salsa he'd liberally spooned on, was nothing short of fiery.

Fiddler grated the cheese then spooned it over the other three tacos Kane had prepared.

Kane swallowed. "Where did you get the cheese?" It wasn't an easy thing to come by because the process was so long and involved. Cheese wasn't one of the staples generally served in Cobaltville.

"Samariumville has prefects in certain outlying areas that

run a black market," Fiddler answered. "I make it a point of being friends with friends of theirs. They still don't know that part of the business they do ends up with me."

Kane sipped the weak beer that Fiddler had ordered for him after he'd turned down the local whiskey and an offer of popskull. The weak beer was mixed into the water, which killed the strong mineral taste. For the most part, it worked and the alcohol content was too slight to get a buzz even in his dehydrated state.

"The rest of the food comes from Lindstrohm," Fiddler said.

"Lindstrohm?" Kane was puzzled.

Fiddler nodded. "Surprised the hell out of me, too. But he meant for food to be here. He sends ships of it occasionally. Doesn't give me jack to buy it myself. Just the food. Some of them, like these vegetables, are perishable."

"Where does he get them?" Kane asked.

"Along the coast. Perhaps from some of the islands in the Ribbean Sea. We get a lot of sugar for the rum from Haiti and some of the other islands that survived the nukecaust and came back to some degree after two hundred years of violent tropical storms and acid rain swept up from the mainland."

"Why does he send food?"

Fiddler shrugged and gave Kane a faint smile. "He just does."

"Bribe," Domi chimed in, her mouth full of food.

Kane looked at the albino, amazed at how she'd already cleaned her plate and was filling it again.

"Bribe," Domi repeated as she sat down with another full plate. "Things bad here. Slavers catch people, sell them to barons. Still, mebbe going to Campecheville too much for some people think about." She gestured at the laden table. "They hear about food. Mebbe hear about ships, Campecheville. At least come down here for food. Mebbe think better of leaving after that."

Kane nodded. Domi had a point, and what she said made a lot of sense. Prospective emigrants working in Fiddlerville got used to eating regularly. No matter how safe Fiddlerville appeared, they were still within striking range of the slavers. After a while, Campecheville probably sounded pretty good.

He looked at Fiddler.

The woman ate fastidiously, not ashamed of her appetite but careful of her manners and fully aware of him watching her.

"How long do people get to stay in Fiddlerville?" Kane asked.

"As long as they need," Fiddler replied.

Kane glanced around the gaudy. "I don't see a lot of extra people in the ville at the moment."

"Most of them decide to take the trip to Campecheville."

"Why?"

"Because they have to ship out or move on," Fiddler said. She returned Kane's gaze full measure, not apologetic about her words in the least. "I don't take these people on to raise, Kane. I'm a way station, and my operation is small. I make a living and believe in what I do, but I know I don't do a fleeing slave one damn bit of good if he or she doesn't get it in his or her head to board one of those ships or get the hell away from here."

"And if they don't leave?"

"I move them out of the ville," Fiddler stated simply.

Kane remained silent, thinking about what she was owning up to.

"Maybe you think that's cold," Fiddler suggested.

"This could be a ville with a lot of work," Kane pointed out.

"One thing I learned while I was doing this business," Fiddler said, "is that there can't be two bosses in Fiddlerville. The first time through, I allowed people to stay that didn't want to leave, either on one of the ships or to another place. It wasn't long before there was enough of them that they thought they could take over my business."

Kane spooned up beans and chewed as he waited. Fiddler

intrigued him, a mixture of vulnerability and ruthlessness that he'd seldom seen.

"You chill them?" Domi asked.

Fiddler turned to the albino and stared at her for a moment, then the woman laughed. "No. Maybe it would have come down to that, but there wasn't time. Even as that group worked to solidify their positions in the ville, the slavers found us and attacked."

Kane knew from the silence around them that Fiddler's story had captured the attention of every person in the room.

Fiddler took a shallow breath, her nose pinching slightly as she lowered her gaze to her plate. "There were a lot of mothers and children in the first Fiddlerville. Lindstrohm's food deliveries were being put to good use. At least, I thought they were." She glanced at Kane with shining eyes. "But do you know what I was really doing to those people?"

"Wasn't your fault, Fiddler," a man said softly from another table.

Ignoring the man, Fiddler kept her gaze on Kane. "What I was doing," she said, "was fattening them up like lambs to a slaughter. While those people were there, three mothers gave birth to children. Two of them named their children, a boy and a girl, after me. As a way of saying thanks for me helping them out. I was stupid, Kane. I let myself take pride in that. When the slavers struck, I don't even know if they survived."

"There was nothing you could have done about them," Kane said.

Fiddler shook her head. "No. There wasn't. As soon as I knew that we couldn't make a stand against the slavers, I gave the order to evacuate the ville. No one that wasn't part of our group could keep up with us. We were gone that quickly." She paused. "Four days later, I returned to the first Fiddlerville. The slavers burned the ville to the ground and hung the people too old or too wounded to travel. Their bodies hung from trees around the ville. They were intended as a message to all the ships' captains that put into port before word got out.''

"Captains got the message all right," one of the men at the nearby table said. "We set up the second Fiddlerville, it took a while for some of those captains to decide they wanted to go back into the slave-running business."

"Some of them had even decided that selling slaves paid better than trying to help them escape," another man said bitterly. "Some of them what we tried to help at the second Fiddlerville ended up on slave auction block anyway. The captain of the ship we loaded them up onto arranged a meeting with some slavers a couple days later and turned over the cargo. Fiddler found out about it from some of the people who escaped the slavers. Next time that ship put into port, we went aboard her in the dead of night and chilled every man on her."

"That was when we lost Hoskins," a man said. "There we had us a ship, never knowing that Hoskins would up and decide he wanted to be a ship's captain. Done real well for hisself, too."

Fiddler pushed her plate back. "I didn't allow anyone to stay at the second Fiddlerville longer than the appearance of three ships. Some of those people wanted to wait on other people. During their escapes, they get separated. But by the time the fourth ship arrived, I made them shit or get off the pot. One way or another, they were leaving. When the slavers hit the second Fiddlerville, we abandoned the ville again. But this time we were able to take nearly every one of the escaping slaves with us."

"It's a good policy to have," Kane said. "It's harsh, I'll grant you that, but it's fair. A hell of a lot fairer than the slavers would be."

Some of the hardness disappeared from Fiddler's eyes. She nodded.

The meal continued for a time without conversation. Kane occupied himself with the food, but his thoughts kept turning to Brigid and Grant. He gazed through the dirt-smeared window overlooking the street in front of the gaudy.

A door on the second floor closed noisily, drawing the attention of everyone in the room. A man in hard-worn clothing and scarred leather chaps ran the fingers of one hand through his dark, dust-streaked hair as he gazed at the people gathered below. His smile was deliberate and cruel.

He whistled and finished buttoning his shirt one-handed as he descended the stairs. A 9 mm handblaster rode in a reverse cavalry holster on his right hip. He carried a cut-down 12-gauge double-barreled shotgun in his left hand. Something glassy and blue glinted at his throat.

Kane was immediately aware of the change in Domi, though he doubted anyone else in the gaudy would notice.

The albino pushed up from her chair as the man reached the bottom step.

"Where are you going?" Kane asked in a low voice that didn't carry.

Domi held up the empty beer pitcher. "Get more."

Kane didn't believe her and shifted slightly in his own chair, getting ready for anything. With Domi, it was sometimes hard to figure out what was going to happen next. But he was certain her moves came as a direct result of the man's appearance.

"Who is he?" Kane asked Fiddler.

Fiddler shrugged. "His name is Craddock."

"Is he part of your regular crew?"

"No," Fiddler answered. "He's a guide. He goes into villes that the slavers have targeted and hires himself out to lead survivors here."

"How long as he been here?"

Domi paused at the bar and passed the empty pitcher across.

"Just got in last night," Fiddler replied. "Barely made in ahead of the chem storm."

Suspicion darkened Kane's thoughts. "How many people did he bring in with him?"

"No one." Fiddler watched Craddock as he leaned on the bar only a few feet from Domi. The albino seemed totally focused on the refilling of the beer pitcher. "He had two men with him who partnered up with him."

Kane scanned the room. "Where are they?"

Slowly, Fiddler glanced around the room, as well. "I don't see them. Maybe they haven't come down from the rooms upstairs yet."

"They were here earlier?" Kane asked.

"They were here this morning for sure. I can ask." Fiddler started to get up.

Kane laid a restraining hand on her forearm. "Not yet." His point man's senses were flaring, but he didn't know if it was because of Domi's actions or something else.

Craddock ordered a drink, laid jack on the table, then downed the shot in one gulp. He whinnied hoarsely and stamped a foot as if in pain. "Damn, but that's good shit." He turned and put his back to the bar. He hooked his elbows on the bar's edge and looked at Fiddler. "Just wanted to let you know that, Miss Fiddler." He smiled again.

Fiddler nodded.

Kane felt even more anxious. Then he spotted the blue stone necklace at the man's throat, realizing instantly where he'd seen one before.

Craddock shifted his attention to Domi. He smiled broadly, showing a mouthful of good teeth. "Hey, Whitey."

Domi looked up at the man. Kane saw the way the albino's body moved, everything shifting fluidly into place.

"When the last time you were rode hard and put away wet?" Craddock asked.

Domi uncoiled like a spring snapping. She twisted her body and yanked the heavy pitcher into motion. Foam sluiced off the liquid and splashed onto the bar.

Surprised, Craddock remained flat-footed as the pitcher shattered across his cocky smile and broke his teeth. He went down to the floor, screaming in pain, bright crimson staining his lower face.

WHEN THE SOUND of the gunshots reached him, Grant turned immediately toward the hill again. He guessed that he was thirty or forty yards short of being parallel with the wag that had stopped for Brigid and the slaves they had freed. But he also knew that he couldn't wait any longer.

The hot sun drew the humidity up from the wet ground and covered Grant in perspiration. The back of his throat burned from his exertion, as well as from the fact that he hadn't had anything to drink since morning.

On his way up the hillside, Grant selected a spot near a gray outcrop. He ran to the south side of the rock and threw himself down to the ground, hoping that the rock would provide as much cover as he thought it would. He crawled to the crest of the hill and peered down into the valley.

The wag had halted crossways on the rutted road and evidently stalled. The big man in the cowboy hat stood his ground and swapped bullets with the advancing line coming from the trees. Brigid Baptiste held her position at the rear of the wag, and Grant heard the familiar chatter of her Copperhead.

Grant swore, surprised at the number of men advancing from the tree line. The push was bigger than he thought it would be. He unlimbered his own Copperhead and brought the rifle's butt plate to his shoulder. He reached into the war bag he carried and brought out a small case that contained the assault rifle's telescopic sights. He and Kane had sighted in all their weapons back at Cerberus, with and without the telescopic sights. They were all marked in and only needed to be locked into place.

Once the sights were attached, Grant popped off the lens covers and sighted on the advancing line of slavers. He figured that he would bag three or four of the men before they knew he was among them.

He picked his targets carefully, choosing them from the center of the advancing line, knowing that soon the rest of the men would be aware of the carnage he was about to unleash.

Grant started with the target farthest down the hillside, knowing the recoil would push the Copperhead into a natural, rising tendency as he shifted to his left to pick up the next target. He placed the crosshairs over the first man's head, took up trigger slack and squeezed off the round.

Keeping both eyes open so he could scope his target and yet keep the terrain in view, Grant saw the man he'd shot suddenly stand straighter and stumble back. The light rounds fired by the Copperhead didn't have much knockdown power, but that wasn't necessary if the target's brain suddenly evacuated the skull.

Grant kept the rest of the shots simple, aiming for the center of each man's body. Still, he scored another head shot on the third target. From the way the man went down, Grant knew he was still alive but he also figured that the man was no longer a factor in the battle.

He had to swing wildly to pick up the fourth man, who'd figured out where the next shot was headed. The man turned and fled back into the brush, but Grant kept his sights on the man and managed to put a round through his right shoulder, knocking him to the ground. The man flailed and tried to pull himself into the brush, but Grant's next round entered through the back of his skull and left him face first on the ground.

Return fire chewed stone splinters from the nearby outcrop and kicked mud chunks and vegetation from the top of the hill. Grant pulled his head down and felt the mud and stone splinters spatter across his back. He crawled on his elbows and knees, the Copperhead resting across his wrists, ten yards past his previous position.

When he peered over the hilltop again, Grant saw that the immediate assault on the stalled wag had broken. But the sight didn't lend any real confidence to Grant. Maybe the slavers had paused in their attack because of the stiff resistance they'd encountered, but that wasn't the only reason.

Grant was suddenly aware of other wag engines rumbling in the distance. They sounded to the north, coming closer.

''C'mon, Baptiste,'' Grant said to himself, glancing back

at the stalled wag. "We gotta get those people out of here."
He briefly worried about Kane and Domi, wondering how
their arrival in Fiddlerville had gone. Then he dismissed that.
The truck had been looking for them, and Grant didn't have
any doubt that it had come from Fiddlerville, and probably
Kane, as well.

He pushed himself up and mentally plotted a course down
the hillside. Then he ran, taking advantage of every piece of
cover along the way. Bullets chopped into the ground just
behind him, scored trees in front of him and clipped off the
tops of bushes.

Lungs burning from the lack of oxygen, Grant remained
fixed on his goal. He became a human avalanche tumbling
down the hillside, gathering speed as he went.

The last twenty feet to the wag were protected by the heavy
tree growth. Bullets ripped through the leaves and branches
as gunners tried to find him, but none touched him.

The big man in the cowboy hat spun toward Grant, bringing
up the assault rifle.

"No!" Brigid yelled from behind the wag. "That's
Grant!"

Not even a flicker of indecision showed in the big man's
cold gaze.

"We've got to get clear of the area," Grant yelled. "More
of them are coming." He reached the cab of the wag, ignoring
the screaming and yelling coming from the people in the
wag's rear.

Wounded and dead were among the human cargo. Nothing
could be done for any of the survivors if they didn't make
their escape.

The wag's windshield existed only in jagged fragments of
chipped safety glass. A corpse sat behind the wheel, half his
face blown away and blood leaking down his chest.

Grant thumbed the release button on the door's handle and
tried to yank it open. The handle came off in his hand and
the door remained locked. Cursing, Grant reversed the Copperhead and slammed the buttstock through the blood-filmed

door window. As soon as the bloody glass was clear, he reached through the door window and found the inside latch release.

The door came open, the hinges squealing as if they hadn't been cared for in some time.

Without hesitation, Grant grabbed the bloody shirtfront and yanked the corpse from the wag cab. Even as he pulled the dead man to the ground outside the wag, Grant spotted the arriving line of wags coming at them through the trees and down the rutted road. He counted five, but he was certain there were more hidden by the brush and the shadows.

Grant slid in behind the wheel and spotted the manually operated foot starter that had been added after the wag had been manufactured. He pressed his left foot against the starter button as his right foot covered the accelerator pedal and pumped.

The starter ground noisily but didn't catch immediately. The strong scent of gasoline filled the wag's cab, and for a moment Grant feared that he had flooded the carburetor. Even as he started cursing and bullets pocked the wag's hood, the engine caught and roared to life.

Checking the rearview mirrors to find Brigid, Grant yelled, "Get in! Brigid, get in the damn wag!" He reached across and shoved the passenger door open.

Bullets suddenly slammed into the passenger door, ripping through the metal and careening through the other side. One of them tore through Grant's sleeve and burned his bicep.

Brigid slid into the passenger seat, already working the reload on the Copperhead. When she had the fresh magazine in place, she kicked out a foot and knocked the rest of the safety glass clear of the passenger side of the windshield.

"Who are those people?" Brigid asked, nodding toward the newly arriving wags.

"Don't know." Grant glanced at the rearview mirror on the passenger side of the wag as he shoved the transmission into reverse. "I think this is more than a simple slaver raid."

The big man in the cowboy hat stepped onto the passenger-side running board. "Not slavers," he agreed. "They come hunting Fiddlerville."

Grant slapped his hands against the steering wheel, cutting the wheels sharply and ramming into the trees behind the wag. The small ones got knocked down immediately, but the wag came to a bone-jarring stop against one of the bigger trees.

"Hope Fiddlerville's all set up to handle unexpected company," Grant commented as he whipped the wheel to the right and shoved the transmission into first gear. He let out the clutch again, feeling the wag shudder for a moment as the spinning tires sought traction. Then they grabbed hold and powered the big wag forward in a lumbering lunge.

The big man in the cowboy hat held on to the side of the wag and fired controlled bursts back at the wags that pursued them. The screaming curses and prayers coming from the back of the wag continued as a constant litany.

"His name's Pilgrim," Brigid said. She caught hold of the wag's windshield area and pulled herself through. "He says Kane sent him."

"Where the hell is Kane?" Grant asked.

"He got detained in Fiddlerville," Brigid replied as she fired smooth, even 3-round bursts with her Copperhead.

"How detained?" Grant asked.

"I don't know," Brigid answered. "We hadn't quite gotten around to that."

Grant moved through the gears, winding each one out to the max before shifting up. The transmission whined in protest. He hoped that it didn't crater and shatter from the stress he was putting it under. He twisted the wheel rapidly, trying without complete success to avoid the larger ruts and potholes in the road. Despite the trouble getting started, the wag ran surprisingly well.

He glanced in the rearview mirror on the driver's side.

The pursuing wags gained ground rapidly. Judging from the men hanging from them, though, they'd stopped briefly to take on passengers. But they were making up for lost time now.

Grant watched the road ahead, swerving hard to the left to avoid a pothole that had become more of a pit over years of hard use. The wag plowed over small trees and snapped off branches. Swerving back at the last moment, Grant caught the front bumper on a tall oak tree. Metal screamed as it caved in under the impact. Fortunately, the wag only shivered and slowed for an instant before the tires found traction again.

Without warning, a small wag burst free of the forest on the left, coming straight at Grant.

Chapter 15

Craddock's screams of agony echoed throughout the gaudy. "Thomas!" He choked and gagged for a moment, then spit up blood as he flailed weakly. "Wilson! Pettit!"

Kane stood up from the table, his gaze raking the gaudy's upper floor.

Domi gave the man no quarter. She dropped the handle from the pitcher and stepped forward. Placing one foot on Craddock's face, she kicked and banged the man's head against the floor.

"What the hell?" one of the men sitting on a nearby stool shouted.

A knife gleamed in the albino's hand. "Kane," she called.

"I got you," Kane growled, remembering the flash of blue he'd seen at Craddock's throat. "I saw it, too."

Craddock clawed frantically for the handblaster at his hip as blood continued to cascade from his broken mouth. Domi's blade licked out, scoring deeply into the underside of the man's forearm. When Craddock touched the blaster, his hand was too weak to grip it.

"Fiddler!" one of the men bellowed, pulling out a blaster and pointing it at Domi as she closed on her victim "She's gonna chill that poor bastard!"

Kane pointed his M-14 at the man. "Point that blaster away or I'll kill you."

The man hesitated only a moment, then he lowered his weapon. He stared at Fiddler.

At Kane's side, Fiddler drew the .40-caliber S&W handblaster and pointed it at the side of his face. She started to say something, but Kane interrupted her.

"Trust me or die," Kane told her, turning to face the big-bore blaster head-on. "Do it now."

Indecision raced across Fiddler's features. She lowered the pistol, frowning uncertainly. "Leave it, Jonas. Let him and the albino play out the hand they've dealt."

Kane returned his attention to the second story. "How many men did Craddock bring in with him?" He had doubt that the woman would know.

"Four or five," Fiddler answered.

One of the upstairs rooms opened and a man shoved a blaster out, following it with his face. "Craddock?" He glanced down into the gaudy's bar. "What the hell's—?" He broke off when he saw Domi standing over Craddock with her bloody knife. The man pushed his handblaster forward, taking deliberate aim.

Kane lifted the M-14 and put the open sights over the man's head, then squeezed the trigger. Even as he was riding out the recoil and the man's head emptied in the hallway above, another man stepped out into the hallway still pulling at his pants.

The second man was covered in tattoos and had unkempt, shoulder-length hair. He dropped his pants and lifted the assault rifle on a sling over his shoulder.

Kane stroked the trigger again. The heavy 7.62 mm round cored through the man's heart, punching him back through the open door. A woman started screaming in terror from inside the room.

Another door opened to the left of the other two, drawing Kane's attention immediately. A naked woman stepped out into the hallway. She was young and hard bodied, her breasts jutting cones capped with large areola. Her dark pubic bush was carefully trimmed in a neat triangle.

She also had a pistol at the back of her head.

"Don't shoot!" the woman screamed. "Don't shoot! I ain't got no blaster!"

Kane swiveled the M-14 to the left, tracking across the woman and settling on the partially open door behind her.

The woman stared at Kane, wide-eyed with disbelief. "He made me come out here! He said he was gonna chill—"

Kane squeezed the M-14's trigger twice quickly. Both rounds cored through the flimsy door and hammered the man hiding behind it. Judging from the slack way the man fell, Kane knew he'd killed him.

Glancing over his shoulder, Kane saw that Domi had Craddock locked into place with a knife at his throat. Despite all the sudden death that had erupted in the room, Domi looked serene and feral. Her bright white teeth showed through her parted pale lips, almost smiling in anticipation.

With a nod, Kane went up the stairs, holding the M-14 at the ready. Fiddler had said four men and maybe five; three were down.

He reached the second-floor landing and knew that Fiddler was at his back. He didn't know if she was covering him or insuring that he wasn't going to get away with the violence he'd just perpetrated. Having her there made him feel uneasy, but it also kept anyone else in the room from risking a shot at him.

At the top of the second-story landing, Kane's Magistrate training took over. He made certain the two men in the hallway were dead, then moved forward and checked the man he had shot behind the door.

The dead man lay stretched out inside the room. One of the bullets had missed the man entirely, but the second had ripped away his throat. Kane returned to the hallway where the naked woman stood.

"Did you know these men?" Kane demanded.

The woman held a trembling hand over her mouth. Her eyes stayed on the dead man in the room. She shook her head, but said, "I knew them a little. They've been in before. That one, his name's Bodine. He ran with Craddock. Bodine always said he liked me."

"What about the other two men?"

The woman nodded. "They ran with Craddock, too."

"How many men were with Craddock today?" Kane

asked. He swung her head so that she looked at his eyes. "How many men today?"

"Four."

"Four with Craddock?" Kane repeated.

"Yeah."

"Where's the fourth man?" Kane glanced around the other rooms.

The woman pointed toward a room at the corner.

"Is he still in there?" Kane watched the door to the room.

The woman shook her head. "I don't know. Gracy, she had some jolt that Fiddler didn't know about. But this guy, he wanted jolt, not just sex. I seen him go in, but I didn't see him come out."

Kane crossed the landing to the room. He took a position beside the door and raised the M-14 parallel to his body. A glance down at the first floor assured him that Domi still had things under control there.

He waved at Fiddler and the naked gaudy slut, motioning them out of the field of fire. Then he rapped his knuckles against the door, drawing them back quickly, expecting immediate shooting.

When nothing happened, Kane turned quickly and lifted his leg. Pain immediately flared through his bruised chest and cut off his breath. Ignoring the pain, he drove his foot into the door, shattering the lock.

The door shuddered open.

Kane let the rifle lead him into the room. A girl lay supine on the swaybacked bed, face up and staring at the ceiling with unseeing eyes. The room's furnishings were simple. Besides the bed, there was a trunk against one wall and a small, mirrored vanity that held a pitcher and bowl for washing up.

Kane strode into the room, his eyes attracted immediately by all the blood staining the bedsheets. A glance at the girl told him that her throat had been cut. Dark bruising across her lower face advertised the fact that whoever had done the cutting had also prevented her from crying out.

The girl was young, not even twenty.

Curtains blew up from the open window.

Kane crossed the room and pulled the curtains aside. He recognized the street in front of Chantilly Lacey's.

Harsh scraping to Kane's left drew his attention and, combined with his quick reflexes, saved his life. He turned and spotted a bearded man with pinpoint eyes staring at him down the muzzle of a shotgun. The man stood on the building's eaves.

Kane ducked back inside the room just as the man fired. The load of double-aught buckshot ripped into the window frame and smashed it to splinters.

Continuing to step back, Kane marked off the distance the man was from the window and the height he'd been at on the eaves. Firing as quickly as he could pull the trigger, Kane stitched a ragged line of holes through the wall, which wasn't thick enough to stop the heavy 7.62 mm rounds.

A hoarse shout of pain followed Kane's fourth shot. He punched two more bullets through the same area for good measure. When there was no return fire, he stepped forward and peered cautiously through the window.

Bullet holes stood out in sharp relief on the wall, and there was no sign of the shotgunner on the eaves. Kane glanced down and spotted the man lying in the middle of the street, barely moving.

Aware that machine gunners on the opposite building were already tracking his movements, Kane pulled back inside the window out of sight. "Your team on the roof of the building opposite us," he said to Fiddler.

The woman nodded and stepped out into the window carefully. She waved, then turned back to face Kane. "It's okay. They saw me."

Kane joined her at the window and peered down at the man again. The man gave a final convulsive shiver, then stopped moving.

Fiddler glared at him. "Are you through chilling people?" she asked.

"If Craddock only brought four people with him," Kane replied, "I am."

"What's the problem with Craddock?"

Kane turned and headed out of the room. "Remember earlier when you said Baron Samarium was sending spies to infiltrate slave-rescue operations?"

"Of course."

"I think Craddock is one of them." Kane walked down the staircase, aware that every eye in the room was on him. If anyone in the room decided to make a move against him, Kane knew the whole gaudy would erupt.

"I've known Craddock for over a year," Fiddler replied. "He's brought in several escaped slaves during that time."

Kane didn't break stride, reaching the bottom of the stairs in seconds. "How long has it been since he brought in slaves?"

"Only a few weeks."

"Longer than normal?"

"Maybe." Fiddler sounded defensive. "Things are getting harder. Baron Samarium is paying more jack than Lindstrohm. Plus, you don't have to worry about being shot by the baron's sec troops if you're working with them."

Kane nodded to Domi.

Somewhat reluctantly, the albino stepped back off her wounded prisoner, but not before she got one last kick in to the side of his head.

"The motorcycle we rode into the ville," Kane said, "belonged to a young woman who died trying to get here. She still had manacles on her wrists. I think she only escaped a slaver recently."

"She was coming here to escape?" Fiddler asked.

"I think she was coming here for something more than that," Kane said. "I think she was coming after revenge. She rode through the worst of that chem storm last night. That's why she didn't make it—the storm killed her. When we found her, we took the motorcycle and Domi took the necklace she was wearing."

The albino lifted the blue gem stone from her throat with the blade of her knife. The blue gem glittered as it caught the light. "Craddock wearing necklace like this one," the albino said.

Holding the man up by his bloody shirt, Kane opened his shirt lapels and showed the blue gem necklace gleaming at Craddock's throat. "I'm thinking that he killed the other person who wore this necklace, then he kept the necklace."

"Fuck...you," Craddock gasped through his ruined mouth. "Stupe bastard. You...you don't know what...the hell you're...talking about."

"Is this necklace yours?" Kane asked.

"Yeah," Craddock replied. "I had that...that fucker for a long time."

"Are you sure he's not telling the truth?" Fiddler asked.

"I'm sure," Kane answered. He centered his attention on Craddock. "I'm also sure that there's another reason he's here now." He locked eyes with Craddock. "I want to know what that reason is."

Craddock hacked a mass of blood and phlegm, and prepared to spit in Kane's direction.

Reacting calmly and efficiently, Kane reached out and tapped Craddock in the throat hard enough to trigger a swallowing convulsion. He watched as Craddock gagged and nearly threw up. Bloody, stringy foam covered his mouth and chin.

Domi held a knife in each hand and stepped into Craddock's personal space. He tried to escape her, but Kane forced him back against the bar,

"Get him up on bar," Domi said. "I make him talk." Her ruby eyes glinted malevolently.

"Fiddler," the bartender said hoarsely, "you can't just let them—"

"Shut up," Fiddler ordered. "If Craddock has turned on us, we need to know about it."

"And if he hasn't?" another man asked.

Fiddler's voice remained flat and neutral. "Then we need to know that, too."

Kane hefted Craddock up on to the bar and laid him out despite his efforts to get up. The damage Domi had inflicted was telling, leaving him weak.

Domi flicked her knives and set to work in a cold-blooded manner. She cut away the crotch area of Craddock's pants, leaving his genitals exposed. Grinning mirthlessly, the albino placed the keen edge of one of the knives against Craddock's sac. "Cold steel not agree with you," she said. "Cause shrinkage."

"Get that...that fucking freak...away from me!" Craddock yelled in fear. He tried to sit up, and he tried to push Kane away.

His own stomach rolling slightly, Kane blocked Craddock's weak blows and yanked the man's jacket back down over his arms, creating an impromptu straitjacket. Stepping behind Craddock, Kane held the back of the jacket against the bar top, restraining the man.

Craddock's feet drummed the top of the bar. Domi easily avoided them and kept her knife in place.

Domi looked at Craddock. "Sac open enough, I castrate you easy. Mebbe you want see how big a man you are."

"Fuck you...you mutie bitch! I ain't done nothing—"

Domi didn't even let him finish. Her knives flashed and a thin, high-pitched scream tore from Craddock's bloody mouth. Crimson sprayed into the air.

"Just nicked sac a little," Domi said patiently. "Haven't done anything really bad. Yet. Will, though." She held the bloody blade up. "Tell about girl, necklace."

Craddock glanced wildly at Kane. "You can't...let her... do this!"

Kane held the man's gaze levelly. "I'm not going to stop her."

Beside him, Fiddler's face turned as pale as paper.

"Fiddler!" Craddock pleaded.

The woman shook her head slowly. "Not my play, Craddock."

The other men around the bar took a step back. They were all hardened, used to the violence that had haunted their lives, but none of them wanted any part of what was happening to Craddock.

Kane couldn't fault them. He couldn't have done what Domi was doing. Even as a Magistrate in Cobaltville, there were limits to the violence. Killing a man—or a woman—was cleaner than what the albino was doing to Craddock.

"One more chance," Domi said coldly, "then you never be daddy. After that, I fix so not even have toy to play with. You piss sitting down."

Kane knew Domi would do it, but he didn't know if he would be able to allow it. However, stopping Domi might not be an option, either. The albino was determined to get the truth. Maybe it was the memory of the dead woman they had found that morning, or maybe it was just the link between the two cheap necklaces.

More than anything else, though, Domi knew she was right, and Kane knew it, as well.

Craddock's nerve broke. He started crying, weeping and screaming. "Don't chill me! Please, don't...let her...chill me!"

"Tell about woman," Domi demanded. She wiped her bloody knife on Craddock's shirt. The knife didn't come clean because blood covered the shirt, but Craddock felt the blade against his skin again.

"My men...found her." Craddock took a deep, rattling breath, sucking his own blood into his lungs and choking on it a moment. "They...chilled her before I could...I could stop them. They were...drunk, stoned out of their heads...on jolt."

"Lying," Domi accused in a thin, unforgiving voice. "I know when lying." She turned her attention to Craddock's crotch again. "No more lies."

Craddock screeched in terror, lifting his head and shaking it wildly. "No! No, no, no! Don't cut me no more!"

Domi looked at him dispassionately. "Tell about girl. Tell about necklace."

"They were…sisters." Craddock hiccupped and crimson bubbles burst in his mouth. "We caught them…a few days back. Some small, no-name…ville northwest of here."

"You were selling slaves," Kane said, "not freeing them."

Craddock turned his head to look at Fiddler. "You don't…understand. They got you. They're coming…coming for you."

Fiddler's face hardened. "Who's coming?"

"Baron Samarium." Craddock's throat worked, swallowing the blood filling his mouth. "There's a whole…detachment of Magistrates…on their way…here now."

Instantly, angry voices filled the gaudy.

"When?" Fiddler demanded.

Craddock swallowed, gazing around the room and finding no sympathy. "Soon. Mebbe only minutes."

Kane immediately thought of Brigid and Grant out on the open road, totally exposed.

"I didn't…have a choice," Craddock said. "Fiddler, I…I swear I didn't. Baron Samarium's Mags…caught me…me and my men. Said they was…gonna chill us…if we didn't…didn't cooperate."

"What did you do?" Fiddler asked.

"They knew…knew about…Fiddlerville," Craddock whined. "I didn't tell them…anything there…that they didn't know…already."

Fiddler drew the big pistol from the cross-draw holster at her waist. She rolled the hammer back, and the man on the other side of the bar got out of the line of fire.

Craddock's mouth opened in a wide, bloody O of surprise and fear.

Without a word, Fiddler shot the man through the mouth, blowing his spine through the back of his neck. Blood sprayed over the age-spotted mirror behind the bar.

Kane released the dead man's jacket and glanced at Fiddler.

The woman holstered her blaster. "Just making a long story short. There was nothing else he could have told us, and every moment we spent here listening to him was another moment we didn't have."

"Could have told us more," Domi argued. "Could have told us how many Magistrates."

"Would it have mattered?" Fiddler asked. "We're already here and they're coming. In the meantime, I've got friends out on the only road leading into this ville. And they're over-due."

"I need to borrow a wag," Kane said. "That motorcycle I rode in on will provide no protection at all."

"You'll get it," Fiddler promised. "I'm coming with you."

"WATCH OUT!" Grant shouted as he pulled the big wag's steering wheel hard right.

The smaller wag darted forward from the tree line like a striking snake. Grant caught a brief glimpse of armed men on the other side of the mud-streaked windshield.

"I see them," Brigid said calmly from atop the wag.

The smaller wag hammered the side of Grant's wag again, sending a shudder down the vehicle's length. Still, the bigger wag's greater weight kept it on course. Grant pulled back to the left, narrowly avoiding the large tree at the side of the rutted road. His path took him back into the smaller wag, and he noticed the man on the passenger side thrusting a shotgun through the open window.

Before the man could fire, Brigid's Copperhead opened up from above. A line of bullets stitched holes across the top of the other wag before Brigid got her aim down. Another short burst caught the passenger and knocked him back inside the wag.

Taking advantage of the driver's sudden loss of control as the corpse stretched out across him, Grant pulled the wheel hard and rammed the smaller wag. Buffeted by the bigger wag's bulk, the smaller one veered off the road and shot ahead. The wag slammed into small group of trees, coming to an abrupt halt that swung the tail end out into the road.

"Hold on!" Grant bellowed, glancing in the rearview mirrors.

The half-dozen wags pursued them in a loose grouping that staggered them two by two, but they were closing fast.

Grant kept the accelerator pinned to the floor. The wag engine strained as it struggled to maintain the pace. The small wag had ended up partially jutting into the rutted road; there was no way to avoid it. Grant held the steering wheel in both hands and aimed for the rear of the small wag, counting on the bigger vehicle's weight to carry it through the impromptu blockade.

Two men tried to scramble from the smaller wag's rear seat through the back windshield. Grant didn't know if the back windshield had already been broken out or had gotten shattered during the initial collision. One of the men reached a standing position on the rear of the wag when Grant drove into it.

Grant's wag bucked for a moment, pushing the smaller vehicle ahead until it got caught in the rutted road. The larger vehicle shuddered for just a moment, then swiftly rolled over the small wag. The man halfway out the back window was crushed beneath the big tire as Grant drove over.

The man who had been standing on the rear of the wag threw himself forward, a determined look on his blood-smeared face. He caught hold of the big wag's hood with one hand and thrust a pistol toward Grant's head with the other.

Reacting automatically, Grant slapped the man's hand and weapon aside. The bullet tore through the passenger door, narrowly missing the big man clinging there and firing his assault rifle at the pursuing wags. Grant grabbed the man by the hair of his head, then yanked him into the cab. The man squalled in pain as part of his scalp tore loose.

"Stupe bastard!" the man roared. He fumbled in the tight confines of the wag cab and tried to bring up his weapon again.

Grant pulled a combat knife from his boot and lashed out, driving the thick blade deeply into the hollow of the man's throat. When the cross hilt slammed against flesh and would go no farther, Grant twisted and shoved the blade around, nearly decapitating his opponent.

The man's blaster dropped from nerveless fingers as his eyes turned glassy.

Yanking the knife from the corpse, Grant wiped it mostly clean on the dead man's pants and returned it to his boot. The wag rumbled on across the smaller vehicle and dropped back to the ground.

"Grant," Brigid called, then leaned her head over the side of the cab to peer through the window.

"What?" Grant yelled over the tortured roar of the wag's engine.

Brigid pointed at a distant dragonfly-shaped silhouette in the western sky.

The afternoon sun robbed the silhouette of any three-dimensional detail, but Grant recognized the shape immediately. It was a Deathbird, one of the most feared weapons in a baron's arsenal. As a Magistrate, Grant had had plenty of experience with the death-dealing machines.

Even as he watched, the attack helicopter swung around on an easterly heading. Grant knew it was moving in their direction.

The slavers hadn't come alone.

Chapter 16

Outside the gaudy, Kane followed Fiddler, who was moving at a jog. The woman called out orders to the nearby men, and Kane was impressed at how quickly the rescue operation took form. They crossed the street, followed by most of the men from the gaudy.

"Hey, Fiddler," one of the machine-gun crewmen yelled down, "what's going on?"

"I think we're about to be attacked by Baron Samarium's shock troops." Fiddler stopped in front of a two-story building across the street. Two massive double doors fronted the structure.

"No shit?" the machine gunner called back down.

"Taylor's passing the word," Fiddler said. "Get your gear together and prep those rooftops. I don't know if we're going to try to hold the ville or leave immediately."

"Where are you going?" the man asked.

"Pilgrim's out there," Fiddler replied. "He doesn't know. He may have walked into a trap."

She glanced at Kane. "Help me with these doors."

Kane bent to the task, finding that although the doors were large, they also moved surprisingly easily on tracked runners. The interior of the building was dark, steeped in shadows, but the metallic surfaces of the large vehicles held inside glowed dully.

"You know what these are?" Fiddler asked as she walked between the two wags.

"Sandcats," Kane said, recognizing them immediately. They were prenukecaust FAVs—Fast Attack Vehicles. Covered in ceramic-armaglass armor, the Sandcats were outfitted with two USMG-73 heavy machine guns. The fighting wags were low-slung and blocky, standing on two tank treads that guaranteed them maneuverability over nearly any terrain. These two Sandcats were even equipped with snorkels that allowed them to travel underwater for short distances. "Usually they're only Magistrate issue."

"Yeah," Fiddler said, "well, they didn't get to keep them all." She reached up and hauled herself onto the Sandcat on her left. "When Baron Samarium's troops hit the second Fiddlerville, we were better prepared. We got out early, like I said, but we waited. Baron Samarium stationed two Sandcats and a small force to hold the ville."

"They were expecting you to show back up," Kane said, hauling himself aboard the Sandcat, as well.

"We did," Fiddler said. "Only things didn't go as they expected. We led them back out into the swamps, and they were so sure of themselves and their equipment that they followed. We blew out one of the first Sandcat's tracks with a rifle gren."

"Standard ops for a situation like that is to stay with the other team," Kane said.

Fiddler opened the top door and dropped down into the Sandcat. "It is. But the Magistrates were too sure of themselves. They thought we'd just gotten lucky with the grenade and that we were still running for our lives."

The Sandcat's 750-horsepower engine turned over loudly, then caused a steady shiver to come to life throughout the big machine. Kane felt the wag's familiar vibration through his boot soles and welcomed it.

"We weren't still running for our lives," Fiddler said as she clambered back out of the Sandcat. "We'd planned on taking out one of the Sandcats, and we'd planned on leading the second Sandcat to its doom. We'd dug a tiger pit. Do you know what that is?"

"A pit in the ground," Kane said. As a Magistrate, he'd encountered such traps and even more inventive boobies. "Usually covered up so that the intended victim can't see it.

Hunters line the bottom with sharpened stakes. Sometimes they kill whatever they catch immediately, and sometimes they wait a few days till it grows weak with hunger.''

"Our tiger pit was different. We dug the hole and covered it over, so the wag driver didn't see it until he was falling through.'' Fiddler watched as the rest of the crew readied themselves for battle.

Kane kept watch, as well, knowing immediately that the men were all well trained.

"We dug our tiger pit in a low area,'' Fiddler went on. "The digging was easy, but the water table made the timing difficult. If we'd had to wait another two or three days, that pit would have completely filled with water and the covering over it would have floated away. The Sandcat rolled into the pit and dropped like a rock. The water level wasn't quite over the top, but we opened a channel we had already prepared from a small swamp area on top of the hill. The water filled the pit in less than two hours.''

Kane listened, amazed by the simplicity of the plan and chilled by the cold-bloodedness.

"When the Mags tried to abandon the wag,'' Fiddler said in a neutral voice, "we ambushed them. None of them made it out alive even with the polycarbonate armor they wore. When the water level topped the Sandcat, the crew inside ran the snorkel up. We covered the snorkel with plastic and ordnance tape. After the crew ran out of air, they swam up and we chilled them all. Then we went back for the other Sandcat crew. They took longer to get out because they had food put up inside the wag.'' She looked at Kane. "But I've always been patient.''

Watching her, seeing how well the men responded to her orders, Kane had no doubts about that.

A man rushed through the double doors. "Fiddler!''

"What is it?'' Fiddler looked at the man.

"Lookout says he's spotted sails out on the horizon.''

"Whose ship?'' Fiddler asked, dropping down from the Sandcat and striding toward the door.

"Looks like Blakeney."

Kane dropped from the Sandcat and followed her. He chafed to be out onto the road, wondering what trouble Brigid and Grant might have already encountered.

Out on the street, Fiddler whistled up at the machine-gun crew on the building adjacent to the one that housed the Sandcats. A half-dozen other semiarmored vehicles, including two six-wheeled Hussar Hot Spur Land Rovers, already occupied the street and stood waiting.

The machine-gun crew kicked out a rope ladder that uncoiled and fell to the street. Fiddler swarmed up the ladder with the grace and speed of a monkey. With slightly less aplomb, Kane climbed up after her, followed by Domi.

One of the machine gunners handed Fiddler a pair of binoculars and pointed out into the Gulf. She stood and brought the field glasses to her eyes.

Kane stared due south, out where the rolling terrain of the sea gradually flowed back up toward the sky, giving the immediate impression that the land was going to be swallowed up by the sea. They were almost at sea level now, and the curvature of the earth always gave that illusion.

The ship looked incredibly small in the distance.

Kane took his own binoculars from his war bag and trained them on the ship. The sails were square-rigged, white standing out against the blue sky. The vessel chased the wind, and even the triangular jib sails belled out.

"The wind is with him," Fiddler commented. "He's making good time."

"How long before he gets here?" Kane asked, putting away his binoculars.

"Forty minutes, give or take." Fiddler started back down the rope ladder.

"Blakeney don't owe us nothing," one of the machine gunners said gruffly. "If this thing spills over into the ville before he gets here, Blakeney's gonna remember that. He'll turn tail and run like a striped ape."

"I know."

Back on the street, Fiddler jogged toward the building with the Sandcats. "Washington."

A big black man with a shaved head and a gray mustache turned to face her from one of the waiting wags. His left hand was missing, but he wore a curved metal hook. "Yes."

"Blakeney's coming in from the Gulf," Fiddler said. "Take a boat out and meet him. If this thing sours, make sure he finds his way here."

"Done," Washington promised, vaulting over the wag's side.

Kane glanced at Domi behind him. "Go with him," he said quietly.

A petulant look filled Domi's face, and she shook her head slightly. "Grant out there. Might need help. Want to help."

"You can help him more by making sure that ship puts in to shore," Kane replied. "I don't know how effective Washington can be about convincing somebody, but I trust you to get the job done."

Domi came to a halt at the entrance to the building that house the Sandcats. She glanced after Washington, who was already double-timing it to the flimsy docks stretching out into the Gulf. She gave Kane a swift nod. "Take care of Grant and Brigid." Then she was gone, a pale ghost drifting through the debris of the wrecked ville.

Kane was already in motion, following Fiddler into the building and slithering into the Sandcat. She already had three other men in the wag with her, completing the four-man team.

Fiddler glanced at him with cool appraisal. "What are you doing here?"

"Coming along," Kane growled.

Fiddler shook her head. "I need an experienced crew for this."

"I *am* experienced," Kane said. "Weps, nav system and repair. Give me the tools, I can strip down one of these and rebuild it for you."

Challenge glinted in Fiddler's eyes. "One of these days, I want to talk to you about where you got all this expertise."

"Not today," Kane replied. He glanced at the pilot's seat.

A Latino with emaciated features and a haunted look in his dark gaze sat there. Knives festooned the front of his shirt.

"I'm driving," Kane said. With all the armor plating covering it, the Sandcat was a blunt object meant for battering infantry or light-wag units to pieces.

"No," the Latino said. "I'm driving."

"Raul," Fiddler called. "Let Kane pilot the Sandcat."

Resentfully, Raul slid from the pilot's chair, brushing forcefully against Kane.

He ignored the man's overt threat. To respond any other way would have meant killing him, and Kane made sure the smaller man knew that by not giving an inch of ground.

Without a word, Raul climbed out of the Sandcat.

Kane sat in the seat and buckled himself in. "Clear," he shouted, slamming a fist against the top of the wag.

"Clear," Fiddler replied.

"Clear," someone called from outside.

Kane engaged the transmission and rolled the Sandcat forward. The tracks clanked against the building's tiled floor, echoing in the cavernous space. As he pulled out onto the street, the polarized ob slit darkened, clearing out the sun's haze. Locking the left track, he turned sharply and headed out of Fiddlerville, speeding up as he took the lead position in the convoy.

He scanned the docks down by the Gulf, catching sight of Domi's pale frost hair on board a speedboat. Most of the other craft tied up at the docks were sailcraft. As Kane watched, the speedboat started out into the tide, slowly gaining speed. Then he switched his attention to the rutted road that had brought him into Fiddlerville and pressed the accelerator.

He glanced over his shoulder and spotted Fiddler stripping out of her clothes, revealing a body that was all taut and curved. The triangle between her thighs was dyed green, as well, and her body showed a few scars.

"Like what you see?" Fiddler asked without conceit or

embarrassment as she gathered her discarded clothing and shoved it into a bin built into the Sandcat.

"Is this some kind of ritual?" Kane asked, only half-serious.

"No." Fiddler took out camou-colored BDUs, pants and a T-shirt, as well as a pair of high-topped combat boots. She belted the cross-draw rig over her hips again, then added a shoulder holster over the camou T-shirt. Turning, she clambered up into the dome-shaped blister at the top of the Sandcat where the weapons controls were for the USMG-73 machine guns. "In case we have to go commando in the woods, I want to be dressed for it. Those pants made me stand out." She strapped herself into the weps seat, then jockeyed the joysticks that operated the two machine guns and the seat itself, which allowed her a 360-degree field of fire.

Kane surveyed the muddy terrain ahead of him. The rutted road slipped and slid under the tracks a little as he moved the Sandcat up near top speed. Even in the specially constructed seats, the team bounced over the uneven road.

"There they are," the copilot said, pointing.

"Got them," Kane replied, having already spotted the wag nearly three hundred yards ahead of them.

Brigid Baptiste lay across the wag's cab, her attention riveted to the wags that pursued them as she fired her Copperhead. Pilgrim hung on to the wag's side, firing his assault rifle with one hand.

At the moment the tree line concealed the Sandcat from the slavers, and Kane counted on that element of surprise. He flicked the Sandcat's lights on and off three times in quick succession, recognizing Grant behind the steering wheel in the same breath.

Grant flicked his remaining light on and off, as well, letting Kane know he'd seen him.

"Hang on," Kane advised as the Sandcat roared down the road and closed on the fleeing wag.

"What are you going to do?" Fiddler demanded.

"Those trees bottleneck the road," Kane explained, holding the mil-spec wag on course. "If we can create a blockage, it will hold them off for a time. Those people are exposed on that flatbed."

"How do you plan on creating the blockage?"

Kane grinned. "Strap in tight," he suggested.

Grant took out the heart of the rutted road, and the wags that pursued him didn't have a clear view of the Sandcat approaching at nearly top speed.

"You're crazy," the copilot yelled, understanding what Kane meant to do. The man gripped the arms of the chair and put his feet against the console.

"The Cat will handle it," Kane said confidently. "I've seen them handle worse than the light wags we've got coming our way."

"If it doesn't," the man said, "you've fucked us all."

Grant broke at the last moment, fishtailing for a moment and looking as if he wasn't going to clear the Sandcat. The wag behind the flatbed was a stripped-down Jeep that sported a roll bar for a top covering. The men riding in the wag stared ahead, and Kane knew that they had only one moment of crystal clarity before he was among them like a wolf in a sheep flock.

The Sandcat roared into the small wag, which shattered like a wave striking rock. The driver had had just enough time to stand on the brakes and try to bring the wag to a halt, but that only lowered the front end. The treads chewed into the muddy ground as the Sandcat actually shuddered to a near-stop, then drove the wrecked wag backward. Not even a heartbeat later, the wag mired up in the mud and wouldn't move.

Kane downshifted on the fly before he lost all momentum. When he released the clutch, the treads clawed into the crushed wag, shredding metal and flesh and blood alike. If the slavers had survived the initial impact, they died in pieces as the Sandcat rolled over them.

"Hit them, Fiddler!" Kane commanded as the other wags skidded to stops, seeking desperately to avoid the tangled wreck of metal the jeep had become and to stay away from the Sandcat's shredding treads.

The USMG-73 machine guns opened up simultaneously, and empties spilled into the built-in brass catchers.

Kane pulled the steering wheel hard to the right, aiming at the next wag in line with the others. The right treads crunched into the second wag and knocked it sideways, hanging it up in the trees. The men inside tried to climb out, but Fiddler hammered them with the twin machine guns.

Bringing the Sandcat to a jerking halt, manhandling the steering wheel, his feet pumping the pedals, Kane whipped the mil-spec into a tight turn. Two other wags skidded into the wreckage of the first wag before they could stop.

"The tires, Fiddler," Kane commanded.

On top of the Sandcat, Fiddler whipped around in the seat and targeted the two wags. Rounds sprayed across the wags, riddling the thin metal and turning the slavers inside them to bloody puppets. Fiddler also chopped the rubber tires to pieces, leaving the vehicles sitting lower on the ground.

"The other Cat is coming through the tree line," the copilot said, pointing.

Kane glanced in the direction the man indicated, spotting the second Sandcat. The driver avoided the large tree, plunging over and tearing through the smaller trees and brush.

"That was a damn stupid thing to do," Kane said.

"Get them in a crossfire," the copilot explained, pointing again to the men on foot following along the trail.

"Yeah," Kane growled, "but it opened a path for the wags to go through around the roadblock we just left."

Understanding filled the copilot's face. "Oh."

The second Sandcat's machine guns opened fire, devastating the uneven line the men on foot had presented. Bodies tumbled and flew as the machine-gun rounds caught the men and knocked them backward. One of the men turned with a long tube over one shoulder, aiming it at Kane's Sandcat.

Kane drove straight for the man, hoping to keep the

weapon's tank-buster round from the Sandcat's vulnerable treads.

Instinctively, the man raised his shoulder-mounted weapon and fired. The rocket leaped across the fifty yards of intervening space and smashed just below the reinforced ob slit. The explosion triggered the reactive armor that covered the Sandcat, blowing chunks of it free as it diluted the warhead's power. Still, the Sandcat rocked back, whipping the steering wheel out of Kane's hands for a moment.

In the next moment, the man dropped the shoulder-fired rocket launcher and ran for his life, narrowly escaping the Sandcat.

Kane recovered the steering wheel and regained control of the Sandcat. He locked the right track and came around hard in a 180-degree turn that threw out great chunks of muddy earth. He kept the accelerator pinned to the floor in between shifting gears, aiming for the path that had been cut through the trees by the second Sandcat's arrival.

"What are you doing?" Fiddler asked as she readied the machine guns again.

"Closing the door," Kane said as he plowed over the trees ahead of him. His course took him perpendicular to the trail the other Sandcat had mowed through the trees and brush. He pushed trees over, collapsing them onto the makeshift passage, effectively closing off any chance the slavers had at continuing their pursuit.

Kane backed out of the forest, locked a track and came around quickly while Fiddler kept the machine guns blazing. He scanned the battlefield, discovering that the other wags that had followed the two Sandcats out of Fiddlerville had set up on the other side of the slaver vehicles Kane had originally smashed up to block the rutted road. One of those vehicles was on fire, sending a wavering column of black smoke high into the blue sky.

Two of the men who had bailed from the wags carried rocket launchers and what appeared to be a good supply of warheads. A motorcycle streaking away from Kane's sudden advance took a direct hit from a rocket and exploded into a ball of boiling flame.

Kane watched the remnants of the slaver forces that had attacked Grant, Brigid and Pilgrim. Despite the overwhelming damage inflicted by the arriving Sandcats, the men did nothing other than dig in and return fire. It didn't make sense.

Unless they knew something, Kane realized. He turned his attention to the air, looking toward the afternoon sun. If he were commanding an air-support unit in the engagement, that was where he would post it.

At first the sun's glare was too harsh to make anything out. Then Kane spotted the familiar dragonfly shape of a Deathbird winging toward the battleground.

The helicopter kept the burning orb behind it for the greatest concealment. Even the Sandcat's protective polarization of the ob-slit glass didn't completely take away the pain of staring into the sun. The polarization circuitry juiced a couple times and turned the screen almost black as the sun hit it directly.

Kane automatically checked the cockpit video feeds. The Sandcats Fiddler had captured were some of the most recent additions to the redoubt rolling stock. Kane and Grant had talked about adding the video to the Sandcat they kept at Cerberus—with Bry's help—but hadn't yet gotten around to it.

"Incoming!" the copilot suddenly yelled.

"Get topside, Eddie," Fiddler ordered from the weps station. "Not everyone has noticed."

Kane estimated there were only seconds left before the Deathbird swooped down on them like a hawk. He knew from past experience that the Deathbirds generally carried Hellfire missiles or rockets attached to the stubby wings. The turret on the underside of the Deathbird's fuselage sported a 30 mm chain gun.

The Hellfire missiles were tank killers out to six klicks. Kane knew the Magistrate pilots would have gladly sacrificed the lives of a few—or all—slavers to take out their targets, which made him think they didn't have the Hellfire missiles. Only dealing with the rockets and 30 mm rounds didn't make the situation any less dangerous.

Eddie opened the hatch above the steering section and climbed up the short ladder. "Get the hell out of here!" the man yelled.

Kane wished they had a working communications frequency between all the vehicles, but obviously that hadn't been an option. He steered the Sandcat away from the remaining opponents on the battlefield, trying to offer Eddie as much cover as possible. Kane hadn't planned on having to get exposed behind the enemy lines.

The lead Deathbird fired a rocket from one of the port-side pods. Kane recognized the rocket's white-gray contrail even as it tore free of the stubby pod. He moved, raising his voice, already knowing he was going to be too late.

"Get—" Kane started to shout, then he voice was lost in the explosion that hammered the side of the Sandcat. With the hatch open, the thundering detonation was immediately deafening. He couldn't even hear his own voice even though he knew he was yelling.

Blood showered down into the Sandcat's interior, then the lower half of Eddie's body dropped back down into the cockpit. In the deafening silence of white noise, there was no sound at all.

Chapter 17

Domi wrapped her arms around her body as she sat in the powerboat heading out across the Gulf. The wind coming across the water prickled her skin.

"Cold?" Washington stood at the boat's wheel and wore a light jacket with a bandolier of rifle magazines and three grens hooked to it. He kept his attention on the ship coming at them from the horizon.

"No," the albino said stubbornly. She didn't like asking for things, and she knew Kane wouldn't be happy if she forced one of the other men aboard the powerboat to take off his jacket at gunpoint.

"Uh-huh," Washington growled, smirking. "You'd probably be a better liar if your skin wasn't speckling up like that."

"Mebbe you'd like to see what your skull looks like," Domi suggested.

Washington started to laugh but caught himself and didn't.

It was, Domi thought under the circumstances, a wise move on his part. She was still angry with Kane for leaving her behind. Even though she understood why he had done it, she didn't like the idea of not being there for Grant. She didn't like not being there for Brigid only a little less.

Washington asked one of the nearby men to hold wheel for a moment, then went belowdecks, returning almost immediately with a small blanket. "Here," he said, holding it out to Domi. "This'll help."

The albino took the blanket and pulled it on, hanging it across her shoulders so that it unfurled and hung down to her knees and knocked off some of the wind.

"Mebbe it'll help some," Washington said.

Domi nodded. As an outlander, she was unaccustomed to the kindness of strangers and always regarded it with suspicion. "Why?"

"The blanket?" Washington asked.

"Yes."

The big man shrugged. "Hate to see anybody uncomfortable." Then he grinned. "And I didn't much care for Craddock. He was always a little hard on my nerves. It was good to see him get his comeuppance."

Domi gazed at the ship as the powerboat slapped against the waves. The sails remained full, and she could see the faces of men gathered along the railing now. "Will Blakeney be suspicious?"

"About what?"

"Us going see him. 'Stead of waiting."

Washington shook his head. "Nah. Usually somebody always takes a run out to the ships' captains before they get into the harbor. Always wanting to see what he's carrying for cargo, mebbe cut a deal before he reaches shore. Of course, that takes a man with jack in his pocket."

Domi swept the ship's deck with her unflinching gaze. The blanket did help cut down on the chill she felt. "Which one Blakeney?"

Pointing with his chin, Washington said, "There. In the stern of the ship. The fattest man standing there."

Domi spotted Blakeney easily. He was nearly two of every other man aboard the ship. He sat in a large chair that had to have been bolted to the deck, because it rolled and moved with the flow of the waves as the ship cut through them.

The ship's sailors waved and yelled out, but they were still distant enough that their voices didn't carry over the noise of the ocean and the powerboat. Some of the men in the prow of the ship waved women's panties in the air.

Washington grinned. "See the panties?"

Domi didn't respond.

"I mean it's obvious what those guys have on their

minds,'' Washington went on, ''but those panties also mean that Lindstrohm must have dug into another mercantile that had clothes put back. The ville we holed up at, all that was already gone. But back during skydark, Campecheville must have gotten hit hard and chilled most everybody outright. Mebbe that's why nobody ever learned about all that oil Lindstrohm knew about.''

''How he know about oil?'' Domi asked.

''Don't know,'' Washington replied. ''Didn't even know he was working that business down there till he sailed into the first Fiddlerville with Narita and offered to start trading.''

Domi thought about that, realizing that Lindstrohm hadn't simply gotten up one morning and known there was oil down in Campecheville. It was something she probably wouldn't have wasted much time considering. Living in the Outlands meant learning to live with next to nothing, or staying on the move and taking whatever wasn't tied down and wouldn't be missed immediately.

Washington throttled back the powerboat as they neared the big ship. He brought the vessel around expertly so it was on course and matching speed with the ship.

Old rubber tires hung from the ship's side to provide cushioning. The vessel rode low enough in the water that the powerboat's prow bumped up against a row of old tires.

''How the hell are you, Washington?'' one of the sailors called down.

''Not complainin' yet, Hogan,'' Washington replied. ''Did you boys have a safe trip?''

''Had some trouble with fuckin' pirates,'' one man snarled. ''Bastards are gettin' thicker all the time. And they got something big goin' on at Campecheville. Lindstrohm was preparing the whole time we were down there.''

''What's going on?'' Washington asked.

''Supposed to have the Tong from the Western Isles in,'' Hogan said. ''Wei Qiang's hatchet men.'' He spit a stream of brown tobacco juice into the water between the ship and the powerboat, missing by inches. ''You ask me, I think all them waters are fixin' to get unsafe if the Tong start sailing it reg-ular-like.''

Domi scanned the sailors crowding at the railing, watching as Blakeney waddled forward. He was an unlovely man, roll-ing in fat and muscle, enough of both to look intimidating and ridiculous all at the same time. His bald head was planted squarely on shoulders that were as broad as an ax handle. Despite the heavy tanning, his face and shaved head still showed pink from the sun. His red coat hung past his knees, with an Uzi machine pistol at his right hip and a Japanese sword at his left hip.

"How's Fiddler?" Blakeney called down. He leaned both hands on the railing and peered down at Washington.

"Doin' good," Washington said, catching the rope ladder that unfurled down the side of the ship.

Blakeney nodded. "She had a ship in lately?"

"Two days ago," Washington said without hesitation.

Blakeney regarded the black man for a moment. "You're lying, you sack of shit," the captain called down good-naturedly, then smiled. "I'll bet it's been a week or more. She'll be ready to trade, and I'll get more than a few bodies to take back to Campecheville." He smiled again. "Gonna be a profitable voyage at both ends this run."

Domi sensed the ship's crew's mood changing even before she realized they were looking past the powerboat now. She looked ahead, toward the shore, and saw black smoke curling into the air.

The smoke was rising from an area well past Fiddlerville, but it was obviously connected.

"What the hell is going on, Washington?" Blakeney de-manded.

"I don't know," Washington replied. "That wasn't there a minute ago." He didn't release the rope ladder.

Blakeney took a step back from the railing, his hand drift-ing down to pluck the Uzi from his hip with surprising speed for someone his size. "You're lying again, Washington!"

Washington stood in the powerboat, obviously at a loss for

words as he stared back at the unmistakable black smoke twisting into the air.

The smoke caused Domi a lot of concern, but she kept her mind off whether Grant, Kane and Brigid would survive—they had to. And when they did, the chances were good that they'd need a ship to leave with.

"I'd heard the slavers were getting close to Fiddlerville again," Blakeney said, motioning to a man nearby. The man passed the captain a pair of binoculars, and he glanced through the field glasses only for a moment. "That's a fucking Deathbird!"

"Shit," Washington said.

"Have you got Baron Samarium's Magistrates walking through Fiddlerville?" Blakeney demanded.

"No," Washington replied. "At least, not yet."

Domi knew there was no mistaking the dragonfly shape that flitted and darted around the twisting columns of black smoke.

"Did Fiddler know they were there?" Blakeney demanded.

"Not until it was too late."

Blakeney glanced at his crew. "Get us the hell out of here. Leave those stupe bastards in the water."

Washington held on to the rope ladder as the crew tried to pull it back. "You can't just sail off. Fiddler and the others may need a way out of there."

"They can fucking swim," Blakeney said. "I don't owe her or you a damn thing. And I'm not going to risk my ass when there's no percentage in it for me." He glanced at his crew. "Get us out of here. If those fucks try to board, chill them."

One of the men started squalling at the top of his voice, giving orders to change the sail.

Domi glanced at the grens hanging from Washington's bandolier. She knew if the ship left that it might take with it the only chance her friends had of getting out of Fiddlerville alive.

With barely a heartbeat between thought and action, because that was the only way a person stayed alive in the Outlands, the albino swiped one of the grens from Washington's bandolier.

"Shit!" Washington yelled, reaching for her. But he was moving in slow motion compared to the albino.

Domi threw herself across the five feet separating her from the ship. The railing was another twelve feet above her, at an incline that further discouraged trying to climb up.

"Kill them!" Blakeney roared, pointing his Uzi in the general direction of the powerboat and opening fire.

The heat of the passing bullets burned Domi's face, then she was against the ship, her feet landing on one of the tires roped to the ship's side and her hand grasping a tire over her head.

As lithe as a dancer and as nimble as an acrobat, Domi turned and scampered up the tires roped to the ship's side. She started toward the bow, hunching and throwing herself up another line of tires, putting herself that much closer to the railing.

A man leaned down, extending a handblaster before him.

Domi balanced on her feet for an instant, ripped one of her knives free of its hiding place and sent it winging toward the man, throwing herself back into her ascent as she worked toward the ship's stern now.

The knife sped fairly, but it missed the center of the man's face, her intended target, and opened a three-inch long cut on his cheek and scored the bone beneath. He jerked back, bleeding viciously and knocking over the small group of men around him, disrupting the aim of several more.

Washington had his blaster in hand, as well, and was firing into the ship's crew. At least one or two rounds from Blakeney's Uzi smashed into his thighs, knocking him down to the powerboat's floor. The man holding the wheel steady instinctively cut the craft away from the big ship.

Still moving, Domi was grimly aware that she'd been more or less abandoned. But even left to her own devices, the albino pressed the few advantages she had. She pulled the pin on the explosive, counted down as she ran across the tires, listening to bullets cut the air around her. Then she heaved the gren into the center of the ship's deck.

"Gren!" someone yelled.

"Fuck me!" another man shouted hoarsely. "Kick the damn thing in the water before it fucks us all over!"

Domi glanced overhead and saw that the railing was almost within her reach. Below her, the greenish brown water sped by, capped by foaming white as the ship rushed through the waves. If she fell, there was nothing but the uncaring Gulf to catch her.

"Someone grab that gren!" Blakeney commanded.

Domi saw the fat man turn his attention to the gren, as well, and made her final play. She leaped upward and caught the ship's deck between the rails. Her arms screamed in protest as they took her weight with a sudden jerk. She hung there, listening for the gren's explosion, knowing that if it was an antipersonnel device the deck was going to get chewed to pieces.

The *bamf* of the gren exploding was anticlimactic.

Domi pulled herself up and peered over the ship's deck, watching as scarlet smoke filled the deck like a sudden fog. Even men only a few feet away were lost in the writhing tendrils of the smoke.

"It's a smoker!" a man yelled. "Bastard useless piece of shit!"

Kicking her feet against the side of the ship, Domi reached up and caught the railing with one hand. She was reaching for the railing with the other hand when the closest men turned and spotted her.

"Fuck all!" a man cried. "That white bitch is still alive!"

Using the forward lunging motion of the ship to her advantage, Domi pulled herself into a full handstand on the railing, then let her forward momentum carry her into a flip. She landed on the deck among some of the men. They tried to turn and bring their weapons to bear, but she met them with elbows to the face and knees to the groin, knocking them out of her way as quickly as possible.

Before she reached Blakeney, the ship's captain raised his Uzi and pointed the weapon at her.

Domi threw herself down, sliding through the curling red smoke given off by the gren still rolling across the ship's deck as the vessel rose and fell on the waves. Blakeney's shots dug splinters out of the deck behind her, striking some of his men even as they were dodging for cover.

The albino grabbed Blakeney's foot, fighting the thick smoke that made her eyes water and burned her nasal passages and the back of her throat. Still, she clung to Blakeney, rising almost effortlessly behind him before he could turn. Her breath was tight in her throat, and excitement burned through her when she realized how close she was to death.

Even now if she was wrong about how the crew felt about Blakeney, she was only heartbeats away from dying suddenly and violently. She drew one of her knives and reached under Blakeney's neck with her other arm.

Blakeney fired the Uzi over his shoulder, spraying bullets into the sails.

Domi raked her knife blade across his knuckles like a cat. Blood spewed from the back of the ship captain's hand and ran down his forearm. For good measure, and to let him know she meant business, the albino bit off Blakeney's left earlobe and spit it onto the deck in front of him.

Blakeney screamed and cursed, then reached for her with his uninjured hand.

Domi pulled herself close into the big man. She wrapped her legs around his waist as far as they would go, as if she were riding a horse. She kept her head tucked into the back of his sweat-covered neck. Then she put her knife against his throat, letting him feel the sharp blade.

"Want me bleed you out like some prize hog?" Domi asked.

A few of the sailors stepped forward, gaining a little confidence as the smoke gren's crimson fog began to dissipate.

"Have them stop," Domi ordered. "Or I'll chill you."

Carefully, Blakeney raised his hands, dropped the Uzi and

ordered, "Stand down! Stand down, or I swear to God I'll chill you myself."

Uneasily, the crewmen stopped where they were and lowered their weapons.

"Good," Domi congratulated. "Now just keep ship headed into docks. Who knows? Mebbe you get live."

KANE TOOK evasive action in the Sandcat, yanking the wheel to the left and stepping hard on the accelerator. The mil-spec vehicle shuddered as the treads bit into the muddy loam. He tracked the Deathbird through the blue sky, aware of Eddie's lower body sprawled on the Sandcat's floor.

"It's coming back around!" Fiddler called.

Locking the left track and coming around in a tight one-eighty, Kane glanced up and spotted the second Deathbird screaming down out of the sky. The chain gun opened up, blowing craters in the muddy ground, tracking straight toward the Sandcat.

"Get us out of here!" Fiddler yelled.

Kane shifted, abusing the hell out of the clutch and transmission, spewing twin roostertails of mud behind the Sandcat. The Deathbird's 30 mm chain gun ripped more craters in the ground only a few feet from the vehicle.

"Aim for the Deathbird's tail," Kane replied. "That's its weakest point." The Deathbird's armor was proof against .50-caliber ammo, and the critical areas were designed to withstand even heavier attacks.

"You've got the first one coming back," the navigator called out.

"Got it," Kane acknowledged. He kept driving, watching as the line of chain-gun rounds smashed divots in the ground to the right of the Sandcat. Waiting until the last moment, he slammed the brakes on to stop the tracks dead, throwing them forward in their seats.

The line of 30 mm rounds barely missed the Sandcat, thudding into the ground and throwing up eruptions of thick, black mud that splashed against the ob slit and stuck, partially obscuring Kane's vision. He threw the transmission back into low gear and surged forward again, driving for the flaming wreckage that blocked the rutted road.

He glanced over at the hillside and spotted the Magistrate Sandcats racing across the uneven terrain. The vehicles sped across the hillside, bringing down avalanches of mud and rock after them.

"They used the slavers to flush us," Fiddler said grimly.

"Yeah," Kane agreed. "You were the target, Fiddler. Not the escaped slaves. They just happened to be in the wrong place at the wrong time." He glanced to the left and spotted the second Sandcat roaring into position behind him.

A handful of survivors lined the flaming wreckage. The contingent from Fiddlerville had already evacuated. The slavers tried to stand their ground in front of the blockade, their assault rifles tight against their shoulders. Bullets ricocheted from the Sandcat.

The line broke at the last moment, fleeing to open ground on either side of the crumpled wags.

Kane kept the accelerator down, feeling the Sandcat shudder as it collided with the wreckage. The tracks never once lost contact with the ground, and forward momentum was slowed for only a moment. Metal screamed, though the sound was partially muffled from the cockpit, and some of the reactive armor exploded as blasterfire raked the Sandcat.

The fiery wag overturned in front of Kane, pushed aside by the Sandcat. He cut the wheel to the left and slipped around the wreckage. Once the flaming vehicle cleared the ob slit, he stared down the rutted road and found it empty. Evidently the other wags had already headed back to Fiddlerville.

"Where are the two Deathbirds?" Kane asked.

"Behind us," Fiddler replied. "They're burning up our back trail."

"What about the other Sandcat?"

"Behind us," the navigator answered.

"The Deathbirds are coming up on us damn quick," Fiddler said loudly.

Kane already knew that. The Deathbird pilots would seek out all targets in the area and begin eliminating them. The Sandcats would be an obvious primary choice, for pride as well as an object lesson.

"If we can make it back to the ville," Fiddler said, "we can shake them. I've got boobied buildings there, as well as places where we can take cover."

Kane silently hoped that Domi had been successful in getting the ship's captain to agree to pick them up at the port. Staying in the ville with this many Magistrates after them would only prove to be a slow death. They were only going to live if they could escape the net that was drawing tighter around them.

He scanned the rutted road ahead of them, searching for anything that he could use to his advantage. As the road descended still more and curved around a thick copse of trees and rocks, he spotted one of the wags from Fiddlerville overturned ahead.

"Here they come," Fiddler said.

Chapter 18

The heavy thumping of the 30 mm cannon pounding the ground echoed in Kane's ears, closing rapidly. He pulled the wheel to the right, steering the Sandcat into the copse of trees to the right of the overturned wag. Trees and branches broke as brush gave way before them.

Glancing up at the clear dome around Fiddler, Kane saw that the forest canopy at least partially obscured the view afforded to the Deathbird pilots. He braked the Sandcat to a halt and pushed himself from the pilot's chair. Shoving away the bottom half of Eddie's bloody, mangled corpse, Kane gripped the floor hatch handle and yanked up.

The hatch lifted, revealing the protected crawlspace beneath the Sandcat. Dropping to his knees, Kane shoved his head and shoulders through the escape hatch and began crawling across the muddy ground.

"Where are you going?" Fiddler demanded over the crash of the 30 mm chain guns.

"I spotted a rocket launcher in that overturned wag," Kane called back, never slowing his forward momentum. "Mebbe it will even things up a little. Those machine guns aren't going to bring those Deathbirds down unless we get lucky."

Rockets tore into the earth along the rutted road. The second Sandcat driver had to have assumed Kane had pulled off into the forest because of mechanical difficulties, because he stayed with the road and swept out around the overturned wag. The Deathbirds powered in pursuit of the Sandcat.

Kane reached the overturned wag just after the second Sandcat roared past on clanking treads. A headless corpse hung from the restraining straps behind the collapsed steering wheel. Another dead man, his body blackened by flames that still burned the grass around him, lay a few feet away. The stench of gasoline was overpowering, and Kane recognized the danger he was facing by going toward the wag.

The Soviet-made RPG-7V rocket-propelled grenade launcher Kane had spotted lay on the road, poking up from one of the ruts. It already had a rocket affixed to the business end of the weapon. A canvas bag of rocket-propelled grenades lay nearby, but a number of them had spilled out and were scattered across the road.

Lying under the overturned wag, Kane watched the pair of Deathbirds scream by overhead. Rockets leaped from the stubby wings of the lead aircraft and pummeled the road in a diagonal approach to the fleeing Sandcat. Craters the size of fighting holes opened up in the ground in a direct line to the Sandcat.

A rocket slammed into the Sandcat's rear, triggering an explosive barrage of the reactive armor. Another rocket exploded against the left track and blew it apart. Having only one mobile track, the Sandcat immediately began going around in circles, looking like a wounded animal caught in a trap.

Kane glanced at the pool of gasoline that had gathered under the overturned wag. Fires still burned in the grass at the side of the road and left smoldering, bright-orange coals snugged up against the muddy loam.

He crawled from beneath the overturned wag on elbows and knees, retreating to the side of the road where he had left the Sandcat. He carried the rocket launcher in one hand and the ammo bag in the other. From the light heft of the ammo bag, he knew he hadn't gotten away with many grenades.

The second Deathbird began its attack on the disabled Sandcat. The top hatch opened as one of the men inside tried to get out, and Kane thought he saw movement beneath the vehicle, as well.

Then the second Deathbird unloaded a dozen rockets that slammed all over the Sandcat. Already stripped of its reactive armor from the first Deathbird's attack, the Sandcat crumpled and tore apart like it was made of straw. No one got out alive.

Standing at the tree line, Kane checked the RPG-7V and made sure it was ready. He watched the Deathbirds heeling around for another pass, no doubt intent on searching out the Sandcat he'd driven into the forest.

Both Deathbird pilots showed combat experience. Young pilots might have made the mistake of assuming they were in the clear after the Sandcat blew and turned quickly, ignoring the fact that they were sitting ducks for a handful of seconds while they hovered. The pilots running the attack kept going as quickly as they could to put themselves out of range of return fire. Then they swept back in on another diagonal approach. Even though Kane was certain they couldn't see the Sandcat hidden in the woods, they were going to be close.

He stood in the tree line and shouldered the rocket launcher. He flipped up the weapon's sights and took aim, sliding his finger inside the trigger guard. The Deathbirds screamed closer, closing in quickly.

Kneeling for only a moment, Kane scooped a handful of mud containing smoldering coals from the road's edge and heaved it toward the overturned wag. As soon as the coals touched the gasoline pool, the incendiary liquid exploded in a *whoosh* that blew heated air back over Kane. The overturned wag jumped and jerked as the gas tank and extra cans of gasoline exploded.

The lead Deathbird's pilot swung around a little to bring his weapons to bear on the overturned wag. The movement also presented the aircraft to Kane in profile.

Kane clapped his muddy hand to the rocket launcher's muzzle to help hold it steady He took deliberate aim at the Deathbird's tail rotor section and squeezed the trigger. The rocket propellant ignited, shooting a stream of super-hot gases from the rocket launcher's exhaust tube.

The 40 mm warhead leaped from the RPG-7V and sped true. It caught the tail rotor section a few inches in front of the spinning rotor itself. As heavily armored as the Deathbirds were, the tail rotor section might have survived the blast but the rotor didn't and blew free as an orange-and-black fireball wrapped the Deathbird's tail section.

Without the tail rotor, the Deathbird spun out of control. On any helicopter-type aircraft, the rear rotor had to be in place and functioning to maintain control over the aircraft. The only chance the pilot had for any kind of safe landing was to cut the engines and hope the main rotor's natural tendency to slow the aircraft fall would save him and his gunner.

But the pilot had been flying too close to the ground. The Deathbird tipped over onto its side and dived into the trees. As soon as the whirling main rotor made contact with the trees, the carbon-ferrous blades shattered into deadly shards.

Kane threw himself to cover behind a shelf of rock. Metal screamed as the Deathbird continued its fall through the trees and came apart. Before it reached the ground, the aircraft exploded and set off the munitions aboard.

A wave of explosions ripped through the forest, blasting whole trees from the ground and hurling them through the air. Fire ran rampant through the trees and brush, quickly building a smoke screen that hugged the treetops.

Kane breathed the acrid air in shallow breaths and felt it burn his nose and throat. He reached into the canvas bag and took out another rocket, shoving it into the still-hot tube immediately.

The second Deathbird passed by and fired a half-dozen rockets in a purely retaliatory gesture. The rockets tore up the road and the surrounding forest, but they didn't come close to the hidden Sandcat. It continued flying and didn't make the mistake of trying to stop to help the downed Deathbird.

As Kane watched, a Magistrate-occupied vehicle roared through the gap he'd created through the blockade. Kane raised the rocket launcher to his shoulder again and took aim. He fired, and the rocket *whooshed* out of the tube and smashed against the Sandcat.

The explosion blew the weapons bubble free and turned the machine-gun snouts into twisted wreckage. The weps officer was blown down inside the vehicle, along with debris from the bubble, as well as the top of the Sandcat.

When the vehicle went out of control, Kane was fairly certain that the debris had had an effect similar to an antipersonnel grenade, and had probably killed or disabled the Sandcat's crew. The Sandcat slammed into another wrecked wag and partially blocked the gap Kane had left when he'd driven through.

The Magistrates behind the stricken vehicle hesitated about ramming through. Magistrates strode through the burning line clad in the black polycarbonate armor and carrying Copperhead assault rifles.

Ruthlessly, Kane armed the Soviet rocket launcher once more, leaving only one rocket-propelled grenade in the canvas bag. Squeezing the trigger, he fired at the knot of men moving through the blockade. The grenade struck one of the men near the center of the group, and the immediate explosion knocked all of the Magistrates to the ground.

Kane reloaded the rocket launcher and glanced at the sky, watching as the other Deathbird came around again. He left the empty canvas bag behind and ran back toward the Sandcat. Enough confusion had been sewn into the ranks of the Magistrates to buy them a little more escape time.

He didn't crawl under the Sandcat when he reached it. Instead, he leaped onto the rear deck and climbed toward the weps blister. The twin machine guns came around so quickly they almost caught him by surprise and knocked him from the Sandcat.

Fiddler brought the machine guns to a halt and gazed up at Kane.

"Drive," Kane said.

Fiddler turned and spoke to the other man in the command cockpit. She stayed in place, but the Sandcat started rolling almost immediately. The driver stayed among the trees, taking advantage of the cover offered there.

Kane glanced at the sky and saw the remaining Deathbird keeping its distance. Maybe it had been ordered to hold its place, or maybe the pilot hadn't wanted to rush in without having a clear view of the opposing force. Kane held on to the Sandcat and kept the rocket launcher handy as he watched the Deathbird hovering in the sky. The canopy of tree branches provided only occasional glimpses of the aircraft.

The Deathbird, Kane knew, would hold back only until the ground forces got up to speed again. Then the aircraft would blitz again. He also had no doubt that the Magistrate force would halt before they reached Fiddlerville. Baron Samarium had evidently given scorched-earth commands. If possible, the Magistrates would kill everyone in Fiddlerville.

FIDDLERVILLE LOOKED abandoned when it came into Kane's view. The streets were empty, and there appeared to be no movement in any of the buildings.

Then a trio of figures broke free of trees to the left of the road as it wound down into Fiddlerville. They yanked lengths of chain from the ground, pulling them clear of the Sandcat's path.

Kane spotted the barbed spike sections attached to the chains and guessed that they were Fiddler's first line of defense in the ville. As soon as the Sandcat had passed, the men moved the chain lengths and spiked section back into position and kicked mud and grass back over them.

The attempts at disguising the chains was obvious to the trained eye, Kane knew, but the Magistrate division roaring on into Fiddlerville wouldn't stop until it was too late. With Craddock feeding the Magistrate commanders information, Baron Samarium and the Magistrates would have known Fiddlerville's defenses were cut to the bone.

The Sandcat didn't stop speeding through the ville until it reached the docks. The ship that had been spotted earlier floated in the harbor. Small powerboats ran Fiddler's people as well as the emigrants fleeing the Outlands out to the ship. The ship's sails, lowered somewhat and turned so they wouldn't catch the wind, popped restlessly.

Domi stood in the ship's stern with a fat man on his knees before her, her pistol tight against the back of his skull.

Grant and Brigid joined Kane as he slid off the Sandcat's rear deck.

"Won't be long before those Magistrates get here," Grant growled.

"I know," Kane said. "That ship moves too slowly to get us out of range of their guns or the Deathbird that's with them."

"Deathbird?" Brigid said. "I saw two Deathbirds."

"I got lucky with one of them," Kane said. "We'll need to take out the second one before we climb onto that ship. Otherwise, it'll follow us and sink us. Survivors will get washed back in by the tide."

"That's not going to happen," Fiddler said. She gazed back up the hill as the first of the Magistrate Sandcats topped the rise. "I prepared for them this time. The first time they hit me, they cost me. The second time, I left early." She released a short breath. "This time—this time *they* pay."

"They'll use the ville against you," Kane said. "The Mag teams will take the high ground and they'll shoot that ship out of the water."

Fiddler shook her head. "Not this time, Kane." She reached back into the Sandcat and took the mil-spec radio communications pack that the navigator handed her. "Let's get to the ship."

Grant looked at Kane. "My vote is to stay ashore. Out on the water we're sitting ducks."

"If you stay here," Fiddler promised, "you're booked on the last train headed west. One way or another. That's an ace on the line." She shouldered the communications pack and headed for the docks at a jog.

Kane glanced at the line of approaching Sandcats. "She said she had the whole ville boobied." He glanced around at the buildings. No one was staying behind to cover the retreat. Even the machine-gun nests had been evacuated. "I'm betting she does." He nodded at the boat that Fiddler was crawling into. "We'll take our chances with the ship." He led the way to the boat.

Brigid clambered into the boat with Fiddler, followed by Kane and Grant.

Kane stood in the stern of the boat and watched as the first wags reached the hidden chains. None of them were Sandcats, and all of them had air-filled tires that were vulnerable to the spikes. The driver suddenly had to struggle with steering. Seeing the problems the lead drivers had, the second rank of wags chose to go cross-country and enter the ville through different streets that were open to passage, but they encountered more buried chains and spikes there. A dozen wags stopped before they rolled across the spikes, saving their tires.

"If they don't have a shitload of replacement tires," Grant said happily, "those guys are going to spend the night fixing flats."

"They don't have that many spares," Brigid said.

"They got a long night ahead of them," Grant said.

Kane silently agreed, but watched as the wag crews bailed from their vehicles and raced toward the shore. Behind the lead wags came four Sandcats. He'd seen more back at the section of the road where they'd encountered the slavers.

"Those spikes aren't going to stop the Cats," he said over the roar of the powerboat as it surged across the waves toward the ship.

"No," Fiddler agreed, "but then they don't have to." She flipped switches on the communications pack, then nodded toward the approaching Sandcats.

The Sandcat drivers didn't slow at all, obviously certain that their treads wouldn't take any damage from the spikes. The machine guns spewed, close enough now to slap bullets against the water in the powerboat's wake. Water jumped up to mark the range and proximity.

Most of the passengers aboard the powerboat dived for cover, but Kane knew the fiberglass hull wouldn't provide any kind of real protection. He stood his ground along with Fiddler and her crew, as well as Grant and Brigid.

Remembering that he still had the Soviet rocket launcher, Kane settled the long tube over his shoulder and took aim. He tried to time the powerboat's rise and fall as it pushed through the waves toward the ship. The Magistrates in the Sandcats were having better luck tracking their prey. As the rocket launcher bounced, Kane spotted movement just above the treetops of the forest, closing fast.

"We're going from the frying pan into the fire," Grant commented sourly.

Recognizing the wicked dragonfly shapes of the three Deathbirds, Kane said, "We're building up to a one-percenter for sure."

The Deathbirds stayed low, running nape-of-the-earth.

"Those damn Deathbirds don't have to worry about spikes at all," Grant said. "That ship doesn't stand a chance."

"Not sure," Fiddler said calmly. "Blakeney outfitted *Jeweled Lady* with antiaircraft guns. He's got four five-inch gun emplacements aboard the ship. The first Deathbird pilot to reach him is going to get surprised."

The Sandcats reached the chain spikes and started to roll across without hesitation. Just beyond the chains, the ground suddenly erupted. All of the fast-attack vehicles jumped and rocked on the ground. One of them tumbled completely over onto its side. Some of the others lost tracks, broken and flapping with a sound of metallic thunder. The rest of the Sandcats slowed, and held their positions.

Kane looked at Fiddler.

"Tank-buster mines," the woman said. "Those were on another set of chains."

"Thorough," Kane said. "I like that."

Fiddler's smile was bitter. "Lessons learned, Kane. When they come hard, you learn and you don't forget. But that's just the opening salvo of the show. Before I'm done, I intend to bring down the house. All the houses, in fact."

"Don't mean to break up the admiration party," Grant said, "but we got incoming." He pointed at the sky.

"Let them come," Fiddler said, watching the attack aircraft. "I've got surprises they haven't seen yet. When they took down the first Fiddlerville, they used Deathbirds to soften up the resistance we managed to put together. In the second Fiddlerville, we didn't stand against them. But I prepared for them this time."

Kane glanced at *Jeweled Lady* and saw that the ship was now less than three hundred yards away. Even with the powerboat running flat out, he knew they'd never reach the ship before the Deathbirds overtook them. He glanced over his shoulder at Brigid.

She returned his gaze coolly, offering no indication of how nervous she might have felt. "We've been in tighter spots," she said.

Kane nodded, accepting that. Her statement was true, but it didn't make things any better. He kept the rocket launcher ready, cradling it in both hands.

Fiddler watched the Deathbirds as they flew toward the abandoned ville now filled with Magistrates dressed in black polycarbonate armor.

Before the Deathbirds reached the first of the ville's buildings, they fired rockets that sped toward the powerboat and the ship. A trio of rockets impacted the water just ahead of the powerboat and threw a wall of water over the boat.

Kane was drenched in the cold brine of the sea, but he expected any moment to feel the heat of a direct hit. He wiped the sea water from his face and watched as the three Deathbirds cruised over the rooftops of the buildings.

Fiddler pressed a button on the communications pack she held. Immediately, at least twenty rooftops exploded upward, throwing debris and concussive force high into the air.

Chapter 19

The maelstrom caught the three Deathbirds by surprise. One of the attack helicopters exploded into a roiling boil of orange-and-black flames. The lead Deathbird plummeted out of control and smashed into one of the taller buildings. The broken aircraft dropped to the streets below in pieces, leaving a gaping hole in the side of the building.

The surviving Deathbird shot out to sea through the swirling debris, smoke and dust. The pilot closed on *Jeweled Lady* immediately. Chattering incessantly, the 30 mm chain gun wreaked havoc with the ship's sails and rigging.

In the next instant, puffs of black smoke appeared in the air around the Deathbird. Then the gunners aboard *Jeweled Lady* got the range. The next salvo of shots struck the Deathbird and broke it into flaming wreckage that dropped into the sea less than a hundred yards from the ship's stern.

In heartbeats, Kane realized, the air battle for Fiddlerville was over. They hadn't won, but they were still alive and had every opportunity to make good their escape.

More rounds struck the water from the shore-based Magistrates standing in the shadows of the ville's buildings. Grant and Brigid returned fire with their Copperheads.

Due to the distance from the shore, and even though sound traveled more quickly over water than over the land, the sound from the next series of explosions didn't reach Kane until after the carnage erupted throughout many of Fiddlerville's buildings. Nearly all the buildings along the shore and the docks blew up and collapsed on the Magistrates below. Many of the structures in the center of the ville collapsed, as well. Broken rock, mortar and debris covered the Magistrates and the wags, beating flesh and blood to the ground and smashing the metal vehicles.

"We mined all the buildings," Fiddler said as she dropped the communications pack to the bottom of the powerboat. "I knew when I left this ville, I wasn't leaving anything behind for them to take."

The rumble of the explosions rolled over the powerboat and faded away out into the Gulf like distant thunder. Along the shore, the Magistrates had vanished, most of them buried beneath heaps of rubble from the broken buildings. Others stayed hidden, because occasional explosions were still evident.

The powerboat pilot guided the craft alongside *Jeweled Lady*. Once the pace was matched, Washington kicked down a rolled-up rope ladder.

Fiddler led the way up, followed closely by Kane, Brigid and Grant. The other passengers and the powerboat crew came next.

Without a word, Fiddler strode to the ship's stern.

"What she did, Kane," Brigid said softly, "was nothing short of amazing."

"I know, Baptiste," Kane replied. "She's a hell of a woman. But she paid a price for what she did." He stared at the dark clouds of smoke billowing from the ruins of the ville. "She moved into that place, however long ago she moved into it, with the intention of making it into a trap. It was never a home or a place that she could relax."

Grant pointed at Domi standing in the stern with her blaster still against the fat man's skull. "Now, that looks like a man who needs a motivational speech."

Kane nodded. "When you talk to him, tell him that we don't need him. Baptiste can plot a course to Campecheville." He glanced at Brigid to make certain.

"I can," Brigid answered. "If there's a ship's compass aboard, it won't be a problem."

Kane nodded, then reached into his shirt pocket and took out a small aluminum cylinder. He opened the cylinder and took out two of the cigars inside, handing one to Grant and keeping the other for himself. He put the cylinder back in his shirt pocket and lit both cigars.

"I'm going to see about that motivational speech," Grant said.

"Let me know how it goes," Kane said.

Nodding, Grant departed and walked toward the stern.

Kane drew deeply on the cigar, then blew it out. The taste of the cigar eradicated some of the stink of the sea. The canvas sails popped and cracked overhead as ship's crew brought them all in line with the wind. They tacked farther west, going with the strength of the wind rather than trying to skirt around it.

The sun had settled lower in the western sky, and reflections danced on the ocean surface. The ship's crew had tied up the powerboat to a stern cleat and given it plenty of length to stay clear of the ship.

As Kane stared out over water, it seemed as though he could hear Balam calling his name. His chest still ached from the heavy bruising, but it was already starting to feel a little better. Lethargy filled him, making his limbs feel like lead.

"Kane."

Turning, Kane faced Brigid. He still seemed to hear Balam's voice on the wind. "What is it, Baptiste?"

"Do you think Campecheville is the best place to head?" Brigid asked.

"Why not?"

"Because if Baron Samarium has decided to wage war against the escaping slaves and the people who are helping them get away, he might have sea-based teams along the way to Campecheville. We could get intercepted."

Kane shook his head and immediately felt dizzy. He took a small, stumbling step that most people would never have noticed, or would have attributed to the rolling carriage of the ship sailing the sea.

"Are you all right?" Brigid asked. She grabbed his arm, ready to help steady him if he needed it.

"I'm fine, Baptiste." Kane drew his arm back from her, removing her hand gently. "I'm just tired."

Brigid looked into his eyes then put a hand against his forehead. "You're burning up, Kane. The fever has come back."

"I'll be fine," Kane said. "Probably whatever bug it is hasn't worked its way completely through my system yet. I get some more fluids and some rest, it'll pass."

"Unless it's something serious."

"It'll pass."

Brigid looked at him doubtfully. "Maybe not if Balam is involved."

"That was just a dream."

"Maybe it wasn't."

"You're worrying too much, Baptiste," he growled.

"And I think you're not worrying enough," Brigid said gently.

Kane looked out at the rolling sea, feeling the deck shifting constantly underfoot, listening to the creak of the rigging and the snap of the canvas overhead, and wished he felt better. It was one thing to be facing all the problems before them while he was well, but being sick was draining.

"I'm worried, Baptiste," he told her. "But mostly I'm worried about these people." He glanced at the ship's passengers, noticing that Angel and Cherub had made it safely. "And I'm concerned about that mat-trans unit that suddenly went online down there."

Brigid stood at his side quietly. "I still think it would be in your best interests to return to the Cerberus redoubt."

"When we get to Campecheville," Kane said, "we can use the mat-trans unit if there's an emergency. At this point, Campecheville is probably closer and more safely reached than any other place we could jump from." He glanced at the stern.

Grant was leaning down into the fat captain's face while Domi looked on with a stone-cold expression. Fiddler watched for a moment, but her attention remained riveted on the burning ville along the shoreline. Sometimes *Jeweled*

Lady dove so deeply down into the next trough that the land disappeared completely.

Kane remembered the room full of clowns that had been in the gaudy. Maybe Fiddler hadn't made the ville a true home, but she'd invested in it. He doubted that she'd get any of those things back—even if they hadn't been destroyed in the explosions.

"And you don't have to be concerned about Baron Samarium posting naval vessels out here," he told Brigid. "Doing something like that would strain his manpower and hardware resources. Plus, any ships he put at sea would be fair game for pirates." He gestured at the ship. "And it takes a crew to man a ship. Magistrates aren't going to do the grunt work aboard one of these things. Taking a crew and getting off to themselves would only guarantee a mutiny later."

"You're probably right," Brigid said.

"I am," Kane said. He peered out at the ocean to the south. The wind whistled past him, and he thought he heard Balam's voice in it again.

Kane. I'll be waiting.

Wait then, dammit, Kane thought, and he hoped he hadn't spoken out loud because he was suddenly very unsure. He walked to the railing and leaned on it to steady himself, hating the weakness that seemed to gnaw at him a little more with each passing second.

Kane.

"LAKESH."

Blinking tiredly, Lakesh looked up from the comp screen he'd been studying. Charts and maps of Campeche, Quintana Roo and the Yucatán peninsula occupied different monitors around him. He glanced at the Mercator map and saw the yellow blips that identified the Cerberus group's locations. They were well away from the Texas shoreline now. The wind had been favorable.

"What is it, friend Bry?" Lakesh asked, then cleared his

throat when he found it had gone dry. He pushed up from his chair and crossed the room to the little man's workstation.

"It's Kane," Bry answered, staring at one of the comp screens in front of him.

"He still has the fever?"

"Yes." Bry consulted one of the digital tables in front of him. "Five minutes ago he just jumped 2.6 degrees."

"That puts him at 103.3," Lakesh said.

Bry nodded.

"He must be delusional," Lakesh said quietly.

"He's also hitting his REM cycle now," Bry said.

Lakesh consulted the stats and figures on the screen. The REM cycle of a person's sleep indicated a heavy dreaming sequence. "True, I talk of dreams, which are the children of an idle brain, begot of nothing but vain fantasy."

Bry looked up at him with a curious expression.

"It's a quote from *Romeo and Juliet*," Lakesh said. "Penned by the illustrious William Shakespeare. I doubt that it's fitting in this instance, but the quote did come to mind."

Unimpressed, Bry turned back to his workstation.

Lakesh pressed a button on a nearby comm unit. He waited patiently. It was only a little after 8:00 p.m., and he was certain that DeFore was either in her med room or in her private suite in the redoubt. "Dr. DeFore."

It took her a moment to answer, and from the slight splashing and the rolling echo in her reply, Lakesh figured that he had caught her bathing.

"What?" DeFore asked somewhat unpleasantly.

"Kane is running fever again, my dear doctor. I thought perhaps you might be interested in witnessing this cycle for yourself."

"I would prefer to see the patient in my exam room," DeFore snapped. Water dripped, and Lakesh assumed she was exiting the tub.

"If I were but able," Lakesh said, "I'd have him there posthaste." Provided Kane was willing to go along with the suggestion, of course.

"I'll be there in a moment," DeFore replied. "But even tracking the fever cycle, I'm not going to be able to tell you if the fever is from a gunshot wound, a snake bite or a virus."

Lakesh nodded, then caught himself and realized that she couldn't see him. "I understand. But since this fever has returned and there hasn't been a chronic condition of some sort throughout the day—although there have been a number of conspicuous adrenaline spikes—I thought someone else would better observe it. I tend to sometimes lock myself into a certain viewpoint—"

"I think it's called pigheadedness," DeFore said. "Megalomania. I've got a few other fancy names I can throw in your direction if you'd like."

"That will be quite all right," Lakesh replied dryly. "Can I expect you soon?"

"I'll be there," DeFore promised.

Lakesh closed the circuit, knowing that DeFore was as concerned about Kane's welfare as he was. Kane didn't have many sick days; he never had. Part of it was his genetic makeup, which Lakesh had had a hand in.

He surveyed the stats relayed through Kane's subcutaneous transponder. The fever was affecting Kane's heart rate, respiration and brain activity. Normal REM took up only twenty percent of an adult's sleep cycle, but Kane had nearly stayed in REM all the previous night before they'd reached the Texas coastline.

During charted sleep cycles at Cerberus redoubt while injured or otherwise convalescing, Kane had never shown a disruption of that pattern. Lakesh knew something was affecting Kane's sleep, but he had no clue what. However, the fever had to be most certainly part of it, because Kane's fever always jumped up a couple degrees every time he entered the deep REM.

Lakesh folded his arms over his skinny chest. He hated mysteries. He especially hated mysteries that all seemed tied in together somehow but yet weren't quite within his grasp.

"What are you dreaming about with such obvious interest, friend Kane?" Lakesh mused.

Of course, there was no answer.

KANE OPENED his eyes and knew he was dreaming when he found himself walking down a narrow hallway that he recognized as being a pyramid corridor. He carried a reed torch in one hand and walked quietly.

"Do you know how it is that the pharaohs make sure they have plenty to eat for themselves, as well as the slaves?" a man's voice asked.

"No," Kane replied before he knew he was even going to speak. He was still acclimating, still trying to get used to the idea of where he was.

"It's because of the machine Set gave to the pharaohs all those years ago," the male voice stated. "It makes the food for them out of thin air when the crops fail."

Kane had no idea what the man at his side was talking about. He glanced at the man, finding him vaguely familiar. The man was roughly the same height as Kane himself. "No machine can make food out of thin air."

"This one can," the man exulted. "I've seen it in operation. I wouldn't bring you here now and risk both our lives if it wasn't important."

"I'm a fool for following you here," Kane replied. "Maybe a dead fool by morning."

The other man grinned, and Kane almost recognized that grin. There was something so familiar about the man. Then he remembered how he'd seen the man before in the tunnels beneath Djoser's pyramid.

Kane held his reed torch high and examined the hieroglyphs on the walls. They were different from the ones that had been put into place in Djoser's temple. And the walls here were covered with them. The work that had gone into carving the hieroglyphs into the stone walls would have taken years.

"This isn't Djoser's pyramid, is it?" Kane asked.

The other man turned suddenly, his hand flashing to the

knife at his waist. He held his torch before him to better light the passageway area around Kane and to use as a weapon. "Ka'in? Is it you?"

Kane stopped moving, falling automatically into a ready position. He touched the knife belted at his waist, as well. In this dream, he was dressed as an overseer, wearing cotton shirt and pants, and sandals, like the man before him. Was he someone else, then? He wasn't sure. His thinking seemed clouded and fuzzy. Part of him knew that he was still aboard *Jeweled Lady* sailing for Campecheville, but another part of him seemed anchored to this time and place.

"Who are you?" Kane asked.

"Are you toying with me again, Ka'in?" the man demanded angrily. "Is this the you from now, or are you here from another time and place?"

"I don't know what you're talking about," Kane said, but the words were automatic, coming from the person whose mind he partially occupied.

The man moved warily. The light from both torches caressed the gleaming edge of the upturned knife held tightly in his hand. The man was young, surely no more than his early twenties.

"Are you here to stop me or to help me this time, Ka'in?" the man asked.

"Stop all this crazy talk," Kane said, but the words were not his. "You took me away from a fine, warm bed and a woman I've not yet had on the pretext of showing me something important. I've got half a mind to turn around and go back to those things."

The young man seemed more nervous than ever. Anxiety tightened his face and fear danced in his eyes with the reflected torchlight. "Whose pyramid is this?"

Kane hesitated for a moment, not knowing how to answer. But his voice answered anyway. "Don't be foolish, Harkhuf. This is the Great Temple of Ramses II."

Harkhuf's eyes narrowed. "If you knew this place was Ramses II, then why did you ask if it was Djoser's?"

"If I did," Kane answered, "it was only because you woke me from a sound sleep after a jug of wine." His words sounded irritated.

"I thought you were with a woman."

"I was, but she was patient. A quality that I find lacking in you." Kane watched the other man relax somewhat. "Now either show me this god's gift you brought me here for or let me return to my home. Your wretched curiosity will be the death of you one day. I promise you that."

Somewhere in the real world aboard *Jeweled Lady,* Kane stirred and felt the pain of his bruised chest. For a moment, he lost contact with the dream, fading out to black.

No, Kane, Balam's voice whispered in his ear, *there is much yet you have to see in order that you might understand. The task that is laid upon you is important.*

"Balam?" Kane called, searching the darkness around him. "Are you here, or are you part of this damn fever?"

Light flooded into Kane's eyes and he blinked. When he blinked again, he was once more in the pyramid. This time, however, he stood with Harkhuf in a large room filled with shelves laden with papyrus scrolls, wax-sealed jars and a collection of furniture.

"Ramses keeps the machine Set gave Djoser in here," Harkhuf said. His voice grew tenser and quieter. "But the Israelites have learned of the machine, as well. Their leader, Moses, has sent spies throughout Ramses II's courts searching for this machine."

"But you have found it?" Kane asked, although the voice was not his own.

"I have." Harkhuf walked to the center of the room where an ornate hieroglyph showing Ramses II's efforts to lead the nation to greater glories. There were pictographs of the pharaoh in his war chariot, standing among conquered peoples, among the pyramids and along the Nile River.

Kane watched, feeling the other man's hesitation and fear in his own mind. Although the dreams again reminded him of the few instances he'd glimpsed into other lives he still wasn't certain if he'd lived, he was certain this was different. He was aware of the other man in the skull that they shared, but he felt certain the other man didn't know of him.

Harkhuf stopped in the center of the mosaic. He drew his knife, then knelt and rapped the hilt against five different tiles. He tapped some of the tiles more than once, and there was a cadence, a blending of sounds that created something more than the individual tones.

When Harkhuf finished, a section of the floor slid open and a dais moved smoothly up into place. The alien machine sat on it. The torchlight glittered along the twisted glass tubing and the curved metal surfaces of the three bowls.

"What is this?" Kane asked, although he'd seen it before. The words that were being spoken still weren't his own. He tried to move and stretch inside the body, but he had no command over it again. The fleeting control made him feel claustrophobic and trapped.

"You haven't seen this before?" Harkhuf seemed amazed.

"No."

"But you have to have seen it before. I've shown it to you."

"I've never seen this thing before."

Harkhuf stepped away from the dais and held his torch high. He shook his head sadly. "Ka'in, are you in there? Can you hear me?"

"The only things I hear," Kane said, "are the words of a drunken fool."

"I'm not drunk," Harkhuf insisted, "and I'm no fool." Absently, his hand touched the hilt of the dagger sheathed at his side. "I'm showing you power. The power that the god Set gave the pharaohs. Don't you see it?"

"I see a contrivance that I don't understand."

Harkhuf pointed at the glittering machine. "That is power. The power to be a pharaoh. Or even more. If you can feed people, you can lead people. That is what the pharaohs have learned. Haven't you learned that famine is the thing the people of this land fear most?"

"The gods willing," Kane said, "there will never be famine in these lands again."

"Not the gods," Harkhuf said. "This machine. That's why Set gave it to the pharaohs, and that's why the Israelite leader, Moses, is so interested in it. He has learned of the machine from his position within the pharaoh's court. Ramses II has been unwise in some respect. Secrets are best kept by one alone."

"Yet you share yours with me now," Kane said.

Harkhuf shook his head. "I thought I saw Ka'in in your eyes."

"You talk madness. I know no one named Ka'in, nor do I know that name. It sounds like an outlander name."

Harkhuf grinned. "An outlander name?" He laughed. "You speak prophecy, and you don't even know it. In time to come, Kane will be an outlander, but the world then will be very different than what you see now."

"Are you a prophet then, Harkhuf, to speak of times to come? Like one of the enslaved Israelite tribes that build our pyramids?"

"No," Harkhuf replied. "I'm only a traveler seeking to understand what my place in the skein of this thing is." He glanced back at the machine. "I was given an understanding of this machine a long time ago."

"You are too young to be speaking this way," Kane said.

"I'm young this time," Harkhuf agreed. "When I get insight through my dreams, I'm not always young. Sometimes I'm a very old man."

"You speak in riddles. I'm going back to my bed and that jug of wine. And maybe if she hasn't gotten totally pissed about me leaving, I'll find the woman there, too." Kane found himself turning to go.

"I can't let you do that." Harkhuf's voice turned cold and menacing in the quietness of the room.

Kane turned, instantly wary. "What are you saying?"

"I'm saying that I'm sorry. I'd hoped seeing the machine

might awaken Ka'in inside you and we might do this thing together.''

''What thing?''

''I'm going to take the machine,'' Harkhuf announced.

''That belongs to the pharaoh.''

''Not anymore.'' Harkhuf drew his knife from his waist and lunged forward.

Chapter 20

Still in the throes of the fever dream, Kane felt the change within the body, like the tension going out of a spring, and found he was no longer trapped in the flesh-and-blood prison. He shifted his weight instinctively, bringing up his left arm to block the knife attack. He slapped against the inside of Harkhuf's wrist, stopping the knife descent immediately.

Harkhuf's eyes widened. "Ka'in? Is it you?"

"I don't know you," Kane replied, holding the man's hand back.

"You know me," the man insisted. "But you've forgotten. Just as I forgot. But I'm remembering now, Ka'in. More and more of what I'd forgotten is coming back. Isn't it coming back for you?"

"No," Kane replied.

The man searched Kane's eyes. "Where are you, Ka'in? Where do you think you are?"

"I don't know what you're talking about."

The man smiled. "You think you're dreaming, don't you?"

Kane didn't say anything. Their torches lay on the floor, and their shadows, long and gaunt, twisted on the walls as they stepped back from each other.

"I used to think I was dreaming," Harkhuf said. "I thought I was going insane. But I was only remembering, Ka'in."

"Who are you?" Kane asked, circling the other man warily.

"I've had many names, Ka'in," Harkhuf explained. "Just as you have. And I've died many deaths. It no longer scares me." He kept the knife low and inside, his elbows tucked in close to his sides, making him less vulnerable to attack. His feet moved in small steps, gliding across the floor.

Silently, Kane mirrored the other man's moves, adjusting his defense every time his opponent shifted in a major way.

"And you're always around the machine, Ka'in," the man said. "Why is that?"

"I don't know what you're talking about," Kane replied.

"I've had dreams like this all my life. Have you?"

"No."

"I think you're lying."

Kane didn't respond. One of the torches guttered and went out, leaving only the remaining torch to light the room. Darkness crept in around them.

"Every time I meet you, though," Harkhuf said, "I never know if you're there to help me or to stop me. You do both, you know."

Kane thought back to his earlier dreams of Egypt. "I've met you only once before."

"When?"

"It was under Djoser's pyramid."

"Yes." Bright excitement burned through Harkhuf's eyes. "You *do* remember."

"Only for a moment. You were an overseer then."

Harkhuf grinned. "And now I am not. That's how the wheel turns, Ka'in. But this is only the price I have to pay to one day be a king. You know about Enlil, don't you? And the baronies? How the barons are all hybrids, a mix of alien and human races, and the way they destroyed the world?"

"Who are you?" Kane demanded.

"Now or then, Ka'in?" Harkhuf grinned as if he just told a favorite joke. "You know how maddening these dreaming memories are. I believed I was going insane until I found the first piece of the machine Enlil gave the pharaohs."

Kane's mind spun, and he knew some of it had to do with the fever that racked his body in the real world. At least, he thought of his existence aboard *Jeweled Lady* as being in the real world.

"And then I found the second piece. Right where the dreams showed me it would be."

"What is this machine?" Kane asked.

"It makes the nectar of the gods, Ka'in," Harkhuf responded. Although he appeared relaxed, he continued moving, circling steadily to Kane's left. "That machine can make food from the very air itself, and it can feed armies of people. And if you can feed a people—"

"You can lead a people," Kane finished.

Harkhuf smiled. "Yes." He paused. "So why are you here this time?"

"I don't know."

Without warning, Harkhuf stopped circling. "I'm going to take the machine now, Ka'in," he announced. "Are you going to let me?"

No, Balam's voice whispered. *He can't be allowed to take the machine.*

"What is it?" Harkhuf asked. "What do you hear?"

Noticing that the torch's flame had frozen and time had stopped again, leaving only himself and Harkhuf free to move, Kane turned, gazing into the shadows around him.

Balam stood nearly ten feet away, clothed in shadows and his robes. His skin was pinkish-gray from the weak light of the torch. When he spoke, his voice resonated within the room, not Kane's mind. "You must stop him."

"Who the hell is this?" Harkhuf demanded.

Kane looked at the two individuals before him, trying to make sense of everything that was going on.

"I am Balam," Balam said.

Harkhuf stepped closer but kept a safe distance. "You're one of the aliens. Like Enlil."

"Not like Enlil," Balam disagreed in a quiet voice.

"What's going on?" Kane demanded.

"The stakes are high in this endeavor, Kane," Balam said quietly. "This man can't be allowed to possess the machine Enlil gave to the pharaohs. It belongs to someone else. At least for a time."

"Who?" Harkhuf demanded. "The Israelites?"

"Things must be as they're supposed to be," Balam said, looking only at Kane.

"Is this the past?" Kane asked. "Or am I only dreaming?"

"This is the past, Kane," Balam said. "But this is a very fragile past that now reaches into the present and can alter the future."

"What are you talking about?" Kane asked, growing frustrated. He shifted again and felt the pain of his bruised chest.

"This man has been tied to the machine that Enlil gave the pharaohs," Balam explained. "That connection has allowed him to find two of the three pieces of the machine in the time/space you now occupy. Given time, he will find the third piece."

"Was it on the German warship in World War II?" Harkhuf asked excitedly. "I've recently dreamed about that."

Balam ignored him.

"Why should I stop him?" Kane asked.

"Because you're the only one who can end the threat of Enlil's machine," Balam answered. "You made a promise to the lady. Only by fulfilling that can you end the menace that Enlil's machine posits."

"What lady?" Kane asked.

Balam didn't have time to answer because Harkhuf launched himself across the distance, the knife gleaming in the torchlight.

Kane reacted immediately, feeling himself slip into the Magistrate hand-to-hand-combat mode. He slapped Harkhuf's knife attack away, then delivered a short roundhouse punch to his opponent's face. However, Harkhuf managed to slip most of the punch's power and spun, sweeping a leg up toward the side of Kane's head.

Unable to avoid the kick completely, Kane rolled with it. Spots swam before his eyes with kaleidoscopic intensity. He moved again at once, sidestepping another kick and rolling into a spinning back fist that hammered Harkhuf across the face and knocked him to the ground.

Blood gushed from Harkhuf's broken nose, looking black in the dimly lit shadows. Still, he was up almost immediately, ending Kane's chances of putting a quick finish to the fight.

Questions spun in Kane's brain even as he struggled to keep his senses focused. If this was real and not some fever-induced dream, what was Balam doing there? And what was the machine?

Harkhuf came at him again with the knife, cutting the air on both sides of Kane's head as he gave ground. Kane focused on his opponent, measuring Harkhuf's reach and stride, getting a feel for how aggressive the man would be if he let him keep coming.

Without warning, the torch on the floor started flickering again.

Kane watched as the warm orange glow cascaded across Harkhuf's face. Then just as suddenly, he realized that more lights had entered the pyramid's room. Stepping back from Harkhuf, who had frozen in place, Kane swept the newcomers with a glance.

They were all hard men, wasted by forced labor, long days and harsh weather. They held sharpened pieces of metal and a few weapons. Their leader was young, his beard fierce and dark, his black hair in disarray.

"There," the leader said. "There is the machine I was given knowledge of through my visions. Come on, my brothers, we have only to take it and unholy wrath will descend upon the lands of our captors and we shall be set free."

Forty men poured into the small room with quiet, desperate haste.

Kane tried to defend himself and resisted several opportunities to kill the men who fought him. Still, there was no escape, and when they saw that he couldn't harm them there were mutterings that they were protected by Moses's divinity. They closed more quickly, drowning Kane in their sheer numbers.

"Balam!" Kane yelled. For some inexplicable reason, the men entering the room hadn't attacked Balam at all.

"Rest easy, Kane. You will wake soon." Balam's voice was soothing. "This is something that happened a long time ago."

"If this already happened," Kane growled, "then why did I have to be here?"

"Are you here, Kane?" Balam asked. "Or do you only dream this?"

"Tell me!" Kane commanded.

"In time, Kane," Balam acceded. "Only in time. You have farther to go. For now, in this time, you've seen enough and done enough."

"What did I do?" Kane demanded as he felt a knife pierce his chest.

"You have prevented Enlil's machine from being taken at the wrong time," Balam said. "That's all that needed to be done here. Enlil didn't see the true danger of the machine he brought to this place for centuries. Then he entrusted the delivery of the world from the machine to a king. Sleep. We will talk again when the time is right."

Blackness filled Kane's vision. Balam's voice and Harkhur's yells grew dim and finally faded, leaving only white noise humming in his ears.

"KANE. Kane, wake up."

Drenched in fevered sweat, the stink of brine filling his nostrils, Kane woke on the pitching deck of *Jeweled Lady* with Brigid at his side. "I'm all right," he growled, shaking off her hand irritably. He was aware that other passengers were awake and watching him. Some of the men watched him with hot, hungry eyes.

"I'm just trying to help," Brigid said coldly, drawing away to put her back against the ship's railing.

Kane's head felt as if it weighed a thousand pounds. He breathed out gently, feeling the ache in his bruised chest. "It's not you, Baptiste. It's the people around us. If they see weakness in Fiddler or any of us, they're going to be scared and uncertain. Like it or not, we're leading this escape attempt, and those people are going to be expecting us to be leaders. Especially in light of the way we left Fiddlerville one step ahead of the Magistrates.''

Brigid remained quiet.

Kane let the silence draw out for a time, listening to the smack of the waves against the boat's hull and feeling the cool night air wash over him. Before he knew it, the heat of the fever drained away and left only freezing temperatures in its place. When he spoke, it was hard to keep his teeth from chattering. ''Returning to Cerberus redoubt wasn't the answer, Baptiste.''

''You're sick,'' she replied flatly. ''The last place you need to be is out here.''

''I don't think so.'' Kane had difficulty swallowing because his throat was so dry. ''We're supposed to be here.''

A curious look flirted with Brigid's beautiful face. ''Is that the fever talking?''

''No.''

''You had another dream.''

Kane hesitated only a moment, knowing he couldn't lie to Brigid. ''Yes.''

''Of Egypt?''

''Yes. But the time period was different. Ramses II was pharaoh. He was the leader of Egypt when the Israelites were there.''

''The story of Exodus, from the Christian Old Testament, begins there,'' Brigid said.

Kane struggled to remember what he knew of the religion. It hadn't been something he'd been terribly interested in while he'd been at Cobaltville, and the fever and pain in his head made it hard to remember things he might have otherwise remembered with no trouble at all. ''There was a man named Moses.''

''He led the twelve tribes of Israel from the lands of the pyramid builders,'' Brigid said.

''I don't know about that, Baptiste, but he was there in my dream.''

"Moses?" The idea seemed to interest Brigid and trouble her all at the same time.

"Yeah. He came after the machine that Enlil gave Djoser." Kane told her about the dream, having an easy time reconstructing it because it was so fresh in his mind.

"The manna machine," Brigid said when he'd finished.

Kane shook his head and regretted it when the pain reached a flashing crescendo that made his vision spot and his stomach roll threateningly. "I haven't heard about that."

"I have," Brigid replied thoughtfully. Her brows furrowed as she searched her photographic memory. "I read about it in the Cobaltville archives. How much do you know about the Christian Bible?"

"Not much, Baptiste," Kane admitted. "I've never read it, but I've heard passages of it in the Outlands in different places. Prayers for funerals and marriages and births still exist in different forms throughout most places. But then, so do all kinds of other religions. Some of them probably weren't even around before the nukecaust."

"There's a story in the Old Testament," Brigid went on, "about Moses and the way he led the Israelites from the pharaoh. Many biblical scholars believe that the pharaoh the Israelites were escaping was Ramses II, although you can find other documentation that the pharaoh was someone else."

"The story, Baptiste," Kane growled. He wrapped his arms around himself in an effort to keep warm.

"You're cold?" Brigid asked, concerned.

"Yes. It's the fever. It'll pass."

Brigid frowned. "If the fever passes."

"It'll pass, dammit. Get on with the story." Anything, Kane thought, to help him forget about the pain filling his head.

Brigid pushed herself up. "I'll be right back."

Irritated, thinking it would serve Brigid right if he was asleep by the time she got back, Kane leaned back against the railing and tried to relax. He and Grant had talked earlier and divided up the watch, neither of them willing to trust the captain and crew, or Fiddler for that matter.

Since leaving the ville and being trapped aboard *Jeweled Lady,* Fiddler hadn't exactly been a social butterfly. As it turned out, she'd lost two members of her crew in the firefight despite her best attempts to keep the upper hand during the confrontation. She hadn't blamed Kane, but she obviously hadn't felt like seeking out his company, either.

Kane didn't fault her, and he had his own concerns. Especially when the fever returned with a vengeance. He'd also noticed that she'd set up her own watch, even though the crew of *Jeweled Lady* didn't seem overly ambitious in the loyalty department.

An uneasy demilitarized zone had settled into place over the ship.

Brigid returned only a few minutes later. She carried a blanket, a bowl and a large tankard. She handed him all three. The bowl contained spicy soup, and the tankard held mulled wine.

Kane looked the question at her.

"*Jeweled Lady* is a cargo ship," Brigid explained. "She's heavy with goods that Harry Lindstrohm, the de facto baron of Campecheville, sent as payment for the help Fiddler had been giving him in procuring emigrants. Maybe it won't be a comfortable trip across the Gulf, but we're not going to starve."

"Tell me about the slave revolt in Egypt," Kane said.

"It wasn't a revolt," Brigid said, resuming her seat at the railing. "According to the Old Testament, the Christian god sent plagues and sicknesses among the pyramid builders. Eventually, fearing the wrath of the god, the Israelites were set free of the city and fled across the lands. The pharaoh pursued them. Then the Red Sea was parted—"

"A whole sea?" Kane asked doubtfully.

"Yes," Brigid answered. "And there was some documentation unveiled to support physical evidence that that event had happened."

"Parting a sea sounds like something Enlil or Balam might be able to do with the tech they had," Kane said. During their search for the truth of the Archons, they had seen a number of amazing things. Parting a sea sounded simple when compared even to a mat-trans unit.

"I don't know. None of the theories I ever read suggested anything like that. Of course, none of those writers and historians knew about the Archon Directive."

"The Red Sea was parted and the Israelites made their escape," Kane prompted.

"The pharaoh and his people followed them into the Red Sea," Brigid said. "Walls of water reportedly stood on either side of them. When the Israelites reached the other side of the sea, ahead of the pursuing Egyptians, the sea closed again, destroying the army that followed them."

Kane waited, savoring the soup and reliving the fever dream.

"According to the Old Testament," Brigid went on, "the Israelites fell into depraved ways and didn't celebrate the god that had freed them from Egyptian tyranny. Moses journeyed up onto Mount Sinai and received the Ten Commandments that later became the cornerstone of that theology. Due to their excesses and failure to recognize the god that had freed them, as well as Moses's own pride during a later incident, the Israelites were doomed to wander for forty years before they were delivered to the land of milk and honey they'd been promised."

Kane glanced up at Grant in the stern. He stood near the plotting desk and smoked, his cigar coal glowing orange against the dark night.

"During their years of wandering in that harsh land," Brigid said, "the Israelites were given the gift of manna. Six days out of the week, but not on the Sabbath because that was ordered to remain inviolate to spend worshiping their god, manna was said to rain down from the heavens."

"Manna?" Kane repeated.

"The descriptions I've read about it were basically that

manna was some kind of confection. It was described as white and fluffy, having taste and texture, but also like milk whey. The Israelites were said to have gathered bushels of it to serve at meals for their families. Some treatises I've read suggest that the manna was manufactured by an alien machine.''

"Enlil's machine," Kane said.

Brigid shrugged. "Maybe. There was never any proof. It was never found.''

"Moses took the machine that night," Kane pointed out.

"Perhaps," Brigid said. "But that doesn't explain why you're dreaming about it now.''

Kane silently agreed. He finished his soup and settled back against the railing, pulling the blanket more tightly around him. He kept thinking about the dreams, turning them around every way that occurred to him, but he couldn't find any explanation that suited him. Whatever the reason, he was sure, Balam knew it. Somewhere in all that thinking, sleep reached out and took him.

Chapter 21

Lindstrohm woke from the dream in a cold, shivering sweat. He peered around the room and found that he'd gone to sleep at his desk. He sucked in deep breaths, willing his heart to slow to something near normal.

He pushed away from the desk and walked toward the balcony. Details of the dream in Egypt threaded through his mind. Ka'in had been there, as well as some other creature that Lindstrohm was certain was somehow connected to Enlil. Ka'in had known the creature; he had called it by name: Balam.

Lindstrohm had never before heard of the creature, nor did he have any clue as to what its purpose in his dreams was. But he was certain it didn't mean him any good.

He paused at the doorway to the balcony and peered out at the moon-silvered water. The sky to the east was lightening, already turning a pinkish purple; soon it would be morning.

Lanterns burned in the morning mist that had descended over the bay during the night. They glowed softly in the streets of the ville, and they glowed distantly on the small cargo boats running barrels of oil in to the warehouses along the shore. He'd deliberately stepped up the production schedule for the night, taking half loads into the warehouses instead of full ones. It would give the Tong spies more to count, and Lindstrohm was certain there were spies.

The Tong junk sat sedately at anchor in the harbor. Its pleated sails lay neatly folded in small stacks along the rigging. Armed crews walked the immaculate decks, and an officer in charge stood in the stern.

The meeting yesterday with Ren and Yip had appeared to

go well. Lindstrohm felt good about that. If an arrangement could be made with Wei Qiang, an arrangement without any duplicitous action on the part of the old Tong warlord, it would benefit them both.

But Vasquez's arguments kept pulling at the logic Lindstrohm tried to build on. With Qiang's ships in the area, the Tong master would show no hesitation at stepping in to take over the oil-reclamation operation if Lindstrohm showed any weakness or proved unfit.

He closed the doors to the balcony and returned to the large desk. Books lay scattered across it, and the oil lantern he'd been working by earlier had exhausted the fuel reservoir. Several of the books in his library had been on World War II, and a surprising number of them were in English. Still, he couldn't help wishing that he had access to the Samariumville archives for a few hours. Then the information he felt he lacked would be at his fingertips.

He refilled the lantern reservoir and lit the wick, only then aware of the shadow that shifted in the main doorway. His heart froze for just a moment, but he made himself sit behind the desk.

"How long have you been there?" he asked.

"Not long," Narita Vasquez answered.

By not staring at her directly, he was able to see her more clearly. When she had trained him to use his peripheral vision in the dark like that, he'd remembered other times in his dreams when he'd known to do it. So many things he now did stirred memories of the dreams.

"I felt you around me today," Lindstrohm said.

Vasquez said nothing.

Lindstrohm turned up the lantern's wick, making the bubble of light around his desk swell until it reached the doorway. "I wasn't imagining things, was I?" he asked.

She didn't answer for a time, and Lindstrohm didn't press her. The one thing he'd never experienced before was the feeling he had for her. She completed him in ways that he'd never imagined, and being away from her yesterday—aware that she was gone not because she'd chosen to go on a voyage, but because she was deliberately staying away from him—had been more painful than he could have imagined.

"No," she said finally. "You weren't imaging things. I watched over you."

"I never saw you."

"You weren't supposed to," she said with a trace of quiet sarcasm. "If you had seen me, Ren and Yip—and their hatchet men—might have seen me, as well."

"Why were you watching me?" Lindstrohm asked, knowing that he knew but only wanted her to say.

"Because I don't trust the Tong as blithely as you seem to." Vasquez shifted inside the doorway, then stepped forward and came on into the room. She wore jeans and a longsleeved shirt with the sleeves rolled up. Her hair was left unbound, cascading down her shoulders. She wore a .40 caliber Smith & Wesson semiautomatic pistol on her right hip, high and tucked into her side.

"And what should it matter if they betray me?" Lindstrohm said. "They might save you the trouble of wishing I was dead."

Vasquez frowned irritably and crossed her arms over her breasts. "Don't be petulant, Harry."

Lindstrohm made himself breathe in and out. "I apologize." He looked away from her harsh glance. "So what arc we going to do?"

She ignored the question and turned her attention to the books, maps and papers on the desk. "What is this?"

"I was researching something."

"What?"

"The U-boat I dreamed about." Lindstrohm glanced back at all the texts scattered across his desk.

"What is a U-boat?" Narita asked.

Lindstrohm blinked as he looked at her, only then realizing that he hadn't had the chance to tell her about the nightmare he'd had the previous night. "A U-boat is an undersea boat.

A submarine. The Germans used them extensively in World War II to take down British ships, as well as cargo ships.''

Vasquez nodded. Her understanding of history had grown a lot during the years they'd been together. She didn't talk as much as he did, and he talked a lot about the way the world had been before the nukecaust. Some of those times had included the events that had led up to skydark.

"I had a dream," Lindstrohm said, "that I was aboard one of those German submarines. It sank, and the man I'd been then drowned." The experience remained vivid in his mind, and he noticed his hand shaking slightly as he moved some of the books around, searching for one of those he wanted.

Vasquez didn't say anything.

"I think the third piece of the machine is aboard that sunken German submarine," Lindstrohm stated.

"And it's lost in the ocean?"

"It's not lost," Lindstrohm said, trying to curb the impact of the strong denial stirring within him. "I've found the other two pieces, Narita. I was guided to them through my dreams. I'll be guided to this piece, as well."

"Mebbe you'll be guided to it," Vasquez said, "but being able to recover it is another matter if it's on the ocean floor."

"That can't be the answer," Lindstrohm said. "I can't have been led this far only to be unable to recover the final piece."

"You're certain it was aboard the U-boat?" Vasquez asked.

Lindstrohm nodded. "I dreamed about it again tonight." That had been before the dream he'd had of Egypt, and Ka'in and Balam. This time, he'd seen through the German officer's eyes as the piece of the machine had been loaded onto the submarine. He'd carefully inventoried and stored the piece of the device. That had been during World War II when the Nazis at Hitler's orders were gathering religious symbols. "It was there."

"And the U-boat went down to the bottom of the sea?"

"It went down," Lindstrohm answered. "Even as I was drowning, I could feel the change in water pressure as the submarine sank. Too many compartments in the submarine had been holed, and the people dropping depth charges onto the U-boat had not given up the attack. They had our depth. There was no escape.''

''Then the submarine lies at the bottom of the sea,'' Vasquez said.

''Mebbe it drifted,'' Lindstrohm said, explaining the thoughts he'd had while researching the war during the previous evening. ''Enough air could have remained trapped in it that it was buoyant for a while. Mebbe years.''

''All that means is that even if you knew where it went down, you wouldn't find the submarine,'' Vasquez pointed out.

''The submarine went down in the Gulf of Mexico,'' Lindstrohm said.

Vasquez glanced at the books. ''You found the submarine you dreamed about?''

''I believe so.'' Lindstrohm gave in to the excitement in his voice. ''During World War II, between the years of 1942 and 1943, a fleet of twenty German U-boats were assigned to the Gulf of Mexico. Their orders were to sink any oil tankers and supply ships coming from Texas and Louisiana.''

''That's not far from here.'' She moved closer.

Lindstrohm smelled her fragrance and longed to touch her, but he kept himself from doing so, afraid to break any of the rapport they now shared. ''It's not far from here at all,'' he said in a thick voice. ''The submarine I was on was the U-166.'' He'd seen the markings in the second dream, as well as been introduced to the captain. ''It was the only confirmed casualty among the German submarines in the Gulf of Mexico. It was sunk twenty miles off the Louisiana coast by what was reportedly a torpedo plane, but it was the depth charges that really put it down.''

''What happened to the other U-boats?''

''They were pulled out of the area once the merchant vessels started sailing with armed convoys after 1943. But before they were sunk, they put down fifty-six Allied vessels. During that time, the United States also succeeded in opening an oil-supplying pipeline from Texas to New Jersey, which meant that tankers were no longer needed to transport the crude oil.''

''Where is the U-166?'' Vasquez asked, studying the nautical map he had located that displayed the Gulf of Mexico.

''No one knows,'' Lindstrohm answered, growing more hopeful as he embraced the facts of the German ship's disappearance again. ''Thirty-nine of the U-boat commanders' confirmed kills still lay in waters just off the coasts of Louisiana, Texas and Florida before the nukecaust.''

''Then they may still be there.'' Vasquez ran a slim forefinger south of Louisiana across the Gulf waters.

''Mebbe. But with all the upheaval caused by the nukes and the changes that took place in undersea volcanoes in the Cific Ocean, not to mention the displacement of the California coastline and the Baja Peninsula when the earthshaker bombs tore them free, that may not be true anymore.''

''It's also true, then, that the U-166 may no longer be there.''

''No, it may not be,'' Lindstrohm agreed. ''It could be somewhere closer to where we are now.''

''Harry—'' Hesitation showed on Vasquez's beautiful face.

''What?'' he asked quietly.

''I don't want you to get your hopes up. Having these dreams the way you are now is bad enough.''

''Having the dreams isn't bad.''

''I worry about you.'' She touched his face with her hand, but Lindstrohm noticed that her other hand was never more than an inch or two from her holstered pistol.

''I'm glad.''

''I'm not.'' Her face hardened a little, but she didn't take her hand away. ''I've got enough to do to worry about keeping my own neck intact.''

''I'll look out for you. Aligning ourselves with Wei Qiang is one way to solidifying our position here.''

''Our position here,'' she reminded, ''is due largely to our ability to feed all the people you insist on bringing to this area."

"There's safety in numbers," Lindstrohm argued softly.

"Not when those numbers are hungry and pissed off."

Lindstrohm gazed into her dark eyes, seeing more than a hint of worry there. "What's wrong?"

"You've been so involved in these dreams that you haven't paid attention to some of the other things going on around you."

"Both times I found the other pieces to the machine my dream cycle intensified. The same way it is now. Only it's never been this intense before." Lindstrohm looked at her. "We're close to the third piece, Narita. I don't know how I know, but I do. Just give me a little more time."

Vasquez looked at him. "The latest shipments are three days late. In the next few days, the people here on this barren piece of rock are going to know that they don't have anything to eat."

The news hit Lindstrohm hard and he tried to remember if someone had told him that earlier. "The ships will be here before then."

"And if they're not?"

"We can send a ship to Fiddlerville or some of the other coastal villes that we've been supporting. It won't take long to get a shipment in. We've got fuel, and everybody around Samariumville trades for fuel."

"Some of those coastal villes have fallen to the slavers," Vasquez said. "That's another thing the ships' captains have been getting upset about. The waters are turning dangerous out there, Harry. The best way to stay ahead of the sharks is to stay fast and mobile. You changed all that when you decided to open up shop here. And then there's the matter of the oil. Everyone would take that away if they could."

Desperation seized Lindstrohm, and he had to work hard to keep the black anger swirling inside him to keep from spilling over. What Narita said was true; he'd always managed to stay at best only a step or three ahead of a famine that would have swept through Campecheville in spite of the oil. That was one of the main reasons no one had settled there, and why it had taken so long to get a community started.

"That's all the more reason to find the other piece of the machine," Lindstrohm said. "Once we have it, food will never be a problem again." He looked at Vasquez. "You do believe the stories that I've told you about it, don't you?"

She looked at him. "I know that you believe them."

"So can you."

She didn't say anything.

"It's true," Lindstrohm said.

Vasquez looked as if she wanted to say something, but she never got the chance. A clanging bell suddenly ripped through the early morning, shattering the stillness and the quiet of the beginning day.

Lindstrohm cursed, resenting the interruption before he got the feeling that things had been put right between them. Still, they were guided by a common goal as they moved quickly toward the balcony doors. The bells were only used to announce an unexpected visitor.

Standing out in the cool morning light, surprised at the heavy, cottony fog that swelled out on the bay and lay heavily over the ville, Lindstrohm gazed out at the sea. Only patches of the dark green water could be seen through the white haze.

But farther out to sea, two tall masts stood proudly, their sails catching the southerly wind.

"What ship is that?" Lindstrohm asked.

Vasquez took up the binoculars she'd thought to remove from his desk on her way. She was more familiar with all of the ships that traded with Campecheville than he was.

"From the cut of her, she looks like Howard's *Kingfisher*," Narita said. "But that can't be."

"Why not?"

"Because *Kingfisher* is rigged with three masts. That one out there only has two."

Lindstrohm watched as the harbor patrol he'd arranged for went into action. Long, narrow boats sporting heavy machine guns, torpedoes and antiaircraft weapons sped toward the arriving ship.

"She's been in a fight," Vasquez commented.

"How do you know?"

"The ship's still smoldering." Narita lowered the binoculars. "This can't be good news, Harry." She looked at him. "And it would probably be better if we tried to contain it."

Lindstrohm's stomach tightened at the mixture of emotions he suddenly felt. Another thing going wrong wasn't what he wanted to deal with, but Narita had said *we,* which made him feel instantly hopeful. Nothing could defeat both of them if they were together.

He followed Narita out of the room.

"FUCKIN' FIREBLAST, Lindstrohm!" Howard yelled across the expanse of ocean between the cargo ship and Lindstrohm's speedboat. "I've got wounded aboard ship that need tendin' to. You can't keep us tied up here."

Lindstrohm stared at the gaping holes in *Kingfisher*'s upper deck. Wounded lay under blankets and thick coats along the powder-burned wood. Most of the cargo ship's railing had been torn away by enemy fire, as well as by grappling hooks. Lindstrohm knew about the hooks, because some of them were still embedded in the wood and entangled in the rigging. Smoke still eddied into the foggy morning from the charred areas aboard the ship. The stench of smoke burned Lindstrohm's nose.

Vasquez ordered the speedboat crew to take them in closer to *Kingfisher.* At her command, despite his own protests over the delay, Howard had his crew roll out a rope ladder. Without hesitation, Vasquez climbed the ladder and stepped aboard the cargo ship.

Lindstrohm followed, aware of the hostile gazes that the crew turned in his direction. "What happened?" he asked Howard as he surveyed the damage.

Vasquez kept walking to the center of the deck, obviously aiming for the hatch leading to the ship's hold.

"We were attacked," Howard replied. "Doesn't it fucking look like it?"

Only then did Lindstrohm notice the blood staining the captain's shirt. "You were wounded."

"Hell, yes!" Howard exploded. "But it's a damn sight better than being chilled the way a lot of these other people were."

"The hold's empty," Vasquez said. "What wasn't taken was damaged by fire and flooding."

"That's right," Howard said. "The bastard coldhearts that did this aimed to see the cargo taken or destroyed. If I hadn't off-loaded it to them, they'd have chilled us all."

"You dumped the cargo?" Vasquez asked, stepping toward the captain.

Howard took a fearful step back. "I didn't have a fuckin' choice, Narita. You see what they've done to this fuckin' ship, and that was with me agreeing to their terms. The only thing that kept them off us entirely was that once they'd loaded up with our cargo, they didn't want to take the chance we'd get lucky and rip out their ship's hull below the waterline. It would have been a slow death, mebbe, but it definitely would have done for the cargo they'd just stolen."

"Who did this?" Lindstrohm demanded.

Shaking his head, Howard said, "I don't know. Most of the men aboard that ship, I didn't know them. But they were well outfitted and not hesitant at all about chilling anybody."

"They knew you were sailing for Campecheville?" Lindstrohm asked.

"I told them," Howard replied. "I told them as plain as a man could tell them. But they didn't give a shit. Nobody gives a shit, Lindstrohm, because you don't have the sense to protect—"

Without warning, Vasquez backhanded the wounded captain hard enough to snap his head around.

Two men standing against the railing reached for their blasters.

The woman swept her blaster from her hip in the blink of

an eye. "If they come out of those holsters," she promised coldly, "you die."

Slowly, nodding their understanding, the two men raised their hands from their holstered weapons.

Vasquez didn't put her weapon away. "If you trade here," she told Howard, "then you'll respect the port."

"If this kind of shit keeps up," the ship's captain promised, "ain't nobody going to trade at Campecheville."

"Then where will they get the fucking fuel you need to trade with the coastal villes?" Vasquez asked.

Howard didn't have an answer for that.

Lindstrohm strode over to the hatch and peered into the hold. He couldn't help wondering how many of the crew would have killed him then and there if they'd had the chance. He felt dozens of hot gazes on him.

The hold was nearly empty. Only a few broken crates and flotsam remained. As he watched, a rat swam through the water that nearly covered the hold's floor. *Kingfisher* had taken on a lot of water. A bilge pump crew remained at work, creating a steady thump of noise as the pumps battled the incoming sea.

"We've been holed," Howard said. "Took a bunch of armor-piercing rounds below the waterline. The bilge pumps can't even break even with it."

"You're sinking," Lindstrohm said.

"Slowly," Howard admitted, "but surely. Campecheville was the closest place to put in for repairs."

"And despite your protests," Lindstrohm said, "you know it's also the most generous when it comes to men and materials. You knew I'd refit your ship and provide the manpower to see it done."

Howard looked away. "You got a vested interest in *Kingfisher*, too."

"That's right," Lindstrohm said, walking toward the man. "We've got a vested interest in each other. You might want to remember that at times other than just when you want something from me."

Howard returned his gaze.

"And you might want to remember that when someone's trying to take a cargo from you that I've already paid for," Lindstrohm said. "I was depending on that cargo to feed those people in that ville."

With the fog hanging heavy over the area, Campecheville could barely be seen on the other side of the bay. But it was clear enough to see that a crowd had turned out to see what was going on. Lindstrohm knew they were going to be demanding answers.

In fact, they were going to be demanding more than that because he'd been depending on Howard's ship to supplement the existing stores within the ville. According to the latest inventory, they had less than two days of food left. There was no choice but to start rationing food now if they were going to make it.

"I bartered for some more immigrants," Howard said. "I still got most of them. But knowing you got even more mouths to feed at a time like this probably isn't something you wanted to know."

Lindstrohm walked away from the man, not knowing what to say. He felt as if he were teetering on the brink of disaster, and it scared the hell out of him. As he peered out across the bay, though, he noticed the movement aboard the Tong ship still sitting at anchor.

"How much longer are the Tong going to be here?" Vasquez asked quietly.

"Three or four more days," Lindstrohm said.

She didn't say anything.

"Long enough for them to watch us start starving if something doesn't happen," Lindstrohm said. "And when they do, when Wei Qiang sees the weaknesses we have here, there won't be an agreement between the Tong and Campecheville—they'll starve us out and feast on us like lions on Christians."

Vasquez looked at him, clearly not understanding the reference.

"It's from an old story," Lindstrohm said. "Mebbe I'll tell it to you one day."

"Okay," she replied.

Lindstrohm looked out at the fog over the bleak sea. "If I could find that third part to the machine, Narita, we'd never have any problems. At least, food wouldn't be a problem. If you can feed people, you can lead people." It was the truth. All he had to do was make it a reality.

His eyes swept the bay, thinking about the missing German submarine. The U-166 had gone down in the Gulf. It had to be out there somewhere. And with it was the missing piece of the machine the aliens had first given the pharaohs.

The machine had also fallen into the hands of Moses and his people. From there it had been protected, not even used. The secret of its operation had died with Moses and the pharaohs. But Lindstrohm still knew how to use it. He had learned about the process while he'd dreamed of the Egyptians, and he'd learned about it again while wandering with the Israelites for forty years while they'd waited for their promised land.

He was probably the only man on the planet who knew how to use the machine. The barons had never even gone seeking it. They had either forgotten its existence or had believed it destroyed. No one thought about the machine anymore.

That is, no one thought about the machine except Ka'in.

The fear resonated within Lindstrohm, sharp and edgy. Ka'in had stopped him from possessing the machine in the past.

Lindstrohm stared at Campecheville. The past didn't matter. It had all been stepping-stones to this place and time. He wouldn't allow Ka'in to stop him again.

Lindstrohm looked to the west, wondering if Ka'in was as close as the missing piece of the machine. In all of the tangled pasts they'd shared, Ka'in always had been.

Chapter 22

"Ambitious project," Grant said, staring down into the dark water of the bay. He flicked ashes from his cigar over the ship's railing. "But they get a hell of a payoff."

Kane silently agreed, staring at the ships and floating oil rigs that worked the Bay of Campecheville. The noise of the generator-powered equipment made it hard to hold a conversation. The water trapped the noise, making it even louder.

"What they doing?" Domi asked, standing beside Grant. Since they'd entered the bay leading to Campecheville, Blakeney, captain of *Jeweled Lady,* had calmed down considerably. It wasn't likely that he'd forget Domi had threatened his life and stripped command of the ship from him, but he hadn't moved aggressively against any of his unplanned passengers from Fiddlerville.

"The oil rigs," Brigid said, pointing at the floating platforms, "are obviously tapping into the underwater and underground wells. But the smaller tugs and platforms must be tapping submerged vessels whose holds are filled with oil."

"And other things," Fiddler said as she joined them. "When the nukecaust hit, there were a number of ships in this area. Lindstrohm told me about it." She nodded toward the bleak coastline of the mainland nearly a mile away.

Kane studied the buildings standing at the water's edge in the distance. He knew that some of the structures lay submerged beneath the waves because he could see the tops of buildings sticking up from the water in different places. Buoys marked other places in irregular shapes, and the tugboats plying their cargoes back to the mainland or returning to the staging platforms steered well clear of those areas.

"Before skydark," Fiddler went on, "this place was a resort ville. A place where people came and spent a lot of jack trying to relax. When the waters rose and the ships went down here, there were a lot of losses. Every now and then, some of the captains told me Lindstrohm's crews manage to get one of the ships sealed off below if the water's not too deep. Then they pump it full of air and float it to the top. They salvage some goods and electronics if they can, though not very much most of the time, and stainless-steel tools and equipment they can use or barter with."

Kane watched the divers work in the water as *Jeweled Lady* sailed on into the harbor. Hardly anyone watched the ship pass through. Evidently the sight was a familiar one. "How many people does Lindstrohm have in the ville?"

"I've never heard any exact numbers," Fiddler answered. "A few thousand, surely. But those numbers change every time a ship arrives. Mostly people who intend to stay, but there are a few who come down here that aren't happy. Farming is too hard for people who are interested in tilling the soil, and they can't grow the things they're used to growing back in the villes they left. So they stay for a while, then they push on. Some join up with ships' crews. Others die." She glanced at the nearest oil rig. "The work out here is dangerous."

"But not everyone works out here," Brigid observed. "There are several people working the shore."

"And farther into the ville." Fiddler nodded in agreement. "Lindstrohm is reclaiming the ville, as well. Campecheville died very quickly during the nukecaust. The stores and mercantiles that didn't go underwater remained dry, and they have a number of supplies that can still be used. Lindstrohm uses those for barter, as well."

Kane took his binoculars from the war bag he carried. He scanned the barren coast, picking up the shelves of limestone rock jutting from the sea and the beaches, as well. Vegetation was sparse, limited to a few palm trees and stubborn brush, broken up by hints and patches of bougainvillea and tropical flowers. He spotted walls farther into the ville. "There are fortifications, too."

"Lindstrohm started getting prepared for an invasion the day he got here and started pumping oil from the first submerged tanker," Fiddler said. "Over the years, he's had to fight off his share of pirates and other coldhearts."

Peering out at the coastline again, Kane spotted the red lacquered Tong warship. A couple moments later, he found the two small air wags tied up at docks. "Wei Qiang's people are here," he stated.

Fiddler peered forward. "Yeah. I'd heard that Lindstrohm might be going into business with him. You know about Wei Qiang."

"Yeah," Kane growled. "He's a tough bastard." He'd first encountered the old Tong warlord when they'd followed up on Ambika after encountering her handiwork in the Utah Territories a few months back. They'd also encountered and ultimately brokered a deal between Tong representatives for Qiang and Tyler Falzone and the Lost Valley of Wiy Tukay, which had actually turned out to be the Silicon Valley of Seattle submerged beneath the sea.

Fiddler stared at Kane. "You have a lot of secrets, Kane. Not many people know of Wei Qiang out here, and here you are sounding like you know him."

"Yeah," Kane replied evenly, "I have secrets. And I keep them." He nodded toward the Tong warship. "If Qiang gets the opportunity, he'll take these oil fields from Lindstrohm."

"Lindstrohm's not in any more danger from Qiang than he is from any other coldheart out here," Fiddler said. "And even with the overland travel routes Qiang's people use to haul the cargoes across Mexico to the Cific Ocean, trying to take and hold Campecheville would stretch him too thin."

"Mebbe," Kane admitted, "but Qiang isn't about to let anyone else take this place if he can help it. Fuel is an addiction to someone making the kinds of empire-building plans Qiang is making."

"Qiang holds the Western Isles," Fiddler said.

"And he'd like to hold more," Grant replied.

Fiddler glanced at Grant, but quickly saw that he wasn't going to be any quicker about explaining how he knew the Tong warlord, either.

"Look at all people," Domi said, folding her arms over her breasts. She didn't sound happy. "Like bunch of locusts running around. Ville this big, they eat too much. Hard put back extra stores for bad time. Fuckin' locusts for sure."

The albino's words rang a bell inside Kane's head, and he thought about the machine he'd seen in Egypt. Harkhuf's words came back to him.

It makes the nectar of the gods, Ka'in. That machine can make food from the very air itself, and it can feed armies of people. And if you can feed a people—

"—you can lead a people," Kane finished again.

"What did you say?" Brigid asked.

Kane shook his head. "It wasn't important, Baptiste."

"Got to be a hell of a butcher's bill for a place this full of people," Grant said. "Domi's right about that."

"Lindstrohm gives food away to the coastal villes that help him with his recruitment," Kane pointed out.

"Not easily," Fiddler said. "I've had shipments come in weeks late before. Even with all the fuel he's tapping into here, Lindstrohm still has to find places and people to trade with. And there are enough coldhearts who've taken to pirating to make these waters more dangerous than ever. Even Narita the Bleeder was a total hardcase when it came to seizing ships before she got involved with Lindstrohm."

Kane looked at all the reclamations operations going on around him. "These people can't eat the oil they're pumping." He brain danced with images of the machine he'd seen. If such a machine truly existed that could make food out of the air, and it could be found here, Lindstrohm would have an empire at his fingertips. No one would be able to stop him from continuing to grow and build.

A cool wind came up out of the west, filling *Jeweled Lady*'s sails and pushing her more deeply into the harbor. Kane felt the residual fever still burning within him. Whatever had been going on within him regarding the dreams hadn't finished yet.

A CROWD OF ARMED MEN met *Jeweled Lady* at the docks. They held back a greater crowd of people from the cargo ship, and most of those people looked sullen and angry.

Blakeney put out planks and a small party of the armed force boarded the cargo ship. The leader, Radkey, was a tall, gaunt man with a pockmarked face and half his right ear missing.

"Lissen up!" the man roared in a voice that was louder than Kane would have expected based on his size. "This here's your welcome to Campecheville. For all of you sailors that has been here before, know that you ain't going to be staying long. Baron Lindstrohm has got needs that need tending to. You'll be getting an immediate restock on cargo—"

"We didn't get rid of the last restock," Blakeney complained. "Samariumville Magistrates down took Fiddlerville. We barely got out of there with whole skins."

"What about the food you were sending to Fiddlerville?" Without waiting for an answer, the sec boss waved two of his men forward.

The two sec men opened *Jeweled Lady*'s hold and stepped down inside. One of them poked his head back up almost immediately. "Looks like he's telling the truth, Radkey. Hold looks pretty full, and there's a lot of fuel drums."

"Strip the food that was going to be left for Fiddlerville," Radkey ordered. "Leave everything else."

"You can't do that," Blakeney said. "My crew and I have got to have something to eat."

Radkey's face hardened. "Fish, fat man. You look like you've been sitting down to one meal too many as it is."

Blakeney sputtered and cursed, but he didn't make an effort to stop the line of sec men that suddenly fell into position to unload the cargo hold.

"The rest of you people," Radkey went on, "can make your choice now. You can stay here and work for your meals doing work that needs to be done around Campecheville, or you can go on this ship when it leaves." He nodded toward the gangplank. "It's time to make your choice."

Grant looked at Kane. "It might be better if we went with Blakeney. From what I'm seeing here, Lindstrohm ain't doing so well."

Kane replied just as quietly so more than Domi and Brigid wouldn't overhear them. "We've come this far. Let's find out about that mat-trans unit." But he knew it was more than that. His dreams had somehow drawn him there, as well. The fever coiled restlessly inside him.

"STARGING IMMEDIATE food shipments to Campecheville will require an audience with Lord Qiang," Ren said.

Lindstrohm regarded the Tong representative across the table in one of the gaudy houses down in the docks. A nearby lantern lit the table area, raising the Tong man's features in buttery gold highlights. They'd gone there to talk, and the ground was as neutral as he could make it. He had no doubt the Tong wouldn't let him on their ship, and he didn't want Ren or his hatchet men escort to set foot in his private offices.

"I've got shipments of fuel that I could send out immediately," Lindstrohm stated. "As a show of good faith." Or desperation, he couldn't help thinking. He knew better than to expect that Ren or any of the Tong wouldn't know how badly the current situation affected Campechcville. Despite how well he paid them or how profitable their relationship with him was, ships' captains would gladly give information for extra jack.

"It's not a matter of your good faith," Ren replied. "It would take time to set up food shipments to Campecheville. Those plans and that time already figured into Lord Qiang's timetable, but he had not guessed that the need might arise so quickly."

"Baron Samarium has stepped up his attempts to keep the slave trade going from this part of the Outlands," Lindstrohm said.

"I understand your problem and your needs, but there is little I can do about it at this juncture," Ren said politely.

It was the Tong man's politeness that nearly drove Lindstrohm over the edge and stripped his control. He forced himself to breathe out, aware that the noise sounded loud in the gaudy despite the dozens of other conversations taking place at the same time. Some of the people at nearby tables even stopped their own conversations to listen more intently.

Ren was aware of the extra attention, as well, and seemed embarrassed by it. "Trust me when I say that I will do all that I can."

"Then send one of the air wags back to Lord Qiang," Narita said. "Have the pilot give the message to Lord Qiang."

Ren leaned back in his chair and shook his head. "I'm afraid that can't be done."

"Why?" Vasquez asked.

"Because, in this matter, Lord Qiang will listen to no one except me."

"Then go with him," she said.

"And tell Lord Qiang that I left this delicate operation unsupervised while there were obvious—*difficulties* underway?" Ren shook his head again. "If I were to do that, my only blessing would be that I wasn't Japanese and wouldn't be expected to adhere to their code of Bushido. However, even though I didn't take my own life as a matter of honor, Lord Qiang would order my life taken for me."

Lindstrohm almost felt beaten. He was certain the final piece of the machine lay nearly in his grasp. He steeled himself and looked Ren in the eyes. "Let's lay all our cards on the table."

Ren spread his hands.

"I'm in a hard place," Lindstrohm said. "To not admit that would be more than foolish—it would be suicidal at this moment. That first supply ship that came in this morning is only the beginning of a trend. There are going to be more ships taken, and I'm not going to be able to feed the people in this ville. When that happens, they're going to turn on me. I'm not stupe.''

"I would never suggest a thing."

"Not to my face," Lindstrohm said. "But if I were you, I'd probably be feeling pretty smug right now. I'm trapped between a hard place and a rock, and I probably need a friend now more than ever. If I was you, I'd settle in for some hard dickering—let me make all the moves and watch my position dwindle as empty stomachs made enemies of friends."

Ren shook his head slightly. "I would never dare presume—"

"The hell you wouldn't," Lindstrohm said. "You're a negotiator for Qiang, and I doubt this is the first time for you to sit down at a table. You don't have to show me your hand—the deck's coming off faceup. But you keep forgetting about the wild card in play here."

"The wild card?" Ren repeated, smiling slightly as if he didn't understand.

"Those oil fields are mined," Lindstrohm said. "Before I let anyone move into this territory and take what I've fought for, I'll see it all destroyed."

"That won't destroy the oil," Ren said calmly. High spots of color showed on his cheeks. Being threatened obviously didn't agree with him.

"No," Lindstrohm agreed bluntly, "that won't destroy the oil, but it will require the next person who comes into this area to invest considerably before they get the operation going that I've got going here." He remained quiet, letting Ren think about that for a time.

Narita Vasquez sat quietly at Lindstrohm's side. Her hands weren't visible above the tabletop.

Lindstrohm had no doubt that she was holding a blaster trained on Ren's midsection. Although no other Tong had taken a seat at the table, several lounged inside the room, as well as just outside the gaudy. Vasquez had surrounded them with men who were loyal to her and to Lindstrohm in turn.

Other men crowded the gaudy near to bursting. Some of

them, Lindstrohm knew, would turn on him the instant they smelled weakness on him. The fuel-reclamation project he'd started up had drawn fierce, bloodthirsty men to his banner, and that fact was working against him now. Any of them might figure that they could step him, kill the immigrants looking at Campecheville as a place to make a home, then hold the ville against outside forces long enough to take a tidy profit.

They couldn't, Lindstrohm knew, in the long run. There was only safety in numbers and in the booby traps he'd set up on the various oil derricks.

"Do you think Qiang is prepared to invest that heavily?" Lindstrohm asked Ren. "Especially since the Western Isles are so far from here?"

Ren hesitated. "No. Lord Qiang would not gladly undertake that task."

Lindstrohm grinned coldly, only showing the expression through a supreme effort of will. "I'm glad we agree on that. At the same time, I know the captain of your ship will probably be sending out teams to try to figure out how to disarm those booby traps."

Ren said nothing.

"Tell your captain that if I find that going on," Lindstrohm said, "the deal with Lord Qiang is off until I get the captain's head on a stick."

"You can't—" Ren began.

"I just did," Lindstrohm interrupted. "I'm trapped here, Ren. I've made my gambles. And this is going to pay off big, or I'm going to die with it. There's nothing else for me to do."

"I'll tell him," Ren agreed.

"Good." Lindstrohm breathed out. "Now there's something else you can tell him."

"Captain Zhao isn't the kind of man to be trifled—"

"Don't let me think I've given you that impression," Lindstrohm warned. "Otherwise we'll both pay for it."

"No," Ren said quickly. "You haven't given me that impression."

"I know Captain Zhao didn't come this far without an escort," Lindstrohm said. "How many ships does he have backing this play?"

Ren hesitated.

"If I have to," Lindstrohm said, "I'll commandeer one of those air wags you have and fly out across the Gulf to check myself. I can find a man who can fly an air wag."

"Of course," Ren said. "There is a small group of ships a short distance from here."

"What's their purpose?"

"To make certain that some kind of arrangement is arrived at," Ren said matter-of-factly.

All the gloves were coming off, Lindstrohm knew. The naked threats hung hot and heavy in the air. "Despite the fact that Lord Qiang is investigating other avenues of oil production, as your partner suggested, he's already committed to this one."

Ren's gaze was unflinching. "That commitment is a double-edged blade, and it cuts both ways."

"That's fine," Lindstrohm said. "I can work with that as long as I know where all the lines are drawn." He paused. "Tell the ships' captains that I want half of their stores."

"They will never agree," Ren replied.

"Tell them what the situation is here," Lindstrohm suggested. "And let them know that if I have an uprising here that I can't control, I'll blow those oil fields just the same."

Ren pursed his lips, obviously not happy.

"I'll trade them fuel for the food," Lindstrohm said. "They'll get bonuses."

"A cargo hold full of fuel isn't going to do a ship's crew any good when they're hungry."

"That's exactly what I'm thinking at this point," Lindstrohm said. "But I'm sure your captains laid on extra stores in case a siege situation they thought they could win arose. Clearing out their larders will serve two purposes. One, I'll have a few more days of food to spread out. And two, you people aren't going to be able to stay out in those waters as much as you want to.''

"No one is going to like this," Ren said.

"I don't give a fuck if they don't like it," Lindstrohm said. "All they have to do is figure it out and realize I'm the best offer they're going to get. Keep me in business, Ren, and I'll supply whatever fuel needs Qiang can ever have. I'm a good investment. Sell the captains on me."

"I'll try."

"Tell them to give up the stores," Lindstrohm suggested. "The amount of time they cut down on the news that I'm going to be doing business with Qiang will allow them to return for more supplies sooner. You don't need to camp out there. I cut a deal with you or I'm dead in the water here."

Ren quietly stared at him.

"Deal with me now," Lindstrohm said, "or die with me later. I'm sure the last thing you want to tell Qiang is that this deal just went to hell in a handcart because some people down here got hungry while you had a fleet of ships out there with food."

"That's not what's going on," Ren objected.

"If I was Qiang," Lindstrohm promised, "one of the first things I'd ask was what you could have done to alleviate the situation."

"The ships' stores—"

"Are fucking expendable where you're concerned," Lindstrohm said. "The oil we're bringing in isn't." He leaned back and let out a tense breath, feeling better and more in control after having said everything he had to say. He glanced at Narita.

She smiled slightly at him, a mere flickering of an amused expression, then she nodded.

"I think we're done here," Lindstrohm said. "I know I am. Get those ships' stores in by morning."

"At best," Ren said, looking away, "you're only buying

yourself a few more days before this crude empire of yours collapses under its own weight.''

"It's a few more days than I had when we first sat down," Lindstrohm said. "I'll take that."

"If Lord Qiang had known how things down here were—"

"He'd still have wanted the fucking oil." Lindstrohm glared at the Tong representatives. "Don't try to shit me about that. We both know the truth when it comes to that."

"Perhaps," Ren admitted. "But dealing with you now is going to be less pleasant than I'd hoped."

"If we both come out of this alive, let's just count our blessings and be done with it," Lindstrohm suggested. He leaned over and blew out the lantern, leaving the table an island mired in the shadows that filled the gaudy. "I expect to see those ships in the morning. No later than noon." He pushed up from the table and forced himself to walk out of the gaudy without turning back.

Vasquez walked at his side. "You did very good in there," she said when they were outside.

"Mebbe." Lindstrohm gazed at the night-dark street and the buildings around them that held pools of shadows. He hadn't forgotten that there were people in the ville who would kill him if they got the chance. Vasquez's personal escort flaring out around them was a grim reminder of that. "I'll believe it if those Tong ships show up tomorrow and start unloading on the docks."

"They will," Vasquez said. "They don't have a choice."

"Neither do we," Lindstrohm said angrily. He gazed at the ville around him. Nearly all of the streets in this area were picked clean, neatly arranged. A few shops had even opened up for trade to ship crews. Campecheville was showing signs of growth. "This is insane, Narita."

"What?"

"I've given these people homes and freedom, and I know they'll turn on me in a moment if they think it's in their best interests. I'm not just offering them their own lives—I'm offering them futures for their children. Children that they can live to see.''

''I know, Harry.'' Her tone was sympathetic.

Lindstrohm blew out his breath. Vasquez did know. And she'd told him that the people he'd imported wouldn't appreciate his efforts. He just hadn't believed her. Now, as he walked through the streets of the ville he'd built from his dreams and hard work, he felt eyes on him, watching his every move.

Chapter 23

"That's Lindstrohm. He's more or less the baron of Campecheville. Only he don't call hisself that."

Kane stood at the second-floor window of one of the temporary housing units that had been established in the structures behind the dockyards. Not all of the structures were completely habitable. Work crews had evidently removed debris from the rooms and cleaned them up to a degree, but repairs hadn't been made yet.

He watched Lindstrohm walk from the gaudy and continue down the street. The low, full moon painted long shadows against the cracked street. Kane nodded to the sec man that had pointed Lindstrohm out to him.

"In the morning," the sec man continued as he stood at Kane's side, "after breakfast, you'll be offered a list of jobs. Everybody in Campecheville works."

Kane nodded, still feeling the heat of the low-grade fever that filled him. The sec men had broken the new arrivals aboard *Jeweled Lady* into groups of ten, then took them to the barracks and started explaining the ville's expectations as well as what was offered.

It had taken hours to clear the sec posted in the harbor before they'd been allowed off the ship. An accounting had had to be made, and Blakeney's complaints had been listened to.

Fiddler's insistence that Kane had only acted in the best interests of all concerned—except for maybe Blakeney and his crew—had gone a long way to seeing them cleared. When the vote had been taken about whether to stay or go, Fiddler had opted to remain on *Jeweled Lady,* intending to go back to the Gulf coastal areas and establish the fourth Fiddlerville.

Kane wished the woman luck, and she'd told him that if he didn't find what he was looking for in Campecheville he should look her up. Kane hadn't commented on the offer. Fiddler stayed aboard ship with Blakeney and his crew while the cargo was off-loaded.

Work crews quickly repaired the superficial damage to *Jeweled Lady*'s sails. She was loaded with fuel drums to replace the food stores that had been taken off, then she was escorted out of the harbor by gunships.

"You got any special skills?" the burly sec man asked. He actually had a small note pad.

"Like what?" Grant asked.

"Machinery operator." The sec man shrugged. "Skilled labor. Something like that."

"Wags," Grant replied. "We've all got wag experience."

"Do repairs on them?" the sec man asked.

"Small stuff. If it's running, I can generally keep it running. If you're talking about a major overhaul, I'm not your man."

"Something's better than nothing," the sec man said, making notations. "You're Kane?"

"I'm Grant," Grant said, jerking a thumb at his friend. "He's Kane."

Kane hadn't seen any reason to sign up under an assumed name. It would have been a pain in the ass to keep up with. Unless they ran into someone from Cobaltville, it wouldn't be a problem. And if they did run into someone who remembered them from Cobaltville, an assumed name wouldn't offer much in the way of protection.

"You willing to work on the floating platforms?" the sec man asked.

"Sure," Kane answered. "Do you get more jack for working the platforms?"

"Some. Enough to make it worth your while if you decide you want to try it on."

"We start work in the morning?" Grant asked.

The sec man nodded. "If you ain't bleeding or injured, it all starts bright and early. When you get up, just follow the crowd that's up and moving. You get where they're going, that'll be breakfast."

"Hungry now," Domi commented.

Kane knew the albino was testing the water more than anything else. They'd eaten well aboard *Jeweled Lady* before the ship sailed an hour or so before dusk.

The sec man pointed to the water barrel in the community room. "Drink plenty of water. Fill up your belly and you'll keep just fine till morning."

"Got plenty food here?" Domi asked in a challenging voice.

The sec man looked only a little defensive. "We got plenty of food. You saw all that unloaded off that ship you come in."

"Thought that was going somewhere else," Domi persisted.

"Well, it's not now," the man said. He looked at Domi, then at Brigid. "There's extra work for women. If you want it. Seem to get more men down this way than women."

"What kind of work?" Brigid asked.

The sec man nodded at the window. "There's a gaudy across the street. And we got more—"

Even though he knew Domi's reaction was coming, the fever aching within Kane's skull slowed him somewhat. He reached for the albino's wrist as her knife flashed for the sec man's throat. The point hovered less than an inch from the sec man's throat.

The sec man dropped his hand to the blaster on his hip.

Grant covered the sec man's hand with his own, restraining the man's hand so the blaster couldn't be drawn. "No," Grant advised in his deep voice. After the sec man looked at him, he slowly released the trapped hand.

The sec man took his hand from the blaster. "Remember

me, you little bone-colored bitch, because if you try something like that again I'll chill you.''

Domi smiled sweetly at the sec man and slitted her eyes. ''I try again, I not have anyone there stop me.''

''Put us down for general cleanup,'' Kane said. ''If we change our minds, we'll let someone know.''

''Sure.'' The sec man made a notation and left.

Head spinning slowly but surely, Kane turned to glance back at the room. Bug-infested pallets and bedding covered the floor, and occupation seemed up to those who were daring. A half-dozen people were in the room: four adults and two children. Only one of the adults and a young child still nursing remained awake.

''What do you know about the food supply here?'' the thin woman with the nursing child asked. She appeared pale and sickly, and only made a halfhearted attempt to cover her breasts.

''Nothing,'' Brigid replied. ''We just know it's got to be hard to feed this many mouths.''

The woman glanced down at the child she held. ''There's more all the time, too. But I been noticing things since I've been here.''

''Things like what?'' Brigid asked.

''Like them taking food back off them two ships today,'' the woman replied, shifting the nursing child to her other breast. ''I've never see that happen before.''

''How long have you been here?''

''Nearly two years.''

''Has there ever been a food shortage?'' Brigid asked.

The woman shook her head. ''We work hard here, but we eat, and nobody bothers nobody else. Baron Lindstrohm won't stand for it.''

''You've met him?''

''No. Just seen him a few times, listened to him talk occasionally.''

''Then why wonder about the food?'' Kane asked.

The woman shrugged. ''There's just been some talk that

mebbe we don't have as much as we once did. And there's new people coming here all the time.'' She stared at the four of them. ''People like you folk what wasn't here when all the real work to clean this place was going on. Mebbe there's a few folks wondering if everybody should keep coming here.''

''Things have gotten worse over in Samariumville,'' Brigid said. ''Are you saying those people should stay there?''

''Not me.'' The woman stroked her child's hair. ''But mebbe there's some that feel those folks should find someplace else to go. This is our place. We cleaned it up and made it what it is. Ain't right somebody else should just up and come along and drink up the gravy of our hard work.''

''And if there's plenty of food for everybody?'' Brigid asked.

The woman shook her head. ''Won't be. There never is. I never been no place where food was always around. You had to chase after it. And if you lit in one spot and tried to grow your own, there'd be coldhearts and other folks by in a short time to come take if from you. Or die trying to get it.''

Kane retreated from the conversation. Just in the past few moments his fever had risen. His skin felt cold and clammy while he was burning up inside. He walked to the corner of the room nearest the window and moved the thin pallets on the floor, electing not to sleep on any of them.

He was well aware that the vermin crawling through the tangle of bedclothes could just as easily crawl across the floor to get him, but he felt a little better at putting the distance between them. He sat in the corner, putting his back to the two walls. He gazed out the window at the big silver moon hanging in the horizon.

Kane, Balam's voice called.

Blinking against the throbbing heat flooding his skull, Kane stared at the moon and tried to will the pain and the fever away. It didn't work. Perspiration covered his body, running down his cheeks to drip from his stubbled chin.

Brigid came to him and sat beside him. She glanced at him worriedly. ''Kane.''

"I'll be all right, Baptiste," Kane whispered. He breathed out constantly, striving for the control he needed. He flicked his glance at Grant. "We need to set up watches."

Grant nodded. "I'll take first up."

"Wake me," Kane said.

"I'll take third watch," Brigid said.

Domi yawned and stretched. "I don't mind all my sleep at one time." She smiled, then curled herself into a ball under the window on the bare floor.

Grant took up a position on the other side of the room, leaving the window on his left and the door on his right. He put his Copperhead across his knees.

Kane shifted against the wall, trying in vain to find a comfortable position. He didn't lie down because he knew his head would throb even worse if he did.

"Maybe we need to find that mat-trans unit tomorrow," Brigid suggested. "We could use it to jump to Cerberus redoubt. DeFore could find out what's wrong with you."

Kane nodded, not wanting to waste the strength to argue. He concentrated on the moon, amazed at the way that he could almost see a face in it.

"THE KING NEEDS YOU! Fight for the king! For Arthur!"

Kane opened his eyes and narrowly avoided a sword swinging straight for his face. He sidestepped, then raised his arm, not entirely surprised to see the sword he gripped himself. His blade flicked out quick as thought and crashed through his opponent's ribs below the small shield he carried.

The Roman soldier knew that his life had been spent and stumbled back, a look of anguished surprise on his face. He was at least thirty years old and had probably spent a lifetime in war. His face and limbs showed terrible scars from past wounds. He stumbled and went to one knee, allowing the man behind him to step forward.

Kane whirled, bringing his sword around to meet that of his newest opponent. The wet ground and loose leaves beneath his boots slipped, and he almost fell. The Roman soldier pressed on against him relentlessly, lifting and swinging the short gladius as if he could do it all day.

Armed with a sword and knife, Kane lifted a foot and drove it into the Roman's shield, connecting high on the shield and knocking it back into the man's face. Blood sprayed from a cut across the man's forehead, dripping down into his eyes and blinding him. Still, being Roman and trained by the harshest taskmasters in the world, he continued to battle.

Stepping in toward the man, Kane blocked the Roman's sword with his knife, then cut his head from his shoulders with the sword. The dead man stumbled back, then sat down slowly as if suddenly fatigued.

Kane took the moment's respite to gaze around at the battle. They were fighting deep in a forest that appeared familiar. Tall trees soared up toward the night sky. Normally battles weren't fought that late in the evening, but he remembered that the two groups had come up on each other unexpectedly.

Wagons filled with hay, bound for the king's stables, blazed now and provided uncertain light for the treacherous and uneven battlefield. The full moon hung above them, streaming down silver light that made the blood look black. Sparks flared when forged iron clashed against forged iron. Men cried out in pain and fear and anger amid the meaty smacks of weapons cleaving bodies, flesh against flesh, and the clangor of shields rattling against shields. Horses snorted and whinnied in the distance, and Kane knew there were those who observed the night's battle from a safe distance.

"For the king!" someone shouted again. "For King Arthur and Britain!"

Mind reeling, Kane remembered a little about the tales of King Arthur, the once and future king. There had been an old man in the Cobaltville Magistrate division that had possessed a fascination with the subject. And Lakesh's and Brigid's own research into different avenues had turned up more information regarding the myths and legends. Even reading up on the Celtic lore of Mother Fand and the Tuatha de Danaan had brought further information about King Arthur and his knights of the round table.

Kane knew of no reason why his dreams would take him to that time. But then, he hadn't known why he'd dreamed of Egypt, either.

He returned to the battle. While the Romans held the line they were so famous and feared for, the knights and warriors who served Arthur picked their battles. Maybe the stories that had been later written of them commented on the honor and bravery of the knights, but Kane saw little of that now. The men were scared, willing to kill anyone who tried to kill them.

The Roman soldier froze suddenly in front of Kane.

Warily, Kane turned, knowing that Balam had to have stopped time in the dream. "Balam."

"Here, Kane."

Following the direction of the voice, Kane gazed more deeply into the forest behind the battle. The camp women hid in the brush and trees there, their faces filled with fear. Those women hadn't been written about in any of the tales of Arthur, but Kane knew it was right that they were there.

When warriors weren't fighting for their lives, their thoughts turned instantly to sex and drink. All the large armies of those times, and even later, had women that were wives, as well as harlots, to follow them around. They looted the dead and took coin from the warriors for their services as cook, tailor or bedmate.

"What do you want, Balam?" Kane demanded. He held on to the bloody sword and knife in his hands, not knowing if they would have any effect on the Archon in this dream state.

"The ending is upon us, Kane," Balam said. "A time when things are won—or they are lost."

"What things?" Kane stepped in front of the robed figure.

With the moon burning down on him, Balam looked like a two-dimensional shadow cutout. "The manna machine. The one that I showed you in Egypt. The one that the Israelites used to feed themselves as they wandered toward their promised land.''

"It still exists?"

"Yes," Balam said. "It was lost to the Israelites. Even until skydark, those people never knew peace. They were always persecuted and destroyed. People who were their friends and allies one day could just as easily turn on them in the next.''

"That's the story of people everywhere," Kane argued.

"Enlil helped them get the manna machine," Balam said. "He whispered the secret into the ear of the right person, and eventually the secret of the machine reached Moses.''

"He stole it from the Egyptians.''

"That's right, Kane, and you were there.''

"Why?''

"So that you would have an understanding of what it was you were searching for, and how important it was. And still remains to be.''

"I'm not searching for anything," Kane objected.

"You're drawn to the manna machine," Balam said, "as the lady knew you would be.''

"What lady?" Annoyance filled Kane.

"Patience, Kane," Balam said. "All will be explained. Contacting you in this manner has been hard on both of us.''

"You've been causing the fever?''

"It's been the only way I could make your mind receptive to the contact I needed. And to take you back through the dream gates.''

"I want you out of my head, dammit," Kane said harshly.

"I promise you, Kane, I don't relish this contact, either. If anything, I find it more draining than you do. You feel ill, but I'm at death's door to make this happen while you're so far away.''

Kane strained to wake himself from the dream. He felt the heat of his body back in the room in Campecheville, felt the weight of Brigid's head on his shoulder and the slack weight of her that told him she was sleeping. He managed to blink his eyes open, and for a moment the darkened interior of the Campecheville sleeping quarters overlaid the forest.

"Don't, Kane," Balam said.

Struggling to get free of the dream or memory or whatever the hell it was, Kane concentrated on the view of the Campecheville sleeping quarters. They gradually become clearer and Balam's voice faded.

"Kane," Balam called, "if you do this, if you ignore this situation, you may be dooming your world."

"The Archons have already doomed it a few times," Kane said, halting his efforts for just a moment. "One more time won't hurt."

"If the manna machine is released," Balam said, "it may well be the end of everything. Think about it, Kane. If you can feed them, you can lead them. That's long been a king's or pharaoh's or president's axiom."

Kane stared at the Archon, wondering if Balam had lifted the thought from his own mind.

"The only reason that's been in your mind," Balam said, "is because you recognize the current situation you're in. You've seen the manna machine work before. Armies and empires have risen around the people who controlled it. If a man can feed people, he can lead them everywhere. That's what Harry Lindstrohm plans to do in Campecheville."

"The people here are trapped," Kane disagreed. "They're on the verge of being starved out. Lindstrohm has brought too many people into this ville to provide for them. Maybe he's got oil, but he lacks natural resources. People can live without fuel a lot longer than they can without food. All Wei Qiang has to do is starve him out."

"Lindstrohm will destroy the oil fields," Balam said.

"How do you know that?"

"Because the barons have a spy close to Lindstrohm. He has overheard Lindstrohm and Narita talking."

Kane wasn't surprised. The barons had become increasingly duplicitous as they'd realized they were going to have to fight for their own continued existence even between themselves. "How is Lindstrohm going to destroy the oil fields?"

"The oil fields are booby trapped."

Kane took in the information without saying anything. Fiddler had mentioned a similar story.

"From his command post there in Campcheville, Lindstrohm can destroy all of the drilling rigs. That destruction will set back possible advancement in this world for decades. When Lindstrohm first set up in the area, no one knew about the oil reserves there. He was able to erect the oil rigs in relative peace. Now that everyone knows the oil fields are there, everyone will fight over it. The force that eventually takes over Campecheville may lack the technical skills to keep the oil flowing."

"Lindstrohm has got trained crews manning those rigs," Kane pointed out.

"And several of them, if not all of them, will be destroyed if Lindstrohm chooses self-destruction. Simply taking over the operation may not be viable."

"The barons want the oil," Kane said.

"If they could get it," Balam agreed, "they would."

"They'll try."

"Eventually." Balam nodded. "But that would happen anyway. However, at the moment, the menace of the manna machine is the greatest thing facing us."

"Us?" Kane shook his head. "You must have a mouse in your pocket, Balam."

The Archon regarded Kane silently for a moment. "I've seen into your mind, Kane, and I've watched you in action. You may not see yourself as a savior for this world, but you have chosen to act in that role several times."

"Wrong. I've chosen to keep my skin intact."

"And you have just as easily risked your life to keep things balanced. You would not willingly let this world backslide again. Even in the past hundred years, there have been improvements in living conditions. Your own existence is as hopeful as...mine."

"We've got different ideas about things," Kane said. He was aware of the frozen tableau of warriors battling to their deaths around him. It made the dream seem even more surreal than ever.

"But we both want the same thing," Balam said, "the continued survival of this world. By seeking the manna machine, Lindstrohm threatens that."

"By feeding people?" Kane let loose his anger. "Dammit, Balam, there are people out there every day in the Outlands who kill each other over their next meal. In some places, the dead person *is* the next meal."

"Food chains are an important part of an ecosystem, Kane. Think beyond simply feeding people for a moment. If you give one people, or a culture, the ability to indiscriminately feed itself, their numbers are going to expand geometrically. And those numbers adversely affect everything around them."

Kane shook his head. "No."

"For the best continued growth of a species," Balam said, "there has to be a system of checks and balances. Enlil's machine circumvents all of those."

"Feeding people isn't wrong," Kane said. Images of emaciated villes filled with scabby children haunted him. Species survival included the ability to reproduce even if it meant the offspring were going to starve to death.

"Haven't you talked with Lakesh about the Heart of the World?" Balam asked quietly.

Kane didn't say anything. Not so long ago, when the barons had taken Lakesh captive, introduced him to the imperator, and returned his youth to him, they had all learned of the Heart of the World and the concept of the world soul.

"Before skydark," Balam said, "there were over six billion souls on this planet. The earth's ability to support those people, especially with the way they depleted natural resources and polluted their own environments, was seriously challenged. That way of life couldn't have gone on much longer. Advances in science and medicine passed the social developments of civilizations around the globe.'' He paused. ''It was only a matter of time until the world imploded.''

''That might not have happened,'' Kane argued, but his words lacked conviction.

''Yes,'' Balam said, ''it would have happened. There was only one other way for it all to end. Skydark pulled the plug on the overdevelopment of the human race. It was the only thing that could have been done.''

Kane looked at the warriors standing as frozen statues around him. War had always been a part of human life ever since the first man had picked up a rock and attacked another.

''Walk with me, Kane,'' Balam said, turning and passing back into the dark forest.

Kane turned and looked at the warriors.

''Don't worry about them,'' Balan said. ''Your part here is done. This battle will finish without you. I want to talk to you of the one still remaining before you.''

''I want out of this dream,'' Kane said defiantly.

''And if you get out of this dream now, Kane, what will you have learned?'' Balam asked. ''Is it enough to allow you to make a choice when the time comes?''

Acquiescing, Kane turned and followed Balam into the deepening forest. The shadows closed in over him.

Chapter 24

"In the beginning," Balam said as Kane fell into step at his side, "when the Annunaki first arrived on this planet, they found only protohumans. They quickly discovered that these protohumans couldn't do the things they needed them to do."

"They didn't make good slaves, you mean," Kane said sarcastically. As he walked, the forest faded out around him. Within three steps, he was walking above a field of stars.

"No," Balam agreed. "They didn't. And so the Annunaki caused the world-altering event that became known as the Flood. They wiped the slate clean and began again. Enlil wanted a more aggressive position to work from. He created the manna machine."

In another few steps, the stars disappeared and Kane was walking through the shifting sands of Egypt.

"Enlil gave the manna machine to the Egyptians," Balam continued. "But the pharaohs became less tractable as they began to consider themselves gods."

"So Enlil arranged for the manna machine to fall into the hands of the Israelites," Kane said.

"Yes." Balam nodded. The desert gave way to a wooded area. "The manna machine sustained the Israelites until they reached their promised land. But you must understand the manna machine, Kane."

"It makes food out of the air," Kane replied. "I know that."

"But do you understand the implications of that?" Balam asked. "If you give any species a seemingly unending supply of food, they will continue to breed. The numbers begin to increase exponentially. That was why Enlil took the manna machine from the Israelites after they'd secured their lives.''

"If the machine is gone—''

"It's not gone, Kane,'' Balam said. "A machine like that is not easy to destroy. Enlil broke the manna machine up into three pieces and divided them among the Israelites. When he'd first created this machine, and others like it—as did others among the Annunaki—he also linked guardians to the machine to serve as protectors of the devices.''

"Watchdogs,'' Kane said. He thought of the memories that sometimes came to him from other places and other times. In those instances, he hadn't remembered through dreams; they had been momentary separations from whatever reality he'd been enmeshed in at the time. "Am I one of those watchdogs?''

"No, Kane,'' Balam replied. "Harry Lindstrohm, known by a hundred other names throughout the ages, is one of those watchdogs. He already has two of the pieces of the manna machine.''

"Then what am I?'' Kane asked.

Balam shook his head. "I don't know, Kane. There is something special about you. Just as you were bound to the Chintamani Stone in some fashion, so you are bound to other things that take place here. And now you are bound to the manna machine.''

"Why?''

"Because of your promise to the lady,'' Balam replied.

"What lady?''

"The one who gave Arthur his sword.'' Balam gestured to the forest that suddenly took shape around them. "Once the three pieces of the manna machine were given into the care of families, Enlil traveled and involved himself in orchestrating the events of humankind. Eventually, he came here to Eire. You know the rest of that story.''

Kane nodded. He'd learned a lot about the background of the Archons and the alien threat when he'd met Mother Fand and the Tuatha de Danaan remnants.

"Over the years, the three pieces of the manna machine were lost. Humankind continued to wage war against itself. In Jerusalem, the topmost bowl of the three that makes up the manna machine added itself to yet another legend. It became known as the Holy Grail." Balam glanced at Kane. "You're familiar with the Holy Grail?"

"The cup Christ drank from at the Last Supper," Kane said. But he couldn't remember how he'd acquired that knowledge. It was suddenly just there with no accompanying source.

"The king, the one who later became known throughout all Britannica as Arthur, chose to seek out the Holy Grail," Balam continued. "He never knew it was once part of the manna machine, nor that it could be used to make sustenance from the very air itself."

"Then why did he seek it out?" Kane asked.

"For any number of reasons," Balam said. "You should know, for part of you was there."

Synaptic twitches suddenly flared through Kane's mind. Image after image, as quickly as a flickering light in a gaudy, followed in quick succession. He saw images of the man he'd known as liege and king at one point, bits and pieces of the battles they'd known together, the feasting celebration they'd had when the knight who later become known as Sir Gawain had returned to them with the Holy Grail and the subsequent ambush by the Roman soldiers that had only come about through the efforts of a betrayer among them.

"He wanted the Grail," Kane said softly, "so that the power could be used to defeat the invading army of Saxons and so that the peace he'd brought to this land would stand forever."

"The Grail, and the manna machine," Balam said, "has been used for many things throughout your history. Even apart, the three bowls that make up the machine contain a tremendous amount of power. Perhaps this king you knew sought only to do noble things with it."

"He was a good man," Kane stated in a hard voice, remembering the king.

Balam hesitated. "I'm sure he was." The Archon reached forward and pushed brush out of the way to reveal a small clearing ahead.

A circle of armored men surrounded another man on the ground.

The man on the ground glanced over at the new arrivals. He was dressed in armor, as well, but much of it had been taken from his upper body. Blood streamed from a wound on his back.

Nearby, another man heated irons in a campfire, holding them at the apex of the flames. Tears glistened down the man's cheeks.

"Ah, Merlin," the wounded man said in a weak, hoarse voice, "you've found Ka'in."

"Aye, my liege," Balam said.

Kane turned to Balam. "You were Merlin?"

"I am now," Balam said.

Kane knew the answer he'd been given was no answer at all, but before he could press the issue, the king called to him. "Ka'in."

Memory of the man's voice haunted Kane. Had he really spent time with the man in the past, or was the familiarity only part of the dream? He couldn't be certain. But he approached the man and dropped to his knees beside the king.

"Aye, my liege," Kane said. Unexpected emotion welled up in him, and unshed tears blurred his vision.

The king was handsome, his face pale in the dark night with the flickering light of the campfire playing over it. His eyes regarded Kane frankly, but there was effort apparent in his attempt to keep them focused. "I lie dying, Ka'in, my old friend."

"Not true, my liege," one of the knights said quickly. "Wilmot is now heating the irons so they may be used to cauterize that foul wound your nephew struck in the battle."

"It's too late," the king said. "I've near bled out." He

breathed deeply and raggedly. "I've little time left, and I've accepted that. As should you."

"No, my liege," the man said. "Not while a breath yet remains within me."

The king glanced up at Kane and held out his bloody hand. Kane clasped it in his own, feeling the chill already seeping into the man's body from the night and from his near death.

"I would have a boon from you, Ka'in," the king said.

"Anything, my liege," Kane replied, and he didn't know if the words were his or if they belonged to whomever he was supposed to be in the dream.

"You went with me as my second when I went to see the lady to get my sword," the king whispered. Pain racked his features, bringing beads of perspiration. "You heard me promise her the return of the Grail."

"Aye, my liege," Kane replied. An image of the sword thrust up from the stone in the middle of the lake filled his mind. In his mind, the woman stood beside the sword in the stone, dressed in a gossamer gown that left her lean and lusciously curved body all but naked even in the moonlight. Her hair was dark, and her eyes were deepest purple. He hadn't talked to her that night, believing her to be some fairy witch that would transform him into a toad at the slightest infraction. Now, however, he thought that his earlier fear had been foolish.

The king stared into Kane's eyes. "You were always the truest and fairest of my knights, Ka'in. See that even a dying man keeps his word to the lady."

"I will, my liege," Kane promised.

Without warning, the king and the knights disappeared, leaving Kane alone in the forest with Balam. Kane fought against the ache in his heart. Everything had been too real, just like the flashes of memory he sometimes had about Brigid and himself.

"Where did he go?" Kane demanded, turning to Balam.

"He's dead, Kane, a long time ago. But the quest he gave you, the boon he asked, still remains to be done."

"The chalice," Kane stated. "It's never been found?"

"Not until now," Balam said. "This evening a group of men found the wreck of a German submarine from World War II. They've journeyed back to Campecheville to tell Lindstrohm that it's been located."

"I don't understand," Kane said.

"Walk with me," Balam said.

Without arguing this time, Kane followed as the forest shifted effortlessly around them. In the next instant, Kane strode along the upper deck of an old German submarine. Water lapped at the sides only a few feet below. It was bright daylight now.

German soldiers in crisp uniforms surrounded them, standing stiffly at attention on the docks surrounding the submarine pen.

Kane automatically reached for the pistol holstered at his hip. Somewhere in there the sword had become his pistol.

"No, Kane," Balam said. "They can't see you. This is a memory of events you weren't present at in any incarnation or memory foisted on you by the Grail's power. I can show you this because of the link I have to the Grail."

Kane relaxed somewhat when he realized that the German soldiers had taken no notice of him. "What link do you have with the Grail?"

"I can sense where it is, Kane, because of the resonance I maintain through the hyperspatial mental energy link I've created with the Grail."

"How did you do that?"

"Once I knew the thing still existed," Balam said, "I searched for it."

"If you found the Grail, why didn't you take it?"

"I wasn't there," Balam said. "Not in physical form, anyway. I wouldn't have found it if I hadn't learned about it through the spy in Campecheville."

Kane stood on the topside of the German submarine and watched as supplies were loaded. A massive boom arm lowered a cargo net of crates to the submarine's deck just behind the stainless-steel antiaircraft gun in front of the conning tower.

"What are we doing here?" Kane asked.

"During World War II," Balam said, "Hitler ordered several religious items sought out and brought back to Germany."

"I'm familiar with that." Kane had brushed up against that fact a number of times through research done at Cerberus redoubt. They'd even found a Nazi stronghold down in Antarctica that had been set up after World War II.

"One of the items that the Nazis found was the chalice," Balam said. "On August 1, 1942, Ensign Henry C. White of Coast Guard Squadron 212 sank the U-166 twenty miles from the coast of Louisiana."

Kane blinked his eyes. When he opened them again, he stood over water.

"This is the Gulf of Mexico," Balam said. "This is where the U-166 went down over 250 years ago. Although several agencies searched for the submarine after the war, the U-166 was never found."

"But you know where it is," Kane said.

"Yes." Balam strode forward.

Trying to ignore the fact that he was walking across a deep ocean, Kane followed. Waves splashed over his boots, but they remained dry.

"The ocean kept the U-166 on its bed for over fifty years," Balam said. "Then skydark occurred. The disruptions to the planet and the underwater volcanoes during the nukecaust and afterward changed several of the current patterns of the oceans. Gradually, the U-166 was picked up again and began a new journey."

Kane watched as the sky darkened and filled with chem clouds. Years sped by in flickers of light. Ahead of them, the German sub suddenly roiled briefly to the surface, then sank again. Other shipwrecks surfaced briefly, some of them heading in the different cardinal points of the compass.

"Only thirty-seven years ago," Balam continued, "the U-166 left the sea."

Kane stared at the coast ahead of them in surprise. "That's Campecheville. Where it's going to be later."

"Almost," Balam agreed. "That is the Yucatán peninsula, where Campecheville will be located. But this is the north side of the coast."

Kane watched as the land suddenly shivered and shook.

"Earthquakes racked these lands, as well," Balam said. "They were aftershocks of other stresses created by past underwater volcanoes, and from the destruction of the Hawaiian Islands only a hundred years ago. Built as it is on a flat karst—a limestone foundation—the peninsula is honeycombed with natural wells and caves. Over two hundred miles of submerged caves were discovered there before skydark. In 1996, an underwater cave system was discovered near the ruins of Tulum that exceeded thirty-five miles. The earthquakes that rocked the Yucatán peninsula opened the tunnels up near Tulum."

Kane kept walking, watching as the mainland came close incredibly quickly. In seconds he was standing nearly forty feet above the turquoise sea crashing into the narrow, rocky beach below. He turned from the sea and stared at the ruins of white stone buildings that lay across the scarp.

With the sea behind him, rolling over the horizon, Kane studied the tall and thick walls that surrounded the ruins of the city on three sides. Jungle covered most of them now. It had been built as a port city, he knew immediately, and had been easily defensible in its day considering what the citizens had been up against. And they would have fought if attacked; there was no doubt of that. With the sea at their backs, there was nowhere to go.

Overseeing the scattering of small buildings was one large building that looked like a cross between a castle and a pyramid. It was blocky and edged, standing out in sharp relief against the blue sky.

"This is Tulum, Kane," Balam said. He looked weary, and

his voice definitely sounded weaker. "Beneath this city is the U-166. The underground river finally carried it into view today. Sec men have already traveled to meet with Lindstrohm. They may already be there in Campecheville." He turned and headed west, directly away from the sea and the tall building. He walked past a building built with pinkish stone and made all in rectangles. Stucco masks marked the corners of the building's facade.

Kane followed, awed by the sense of history that clung to the city.

The western wall had been torn apart by a massive tremor that had left a crack deep in the earth. Peering through the crack, Kane saw the caverns below.

"Kane," Balam's voice sounded strained. Pain showed on his face. "I can't stay any longer. You must get here and take the chalice. Return it to the lady. If Lindstrohm succeeds in reassembling Enlil's manna machine, we may all be lost. If Lindstrohm can feed them, he will draw an army to his cause, an army even greater than the ones the barons have been able to amass and control. Not everyone will flock to his banner, but enough will to overthrow the slight balance we now have against the barons."

"Why don't you do this yourself, Balam?" Kane asked.

"Because I can't," Balam replied. "Pay attention to the dreams you've had over the past two days. I've not put them there—I've only dredged them up to help you remember. Why else were you already headed in this direction?"

Kane wanted to mention the sudden unexpected appearance of the mat-trans unit going on-line had had a lot to do with it, but he couldn't. If Balam didn't know about the mat-trans unit, Kane wasn't about to educate him.

"You're linked to the chalice, Kane," Balam said. "And you're bound through the king by his promise to the lady. Trust that."

"What lady?" Kane demanded. "How do I find her?"

"The same way you found her with the king's sword,"
Balam said.

Before Kane could ask another question, the world exploded around him.

Chapter 25

Kane sucked in a sudden ragged breath and opened his eyes, not knowing whether he should feel relieved that he was still sitting against the wall in the housing building in Campecheville. It would have been better if he'd woken in Cerberus redoubt and discovered everything he'd experienced in the past couple days had all been a dream.

"Are you all right, Kane?" Brigid asked quietly. She pressed a hand against his forehead as if he were a child.

"I said I was all right, Baptiste," Kane growled irritably. He brushed her hand from his forehead and stood with effort. His bruised chest still pained him and caused only a little hesitation in movement.

"You're drenched with sweat," Brigid said, coming to her feet, as well. "I wouldn't call that—"

"The fever finally broke, Baptiste," Kane said. "That's all it is."

"You're sure? What about Balam?"

"I'm finished with him." Kane sorted through his gear, quickly arranging it, watching Grant working to get ready on the other side of the room. One of the things he liked about working with Grant was that when it came time to go, Grant didn't ask a lot of questions.

"What makes you sure you're through with Balam?" Brigid asked.

"Because he told me everything I need to know," Kane said. He hoisted his M-14 over his shoulder.

"How can you be sure Balam wasn't a figment of your imagination brought on by the fever?" Brigid asked.

Other people in the quarters snarled curses at them, demanding quiet so they could sleep. A child woke and started squalling.

Kane looked at the people in the room, knowing they'd all be hungry by morning. He felt suddenly guilty about what he was planning on doing. What he planned to do affected them all. But he saw the need for it. "Because he wasn't, Baptiste." He nodded at Domi and Grant, who were up and already moving. "Let's go. I'll explain along the way."

"BALAM COULD BE lying to you, Kane."

"Why would he do that, Baptiste?" Kane led the way through the shadowed streets of Campecheville. Lanterns burned in several windows and buildings along the way down to the docks. Despite the late hour, there were still a number of gaudies open and doing business. Music from instruments, mostly on key, spewed out into the streets, mixing with loud voices and raucous laughter.

"I don't know," Brigid answered. "Yet. But I've got the feeling that by the time we find out, it will be most likely too late to do anything about."

"This is the truth," Kane said stubbornly. "You didn't have those dreams when I did." He marked the leather goods shop at the corner of the next street and turned his steps downhill toward the docks. An earlier recon had revealed the location of the ville's motor pools. The one they were headed for now was one of the smallest, and hopefully the least guarded.

"Those dreams could have been nothing more than the fever," Brigid said.

Kane stayed within the shadows, waiting until a trio of hard-faced men wearing stained clothes from working on the tugs coming in from the offshore drilling rigs passed by. The men looked at them, obviously taking notice of Brigid's sex. Kane had dropped his hand to the trigger action on the M-14 meaningfully.

"Then let's go out there and see, Baptiste," Kane said. "It's little more than two hundred miles. Even in rough country, we can be there by morning." He'd checked the map he'd gotten from Blakeney's captain's quarters. It was a preskydark courtesy map from a car-rental agency.

"Once we steal one of Lindstrohm's wags," Brigid said, "we're not exactly going to be welcome company when we return."

"Only if they figure out who took the wag, Baptiste. If we don't turn up anything in Tulum, we'll leave the wag outside the site, wait till another ship unloads passengers and slip back in during the night. Mebbe Lindstrohm keeps a list of the people who come into the ville, but he can't keep up with them after they're here."

"He may be better than you think he is."

Kane shook his head. "It's just as likely we'll miss the revolt the people throw when they find out the food bank has gone bust. There'll be even more confusion then. Once we find the mat-trans unit on this island, we won't have to stick around for that." He peered ahead, spotting the first of the guards standing watch over the building that housed the motor pool.

"I don't know if I buy into Balam's reasoning to get rid of the manna machine," Brigid said. "If there was a means of feeding all the people on this planet, that would be a good thing."

"Depends on who's handling the machine," Kane said. Shadows moved between the ships down in the harbor. Lanterns hung from the various vessels, and lines slapped against the masts as the wind blew. "Mebbe we could turn it over to Lakesh." He kept moving forward.

"No," Brigid said a moment later. "Lakesh could be a problem."

"Do you want to take on the responsibility of feeding the world?" Kane asked. "Of course, that's assuming someone who figures he's more fair than you are about it doesn't come along and blow your brains out."

"Okay," Brigid conceded. "If this machine can do what you claim it can, having it around is a problem."

"Exactly, Baptiste." But Kane's primary motivation was his promise to the brave king he might have fought with all those years ago.

"I want to think about this a little more before we make a decision," Brigid said.

"Let's just find out if the damn sub is there first," Kane suggested. "If it turns out that I've just gone insane, worrying about what to do with the chalice is just going to be wasted effort." He fell into position against the side of the building, then looked back at Grant and Domi, watching them disappear from sight behind the building.

He waited, watching the ships out in the harbor for a moment, listening to the voices of the people yelling to one another across the water. Catcalls screamed up from the darkness. Evidently, the gaudy sluts had just hit the beach.

After a slow thirty-count, Kane turned and walked toward the front of the building, drawing the instant attention of the sec man stationed there.

"YOU THINK Kane's gone stupe?"

Pausing at the back door to the motor-pool building, Grant watched Domi pick up a brick from a small pile nearby. "What the hell kind of question is that?" he whispered.

Domi hefted her weapon. "You heard story he told us. Make sense to you?"

"The Chintamani Stone didn't make sense to me," Grant argued quietly. "But we were there. I saw those other worlds. If the Archon, Annunaki or the Tuatha de Danaan can create gateways to other worlds and all the other shit I've seen them do, I'm not going to worry about believing the Holy Grail is aboard a German submarine that just washed up in an underground river on the other side of this peninsula." He slid his thick-bladed combat knife into the crack between the door and the jamb, then lifted it to clear the bar that had locked it from inside.

Light from inside poured out into the small alley behind the building.

Grant made sure he stayed out of the light from the lantern as he stepped into the building. He kept the Copperhead loose and ready in his hands. The way they'd planned it was for no one to get permanently hurt, but things didn't always go according to plans. Being shot up some, Grant knew from experience, was preferable to being dead.

"Beside," Grant whispered as they walked into the small building, "if we get to Tulum and there's no German submarine there, we'll know to bag Kane and get him back to DeFore. And hope that she can save whatever's left of him."

Even though his tone was joking, Grant was concerned about his friend. During the time they'd left Cobaltville, things had been decidedly different. He'd seen things, and learned of things, that he'd never even imagined before. And he knew Balam had found a way in the past to communicate telepathically with Kane.

This wasn't much of a stretch.

"I think it's stupe," Domi whispered back.

Grant ran an appraising eye over the three wags that were inside the building. Two of them were jeeps, which were good enough vehicles on their own, but they didn't have much storage space for extra fuel, which he knew they'd want to take along.

The third vehicle showed more promise. In its day, the wag had been a full-size sport utility vehicle. It showed obvious signs of care despite the pitted exterior and dented quarter panels. The rear right quarter panel was missing entirely, exposing the tire and strut. There were two bucket seats in front, and two bench seats behind, followed by a large transport area.

Looking at the front of the building, Grant saw Kane talking to the sec man there.

Another sec man sat to Grant's immediate right, on the other side of Domi. The man sat slack-jawed in a folding chair, obviously expecting no trouble at all, and watched the conversation between Kane and the other sec man.

As quiet as a shadow, Domi strode across the building just

out of the sec man's sight. At the last minute, some primitive instinct had to have warned the man. He turned and looked up, but it was too late to stop the albino. Domi smashed the brick against his head, and Grant heard the hollow thud all the way across the building.

The noise drew the other sec man's attention, and he turned from Kane.

Uncoiling like a spring, Kane stepped into a short jab that caught the sec man behind the ear and dropped him unconscious to the ground.

"Well," Kane said, grabbing the unconscious sec man by the back of the shirt and pulling him out of sight inside the building, "that went well enough."

Domi dropped her rock onto the man's chest at her feet.

"Is he still breathing?" Grant asked. With the situation the way it was in Campecheville, there were no clearly defined opposing forces, though everyone there would turn on them if they knew what Kane was contemplating.

"Yes," Domi said. She sounded disappointed.

Grant checked the big wag and found the keys in the ignition, which hadn't really been a problem because he could have gotten it started. Then he walked to the rear of the wag.

Kane appeared still somewhat unsteady on his feet, but he immediately started loading extra jerricans of fuel into the back of the big wag. Brigid helped him, adding coils of rope because facing the unexpected made rope of any kind worth its weight in gold at times.

Grant turned his attention to the wag's rubber. All the tires appeared to be in good shape. He looked around the building and found three more tires that looked as if they would fit the vehicle.

Sometime during the wag's history, someone had welded on supports for four spare parts on the sides and two across the engine hood. Grant put two of the spares on the hood, then two others on the passenger side of the wag, thinking they'd probably be safe there.

In less than three minutes, they rolled out of the building

with Grant behind the wheel. Kane took the passenger seat with Brigid and Domi riding behind.

Grant kept the speed low as they passed through Campecheville. There was little traffic, and he wondered if they were going to draw the wrong kind of attention. Another thought struck him. "Should have got some supplies. No telling what we'll find out there in that jungle. If anything."

"Already taken care of," Domi said. "While you loaded tires, I scavenged." She opened up a paper bag to show self-heats and fresh fruit that had evidently arrived on *Jeweled Lady*. She passed out apples.

Grant drove cautiously, sweeping the street, feeling tight in his own skin because he was certain they were going to be stopped at any second. He noticed Kane's head tracking something out in the harbor. "What is it?"

Kane answered without turning. "Caught a reflection from out on the Tong ship. Looked like someone with a pair of binoculars. A double reflection, like both lenses of binoculars."

"Probably was." Grant grinned. "As much as they want to do business together, I bet Lindstrohm and Wei Qiang's people spy on each other all the time."

A few minutes later, Grant followed the northbound highway out of Campecheville and drove into the night-black jungle.

"I NEVER SEEN a boat like this, Baron Lindstrohm. It was all enclosed like. From what I could see of it, it weren't nothing but a long cylinder shape. Looks old, mebbe from even way back before skydark."

The description set off a wave of excitement that thrilled through Lindstrohm. The man had just arrived at the ville and was excited about his own find.

Although Lindstrohm hadn't known about the U-166 at the time he'd sent out the scouting teams, the man had obviously known that the German submarine would be important. He'd come knocking on Lindstrohm's door, certain that he wouldn't be waking anyone.

Without another word, Lindstrohm crossed the office in the Spanish fort and took down one of the books he'd been studying about German submersibles since the previous night. He flipped the book open to a picture of one of the deadly sea machines. "Is that it?"

Narita Vasquez stood in the doorway leading to the rooms he kept as his personal quarters. She'd dressed in less time than it had taken him. Both of them were still covered in perspiration from making love only moments ago.

The man looked at the picture. He was dressed in clothing that was near rags and had a beard that hadn't had attention for weeks. Standing downwind of the man wasn't pleasant, either.

Since setting up the operation in Campecheville, Lindstrohm had ordered regular sweeps to be made across the peninsula. The landmass was a little more than two hundred miles across from east to west, and the patrols ranged as far as Guatemala to the south. Even before the nukecaust, few roads had traversed the peninsula. Maintaining sec stations along them and the coastal areas hadn't proved difficult, but Lindstrohm had felt they were necessary.

"If that's not the boat we found," the man declared confidently, "it's just like it."

"Did you see any numbers on the boat?" Lindstrohm asked.

The man shrugged. "Don't know from numbers. Never learned my readin' and writin'."

Lindstrohm smiled at his own question. "Don't worry about it, Tillman. You did good. How many fucking German World War II submarines could suddenly show up down here?"

Tillman blinked, obviously thinking the question was meant for him. "I don't know. We only seen the one."

Despite the nervous energy filling him, Lindstrohm laughed. "One is plenty. I want to go out there."

Tillman nodded. "Want me to meet you here in the morning?"

"No," Lindstrohm said. "I want to go right now."

"Now?" Tillman looked stunned. "I just got into the ville. Ain't even blew the froth off a glass of beer. I figured you'd want to know about the boat. I thought mebbe I could—"

"I'll have a case of beer brought for you," Lindstrohm said. "We're leaving now."

"I can give you directions to that underground cave system," Tillman offered. "Hell, you can't get lost out there. Once you find Tulum, ain't no way you can go wrong."

"I'm not taking the chance," Lindstrohm said with a hint of steel in his voice. "This is triple important to me."

"Sure," Tillman said, wiping wearily at his grimy beard.

"Narita," Lindstrohm said as he headed through the door to the hallway, "we'll need some of your people along on this expedition."

"They will be," the woman promised.

Lindstrohm barely managed to keep his stride from lengthening into a run by the time he reached street level. Vasquez trailed at his side like a shadow, only a step behind him. Tillman clumped down the stone steps.

In minutes, the sec men standing guard around the Spanish fort got a convoy together. Five wags filled with armed men rolled to a stop in front of the fort. Their headlights cut swaths through the dark night and attracted the attention of several people still out on the streets.

"There are some people," Vasquez pointed out quietly, "who are going to wonder if you're running out on them." She clambered up into the lead wag behind Lindstrohm.

Lindstrohm shook his head. "If I was running out on them, I'd head out in a ship, not a wag. Hell, there's nothing in the interior of this peninsula. Or even farther south. They know that from personal experience or from stories other people have told."

"They're not going to be thinking logically," Vasquez

said. "Stories are already circulating that there isn't enough food in the ville."

The wag driver got under way at Lindstrohm's impatient command.

"When they see the Tong ships arrive in the morning," Lindstrohm said, "they'll think differently."

"Yeah," Vasquez agreed. "Probably that you've run out just ahead of the Tong invasion."

Lindstrohm shook his head and looked at the woman. "Narita, the final piece of that machine is aboard the U-166. I dreamed it. And now that submarine is here. After 250 years and the near death of a world. This is fate. It's meant to be. By tomorrow afternoon, when we get back with the final piece from Tulum, we'll never have to worry about food again. Nor will anyone else who throws in with us." He smiled at her and touched her face gently with the back of his hand. "Trust me."

She captured his hand in both of hers. "I do," she said as softly as she could over the grumble of the wag's transmission.

Then Lindstrohm realized she had let him touch her without flinching. Memory of the night when he'd hit her was still there, but she'd let him touch her anyway. He turned back to look at the street as the driver wound down toward the docks where the food was kept under lock and key. He noticed all the activity going on at one of the auxiliary wag stations.

"Wait," Lindstrohm ordered when a sec man helped another man stagger from the building. Anger blazed up in Lindstrohm. The last thing he needed this night was men getting drunk at their posts. He slid from the wag and walked over to the two men.

The man supporting the other man straightened. "Baron Lindstrohm," he said.

"What the hell is going on here?" Lindstrohm demanded.

"Got broke into," the sec man said. "I was making my rounds and found these two bastards all stove up."

Moonlight glinted from the bloody wound on the other man's head.

"Was it the Tong?" Lindstrohm asked. The pilots had left earlier, presumably to fly Ren back to the other ships and let them know what had to be done. He didn't know what Ren or his people hoped to prove by breaking into a wag station, but nothing else made sense.

"No," the wounded man said. "It was a group from *Jeweled Lady*."

"Blakeney's ship?" Narita asked.

"Yeah," the man answered. "Remembered because I went aboard and helped sort out all the new arrivals. They came from Fiddlerville. One step ahead of the Samariumville Magistrates." He took a deep breath and touched his wounded head gingerly. "You could tell all four of them were hardcases just from looking at 'em. Especially that albino bitch that hit me. But I wouldn't have figured them for stealing a wag. Where the hell would they go out here?"

Lindstrohm dismissed the matter from his mind. Thieves were dealt with harshly in Campecheville. Gulls and pelicans picked their bones clean down on the south beaches. "Tell your sec boss I want those people hunted down, and I want an example made of them." He started to clamber back into the wag.

"I will," the other man said. "With that albino bitch along with them, they ain't gonna be hard to find. I'll ask some of the other recent arrivals about him."

"I remember his name," the wounded man said. "I was on *Jeweled Lady* when Radkey took down his name for the record. Called himself Kane. Other man was—"

Lindstrohm stepped down to the ground again and turned to face the sec men. "His name was Ka'in?"

The sec man took a step back. "Yeah. Only he didn't say it like that."

For a moment, the world swirled around Lindstrohm. Ka'in was here. How was that possible? Then he wanted to laugh in self-mockery. Now that the final piece of the manna machine had shown up, how could he not *expect* Ka'in to be present?

"Which way did they go?" Lindstrohm asked.

"North," the sec man said. "I saw the wag drive out of the station, but I didn't think anything of it at the time."

Lindstrohm started back for the wag, feeling the anxiety level rise in him. North led not only to the coastline, but also to the remnants of Highway 180, which was still the best way to get across the peninsula. "Let's go," he commanded gruffly, hauling himself into the seat. He turned back to the sec men that had stumbled from the wag station. "How long ago did this happen?"

"About an hour. Near as I can figure."

An hour, Lindstrohm thought. He turned to Tillman. "How long does it take to get to Tulum?"

The man shrugged. "Seven, eight hours. If they drive straight through. Probably be slowed up some since it's night. Gets dangerous out there in the jungle when it's dark, and them roads ain't worth shit. Barely better than going cross-country."

"You know the way to get cross-country?" Lindstrohm said, feeling trapped by circumstances. And by Ka'in, he had to admit to himself.

Tillman shook his head. "You don't fucking want to do that. Especially at night. You'll bust an axle, mebbe break your damn neck. Best way to go is the highway, and even then you're going to have to be bastard careful."

Lindstrohm nodded, chafing under the delays.

"It's only a head start," Vasquez said from behind Lindstrohm. "Even if they get the chalice, where are they going to go with it?"

Lindstrohm didn't answer. Ka'in was more dangerous than that, and more clever. He didn't know how to convince her of that until she'd seen him in action.

"We need to get supplies," Vasquez said. "Extra tires and gasoline. There's nothing on that side of the peninsula except the Caribbean."

Reluctantly, Lindstrohm agreed. Even now Ka'in was gaining precious minutes.

"You don't have to worry about them getting to the boat too easy," Tillman said. "It's pretty deep in the water in them underground caves, and there's seven men guarding it. All of them men are coldhearts. Anybody they don't recognize is going to get chilled. More'n likely, you'll get to drive up there and identify their bodies." Tillman took another drink of his beer. "That is, if identifying them is possible afterward."

KANE PULLED the wag over to the side of the winding road leading up to the promontory where the map indicated the Mayan ruins of Tulum would be. The sun was already coming up, staring at him straight in the face because of the easterly heading they'd been on for the past two hours.

Grant had driven most of the night while Kane slept, totally fatigued. When he woke, for the first time in days there'd been none of the fever that had usually racked his sleep.

Grant woke as soon as Kane slowed and went off-road.

"Problem?" Grant growled, taking up the Copperhead from between his knees and peering at the dense jungle that surrounded them.

"I thought it would be better if we walked the last mile or so," Kane said. "The wag engine will give us away if we don't." He switched off the rumbling engine when he was certain they were far enough into the jungle to hide the wag.

Brigid and Domi woke easily.

"Are we there?" the archivist asked, looking at the dense canopy overhead.

"Near enough," Kane said. He and Grant used their combat knives to hack branches from nearby trees, then used the branches to cover the wag. He took a hundred-foot coil of rope from the wag and slung it over a shoulder.

Brigid passed out self-heats from the supplies they'd taken back in Campecheville, and they started the last leg of the trek to Tulum. The old road they followed had a gradual incline.

Even though it was early morning, just past gray dawn, the day was already starting to heat up. Due to the heat and the humidity, Kane was drenched in sweat within minutes.

They buried their self-heat containers along the side of the road as they finished them. It wasn't a meal—more of a necessity. At least Kane didn't feel hollow inside after he'd finished. He couldn't even taste what it was.

Less than ten minutes from where they'd left the wag, they walked through the first of the low-slung arches in the three-sided wall that guarded Tulum. Trees had overgrown the wall and threaded through some of the stones, loosening the mortar and causing them to tumble to the ground.

"Place must have been an invader's nightmare at some time," Grant said. "If they'd kept the trees and brush back from the walls, it wouldn't have been easy to get over. Seem kind of short, though."

"Mayan people," Brigid said, "weren't much above four feet in height."

"Okay," Grant admitted, "that would have been a hell of a climb for those guys." He reached out and touched a cracked stone. His fingers dug at something lodged there, finally freeing it. He tossed it to Kane. "Not all the battles here were fought that long ago."

Kane caught the object, feeling the weight immediately. He looked at it, finding that it was a flattened bullet. "It's still a port area. Mebbe pirates put up here from time to time, or people that Lindstrohm has problems with." He stepped through the gate, watching the terrain ahead for any signs of movement.

"Is this what you saw in your dream, Kane?" Brigid asked quietly as they continued into the ancient ville's interior.

"Yeah," Kane said, staring up at the massive white stone building perched at the cliff's edge. He couldn't see the Caribbean Sea on the other side of the cliff because of the angle, but he had no doubt that it was there. The sky continued to lighten, going from steel-gray with hints of color from chem clouds in the distance to robin's-egg blue.

"Tulum," Brigid said, "wasn't the original name of this place. Scholars think it was first called Zama, which was a bastardization of the word *zamal*, which meant 'morning' in the Mayan tongue."

Kane nodded at the rising morning sun. "The name would have fit."

"*Tulum* means 'fence' or 'wall,'" Brigid said. "Tulum was also used as a base of operations during the Mayan War for the Castes, which lasted from 1847 to 1901."

"That bullet was from more recent than that," Kane said, striding along the wall to his left to keep some cover handy.

"Less than ten percent of the people lived within the walls," Brigid said. "The houses outside the walls were huts, not made of stones. That's why they're not here now."

"This place was ten times bigger than what it looks like now?" Grant asked.

"Yes," Brigid replied. "Only the wealthy, the religious and the important people lived within the walls. Tulum was the only Mayan city on a coastline in the empire."

"Do trading here?" Domi asked.

"That's the general consensus," Brigid agreed. "Cozumel is an island farther east. They believed other trading took place there, as well. But the tall building there, called the Castillo—or Castle—might have been used as a lighthouse to light the way for ships."

"Anybody live here now?" Domi asked.

Kane shook his head. "I don't think so." He glanced down at the wag tracks marring the soft, rocky ground. "But there have been people through here lately."

They passed across from the rectangular building with the pinkish stones and the faces at the corners.

"Did you see the faces on the building, Kane?" Brigid asked quietly.

"Yeah, Baptiste. They were in the dream, too."

"They look like representations of Chaac, the Mayan god of rain, or Itzamna, the creator and life-giver."

"They kind of look like a lizard, too," Grant said. "Reminds me of our old friend Enlil."

Kane continued leading them through the dense growth that had invaded the courtyard. They passed a rectangular hole in the ground overgrown with weeds that Brigid said had been a gravesite. Only a little farther on, he saw the ragged hole in the north wall where the earthquake had torn through the karst. Limestone rocks lurched up from the ground, looking like fangs left by an unknown beast in the flesh of the earth.

As he went more deeply into the jungle, Kane noted the worn trail between trees. He stayed off the trail and went slowly through the brush so he wouldn't be easily seen. Grant, Domi and Brigid followed his example.

Only a few feet farther on, less than thirty yards from the broken section of the north wall, Kane heard the unmistakable sound of running water. He waved the others down, wondering if their slight movement across the terrain could have been picked up by the cavern he'd seen below in the dream. A covey of brightly colored birds launched themselves from the treetops around the split in the earth and took wing.

Kane waited quietly, feeling almost smothered in the heat and the brush. Occasional gusts of cooler air drifted in from the cliff behind the tall, white building, but the prevailing winds were from the wrong direction.

After a few minutes passed without incident, Kane looked at Grant and nodded. Grant nodded back. Cautiously, Kane crept forward, keeping his rifle tucked in close to his body. He halted at the edge of the hole opening to the cavern system below and peered down, careful to keep his head in line with overhanging brush so he would be limned against the dawn sky.

A surprising amount of light filled the cavern below, rendering the huge chamber a little lighter than twilight. Kane guessed that the white limestone reflected most of the light that entered the caverns, trapping the majority of the light and making the most of it.

The German submarine lay in the deepest part of the water

that partially filled the cavern system. It heeled over on its starboard side against a shelf of rock that rose out of the underground water. Seven armed men sat on the rock shelf around a campfire. The smoke chimneyed up and flowed along the cavern roof, heading away from the opening where Kane was and going farther down the tunnel. Kane assumed the smoke was following the wind passing through the tunnel, evidently coming out somewhere on the other end. The water below was crystal and placid. Even from thirty feet up, Kane saw multicolored fish swimming lazily through the water.

Open wooden crates, warped wood showing obvious signs that they'd been underwater for some time, sat in piles around the men on the rock shelf. Not much had apparently been worth salvaging.

But somewhere down there was the chalice.

Kane drew back, keeping the sun from casting his shadow down across the crystal-clear water below. He waved to Grant, drawing him close.

"I count seven men," Kane whispered, sliding the rope coil from his shoulder. "But I don't figure they'll give up whatever they've found easily."

"We can chill them," Grant suggested.

Kane shook his head. The men were like any of the others in Campecheville, just trying to stay alive. "They haven't done anything to us."

"That all changes after the first shot," Grant replied evenly. "Unless you just want to walk away from this."

"No," Kane said. "I can't."

"If we announce ourselves, we give away the advantage of surprise."

"I know, but I can't do it any other way. Not and keep it clean."

Grant nodded. "We'll do it your way. Whichever way it goes, we'll handle it."

Kane crawled back to the hole in the ground. Then he raised his voice. "You men down there!"

Instantly, the seven men took cover behind the stalagmites

thrust up from the rocky shelf, as well as the water-warped crates.

"Who the hell are you?" one of them demanded.

"It's not important," Kane replied.

"What do you want?"

"The submarine," Kane answered. "You people get clear and we'll let you go."

"Fuck you!" the man yelled back. "We already declared salvage rights to this son of a bitch!"

Grant glanced at Kane. "Ain't nothing left to do but take this one the hard way. Unless you want to walk away."

Kane considered that option only briefly. The dreams and Balam's information had left him little choice in the matter. Before he could say anything, a humming drone echoed through the air above. He glanced up.

A crimson-lacquered air wag shot by overhead, the wings tilting slowly as the pilot scouted the ground.

"Wei Qiang's people," Grant said. "They're taking a hand in this."

"Why?" Kane mused.

"They spy on everybody," Grant replied as the air wag heeled around out over the sea to the east. "Mebbe they already knew about Lindstrohm's hunt for the chalice."

"But why come here now?"

"Mebbe they found out about us leaving," Grant said.

Kane turned that over in his mind for a moment, then shook his head. "They followed Lindstrohm. He must be somewhere behind us." He turned and gazed back to the west, the way the road lay that had led up to Tulum.

"That means we got two groups bearing down on us," Grant said. "Getting on toward a one-percenter here."

Kane watched the plane circle around and head back to the west.

Abruptly, machine-gun fire sounded in the distance, echoing over the hills. The little crimson air wag turned away, skirting a section of the jungle.

"We could go back," Grant said. "There's a good chance

we can get around Lindstrohm's people in that jungle. Or just hide out until they're gone.''

"Not without the chalice," Kane said. He grabbed the coil of rope and started tying it around his feet. "If Balam is right about that being part of the manna machine, I can't allow it to stay here." But there was more, he knew, although he didn't tell Grant. There was also the promise he'd made to the dying king, and to the lady. Maybe he would tell Grant at a later time, but he wasn't going to say it now. "Secure the line to the tree."

"You're going to rappel down into that cave?" Grant asked in disbelief.

"You saw the ropes alongside the cave opening," Kane said. "That's a steep grade. If we try to go down that way, they're going to pick us off." He finished tying a quick-release knot that held his booted feet together. "Drop me halfway to the water."

"And how far is that?"

"Twenty, twenty-five feet should do it." Kane pulled himself to the edge of the opening. "I'll need to use your Copperhead."

Grant tossed over the weapon.

Kane sat up, peering briefly down into the cavern below and hoping that the sides were as straight as he thought they were. Otherwise the cavern walls were going to beat the hell out of him. He held the Copperhead in one arm, checked the magazine and accepted the bandolier of spares that Grant handed across. He snapped the security strap on the .45 at his hip.

Grant finished hauling the other end of the rope around a nearby tree, making certain he could control the rope easily. "I've got you secured."

The sound of wag engines in the distance came closer.

Kane glanced west again and spotted dust plumes rising from the trail above the jungle canopy. "We're not going to have much time to pull this off."

"Less, if you keep talking," Grant told him.

"If it comes to it," Kane advised, "leave me below and get clear."

"If I have to," Grant agreed.

Without another word, Kane placed his back to the opening to the cavern and toppled inward, falling like a rock.

The gunners below started shooting at once.

Chapter 26

"Wei Qiang is trying to fuck us over," Harry Lindstrohm declared angrily as he stood in the wag's rear deck and swung the .50-caliber machine gun around to track the crimson air wag cleaving through the air to the south. The rounds thundered through the machine gun, sending spent cartridges into the brass catcher.

None of the rounds appeared to touch the air wag, and it continued on its way serenely through the blue, cloudless sky.

"Son of a bitch!" Lindstrohm roared. He released the machine-gun trigger and slapped the weapon angrily.

"Mebbe they're only watching," Narita Vasquez suggested.

Lindstrohm remained standing, watching as the air wag disappeared in the distance. "This might not be the first pass through for those air wags. They could have already spotted Tulum. Wei Qiang's people, Ren or one of the other Tong commanders could already be en route."

"Then we'll deal with them," Vasquez stated calmly. "If they think they can take us here, they've made a fatal mistake."

Lindstrohm didn't say anything. He shifted his weight unconsciously as the wag rumbled over the uneven road.

"The gates are too narrow to get a wag through," Tillman said from the rear seat next to Vasquez.

"Not for long," Lindstrohm said. They hadn't seen the wag that Ka'in had taken, and he couldn't help hoping that the man had gone another way and encountered more trouble than they'd had while trying to make up lost time.

The driver halted a hundred yards from the entrance to the ruins.

"Johnson," Lindstrohm ordered, "make me a door." He swiveled the machine gun around to cover the entrance. Other men in the rest of the wags did the same.

One of the men from another wag ran forward and pushed a plas-ex satchel charge on either side of the entrance. He trotted back to the wag.

"Ready," Johnson called.

Lindstrohm gazed back to the west, the way the air wag had disappeared, and saw it appearing again on the horizon. There was also a smudge of dust clouds hanging over the jungle canopy. He had no doubt that the Tong had managed to put together a ground-assault team, as well.

"Bastards," he snarled to himself. This far out from the bay, there was no way to set off the radio signal that would destroy the floating oilrigs. But the last laugh would be on them if he didn't make it back. If he wasn't back in twenty-four hours, the timer was set to automatically send the signal.

"Baron," Johnson prompted.

"Do it," Lindstrohm ordered.

KANE FELL, keeping his legs loose as the bullets from his opponents chopped the air around him. His eyes raked the upside-down view of the cavern to orient himself.

He kept his body loose, hoping not to get hurt in any way when he reached the end of the rope around his ankles. He glimpsed the dizzying array of stalactites and stalagmites swirling around him, the crystal-clear water below him, which looked like *up* in his present frame of reference.

The men on the rocky shelf scrambled to new positions.

If Grant hadn't been busy manning the rope, Kane knew he could have picked off two or three of the men guarding the submarine while they were in motion.

Then the rope drew tight around Kane's ankles. Grant handled the rope expertly, working it so the drag didn't stop suddenly and take a chance on yanking Kane's legs out of the sockets or whipping his back.

As he slowed to a halt, hanging at least forty feet down from the cavern roof and now another thirty feet above the underground lake, Kane let the Copperhead fall into position at the end of one arm, then secured it with the other.

He fired controlled 3-round bursts, catching two men in the center of the bodies with not even a heartbeat between the two actions. Their bodies spun to a halt on the rocky shelf. Bats suddenly fluttered from among the stalactites, their dawn slumber disturbed by the riot of noise.

Bullets from the sec men's weapons scoured sparks from the cavern roof.

Kane drew a bead on a man behind one of the warped wooden crates. His line of fire ripped splinters from the fragile wood, then he adjusted and targeted the sec man's head, which erupted in a rush of ruby blood and gray-pink brain matter.

Three, Kane told himself, keeping track. His thoughts swung constantly to the location of the final piece of the manna machine. This was the chalice, the part the king had promised the lady in exchange for the luck and aid she'd given him during the years.

Kane scattered more shots among the surviving sec men, driving them to cover and keeping them stirred up as he swung at the end of the rope. His motion through the air made it more difficult for him to acquire targets, but the surprise maneuver had netted him three confirmed kills.

He roared through the rest of the clip, blazing rounds across the rocky shelf and aiming at the cavern wall just behind one of the men taking cover behind a crate.

The bullets ricocheted from the limestone wall. Not all of them struck their target, but enough of them hit the man that they slapped him to the ground. He lay twitching, dark red blood suddenly staining the limestone.

Then the Copperhead blew empty, and the sudden silence of the roaring automatic weapon was at once noticeable.

The three survivors took heart in Kane's apparent helplessness while dangling at the end of the rope. They stood and took more deliberate aim at him.

Kane transferred the assault rifle to his left hand. He bent at the waist with effort, having to overcome the weight of his upper body, as well as gravity, and grabbed the loose rope he'd left in the knot. "Clear!" he shouted.

"Clear!" Grant responded immediately.

Kane yanked the rope, loosing the knot. He plummeted toward the crystal-clear water below, angling his body so he'd go deep. If he remained near the top, the three survivors would shoot him easily.

Then he hit the water, finding it only slightly chilly. It closed over him, drowning out the sharp staccato reports of his opponents' weapons as they searched for him. Bullets zipped through the water, leaving visible contrails thanks to the light coming from the hole in the earth above.

Kane swam, knowing the gunners could easily see him.

THE EXPLOSION THAT BROKE through the western wall of Tulum caught Brigid Baptiste off guard. She'd been intently watching the sky, spotting the crimson air wag in the distance as it came back around.

As the blast filled the air with broken rock and flying debris, Brigid dived to the ground behind a line of boulders. Rocks shattered against the boulder with sharp cracks, and smaller rocks rained down around her like grapeshot from a cannon.

Domi cursed, her words unrecognizable but the tone unmistakable.

Lifting her head from the ground, covered with dirt and fine debris, Brigid looked back at the western wall. A huge hole had been blown through the stone bulwark. Dust swirled in the opening, obscuring it for a moment, but there was no mistaking the wag that suddenly roared through the gap in the wall.

The vehicle jumped and jerked as it rolled over huge chunks of stone and mortar.

Domi reacted instantly, lifting her .357 Magnum blaster in a two-handed grip. She fired as quickly as she could, aiming at the driver's side of the wag. The windshield glass chipped, showing holes as the bullets punched through. One of the trees in front of Domi took two direct hits, leaving white pulpy scars in their wake.

The wag rolled to one side and slammed into a tree, coming to a reluctant stop.

Brigid recognized Harry Lindstrohm pushing himself up on the rear deck of the wag. The man fit himself behind a .50-caliber machine gun and started raking the jungle with heavy fire.

Other wags roared through the opening in the wall and spread out.

Brigid's immediate guess was that at least forty men were aboard the wags. The rising dust cloud skimming along in the valley that held the road leading to Tulum told her that even more were on the way.

She turned to Grant and yelled at him.

"I see them," Grant growled, eyes raking the situation. "Well, it's a damn fact that we're not going back the way we got here."

Brigid glanced at the yawning mouth of the cavern near Grant's position. "From what Kane said that Balam told him, there's another opening in that cavern system."

"That's a hot zone down there right now," Grant said.

Brigid look back at the advancing line of men. "It might be safer there than here."

Without warning, the first crimson-lacquered Tong air wag was joined by a second. Both of them streaked toward the inner courtyard of the ruins, locking into an attack path.

KANE SWAM underwater as long as he could. By the time he surfaced, his lungs begging for air, bright pinwheels spun in his vision. He came up behind the bulk of the listing submarine, using it as cover from the hostile guns on the rocky shelf.

"Fucker's behind the boat!" one of the men yelled.

Running footsteps spanged off the limestone, echoing within the cavern. But that sound was partially masked by the roar of the explosion from above.

Kane kept himself focused with difficulty. Evidently, Lindstrohm and his squads had been closer than any of them thought. He crowded up against the submarine, working hard to tread water in his boots and clothing. He slipped a magazine from the bandolier Grant had given him and rammed it home into the Copperhead.

Three men—at least, he reminded himself, because that had been how many he'd been able to visually confirm—still remained in the cavern with him. His bruised chest hurt as he breathed, and the air inside the cavern seemed thick, hard to get into his lungs.

Bats fluttered against the cavern roof, darting in between the stalactites and shadows where the natural light didn't touch even after being reflected from the limestone surfaces. Kane knew none of his opponents could hide up in the stalactites, but the movement kept pinging his point man's radar.

"Did we get him?" another man yelled.

"We fuckin' filled the air with rounds," the first man said. "If we didn't get him, the fucker's got all the luck a man would ever need."

The statement wasn't true, Kane knew. None of the shooters had tried to lead his plummet into the water. They'd all shot where he'd been, and even at the distance and factoring in the speed of the rounds, he hadn't been there when the bullets had arrived. He'd counted on that for survival. A scared man always tried to catch up, never taking a split second and working ahead of a situation.

"Cover the ends of the boat," a man yelled. "Bastard will probably try to come around if he's still alive."

Kane felt something bump into his left leg at mid calf and jerked in the water, thudding up against the submarine. He glanced down, his hand already streaking for the combat knife in his boot.

A fish as long as his arm looked up at him briefly, then turned and darted away, disappearing in the crystal-clear water.

Kane forced himself to breathe out. Machine-gun fire echoed into the cavern from the battlefield above. Brigid, Domi and Grant were seriously overmatched.

"He's still over there," a man said. "I heard him."

"Gonzo, climb on top of that fucking boat and see if you can get a bead on that bastard."

"Fuck you," another man said. "I ain't climbing up there."

"It's the high ground, you fuck. You'll get him for sure."

"*You* get him then," the man replied.

Kane spotted movement at the forward end of the submarine. He lifted the Copperhead, letting the water drain from the muzzle so he could fire without worrying that it would jam.

A small outboard drifted into view. A rope tied it to the prow of the submarine. The gentle current that swept through the water trapped in the cavern system had pulled the outboard around the front of the sub. No one was aboard it.

"Stupe bastard probably drowned," one of the men said. "That's why we ain't seen him no more. Musta hit his head on a rock when he went into the water."

"That water's over a hundred feet deep."

"Fuck it. Mebbe he was so weighted down he just didn't come up again."

Kane tried to figure out where the three men were from the sound of their voices, but it was almost impossible in the rolling echoes of the cavern. He took a few deep breaths to charge his lungs, then took a final breath and submerged.

The water was so clear that even in the half-light he had no problem seeing the bottom below. White powdery sand caught the light there, as well, illuminating the lower reaches of the water. He didn't know if it was really a hundred feet deep; the refraction of the water made it impossible to guess, but he supposed it was possible. The size of the caverns was impressive as hell.

The water didn't carry the salt of the ocean, either. It was pure and clean, but had smelled strongly of minerals when Kane had been on the surface. He kept his eyes open in it easily. He swam to the bottom of the submarine, feeling the pressure tighten in his ears and bruised chest, knowing he was going deeper than he realized to get around the German vessel.

He trailed his free hand above him, following the curvature of the submarine's outer hull. He didn't see any real signs of damage aboard the boat and guessed that whatever damage had been inflicted had popped open seams that had let the sea in and dragged it to the bottom 250 fifty years ago. The vessel was surprisingly intact for having shifted around in the sea for all that time.

His lungs near bursting again, not able to get fully acclimated to the humid air trapped in the cavern, Kane felt relieved when he finally reached the apex of the hull and started up again. The submarine lay next to the outcrop the men had camped on. Less than six feet separated it from the outcrop's edge.

Kane swam up, already tracking the movement of two men in front of him. While swimming, he pulled the Copperhead over his shoulder, leaving the muzzle pointed down. With the angle involved in shooting up, he knew he might not be able to get the barrel clear of water in time to use it. He fisted the .45 at his hip.

He came up out of the water quietly, hardly making any

noise that could be heard over the crash of gunfire and explosions coming from overhead. The first of the men was only ten feet away, standing behind the cover of a stack of crates that contained machinery parts.

The preternatural senses of a predator had to have warned the sec man, because his head swiveled around toward Kane. "He's over here!" the sec man squalled. "The fucker's over here!" He tried to bring his assault rifle around, tightening his finger on the trigger.

A line of jacketed rounds struck sparks from the submarine, closing in on Kane's position.

Kane raised the .45 clear of the water, tilting it quickly to drain the water from the barrel, then hoped all of it had spilled free as he dropped the sights over the center of the sec man's chest. Kane squeezed the trigger three times in quick succession, riding out the recoil each time and keeping on target.

The heavy .45-caliber rounds smashed into the man's chest and drove him backward from cover. Blood suddenly masked his lower face, coming from his ruined lungs as his heart pushed the crimson fluid through his system. He stumbled backward and tripped over the ring of rocks that had been set up around the campfire. A silver bowl containing some kind of fish stew shot out of the fire and overturned nearby. Stew mixed with spattered bat guano, creating a mosaic across the rocky limestone ledge.

Kane heaved himself from the water, staying in a low crouch that nearly blinded him with pain from his bruised chest. He kept the .45 loose and ready before him, following his line of sight with the weapon just like he'd been taught back in the Cobaltville Magistrate division.

Another man at the other end of the ledge peered over the barrel of his weapon at Kane.

Without hesitation, Kane snapped off two rounds, knowing there was no way to avoid the sec man's aim. It boiled down to who killed whom first. One of the .45 rounds missed the man, but the second crashed through his skull and knocked him down.

A line of bullets smashed into the cavern roof as the dead man fell backward. A half-dozen chunks of bats splatted onto the rocky ledge and the submarine.

The man lying in the fire continued to struggle weakly for a moment. He lacked the strength to raise his weapon. The stink of his burning hair and flesh filled the cavern.

Kane put a mercy round between the man's pain-filled eyes. The corpse dropped back into the fire and continued to cook.

The third man stepped out from behind a jagged section of the cavern wall at the back of the rocky ledge that had provided an inspired hiding place. He brought up the shotgun he carried and locked it into his shoulder.

Kane took one step to the right, toward the back of the ledge, and threw himself into the air, knowing he'd never avoid the shotgun's discharge by trying to run.

The sec man was practiced at his killing craft. He kept the shotgun blast low, toward the center of where Kane's body had been. Most men would have been caught flatfooted by the deadly swath that ripped through the air. Only Kane wasn't there when the double-aught discharge arrived, and it ripped through the side of a waterlogged crate.

Still in the air, arcing his body, hoping to land somewhere near his feet instead of on his head as he flipped, Kane pointed the .45 at the sec man and squeezed off the last two rounds in the pistol. He'd tried to keep both shots onto the center of the man's chest, trusting the knockdown power of the .45 round to at least keep him in the game and provide him a chance to recover after hitting the ground.

Neither round hit the sec man's chest. One struck the man in the left shoulder, spinning him and knocking him a foot to the right. It was a combination of skill and luck that put the second round through his throat, ripping it out in a crimson spray that painted the cavern wall beside him.

Kane slammed against the ground, landing on his back and

not even coming close to landing on his feet. The impact drove the wind from his lungs and almost sucked away his conscious mind. His bruised chest felt as if it were covered in red-hot brands.

It took two attempts to get to his feet. He shucked the empty magazine from the .45, pushed a fresh one into place, then holstered it and took up the Copperhead. A brief recon of the rocky ledge assured him that no one remained in the cavern.

Kane turned his attention toward the gaping hole in the cavern roof. "Grant!" But his voice was lost in the sudden hammering of explosives. Rock broke free of the cavern roof on the other side of the hole. He raised his voice again. "Grant!"

LINDSTROHM TOOK COVER as the Tong air wags continued their bombing run across the ruins.

The two pilots had obviously worked together before, because their movements were fluid and certain. They fired the twin machine guns mounted on the front of the small air wags and strafed the ground while the passengers dropped impact-triggered bombs over the side.

"Ren and the others must have seen us leaving Campecheville," Vasquez said over the roar of the bombs and the 7.62 mm machine-gun fire hammering into the jungle and ground. "They decided it would be better to take you out here, away from the ville, than try to deal with you there. Probably have the ville under a full-scale invasion right now."

Lindstrohm knew her assessment was likely correct. Even if the Tong couldn't take the ville by force, it wouldn't take long for them to starve everyone out. Dark rage filled him, and he desperately hoped that the sec teams he had in place in Campecheville could hold out long enough for the preset timers to run their course and explode the bombs aboard the oil rigs.

He ducked his head as one of the impact bombs landed less

than thirty feet away. The ground vomited up, sailing high into the air and crashing back down a few heartbeats later. He was pelted with dirt and rock, some of the chunks large enough to leave fist-size bruises. Blood streaked his face from a cut on his scalp.

Lindstrohm's thoughts raged around Ka'in. Every time in the past he had failed at getting the manna machine because of something Ka'in had done. Sometimes they'd worked together to free the chalice from enemy hands, as they had when they'd acted as agents for the Celtic king on behalf of the Tuatha de Danaan. They'd recovered the chalice then and returned it to the king. Lindstrohm had returned the device under protest because he didn't want to confront Ka'in, but he'd set up their betrayal to the Romans. He just hadn't counted on getting killed as part of the bargain.

Machine-gun fire from one of the wags pursued the air wags. The gunner was even getting closer, starting to lead his target, when the air wags returned. The 7.62 mm machine guns chewed through the jungle and across the ground, leaving small craters in their wake, and clouds of dust and debris rose from the earth.

The gunner in the wag stayed with his target, scoring on the lead air wag. Smoke belched from the front of the air wag, then flames flickered to life. The air wag's twin machine guns chopped into the wag and the gunner, jerking him like a puppet at the end of its strings. Then the air wag passenger tossed an impact bomb over the side that scored a direct hit.

The wag erupted in a *whoosh* of flames.

The air wag streaming smoke and fire, tried to recover, but was visibly slowed by the damage it had taken. Before it could gain altitude, the landing gear snagged in a cluster of treetops. The air wag stopped suddenly and flipped, pancaking into the trees and breaking into pieces like a child's toy.

The other air wag lifted, having no choice but to leave his wingman.

But Lindstrohm knew the pilot hadn't abandoned the battlefield when it started climbing again and coming back around in a looping circle.

In almost the same instant, wags poured through the yawning gap that had been created by Lindstrohm's munitions man. All of them carried Tong hatchet men. Two of the wags were fast-attack vehicles similar to Sandcats that Lindstrohm hadn't seen before. Besides having a .50-caliber machine gun, the wags also sported a 75 mm cannon as part of the armament.

As Lindstrohm watched, the lead wag turned its long gun on a pair of wags parked under nearby trees. The wag crews scattered immediately while the drivers tried desperately to clear the area.

"Bastards had the war wags already put ashore somewhere outside Campecheville," Vasquez said. "We missed that."

Lindstrohm cursed. He'd guessed about the extra ships, since Ren's vessel hadn't had any severe problems with pirates. The only reason pirates wouldn't have attacked would have been if the force was too large or too well protected with on-board artillery. Evidently the ships from the Western Isles had possessed both. "Didn't expect those fuckers to be so bold."

"They want the oil fields," Vasquez said. "And they don't want to have to deal with anyone else."

Glancing back at the opening in the cavern, Lindstrohm said, "The U-166 is down there, Narita." He glanced at her desperately. "We can still make this work. Those three people up there must be part of Ka'in's group. He hasn't left yet."

The war wag's main gun belched flame, and the scream of the shell filled the air for one instant before the resulting explosion deafened everyone. Shattered trees toppled, bringing down still other trees and brush, as well as men who hadn't cleared the area quickly enough.

The sound of the main battle gun echoed over the bowl-shaped depression that Tulum occupied on the karst above the Caribbean Sea.

"Tillman!" Lindstrohm shouted.

The man looked over from where he was hiding behind a boulder a few feet away.

"You said the caverns had another opening," Lindstrohm reminded.

"Yeah. About thirty miles away. There's at least one boat down there. Tied off at the submarine. At least, it was there when I left."

Another salvo of cannon rounds spewed from the long guns aboard the war wags. Thunder rolled over the immediate area, then dirt and debris filled the air as more trees shivered and fell. Flames raced across the canopy of the trees from the air wag that had been shot down, bleeding black smoke up into the blue sky.

"The caverns are our only way out," Lindstrohm told Vasquez. "Order your men to charge that area."

She hesitated only a moment, staring at the area near the opening in the earth. Then she raised her voice and yelled orders.

Lindstrohm led the charge, pushing himself up from the ground and racing forward. Some of Vasquez's sec men passed him, spraying the area around the cavern mouth with autofire.

A black man leaned around a tree with an M-14 in his hands. Coolly, he shot into the approaching sec men, picking off targets as if he had all day to do it.

An albino rose from hiding, grens in both hands, and flung them at the advancing sec men.

"Gren!" a man yelled, diving to cover.

But there was no time. The albino girl had obviously pulled the pins and counted down part of the time. The grens exploded while they were still in the air. It was a dicey move, because she could have been caught up in the twin blasts, as well. Instead, she vanished from sight just as Lindstrohm threw himself down.

The grens exploded, one only a short time after the other. One of them was an antipersonnel munition that threw out shot in all directions and ripped men unlucky enough to get caught up in the blast to bloody caricatures of anything human. The other gren was a smoker that unleashed white tear gas that filled the area and stayed put because the breeze was nonexistent.

The three people near the cavern's mouth got to their feet again. The white-haired albino threw herself into the cavern opening as if she were diving from a cliff. The black man offered covering fire as the woman with red-gold hair started for the opening.

Filled with desperation, certain that Ka'in was again about to put the manna machine part from his grasp, Lindstrohm shouted, "No!" and ran toward the woman.

"Harry!" Vasquez shouted, breaking cover and bringing up her CAR-15. "Dammit, that was stupe!"

The black man didn't hesitate as Lindstrohm charged across the distance. The M-14 rose swiftly and surely to his shoulder, and Lindstrohm could almost feel the crosshairs on him. Lindstrohm fired his handblaster instinctively, but knew none of his rounds even came close to their target. He ached, waiting for the bullet that would surely kill him even as he drove his feet hard across the uneven, rocky ground. He held his breath, but the tear gas was already burning his eyes and nose.

Vasquez's CAR-15 blasted behind Lindstrohm, and the black man spun away.

The woman with red-gold hair tried to bring up her weapon. Not daring to slow down, Lindstrohm threw himself at the woman, watching as the assault rifle in her hands came up. He caught her quickly enough, though, that the rifle was trapped between their bodies when he slammed into her.

Lindstrohm's forward momentum carried them both over the edge of the yawning cavern mouth. He spotted the albino hitting the crystal-clear water below them as they dropped.

KANE WATCHED as Domi hit the lake cleanly, then plunged beneath the surface. Then he watched anxiously as Brigid came spilling over the side of the cavern mouth with a man wrapped around her. They fell to the underground lake, and there wasn't a damn thing Kane could do except watch helplessly.

Then some kind of explosive round landed near the open mouth of the cavern. The edge around the opening crumbled, spilling huge rocks from the cavern roof. If Brigid survived the plummet to the hard, unforgiving surface of the lake, Kane knew there was a good chance some of the falling debris might kill her.

Domi's head popped up above the surface nearly to the submarine's side by the time Brigid and the man hit the water.

Kane ran across the rocky ledge and leaped onto the listing submarine. It was the highest vantage point possible. His footsteps sounded hollow, letting him know the vessel was no longer filled with water. He trotted to the stern of the submarine, boots rasping against the pitted surface, and peered down into the water.

More debris rained down from above, creating dozens of ripples and impact areas. Brigid and the man who'd been holding her had disappeared.

Grant leaped through the yawning opening above and dropped in a clean dive, but Kane could tell by the way the other man had hit that he was hurting.

Domi reached the rocky ledge and pulled herself up, filling her hands with her blaster as other sec men threw themselves into the cavern.

"Tongs," Domi explained. "They attack Lindstrohm."

Kane nodded. Attacking Lindstrohm while he was away from Campecheville and couldn't trigger the self-destruction among the oil rigs was only good strategy, something he would have done himself. He peered into the lake, looking for some sign of Brigid.

An instant later, her red-gold hair caught his eye as she surfaced fifty yards out. She brushed water from her face and started to swim, but before she could move, an arm snaked around her neck from behind.

Lindstrohm surfaced behind Brigid, holding her hostage with a knife at her throat. His wet hair matted to his head and he grinned malevolently at Kane. His eyes held mad cunning.

"I'll chill her, Ka'in," Lindstrohm threatened over the roar of explosions that echoed in the cavern. The knife glinted at Brigid's throat, fisted tightly in his hand. "You know I will."

Grant came up only a few yards away, then glanced around and spotted Lindstrohm holding Brigid. Other heads popped up quickly after that, all of them belonging to Lindstrohm's sec men.

Rocks and debris continued falling into the underground lake from the cavern mouth above. More fractures showed in the cavern rooftop and walls, and Kane felt certain the whole place was about to come down as the Tong shelling above remained constant.

"I know you will," Kane said. Half-buried dreams and memories of other atrocities Lindstrohm had engineered over a score of lifetimes pushed at Kane's mind. Maybe in this life he'd professed good intentions about Campecheville, but Kane couldn't forget the things the man had done in the past. Lindstrohm, under another name, had been responsible for the death of the king who had served the lady.

"Where's the final piece, Ka'in?" Lindstrohm demanded. Water lapped up to his nose, causing him to splutter. Treading water while holding on to Brigid for cover was demanding. Brigid kept sinking into the lake and having to fight her way clear, as well.

"I don't know," Kane replied. "I haven't had time to look."

"Find it," Lindstrohm suggested. "Mebbe I'll let her live."

"If you don't let her live," Kane promised in a cold voice, "you'll die next." He swept the lake with his gaze, discovering that eleven sec men had survived the plunge from the cavern opening. And there was the woman that had been with Lindstrohm back in Campecheville—Narita the Bleeder.

"Get the chalice, Ka'in," Lindstrohm ordered in a belligerent voice.

Kane turned, knowing the sec men were going to head for the outcrop and clamber to shore. The sounds of the battle above continued. Small-arms fire punctuated the barrage of big guns. More rock and debris tumbled from the cavern roof.

Searching quickly, Kane looked through all the crates that had been opened on the rocky ledge. Most of what had been taken had been ruined by the centuries of lying at the bottom of the ocean. There were also spare assault rifles and a couple of RPG-7 rocket launchers.

Nothing looked like the bowl he remembered from the dreams.

Then Kane remembered the fish stew the men had been cooking over the campfire when he'd arrived. In disbelief, he walked over to the dead man still being burned in the campfire. Flames clung to the man, burning his clothes off and sizzling the fat from his flesh. The stench of burning hair filled Kane's nose.

He walked past the dead man and knelt to pick up the bowl that had held the fish stew. He turned just as the first of the sec men reached the rocky ledge and pulled themselves up. They stayed back from Kane.

Holding the Copperhead in one hand and the chalice in the other, Kane turned toward Lindstrohm, who remained floating behind Brigid. Kane noted in grim satisfaction that Domi had hauled herself up onto the submarine and had taken a position behind the conning tower.

The albino thumbed fresh cartridges into her blaster and kept a wary eye on the sec men occupying the other end of the rocky ledge from Kane. So far, none of them seemed really intent on encroaching on Kane's space.

Grant crawled up onto the submarine, as well, and took up

a position beside Domi. Blood streamed from a wound in his upper left arm.

"You okay?" Kane asked.

"Been better," Grant growled, adding another stripper clip to the M-14.

"The Tong?" Kane asked.

Grant shook his head. "No going back that way."

Kane nodded toward the front of the sub, knowing Grant would spot the motorboat tethered there.

Grant nodded, indicating that he'd already noticed it.

"Ka'in," Lindstrohm said.

Kane lifted the silvery bowl into view. When he'd looked at it earlier, he hadn't noticed the fine webwork of circuitry printed into it. Perhaps other cultures, thousands of years in the past, had believed the circuits were only a design affected by the maker.

"That's the chalice," Lindstrohm said.

"Yeah," Kane replied. "You killed the king for it."

A small smile played on Lindstrohm's lips. "You remember that from all those years ago?"

"He was a good man," Kane answered. "He deserved a lot more than the betrayal you showed him."

"He was a fool," Lindstrohm said. "He was going to give that back to the lady."

"What lady?" Narita Vasquez asked suspiciously. She stood at the forefront of the men, both hands extended with pistols filling them.

Kane ignored her.

"That chalice is pure power, Kane," Lindstrohm said.

"If you can feed them, you can lead them," Kane quoted.

"You remember," Lindstrohm said, smiling.

"Can't forget," Kane replied. "A lot of people have died while you've tried to put your hands on the chalice and its other component parts."

"They had to die," Lindstrohm said. "You know that I was linked to that device, don't you?"

Kane said nothing.

"I finally saw that in my dream," Lindstrohm went on. "Enlil was afraid the manna machine would fall into the wrong hands. He marked me through genetics, as well as pre-programmed memories. The manna machine is mine by rights." He treaded water with greater vigor, coming out slightly from behind Brigid.

Vasquez pointed a handblaster at Kane. "Give him the chalice. And throw down your weapons." She brimmed over with hostility.

Kane looked at her. "No," he replied calmly. "I'm not giving up my weapons. They're the only things keeping us even."

Narita Vasquez stood silently for only a moment, then she smiled slightly. "You're going to get somebody chilled."

"Once we start," Kane promised, "there's going to be a long line."

Vasquez pointed her pistol at Kane's head. "Do you think you can get that assault rifle up before I blow your brains out?"

"Mebbe," Kane replied. "But if I don't take you out, they will." He nodded at Domi and Grant, who held their weapons trained on her.

Vasquez laughed. "You're going to get everybody chilled."

"If it comes to it," Kane said agreeably, "I'll settle for that. How do you want to play this out?"

"Leave him alone," Lindstrohm said. "All we want is the chalice, Narita. They can walk out of here." He paused. "If that's what Ka'in really chooses to do."

"And if he doesn't?" Vasquez asked.

"Chill him," Lindstrohm said, "then I'll chill this woman."

"Okay," Vasquez said.

"Did you hear what I said, Kane?" Lindstrohm asked.

"I heard," Kane said. He was aware of a lull in the action

aboveground, saw shadows shifting around the yawning mouth of the cavern. Tong hatchet men lined up around the opening, evidently triumphant over the forces Lindstrohm had brought.

"Give me the damn chalice," Lindstrohm ordered. He yanked Brigid's hair and pulled her head back, exposing her throat to his keen blade.

Without a word, knowing the scenario was playing out to a deadly close, Kane flung his arm out, throwing the chalice in Lindstrohm's direction. The silvery metal bowl spun through the air, catching glints of light.

Using the motion of the chalice flying through the air, Kane brought the Copperhead to his shoulder and sighted deliberately. The chalice was still in the air when he took up the trigger slack and squeezed on through.

Lindstrohm's eyes were locked on the silver chalice as it flashed through the air.

Kane felt the Copperhead buck against his shoulder and saw flesh fly in a bloody eruption from the side of Lindstrohm's head: he'd missed hitting the man flush. Still, the impact of the bullet drove Lindstrohm backward and broke his hold on Brigid.

Brigid wasted no time in swimming toward the submarine.

Kane swung back to his left, keeping the Copperhead up and at the ready. Before he could fire again, two bullets smashed into his side with stunning force. Knocked off balance and the wind driven out of him, Kane fell back heavily to the ground. For a brief moment, he wondered if one of the bullets had found his heart, then he rolled over and opened fire, joining the firepower Grant and Domi were unleashing.

The ranks of the sec men dwindled quickly. Most of them were unwilling to fight standing toe-to-toe. They broke and ran, and Kane swept the Copperhead's deadly swath over them. The bullets chewed into the sec men, sending them tumbling, knocking down men who'd suddenly decided to stand and fight.

Either Grant or Domi put a round into Vasquez's face, exploding it into bloody ruin. She sat down heavily on the floor, a look of surprise on her features until it was covered by blood.

In the next instant, the cavern filled with the bull roar of a .50-caliber machine gun.

Glancing up, gathering his feet under him, Kane saw that the Tong hatchet men had maneuvered one of the wags around to take advantage of a full-size .50-caliber machine gun. The tracer rounds sizzled when they hit the water and threw up two-foot-high geysers.

Brigid came up next to the submarine, gasping for breath.

"Baptiste," Kane called.

"What?" she gasped.

"Get the outboard." Kane tossed the Copperhead toward Grant, then ran for the water's edge. The wounds in his side burned like hell, but they weren't terribly debilitating. He dived into the water, ignoring the floating dead men who had fallen from above and hadn't remained in one piece.

The salt water burned Kane's gunshot wounds and stung his eyes when he went under, and his bruised chest screamed as he swam as hard as he could. He threw his arms forward, cleaving into the water and pulling himself forward. He glanced up, seeing the silvery chalice floating on the water right side up, riding out the ripples that crossed the surface of the underground lake.

"Kane," Grant called. "What the hell are you doing?"

Kane kept swimming, knowing he couldn't have explained the need that pushed him toward the device Enlil had given the pharaohs thousands of years ago. The manna machine was directly linked to the Gaia force that filled the world, and the king Kane had fought with had given his promise to the lady. But Grant wouldn't have understood any of that.

Bullets from the Tong machine guns slapped the water around Kane as he swam. He glanced back as he stroked again, spotting Brigid aboard the outboard boat pulling at the engine. He barely heard the blat of the engine starting.

Then he reached out and seized the chalice as it floated on the water. The metal felt cold and hard in his grip. He treaded water for a moment, taking a deep breath, then turned to swim toward the outboard.

Domi had already climbed aboard the small boat with Brigid, but Grant stood on the submarine with a rocket-launcher tube over his shoulder. The Tong machine-gun fire reached fever pitch, burning down into the lake.

"Fire in the hole!" Grant yelled.

Kane swam for the outboard, sucking in air now, his lungs burning from exertion and his chest throbbing. Swimming with the chalice was difficult because it slapped and pushed against the water every other stroke. He was grimly aware of the rocket leaving the tube over Grant's shoulder.

Mesmerized, Kane stopped in the water to turn and watch the rocket streak across the distance toward the opening in the cavern roof. The warhead missed the Tong hatchet men standing around the opening and slammed into the cavern roof itself.

The resulting explosion was almost deafening in the enclosed space of the cavern. Kane watched incredulously as the cavern roof went to pieces under the weight of the Tong war wags. Almost in slow motion, the cavern roof collapsed, sinking down and sucking men and machines after it. The roar of breaking earth filled the cavern, and the impact of the rock tonnage as well as the war wags, created huge swells in the lake. Kane was slung forward like a rag doll in the grip of a giant.

The water rolled over his head for a moment, submerging him. He held his breath and peered up at the cavern roof to keep his bearings.

Without warning, Lindstrohm suddenly shot by overhead. The man caught Kane's shirt with his free hand and brought his other hand—with the knife still held tightly in it—streaking toward Kane's throat.

The whirling water lifted Kane and Lindstrohm clear for an instant. Kane reluctantly released the chalice and grabbed his opponent's knife arm.

"Time to die, Ka'in," Lindstrohm shouted hoarsely.

Kane held the knife hand back, the blade only inches from his face. "No," he said coldly, remembering how Lindstrohm had betrayed the king and the other warriors who had stood so valiantly with him.

A hesitant look filled Lindstrohm's face.

Kane drew the .45 from his hip. He stayed locked together with the man as the swells rippling through the underground lake pushed them up. He thrust the .45 into Lindstrohm's face.

Insanity gleamed in Lindstrohm's eyes. "Go ahead, Ka'in. Chill me again. But I'm linked to that chalice by Enlil. I'll just get it next time."

Kane looked at the man. "No," he said with grim certainty. "There won't be a next time." Then he thrust the pistol into Lindstrohm's mouth, breaking teeth. Before Lindstrohm had time to struggle or gag, Kane pulled the trigger, blowing out the back of the man's skull.

Lindstrohm's head sagged, like a sack emptying its contents. Life left his eyes, but they remained open.

Kane pushed the corpse from him and swam after the chalice again, catching it easily.

"Kane."

He glanced up as Brigid Baptiste brought the outboard around through the choppy water. Grant shoved out a hand, caught his, then drew him aboard.

Overhead, the cavern roof continued to crumble, and the tear in the earth above the underground lake continued, pulling down some of Tulum's ruins, as well.

Brigid turned the outboard in the other direction, following the path of the huge cavern system as the water level rapidly started to rise. Kane gazed at all the destruction, dimly aware that Brigid had turned control of the outboard over to Grant as she started dealing with the wounds in his side.

"It's okay, Baptiste," Kane said in a hoarse voice. "They're through and through. Didn't deflect off a rib and bounce inside."

But she cut his shirt off anyway and started working to staunch the bleeding.

Kane watched the destruction raining down from the cavern roof. There was no sign of pursuit from the Tong. Thankfully, the outboard also carried a large, mountable light on the bow. Domi switched it on and the bright light chased away the dark, allowing Grant to safely steer their craft through the caverns.

Relaxing a little, Kane leaned back as Brigid continued examining his wounds. His mind drifted, recalling the images and events he'd seen in the dreams Balam had sent him. Some of them seemed so far away now, like memories of things other people had told him, but he remembered the lady and the king's promise to her.

He gazed at the chalice in the bottom of the boat and knew what he had to do.

Epilogue

Kane gazed up at the opening they'd reached at the other end of the cavern systems. The trip had covered every bit of the thirty-plus miles Brigid had mentioned, and the sights throughout the underground world had been awe-inspiring.

Brigid had bandaged Kane's and Grant's wounds as well as she'd been able to. None of them were life threatening, and DeFore could clear up any complications once they got back to Cerberus.

Grant steered the outboard toward a rocky shelf with steps carved into the side of the stone wall. Iron rings set into the stone offered mute testimony that the shelf had been used as a dock in the past.

Domi leaped from the outboard and tied off the line to one of the mooring rings.

The hole in the cavern roof showed a deepening, twilight-blue slate sky shot full of diamond-bright stars. The shadows inside the cavern system had lengthened, and during the past twenty minutes the battery-powered light on the outboard struggled against the darkness that filled the caverns.

Kane clambered aboard the rocky spit of land stiffly. His chest felt as if iron bands had wrapped it, and he knew from experience it was going to take a few days before he got back to one hundred percent. He carried the chalice in one hand.

"Ladder here," Domi said, pointing a small flash that had also been in their confiscated boat at an iron ladder punched into the wall. She took the lead, swarming easily into the sixty-foot climb.

A chill wind blew against the back of Kane's neck. He

thought for a moment that he heard his name. He stopped and turned back toward the deep lake.

The water was as smooth as glass, picking up pink and light purple coloring from cavern walls. Nothing moved out in the water. There'd been no sign of pursuit, or that anyone that had fallen through the cavern roof had survived. It had been hours since a corpse had been within sight of the outboard.

"What's wrong?" Brigid asked, stopping beside Kane.

"Nothing, Baptiste." Kane surveyed the still water, feeling more certain of his decision.

"Did you hear something?" Brigid played the small flash she'd gotten from one of the war bags they'd managed to hang on to over the smooth water.

"No." Kane took the chalice in one hand, torqued his body, then threw it out into the lake.

The silvery bowl flew out over the water, then started down toward the surface of the lake. For a moment, Kane had thought he was wrong and thought he was going to have to get wet again just after having gotten dry at last.

Then, amazingly, a column of water splashed up from the lake and caught the chalice. Instantly, the chalice was dragged below the lake's surface and disappeared.

"Was that an arm?" Brigid asked quietly.

Kane studied the lake, but no trace remained of the water column or the chalice. "Did it look like an arm, Baptiste?"

"For a moment," the archivist said, "that water column looked exactly like a woman's arm."

"Mebbe it was a trick of the light," Grant suggested.

"Not trick of light," Domi said. "That was a woman's arm. Saw it myself. No mistake. What's a lady doing in the lake?"

"Making sure a promise was kept," Kane said, feeling suddenly lighter and more energized. He saw the king's face in his head. Then he turned and headed for the ladder on the wall. "Let's go."

KANE SAT on his haunches in the hills ringing Campecheville thirty-eight hours later, his gaze raking the ville through binoculars. They'd taken their time during the trip back from Tulum, traveling at night to avoid the heat of the day and to give their wounds time to heal over a little. They'd also been on the lookout for the survivors of the Tong group, as well as anyone who might have come back looking for Lindstrohm and Narita Vasquez.

They'd passed no one.

Dawn rose in the sky behind Kane, spilling down into the sloped bowl that held Campecheville. Out in the bay, only crumpled wrecks remained of the floating oil rigs. Many of them were still burning, and huge spills that flickered with low-level fires continued burning, as well.

"Automatic timers," Grant said, seated beside Kane. "Only thing it could have been."

Kane nodded and put his binoculars away. "It's going to be a long time before anyone rebuilds this area into what Lindstrohm had it operating at."

"Yeah," Domi said, "but for oil, somebody will try."

The red-lacquered Tong warships sat at anchor out in the distant western horizon. Evidently, they hadn't been able to negotiate with the people still surviving at Campecheville. A skirmish line of crates and wags formed along the docks, and small boats patrolled the harbor.

"That's an armed camp down there, Kane," Brigid said.

Kane nodded and rubbed at the whisker stubbles covering his chin. "I know. Mebbe they'll be able to make a go of it. Even against Wei Qiang's ships." He pushed out a breath, planning their next moves. "We'll rest up here, then go down after dark. With all the confusion going on down there, we should be in good shape."

"Because we're obviously not Tong men," Grant said.

"Right." The fact provided a flimsy cover at best, but Kane felt certain it would prove enough. "We'll locate the mat-trans gateway and use it to get back to Cerberus. And if that doesn't happen, we can take a ship out of here.''

"Sounds like a plan," Grant said. "What do we do until then?''

"We rest," Kane said. "We might not be the only ones who decide tonight would be a night for skulking through Campecheville. I'll take first watch.''

Grant didn't argue. Despite the leisurely trip back from Tulum, all of them were still worn from the past few days of hard traveling. Grant crawled back up into the tree line where they'd left the wag they'd recovered from the Tulum site and went to sleep under the vehicle. Domi joined him.

Kane remained where he was, looking out over Campecheville and the burning oil wells.

"What Lindstrohm was doing wasn't all bad," Brigid commented quietly.

"No," Kane agreed.

"If it had worked, it would have been a good thing he was doing.''

"It wouldn't have worked," Kane said. "There's an old saying they teach Mags. Kill a man's enemy, he's free for the day. Teach a man to kill, he's free forever.''

"There's one about fishing, too," Brigid said. "Give a man a fish, he eats for a day. Teach a man to fish, and he eats every day.''

"Till somebody comes along and takes his fish away," Kane agreed. "Makes you wonder which saying came about first, doesn't it?''

"Why did you throw the chalice away?''

"I didn't throw it away, Baptiste." Kane started to tell her what had happened, but he didn't. Somehow, putting it into words took something away from it. What had happened…had just happened. "It was a promise that was made a long time ago.''

"If the machine would have worked, those people down there could have used it. They're going to starve.''

"Or they'll leave," Kane pointed out. "Or mebbe they'll broker a deal with Wei Qiang's people or some of the local pirates or traders."

"Having the machine would have made it easier."

Kane looked at Brigid. "The machine would have made it too easy, Baptiste. That's what Balam was telling me. Enlil was able to lead the pharaohs and everyone else he needed to control later, through the manna machine. If you can feed them, you can lead them. That's a basic law in any beginning society. People who rise to power do so because they're smarter than the rest of the population and can provide knowledge they need. Or mebbe they're stronger, or kill easier. That way they're more able to protect the group they're leading. But those people don't make the other people dependent—they teach them things. Either knowledge, or the conviction to stand up for themselves."

"The machine makes them dependent," Brigid said.

"Yeah. If Lindstrohm chose to freeze out certain segments of his society, the others would have no choice but to go along."

"It gave him absolute control over them," Brigid said.

"It would have." Kane was silent for a moment, watching the streaming black smoke dissipate out toward the horizon, lingering over the Tong warships waiting in the distance. "What I did was right, Baptiste. There are some people who are going to be hurt by my decision, but I believe that they'll be better off in the long run." He paused. "I have to believe that."

Brigid was silent for a moment. "A Magistrate wouldn't have to believe that."

Kane nodded. "Yeah. But I haven't been a Magistrate for a long time, Baptiste." He pushed out a breath from his sore chest as he gazed down on the ville where factions were already squaring off against each other in the streets. "Things were easier when I was a Magistrate. Simpler."

"Simpler isn't always better, Kane," Brigid said. She slid her hand into his.

Kane held on to her, felt her warmth and drew it into the cold places of his heart. His world had changed as surely as those people in Campecheville, and none of them could go back to the way things were.

Brigid leaned her head on his shoulder, and he let himself go distant from the violence breaking out in the streets of the ville below. But he couldn't help thinking about the way the chalice had disappeared. Part of him didn't want to believe an arm had reached up and taken it below, but another part of him knew that was exactly what had happened. The Lady of the Lake—maybe a manifestation of the Gaia force of the planet itself—had taken the chalice back where it had come from. Enlil had used the earth's own electromagnetic fields to create the device, and the lady had reclaimed what had been taken from her.

The king had told Ka'in that.

And Kane believed it. But thinking about the Gaia force able to interact on a personal level left him feeling very confused. Especially when he had to wonder about his own ties to it.

After a while, Kane let it all go and simply drew comfort from Brigid's presence. For now, that was enough.

JAMES AXLER

DEATH LANDS®

Breakthrough

Deathlands is a living hell, but there is someplace worse: a parallel Earth where the atomic mega-cull never happened. Now, this otherworld Earth is in its final death throes. Yet, for an elite few, the reality portal offers a new frontier of raw energy, and expendable slaves—a bastion of power for Dredda Otis Trask. Her invasion force has turned the ruins of Salt Lake City into the deadly mining grounds of a grotesque new order—one that lies in wait for Ryan and his companions.

In the Deathlands, danger lurks beyond the imagination.

*Available in March 2002
at your favorite retail outlet.*

Or order your copy now by sending your name, address, zip or postal code, along with a check or money order (please do not send cash) for $5.99 for each book ordered ($6.99 in Canada), plus 75¢ postage and handling ($1.00 in Canada), payable to Gold Eagle Books, to:

In the U.S.
Gold Eagle Books
3010 Walden Ave.
P.O. Box 9077
Buffalo, NY 14269-9077

In Canada
Gold Eagle Books
P.O. Box 636
Fort Erie, Ontario
L2A 5X3

Please specify book title with order.
Canadian residents add applicable federal and provincial taxes.

GDL57

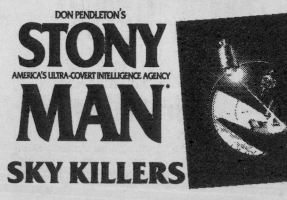

James Axler

OUTLANDERS®

PRODIGAL CHALICE

The warriors, who dare to expose the deadly truth of mankind's destiny, discover a new gateway in Central America—one that could lead them deeper into the conspiracy that has doomed Earth. Here they encounter a most unusual baron struggling to control the vast oil resources of the region. Uncertain if this charismatic leader is friend or foe, Kane is lured into a search for an ancient relic of mythic proportions that may promise a better future…or plunge humanity back into the dark ages.

In the Outlands,
the shocking truth is humanity's last hope.